SHE BELONGED TO HIM

Slowly, her head lifted, her eyes fastened on him, absorbing the finely etched features, the well-shaped mouth, the thick pelt of hair tied back with a ribbon. But it was the promise in those glittering green eyes that made her shiver. "It's you," she breathed hoarsely. "It's you."

He was studying her silently. Where his eyes touched, her skin grew cold. Her hands clenched around the rim of the tub. "Oh God, it's you," she repeated.

"It's all right," he soothed, and the words surprised him. Slowly, inexorably, he pulled her into his arms.

His lips found hers. She did not respond, but she did not resist him either. Adam pulled back and studied her wide-eyed expression. There was feminine wariness in her eyes.

Something primitive, something savage and totally masculine seemed to have entered his bloodstream. His skin was fever hot; his breathing was difficult. He seemed to have lost his grip on reality. Philippe Duhet was forgotten, as was the elaborate charade that had brought him into Rouen. The only thing that Adam was conscious of was the woman in his arms and the driving compulsion that urged him to prove to her that she belonged to him.

He swept her up in his arms and carried her to the bed.

Elizabeth Thornton

Velvet is the Night

PINNACLE BOOKS
WINDSOR PUBLISHING CORP.

For Ellen Kemp Black
dearest friend, best of sisters,
with love—

To Maureen Taggart, librarian, University of Winnipeg.
Every writer should be so lucky!
Without your help,
the research would have been a formidable task.

PINNACLE BOOKS

are published by

Windsor Publishing Corp.
475 Park Avenue South
New York, NY 10016

First printing: April, 1992

Printed in the United States of America

Prologue

The fight was over in a matter of minutes. The palace guards put a stop to it, but only when it became evident that the melée was no boyish prank but a contest which was as deadly as any duel fought on the field of honor.

Adam was dragged from the other boy, then he darted away before the guards were aware that he was an outsider, a boy on the periphery of court life. In his best suit of clothes, he had been taken by the guards for one of their own, or a page attached to one of the great noblemen who was present at the king's masquerade that evening. The other boys had known better. They were used to seeing Adam come and go as he pleased. No one was *his* master. Adam Dillon waited on no man unless it suited him, and the other boys hated him for it.

He'd been expecting trouble, but when it came he'd been taken off-guard. It wasn't the pages who had ganged up on him. The attack, a verbal one, had come from Philippe Duhet, the young heir to the Comte de Blaise. Duhet was older than Adam by a year or two, but in many a fight, Adam had outmatched boys of far superior weight and build. Adam was no coward. He also had the advantage of

5

experience. In Paris, among his own kind, Adam's reputation as a fighter went unchallenged.

Whore, Duhet had called Adam's mother, and for some few seconds, surprise rooted Adam to the spot. He had no quarrel with young Duhet. Their paths seldom crossed. The only time they had exchanged a few words was when Adam had delivered a note to the boy's father in the fashionable Rue St. Medéric. Yet, on reflection, Adam had to admit to a vague uneasiness whenever he had found Duhet's eyes trailing him of late. He had shrugged it off as a figment of his imagination. As far as he was aware, he had done nothing to earn the boy's hostility. He was coming to see that he was in error. From the snickers and catcalls of the pages, it seemed that he and Duhet must be sworn enemies.

In the next breath, Duhet had flung the word *bastard* in his teeth, and Adam had launched himself at the bigger boy. In the fray, he had taken a black eye, but Duhet had not had everything his own way. Adam had bloodied the young aristocrat's nose.

An icy blast of March air stung his cheeks, and Adam turned up his coat collar and bent his thin shoulders into the wind, his swift steps taking him farther away from the palace environs to the less elegant quarter of Versailles where his mother had taken up lodgings.

Versailles. The town was too staid for Adam's liking. Paris was his milieu. The capital was dirtier, noisier, more crowded. In Paris, he had friends, boys like himself who knew how to earn a living by their wits, boys who skirted the law and stopped short, barely, of embracing a life of crime. For the most part, they were the sons of "actresses" or kept women who had fallen on hard times. The succession of men who passed through their young lives were shadowy figures and temporary at best. When the word "father" came to Adam's mind, his first thought was of Mother Church.

Ducking into the doorway of an elegant town house, Adam felt in the pocket of his breeches and withdrew his night's earnings. The gold ducat glinted wickedly in the light of an overhead lantern. He bit down on it and grunted in satisfaction. The ducat was real. He grinned, thinking that it was the easiest money he had ever made in his young life. He had earned it by acting as courier for the elderly Maquis de Narvenne and the young Madame Caron, the wife of one of the town's foremost citizens, Caron the church warden. Versailles, Adam was thinking, had one point in its favor. It was where the aristocrats hung out. An aristocrat bent on pleasure was easily parted from his money.

One day, when he reached manhood, he thought he might like to be an aristocrat. From what he had observed, they had a soft life. The pages always had plenty to fill their stomachs; their masters wore fine clothes; they rode in gilt carriages; they lived in elegant châteaux; they pursued a life of ease and pleasure. An aristocrat's life might be quite the thing, thought Adam idly.

With a surreptitious look over his shoulder, he carefully eased the ducat under the top of his silk stocking, knowing full well that the coins in his pockets would be confiscated by his mother the moment he walked in the door. Every sous, every livre was needed to pay off their mounting pile of debts, so his mother avowed. Adam did not doubt it. Everything in Versailles was more expensive. Even so, he knew of his mother's fondness for cheap cognac. A ducat would put food on the table for some weeks to come, if they were careful. He wasn't sure how much brandy it would buy, nor did he care.

As he entered the courtyard of the Chasse Royale, his eyes unerringly found his mother's room in the unheated garrets of the inn. A candle flickered at the window, the signal that his mother was entertaining company and must not be disturbed.

At ten years of age, Adam was wiser than his years. He had no illusions about the "company" his mother was entertaining. He hated the succession of men she brought home to their lodgings, but not out of any moral consideration. The arrival of some gentleman always necessitated his quick removal from the scene. Mara Dillon had no wish to advertise the fact that she had a half-grown son, not when she was promoting the fiction that she was younger than her years.

Cursing under his breath, Adam detoured to the back of the inn, avoiding the noisy throngs in the inn's public rooms. The night was raw. His eye was sore. He longed for his bed. Ducat or no ducat, he resolved to take the pauper's privilege and bed down in one of the outhouses. If he was lucky Cook might give him permission to curl up in front of the kitchen grate. And if his luck held, he might even cadge a bowl of rabbit stew. Like himself, the cook was half-Irish. O'Murphy claimed that his father was one of the Irish Jacobites who had sought sanctuary with his family in France to escape retribution from the Hanoverian kings of England. Adam's line was of more recent vintage, beginning with his mother. Nevertheless, their common heritage gave O'Murphy and Adam a feeling of camaraderie.

"Black Irish," O'Murphy called him. It was meant as a compliment. More and more of late, Adam was beginning to wonder about the other half of his patrimony, the part that came to him from his unknown father. *Bastard*, Duhet had called him. He flexed his hand, observing the abrasions to his knuckles. Whistling, smiling, he sauntered into the inn.

Two days later, the ax fell. Adam was in the inn's kitchens, ostensibly to keep an eye on the succulent whole pig which was roasting on the spit. O'Murphy

8

and his helpers were preparing the other courses for the influx of guests which had descended on the inn, mostly the finicky retainers of aristos who had found more elegant lodgings for themselves.

The tantalizing odors, the blast of heat from the grate, the rhythmic clatter of pots and pans—all conspired to make Adam fall asleep at his post. He was awakened when O'Murphy put a hand on his shoulder.

Adam always came awake instantly. There was no telling what he might awake to. It wouldn't be the first time that he and his mother had crept out the back door in the middle of the night as their creditors burst in the front.

Hearing O'Murphy's soft Irish lilt, so like his mother's, Adam untensed his muscles. "Up with you, boy. Your mother's been asking for you. Something's afoot," and O'Murphy gestured to the window. A gilt carriage with liveried coachmen had drawn up in the inn's courtyard.

A weight seemed to lodge itself in the pit of Adam's stomach. He was almost sure that Philippe Duhet had sent his minions to punish him. Those minions must be with his mother.

He took the stairs two at a time and burst into the room. Breathless, he pulled up short.

A gentleman in court finery occupied the only chair in the small room. His folded hands, with a profusion of lace at the wrists, rested upon a gold-tipped walking cane which he held out in front of him. At Adam's precipitous entrance, his dark eyebrows lifted.

Adam's glance swiftly moved to his mother. She was seated at the end of the bed as if she were a queen holding court, and she was attired in her most flattering gown, a blue brocade with a white lace fichu around her shoulders and tucked in at the low bodice. For once, she was completely sober.

"Mother?" Adam spoke in English.

She answered in French, as was her habit when there was company present. "Comte, may I present my son, Adam? Adam, make your bows to the Comte de Blaise."

Mara Dillon lowered her long lashes and covertly observed her son as he obeyed the faint warning in her voice. If ever there was a time for Adam to demonstrate the elegancies she had tried to inculcate in him over the years, that time was now.

Adam bowed. The comte inclined his head. Mara let out the breath she had been holding. She had hardly dared to hope that her plan would succeed.

For years she had sent letters of entreaty to the comte, begging his assistance for a son he refused to acknowledge. She'd received not one word in reply, until she had hit upon the brilliant notion of sending the boy to him in person. The resemblance between father and son was striking.

Mara Dillon found herself praying to a deity she had ignored for years. The last time she had prayed for deliverance was when her father had thrown her out of the house for bringing disgrace to the family name. At fifteen, she'd been pregnant and unable to name the father of her unborn child. Fortunately, her prayer had been answered. She'd miscarried, and shortly after she'd found a protector, the leading actor-cum-playwright of a troupe of players based in Dublin.

In the summer of '62, the troupe had gone on tour. In Paris, in the title role of Racine's *Iphigénie*, Mara had come to the notice of the Comte de Blaise. When the company had moved on to the provinces, Mara had stayed behind as the comte's mistress.

She'd been too young, then, to appreciate her good fortune. The tributes she'd received from so many admiring gentlemen had gone to her head. She had committed the unforgivable folly of being too free with her favors. Blaise had discovered it and had cast her out without a sous. Much she had cared! She was

10

young, she was beautiful, she was courted and flattered by a host of wealthy aristocrats. Her next protector was waiting in the wings. She'd thought, quite genuinely, that the child she was carrying belonged to Pascale. And by the time her son was born two months early and indelibly stamped with his father's likeness, it was too late to procure an abortion.

In the last number of years, life had not been kind to Mara Dillon. Youth and beauty had quickly faded. The hosts of blue-blooded gentlemen had quietly melted away. There were no admirers now, only a string of men of dubious background who were willing to pay for an hour or two's pleasure. Mara was becoming desperate. She had one asset—Adam and his connection to the Comte de Blaise.

Green eyes locked on green eyes as the indolent aristocrat and the half-fearful, half-defiant boy assessed each other across the small room. It was the comte who broke the silence.

"You are my . . . ward, Adam Dillon. Do you understand what this means?" The aristocrat was not angry. Evidently, he did not know that he, Adam Dillon, was the boy who had given his son a bloody nose. Adam unbent a little and said, haltingly, that his one wish was to serve and that if the comte had some office . . .

The comte waved him to silence. Amusement coloring his voice, he told Adam that he had come to an arrangement with his mother. "You are to become a member of my household. I shall provide you with the privileges befitting one of your station in life. With my influence, who knows, you may go far."

When Adam finally understood what his fate was to be, he threw himself down at his mother's knees, pleading for her to intercede. He could not know that his mother had sold him outright for a substantial lump sum. Mara Dillon loved her son, after a fashion. If it had been possible, she would have kept

11

the boy with her. But the offer from her former protector had been unequivocal. He wanted all or nothing of his bastard son, and her problems were too pressing to forgo the rewards he offered.

The comte left to fetch his coachmen, and Mara soothingly tried to convince her young son of all the benefits he would enjoy as the ward of a rich nobleman. To every blandishment, Adam found a ready rejoinder. He didn't want to live in a rich man's house. He had no use for fine clothes or refined manners or a gentleman's education. He was happy to go on as they were. He wanted them to return to Paris. He wouldn't be a trouble to her. From that moment on, he promised to hand over every sous he earned. He felt in his stocking for the precious ducat and pressed it into his mother's hand.

What Adam failed to convey, because he, himself, did not understand it, was the shadow of foreboding which lay over his heart. In the household of the comte, he was bound to meet up with Philippe Duhet. Adam was not afraid of the older boy. What he feared he could not put into words.

Mara was close to the end of her tether. She needed a drink badly. She could not understand Adam's misgivings and she was terrified that the comte would take umbrage at her son's defiance and withdraw his offer.

More cruel than she meant to be, she seized Adam's arms and administered a rough shake. "Blaise is your father! You are his son! You should be grateful that he has finally condescended to acknowledge you. If you won't think of yourself, think of me. I'm warning you, Adam, don't think to run away. You won't find me. I'm going back to Ireland. Those were his terms. Do you understand? He's given me money to start a new life. If you spoil this for me, I shall never forgive you."

Stricken, Adam stared into his mother's eyes. There was a sound behind him. The comte was standing in the open doorway, flanked by two burly coachmen, the faintest sneer curling his lips. In fear and trembling, Adam straightened.

"Do you play the man or shall I order my men to carry you like a screaming infant to the waiting carriage?"

Adam searched his mother's face for a sign, any sign, that she might be open to persuasion. Her features had hardened into an implacable mask, her eyes flashing, warning him not to make the attempt.

Adam's life with Mara Dillon had not been an easy one. For the most part neglected, Adam had learned early how to fend for himself. But it was the only life he knew. The familiar exerted a powerful hold on him. Again, he thought of Philippe Duhet, and shivered. He felt as if someone had just walked over his grave.

His mother rose and moved to the small window, presenting her back to her son. She was trembling, but Adam did not notice.

Dazed, he allowed himself to be led from the room.

The Château de Blaise, the ancestral home of the Comtes de Blaise for more than six generations, was situated in the beautiful and fertile Loire Valley and far enough distant from Paris to deter young Adam from any hastily contrived plan of escape. Adam knew Paris like the back of his hand. The château and its rural setting had all the oddity of a foreign country.

The Duhets, themselves, were like creatures from another world. In those first few months, Adam could not conceive why the comte had taken it into his head to make him his ward, unless it was a rich man's whim. No one wanted him, least of all the comte, as far as Adam was able to deduce. The comte and his comtesse were scarcely ever in residence, and never together at the same time.

The comtesse, when she could tear herself away from the pleasures of Versailles, would periodically descend on the château like a beautiful godmother dispensing gifts and favors. In some trepidation, Adam waited for a summons to the august presence. None was forthcoming. Not only was he excluded from the comtesse's charmed circle, but when they chanced to come face-to-face on the odd occasion, she looked through him as if he were invisible. Adam withdrew more into himself and pretended to an indifference he was far from feeling.

Through servants' loose tongues, he gathered that the comte and his comtesse had long since decided to go their own ways. The comte kept a stableful of mistresses. The comtesse had a string of young lovers. In the theater world in Paris, men and women conducted themselves in much the same manner. Adam accepted these modes as the natural way of things.

A staff of more than one hundred liveried footmen catered to the needs of a handful of people. Presiding in the absence of the comte and comtesse were Monsieur Perrin, the tutor, and Mademoiselle Cocteau, governess and chaperone to the daughters of the house.

Philippe Duhet had two younger sisters, pudding-faced, graceless girls, in Adam's opinion. He supposed that they must be his own half-sisters. Again, it was servants' gossip which put him wise. "The two suet dumplings," as Adam contemptuously referred to them in his own mind, were not the comte's children, but the issue of the comtesse and her several lovers over the years. For all the airs and graces these ugly ducklings adopted, one would have supposed them princesses of the blood, so Adam muttered to himself, and not the offspring of dubious parentage.

That first year, Adam had more thrashings than he'd had in the previous ten years in his life, and far more severe. The first beating, as Adam expected, came from Philippe Duhet. He'd been lured to the stables on some pretext or other. When he entered, a couple of the stable lads laid hold of him, pinioning his arms behind his back. Only then did Philippe step out of the shadows.

When he left, one of Adam's ribs was cracked, though not a scratch or bruise showed where it could be detected by a casual observer. As the weeks wore on, it became evident to Adam that Philippe was as sly as a fox, and twice as deadly. There was a streak of cruelty in the boy which he hid behind an easy charm and impeccable manners. The passing of time would amend Adam's opinion. Philippe Duhet was not merely cruel. He was demented.

As far as was humanly possible, Adam took to giving Philippe a wide berth. There were times, however, when they must be together. They shared the tutor. They sat facing each other at the dinner table with Monsieur Perrin and Mademoiselle Cocteau presiding. On such occasions, knowing he was not welcome, Adam was taciturn. Philippe was all charm and good humor—a born actor. Adam despised the older boy. The feeling was mutual.

For all the luxuries the Duhets enjoyed, theirs was not a happy household. Discipline was ferocious. Adam chafed at the restrictions. He missed his mother—not that Mara Dillon had been an affectionate mother. But when she was sober, she was entertaining, a fund of stories, and good company. Adam felt estranged. No one at the château made overtures of friendship. Philippe's sisters went out of their way to avoid him. The reason was not hard to find. Like the servants, they went in fear of the heir's unpredictable temper, and Philippe had made it known, though not overtly, that Adam Dillon was beyond the pale.

That lesson was brought home to Adam in a particularly brutal way. One of the coachmen, taking pity on the boy, presented him with a pup, a black mongrel bitch, which lavished the solitary youth with an indiscriminate affection. Adam was captivated. He named his dog Sheba and spent every spare moment schooling his pet to his commands. The loneliness became a little easier to bear. Sometimes he was surprised to find that he was almost enjoying himself.

Ever afterwards, he was to curse himself for underestimating Philippe Duhet. He should have foreseen the lengths to which the boy would go in his lust to avenge the slur of having his father's bastard foisted upon him.

Sheba was missing. A presentiment of disaster gripped Adam. Ignoring the summons to meet with his tutor in the music room, he dashed aimlessly about the grounds of the château, shouting Sheba's name at the top of his lungs. He found his pup floating in the moat. Sheba had been deliberately drowned. No one had to tell Adam who was responsible. As he gathered the small, miserable bundle into his arms, something inside Adam snapped.

He found Philippe in the music room with their tutor. As Adam entered, the tutor's hands on the keyboard of the harpsichord stilled. Philippe rested one hand idly on the edge of the instrument, a telling smile curling his lips, triumph glittering in his eyes. Adam wanted to kill him. Slowly, deliberately, he approached the older boy. Without warning, Adam grasped Philippe's wrist, holding his hand steady where it rested. In the next instant, he slammed the lid of the harpsichord down on Philippe's hand.

The beating the tutor administered was savage. Adam was past caring. He was heartbroken. He could not even be glad that he had broken two of Philippe's fingers.

The thrashing was only a small part of his punishment. He was confined to his room on starvation rations until he came to his senses. That day never arrived. Adam refused to apologize, nor would he divulge the reason for the attack. In his circles in Paris, boys disdained to tattle on one another, whatever the provocation. A boy fought his own battles, meted out his own brand of justice, or else he became the runt of the pack, an object of ridicule or abuse. The adults in Adam's life rarely interfered. Their interest was careless, and desultory at best. The tutor, who grudgingly commuted Adam's sentence when it seemed that the boy would starve before he would beg his half-brother's pardon, was a new experience for Adam, as was Philippe Duhet.

In the succeeding months, as he observed Philippe's covert cruelties not only to himself but also to anyone who incurred his wrath, Adam was struck anew by the thought that the boy was a born actor. No one observing that cultured, charming exterior would credit that Philippe Duhet was anything other than he appeared, except, perhaps, his victims. There was only one way to fight him and win, and that was by emulating his example. In the interests of self-preservation, Adam, also, became something of an actor. In the public eye, both boys pretended to a distant though polite amity. In private, they followed a more vicious course. For every deliberate transgression on Philippe's part, Adam evened the score. Before long, an uneasy truce prevailed.

When Adam was fifteen years of age, the fiction that he was the comte's ward deceived no one. The resemblance between father and son was remarkable, but not so remarkable as the growing resemblance between Adam and his half-brother, Philippe. The aristocratic bearing, the high forehead, aquiline nose, finely chiseled features—all gave proof of their common patrimony. But it was those extraordinary Duhet eyes which put an end to idle speculation, eyes as green as grass, sultry, and half veiled with a fan of dark, curling eyelashes.

Both boys possessed a muscular physique, the result of the various accomplishments which men of fashion were obliged to acquire. Hours in each day were devoted to the mastery of the manly arts—riding, hunting on the comte's vast estates, fencing, athletics. And both boys had an eye for the girls.

At sixteen years of age, Adam fell in love. The object of his devotion was Jeanne, the beautiful daughter of an innkeeper in the city of Tours. The Épée de Bois was the inn where all the Duhets put up when they had occasion to visit the city. Adam was a little ashamed. There was only one thing which drew him to Tours. His father had arranged for him to visit, periodically, one of its better brothels. Jeanne, in Adam's opinion, was as far removed from the wenches who catered to the carnal side of his nature as is the sun from the moon. Jeanne stirred the boy's softer emotions. She was as pure as she was beautiful. He worshipped her.

The romance blossomed. When Jeanne could slip away from her numerous duties, they went for long walks or found a quiet nook where they could be private. Jeanne was a good listener. Adam told her things about himself he had never told another soul. Occasionally, he held her hand. Once, he kissed her fingers.

Somehow, word of Adam's partiality for the girl got back to Philippe. When Adam next visited the Épée de Bois, the comte and Philippe rode with him. Adam was wary, but not in his worst nightmares could he have conceived what followed.

The comte and Jeanne's father entered into negotiations to establish the girl as Philippe's mistress. Adam was beside himself. The hatred which had smoldered beneath the surface for years erupted like an exploding volcano. He went for Philippe. When the comte tried to intervene, Adam turned on him, too. It took three of the comte's men to hold him down. Jeanne was summoned. For

Adam, she spared scarcely a glance. Philippe made his offer. Jeanne prevaricated but quickly accepted terms when the question of her duties at the inn was raised. For the first time, Adam learned that Jeanne's favors were available for any gentleman who could meet her price.

Something inside Adam died. He thought of all the women he had known in his life, not least his own mother. Heartsick, he told himself that he had learned a valuable lesson. Beneath their fine clothes and genteel manners, all women were alike. Never again would he make a fool of himself over any female.

The hatred which had always existed between Adam and Philippe was now out in the open. The comte would not countenance it. As the heir, Philippe must be protected. The bastard son must be sent away.

Adam was destined, a befitted his station in life, for a career in law or the army. To further this end, he was enrolled at the famous Lycée Louis le Grand in Paris.

It was here that Adam was introduced to the philosophy of Rousseau and the new ideas which were beginning to gain acceptance in France, ideas which one day would be taken to extreme. The Revolution was already in the making. De Robespierre was a fellow student.

As Adam approached his eighteenth birthday, it was not French politics which fired his imagination, but events in America. The American War of Independence was in progress. Benjamin Franklin, the American ambassador, was the most celebrated man in France. His commentary on American life was widely reported in the press, and eagerly received. The young Maquis de Lafayette had recently returned to an ecstatic welcome and was vigorously recruiting volunteers for the American cause. For young men of ambition such as Adam,

America offered rewards which were denied them in France by an entrenched aristocracy. Adam toyed with the idea of offering his services to Lafayette.

Events moved swiftly to force his hand. While on a visit to relate the news of the death of Adam's mother in Ireland, the comte was ambushed near his town house and brutally murdered. The trail of evidence led straight to Adam. It was known that there was no love lost between Adam Dillon and any member of the Duhet family. Moreover, only hours before the murder was committed, witnesses swore that there had been a violent quarrel between father and son.

In everything, Adam recognized the hand of his half-brother. Philippe would not be satisfied until he had erased Adam Dillon from the face of the earth. One day, Adam promised himself, there would be a final reckoning. For the moment, he was powerless. To remain in France meant arrest and certain death. His destiny lay in America.

Book I

The Masquerade

Chapter One

It was one of the first parties of any note in New York since the sweltering heat of summer had given way to the more moderate temperatures of autumn. Mrs. Sarah Burke, one of New York's foremost hostesses, calmly surveyed the throng of people in the ballroom of her magnificent mansion on Broadway. Tall pier glasses, strategically placed around the room, caught the candlelight and reflected her galaxy of glittering guests, giving the impression of airiness, space, and a party almost double its actual numbers.

A moment later, Sarah's slim, straight-backed figure was observed slipping away from the crush of people. She entered the grand dining room which was reserved for formal occasions only. Here she conferred with her French chef. Having ascertained that the éclairs and petit fours as well as a selection of French bonbons had arrived from Joseph Corré's pastry shop on Wall Street, Sarah smiled her approval and returned to her duties as hostess. In the foyer, she met her husband.

John Burke, for all his five and fifty years, was a handsome, virile-looking man. His dress was formal, following the old fashions. His powdered hair was tied in back with a black ribbon. And Sarah, for all the years of their long and happy union, still experienced a little leap of pleasure every time she looked at him.

He greeted her with an expression of acute agitation. "Aaron Burr arrived not five minutes ago."

Sarah understood at once the cause of her husband's alarm. Aaron Burr and Alexander Hamilton, two prominent gentlemen in the upper echelons of government circles, could never be civil to each other for more than five minutes at a time. She had made it a rule never to invite both gentlemen to the same party. Fortunately, Congress was meeting in Philadelphia. Before long, Hamilton and Burr must take up their duties there.

In her usual calm manner, she put her husband's mind at rest. "The Hamiltons were invited to our last do, dear. They won't be here this evening."

The antagonism which existed between Aaron Burr and Alexander Hamilton put Sarah quite out of patience. In the uncertain times in which they lived, old hatreds, in her opinion, were best forgotten. It would seem that her guests agreed with her. At her soirées were to be found men and women of widely different persuasions—patriots and those who were once decried as traitors, "rebels" as well as former Tories. There was even a sprinkling of British officers who had fought against the armies of the Revolution. But that was all of ten years ago. They regarded themselves now as American citizens, having long since turned their backs on England to wed with American girls.

And then there was the French contingent. They were a little more volatile, but Sarah prosaically told herself that this was to be expected. Not only did the American government welcome official representatives of the new Revolutionary Government in France, but fugitives from the French Revolution, as many as twenty-five thousand some reports said, had also found a welcome on American shores. It was only to be expected that when men of such disparate views came face-to-face, sparks would begin to fly.

Her sympathies were all for the refugees, not that she would say as much in public. Her husband would not thank her for it. John Burke was a diplomat to the tips of his little fingers, even supposing he had long since resigned from Congress to return to his law practice in New York. John understood her sentiments and sympathized with them.

It was inevitable that her thoughts would shift to happier days in France, when she and Mr. Burke had paid an unofficial visit to Benjamin Franklin. They had been taken up and fêted by King Louis and his queen, as well as by the French nobility. And now King Louis had found a felon's grave, and Marie Antoinette was incarcerated in the infamous Conciergerie awaiting an uncertain fate.

Sarah shook her head as if to dispel her gloom. Her eyes chanced to fall on the tall figure of Adam Dillon, and her thoughts were given a more pleasant direction. Adam was the most sought-after bachelor in the state of New York. The girls made fools of themselves over Adam, and who could blame them? Even without the advantages of his wealth and standing in the community, those arresting good looks, that devil-may-care Irish charm were enough to turn any girl's head. But at thirty-one, Adam was in no hurry to tie himself to any girl, at least, not to the eligible ones. His preferences, his peccadilloes, were widely reported. Sarah forgave them easily. Adam was a single man. But she deplored the scandals which attached to a number of the married gentlemen who were present that evening.

In her day, a wife would have created mayhem if her husband had dared to stray. Modern modes did not sit well with Sarah. Well-bred girls were too insipid, too spineless by half. Naturally, husbands applauded submission in a wife. It suited their purposes. But when those same husbands chose their mistresses, they looked for something quite different. Happily, her own husband had never given Sarah an unquiet moment. Their love was enduring and based on implicit trust.

No, decided Sarah, she liked Adam Dillon too well to wish on him any of the insipid, whey-faced young eligibles of her acquaintance. What Adam needed, whether he knew it or not (and here Sarah had the grace to laugh at herself), was a good-hearted girl with some spunk, a girl who would see beyond Adam's facile Irish charm to the rather solitary, mistrustful man who never allowed anyone to get too close to him.

Few people understood Adam Dillon as Sarah did, and Adam would have been mortified if he had known that she was privy to things about himself he wished to conceal. Sarah had come by her knowledge when Adam's guard was down, when he had been sedated with laudanum while recovering from a bayonet wound he had taken at the seige of Yorktown.

Adam was only twenty, but he'd made a remarkable impression on John Burke, who was serving with General Washington. Adam's wound healed, but he had come down with a fever. It was only natural that John would send him to recuperate at his sister's house at nearby Williamsburg where Sarah had taken refuge for the duration of the war with her children.

Sarah had spent several nights nursing the delirious young soldier, trying to bring his fever down. What she had learned of the boy's early life had stirred her maternal instincts. Adam had no use for pity. Nor would Sarah have insulted him by betraying such an emotion. Her abrasive, no-nonsense manner seemed to strike just the right note with Adam. Before long, he felt so much at home with the Burkes that he might have been a member of the family. When the war was over and the Burkes returned to New York, Adam went with them.

Sarah's eyes narrowed on the beauty who claimed Adam's attention. Mrs. Lily Randolph, in Sarah's opinion, was something of a barracuda. She ate little whey-faced girls for breakfast. She was also reputed to be Adam's mistress. There was no love lost between Sarah Burke and the wealthy young widow. But Sarah knew her duty. Lily Randolph was related, both by birth and marriage, to some of the great families in and around New York. To leave the lady off her guest list would occasion gossip. A diplomat's wife avoided such unpleasantness at all costs.

"Old harridan!" Lily Randolph muttered the words under her breath, but Adam heard them, and his dark brows lifted. Lily pouted, and throwing a sulky look in the general direction of her hostess, made to answer the question in Adam's eyes. "Who does she think she is? I swear she puts on more airs and graces than the queen of England. Someone should tell the old harridan that it isn't polite to stare. She hates me, and I can't think why."

Adam's eyes glinted with amusement. He understood the reason for Sarah's antipathy to his mistress. As much as he could be fond of any woman, Adam was fond of Sarah. She took a motherly interest in him, and like any mother, she was angling to see him settled with the right sort of girl. Sarah did not think that Adam could ever be happy with someone like Lily.

But that's where Sarah was wrong. Lily suited him admirably. She was a beautiful, sensuous woman, and wise in the ways of the world. If she was ever jealous of her rivals, and sometimes there were rivals, Lily never betrayed it. Nothing would have put Adam to flight faster than a display of jealousy, except, perhaps, the mention of marriage.

Women had their place in Adam's life, but it wasn't a very significant one. Sarah could never be persuaded of that truth.

"Why shouldn't Sarah stare at you?" began Adam, disguising his cynicism behind a false charm. "You are the most beautiful woman in the room. Sarah, in her day, could claim that distinction." His eyes drifted to Sarah. He considered Sarah Burke, even at something close to fifty, as one of the handsomest women of his acquaintance. Her figure was trim, almost girlish, and this in spite of being the mother of five grown-up daughters, all of whom took after their beautiful mother and had made brilliant matches. He did not think that the passage of time would deal as kindly with his companion as it had dealt with Sarah Burke.

Sensing that he was expected to say something more, Adam stifled a bored sigh and went on. "You're the envy of every woman present tonight. Your beauty is peerless."

The flattery smoothed Lily's ruffled feathers as Adam knew it would. God, women were so predictable! A few choice words (preferably "I love you"), and a few extravagant tributes (preferably of monetary value), and they became putty in a man's hands. A man would be a fool not to use every weapon in his arsenal in his dealings with women. And where women were concerned, Adam considered himself a sage.

Adam noted that people were beginning to idle their way toward the dining room where Sarah's French chef would have set out a sumptuous supper to tempt the most fastidious palate. Adam's appetite was whetted, but not for what was laid out in Sarah's grand dining room.

Lily, with her voluptuous, sultry beauty, was every man's fantasy. An octogenarian on his deathbed would have been unable to resist the pull on his senses. Adam wasn't an octogenarian, and he wasn't on his deathbed.

He whispered something in Lily's ear, then held

28

her gaze with eyes full of sensual promise.

"You wouldn't dare," she breathed.

One eyebrow quirked. "Oh wouldn't I?" He bent to her, and whispered some more in the same vein.

A dazzling smile tilted the generous curve of her mouth. "No, Mr. Dillon. I have not yet had that pleasure." She giggled. "The lavender room, you say?"

"It's worth a visit," said Adam, grinning roguishly. "It's upstairs and right next to the room reserved for the ladies' wraps. You take the main staircase and I'll take the back. No one will miss us."

"You are *brazen*," she whispered. Already her eyelids were becoming heavy as desire stirred her.

"And you love me for it," he laughed softly, confident of his power to reduce her to a shivering, quivering passion without laying a finger on her.

The pleasant interlude took no more than a few minutes. Lily was on fire for him. Adam had scarcely locked the door to the lavender room when she launched herself at him. Her hands moved quickly to the waistband of his breeches, deftly releasing his hard shaft into her hand. Lily was no novice. She knew how to pleasure a man.

Adam was equally busy. With his mouth fastened to hers, he swept aside her skirts. Adam approved of the new fashions for ladies. There were no hoops, now, and fewer petticoats. Lily wasn't wearing drawers.

His hand slid between her soft thighs. When he found her damp woman's core, one finger easily slipped inside. Lily moaned and threw back her head. Her breasts were heaving. Her hips began to gyrate wildly. She was teetering on the edge.

Quickly, Adam lowered her to the bed. In one smooth movement, he entered her. He withdrew, then thrust deeply. Lily whimpered then cried out again as her release convulsed her. A moment later Adam quickly pulled himself from her body before he gave himself up to his own release.

He rolled from her immediately and began to adjust his clothes. Lily gave a sigh of repletion and reluctantly began to follow his example.

"You were right," she said, and smiled languorously.

"Mmm?"

"The wickedness of our situation—it added a certain something. We must do this again sometime. I found it almost unbearably . . . exciting."

"Few women can match you in passion," said Adam absently.

Something flashed in her dark eyes then was quickly gone. She flounced off the bed. "I thought you loved me," she said.

Adam could barely tolerate the predictable ending which all women expected after such encounters. Without a ripple of conscience, he voiced the practiced words. In his time, he'd offered them to dozens of women. It was all part of the game.

"You know that I love you," he said, and adroitly changed the subject. "But I am also partial to Sarah's lobster mousse. If we delay, we'll miss it."

Abruptly, he shut his mouth when it occurred to him that he really had been thinking of Sarah's lobster mousse. His lips quirked. He had just made love to a beautiful, passionate woman and immediately afterwards all he could think of was filling his stomach. He must be more jaded than he knew.

Shaking his head, smiling, he said, "Give me a few minutes before you follow me down. It's probably more discreet if we avoid each other for the rest of the evening."

"Adam?"

He had one hand on the door. His thoughts had drifted.

"Mmm?"

"You'll visit me later?"

His hesitation was barely noticeable. "I shall do

30

my best.''

As it turned out, Adam did not pay a visit to his mistress's house that evening, nor did he taste one morsel of Sarah's delectable lobster mousse. He had barely descended to the foot of the staircase, when the door to John Burke's bookroom opened. John's tall frame filled the doorway. His expression was grave.

"Adam, would you be so kind as to spare me a moment of your time?"

"Of course." Adam entered the bookroom noting that several gentlemen were seated about the room. He recognized three of those gentlemen as recently arrived refugees from France. After the introductions were made, he accepted a chair.

It was John Burke who led off with the first question. "Adam," he said, "what do you know of Philippe Duhet, the former Comte de Blaise, and now one of Robespierre's right-hand men?"

Long after Sarah's guests had gone home to their beds, Adam and John Burke lingered in the book-room over a decanter of whiskey. Adam's ready smile and easy charm had long since given way to an intensely brooding look. For some time past, silence prevailed.

Adam's mind was sifting through the conversation which had taken place earlier. Much of what had been related to him, he already knew. There was an escape route for French refugees operating out of Rouen. It was financed by American money. Selected ships were the means of transporting this human cargo to sanctuary in the United States.

Adam and John Burke were only two of the many backers of this venture. Adam's ships, the *Sheba* and the *Mariner*, regularly plied a course to various Mediterranean ports. It was a dangerous business. Frequently, both English and French warships arbitrarily seized or boarded American vessels which crossed their paths. Many American merchant ships were, at that very moment, languishing in French ports. Adam's ships took more chances than most. They unfailingly made a detour and anchored in the lee of a small island just off La Rochelle. When they made the return voyage to New York, they sometimes carried more than the silk, lace, and fine French furniture which packed their holds.

It seemed that the escape route was in jeopardy. In its wisdom, the Convention had instituted a new office with wide-ranging powers—the office of commissioner. One of those commissioners, a man who was notorious for his brutality, had been appointed to the City of Rouen. His name was Philippe Duhet.

John Burke cleared his throat. "If I thought, for one moment, that you had accepted this assignment out of some misguided sense of obligation to me, I should absolutely forbid it."

At these gruff words, Adam flashed one of his rare, natural grins. "No," he said. "Our friendship has nothing to do with my decision."

In this, he was not quite honest. The older man's friendship was something that Adam did not take lightly. For some reason that Adam was never able to fathom, John Burke had taken an instant liking to him from the moment they had come face-to-face outside Yorktown in a hastily dug trench which was under British fire.

In the intervening years, John had assumed the role of patron to the younger man. It was John's capital that had given Adam his start in the fur trade, and John's advice which had encouraged Adam to invest his profits from that venture in property in and around New York. One enterprise led to another. There was an iron foundry in Boston and a shipbuilding yard in Charleston. Adam was a rich man. He never forgot the debt of gratitude he owed to John Burke.

John shifted in his chair and glanced consideringly at the younger man. "This brother . . ."

"Half-brother," corrected Adam.

"This Philippe Duhet . . . I wonder if we are deluding ourselves by thinking that it is possible for you to impersonate him?"

"It's entirely possible. You heard Millot. Philippe and I might easily be taken for twins."

"Even so, there's more to impersonating a man than simply showing his face to the world and donning his clothes."

"Millot will keep me right." Adam's expression turned speculative. "You sound as though you are having second thoughts. I understood that you endorsed Millot's scheme?"

John Burke took a long swallow from his glass before replying. "Naturally, in common with all right-thinking men, I am sickened by the recent turn of events in France. According to our sources, things are going to get worse. Can you believe that? The fate of Marie Antoinette is almost a forgone conclusion. In the next few months, we may expect a flood of refugees. The escape route must continue to operate. When we heard that Deputy Duhet had been appointed as commissioner to Rouen, you can imagine our consternation."

"I can imagine." Adam's tone was dry. "But that was before someone remembered the uncanny resemblance between Philippe and myself."

"Not I!" exclaimed John, straightening in his chair. "To my knowledge, I have never set eyes on Duhet. And as for your connection . . . ," he shook his head, " . . . that took me completely by surprise."

Adam adroitly avoided this moot observation. "You still haven't answered my question. Are you having second thoughts, John?"

"I would not put it quite as strongly as that. Desperate situations call for desperate measures. But I would not be human if I did not entertain some reservations." Before Adam could interrupt, he went

33

on, "Philippe Duhet is a powerful figure in the Convention. He is well known."

"But not in Rouen," cut in Adam. "And that is where the substitution will be made."

For the first time in a long while, a smile creased the older man's cheeks. "To hear you talk, Adam," he said, "anyone would think that it is *you* who is having second thoughts. When Millot put his plan before you not thirty minutes ago, you were as chary as . . . well . . . as a fly walking over a spider's web. And yet, you agreed to involve yourself in the affair. Do you mind telling me why?"

Adam gave his attention to the amber liquid swirling in his glass. His mind was searching for answers that would be acceptable to his friend.

The project was almost impossible to bring off, in his opinion, at least for any length of time. But there was something about it that pulled at him like a magnet with a compass. He had always sensed that there would come a day when his path and Philippe Duhet's would cross. But it had never entered his head that he would be the one to bring that day forward.

Looking up, he said in that easy way of his, "As you say, all right-thinking men must be sickened by events in France. Few of us are in a position to do anything about our convictions. This evening, it seems that Fate, or Providence, touched me on the shoulder." To his friend's patently disbelieving look, he laughed before answering. "All right, I'm a young man. I'm bored. I'm restless. Does that answer your question?"

John Burke was not quite sure that it did, but he knew from experience that Adam would satisfy his curiosity only when it suited him. Nevertheless, he had learned a thing or two about his young friend that evening which had staggered him. Adam Dillon the half-brother of the notorious Deputy Duhet? And it was very evident that there was no love lost be-

34

tween these offshoots of the Comte de Blaise.

The next little while was taken up with reminiscences about France. John Burke had visited the birthplace of his ancestors on a number of occasions. His people had been French Protestants, Huguenots, who had sought refuge from the religious persecutions of the seventeenth century, eventually settling in the New World. Bourque was John's surname, long since Anglicized to Burke. John Burke, a lawyer by profession, was one of the fathers of the Constitution. He was a member, for want of a better name, of the French-American aristocracy, those influential families of French descent—the Burkes, the Jays, the Delanceys—who had settled in and around New York in the latter part of the previous century.

Adam's thoughts had wandered. Abruptly, he became alert when he sensed a certain change in the timbre of his companion's voice. The words were coming more slowly, as if John were having difficulty in expressing himself. Where were they? Oh yes. John was describing his visit to France in the summer of '72. Sarah was pregnant with their fifth child and had chosen to remain behind in New York.

"Her name was Juliette Devereux," said John, then seemed to retreat into a place where he was alone with his thoughts. A moment later, he bolted his drink, and poured himself another. "There was a child, a girl, I was given to understand. She would be all of twenty today, if she is alive, that is. I have no way of knowing. The Devereux, as you may understand, have never forgiven me for what I did. Juliette died in childbed. And there was the duel, you see."

"Devereux?" said Adam, stunned. "The international banking family?"

"The same."

"And you . . . fathered a child on a daughter of the

35

house when you were a married man . . . and Sarah . . ." Belatedly, Adam closed his mouth, annoyed with himself for having betrayed his shock.

"I wasn't in my right mind—isn't that what every man says?" Again, that grim smile hovered on the older man's lips. By this time, Adam had recovered his equilibrium. He had the sense to remain silent.

"I never stopped loving Sarah. But I loved Juliette, too. She was the most beautiful woman I have ever known. She was innocent. She was spoiled. She was headstrong. In a weak moment, I took what she was offering. God, I must have been mad!"

Adam understood perfectly. In his time, he'd had his share of virgins, most of whom had been more than a little eager to rid themselves of their tiresome condition. Some men, Adam knew, scrupulously avoided virgins as if they had the pox. He thought that the girl who had seduced a man of John Burke's principles must be the veriest Jezebel.

Something of Adam's reflections showed in his face. "Adam, you don't understand. The girl was not yet twenty. I was fifteen years her senior. She was an innocent. I had a wife whom I dearly loved." Wearily passing a hand over his eyes, the older man shook his head. "God, if Sarah were ever to discover that I had betrayed her . . ."

The silence lengthened. Adam replenished his own glass from the crystal decanter. He waited. Finally, John Burke raised his head.

"Leon Devereux is Juliette's brother. He has a wife and young family. He hates me, and with good reason, as I have already explained. Twice since, I've been to Paris. He refused to see me. There are reports that the Devereux are out of favor with Robespierre and his clique. At any moment, they could find themselves under arrest and facing execution. As a favor to me, I ask you, no, I beg you, if it is ever in your power to offer assistance to any member of this family—do so! As for Juliette's daughter, you must know I would move heaven and earth to have her here safely with me."

"And Sarah?" asked Adam quietly.

John Burke turned troubled eyes upon his companion. Adam looked away. "Sarah will understand," said John. "At all events, Sarah would never vent her wrath on an innocent girl."

Adam returned to his rooms in Wall Street at four of the clock in the morning. He didn't bother with a candle, but deftly peeled out of his garments with only the light of the moon to guide him. His nerves, he decided, were taut with excitement. His heart was racing. Soon, very soon . . . He shook his head, not fully understanding the reason for the furor which raged within. Naked, he stretched full-length upon the bed, his hands laced loosely behind his neck. He did not believe in fate, he reminded himself. Those words he had spouted to John were for effect only, nothing more. A man made his own choices, forged his own destiny. Wasn't he proof of it?

Philippe. He had been appointed commissioner to Rouen. His powers would be wide-ranging. In the provinces, the commissioners were to stand in place of the Convention. They were the only law. It did not seem possible, in the political climate of modern day France, that a man of Philippe's aristocratic background should go so far. God! Was there anything more ironic than Philippe Duhet, blue blood among blue bloods, carving a career for himself out of the ashes of the *ancien régime?*

Rouen. In Rouen, Adam would be the one to play the role of commissioner. His power would be almost absolute. For as long as the fiction that he was Philippe Duhet could be maintained, the escape route for fleeing refugees would remain open. Hundreds of lives, thousands, might be saved. He was doing a very fine thing. "Noble," Millot had called it.

Adam smiled, but there was nothing pleasant in the gesture. To be thought "noble" was a worthy ambition, he supposed, but it was not his. He was thinking that when the game was over and his half-brother resumed his rightful place, Philippe Duhet was going to find himself in a very awkward position. He, Adam Dillon, would make damn sure of it.

He turned on his side. By degrees, his eyelids became heavy. One thought drifted into another. Juliette Devereux. She was an innocent. She was beautiful. She was spoiled. She was headstrong. Even in sleep, Adam's lip curled. It was John who was the innocent. For Sarah's sake, he devoutly hoped that he would find no trace of Juliette Devereux and her child.

Chapter Two

The girl's name was Claire Devereux. She was the eldest child of the financier Leon Devereux and his wife, Elise. She was twenty years old. She was startlingly beautiful. She was spoiled. She was headstrong. And she was more afraid than she had ever been in her young life.

At any moment, she expected to come face-to-face with Philippe Duhet. The commissioner would step out of his office in his headquarters in Rouen's Hotel Grosne, and his eyes would sweep over the crush of suppliants in the anteroom. Unerringly, his gaze would single her out. It had happened once before, when she had been interrogated about her papers. This time, she was here by choice. Philippe Duhet would know it, and he would gloat.

Involuntarily, Claire huddled a little more deeply into her cloak. There was no fire in the grate in the commissioner's waiting room, but the heat from the crush of bodies took the chill off the air. She pitied those who were pleading with stony-faced officials for information on the fate of friends and family. They lived in desperate times, and the faces of those around her showed it. Everyone spoke in whispers. The smell of fear polluted the air.

It seemed beyond belief that she, Claire Devereux, a girl whose pride was almost legendary in her own circles, should have come to this. She was prepared to barter her pride, her beauty, her body, her favors, for two small pieces of paper—those coveted and almost impossible to obtain passports which promised their fortunate possessors safe-conduct out of France.

Oh God, how her detractors—and there were many of them—would mock her if they could see her now. *Proud,* some called her. Others were not so kind. *Arrogant,* they said. *Full of her own consequence,* said others. *A haughty beauty,* she had heard herself described on more than one occasion. And the man she had petitioned for an interview had once promised that he would take great delight in humbling that pride beneath his heel.

She *was* proud, but not in the sense that most people assumed. Her beauty did not hold her in thrall. Perversely, nature's gift had turned into something of a curse. It attracted men like moths to a flame. Her beauty, she knew, seduced their senses. Men wanted to possess her.

Wise to the ways of gentlemen, she held herself aloof. Their flatteries amused her. For all they cared, she might as well have been an empty-headed widgeon. In point of fact, they probably wished that she *was* a widgeon. When provoked, her tongue was rapier sharp. Her wit was scathing. She had the temper to match her red hair. Some gentlemen had discovered these unpalatable truths to their ever-lasting mortification.

Her mother had observed her elder daughter's growing cynicism with a troubled eye. She'd tried to remonstrate. It was imperative that Claire accept one of her suitors as soon as possible. Leon Devereux and his vast financial empire had excited the envy of some powerful deputies in the Convention. Anything might happen. A husband with the right con-nections could shield not only his wife but her family also.

Claire would have none of it. She was too proud to

40

accept a husband on those terms, and too headstrong to heed her mother's advice. Leon Devereux had aided and abetted his beautiful elder daughter. He could not credit that he stood in any real danger. His wife prevailed upon him, however, to set things in motion should the worst come to the worst.

Under assumed names and identities, with forged papers, they were to hide out in Rouen. His daughters were to take up residence in Madame Lambert's School for Girls. Claire, too old to pass herself off as a schoolgirl, was to be a teacher of piano and voice. Leon, named for his father, a youth of fifteen summers, was to be enrolled at a boys' school nearby. The parents would take their chances hiding out above a locksmith's shop. The arrangement was to be temporary. Leon Devereux confidently expected that escape to England or some other friendly country would be easily contrived. He had connections and money. What could go wrong?

Claire stifled a sob. Nothing had gone right! They had been taken completely off guard. In October, suddenly, the queen was tried and executed. Moderates in the Convention were denounced and swiftly followed Marie Antoinette to the guillotine. By the time Leon Devereux decided to put his plan of escape into motion, it was too late.

Deputies from the Commune arrested her parents the very night before they were due to leave for Rouen. Leon Devereux and his wife were an example that Claire would remember to her dying day. Calmly, they embraced their children in turn. Leon Devereux managed a private word with his eldest child before he was led away.

"Everything rests with you now," he said softly. "You are the strong one, Claire. I rely on you to take care of Zoë and Leon." He would have said more, but the deputies came between them.

Claire would never forget the hours that followed. Zoë was subdued. But Leon was in a passion, and all for organizing an escape attempt on the Abbaye where their parents were to be incarcerated. Claire was consumed with remorse.

She blamed herself for bringing them all to this sorry pass—she and her overweening pride. If she had only listened to her mother, if she had only accepted the hand of one of those well-connected suitors, it might have been possible to avert the catastrophe which had overtaken them.

When she came to herself, she knew exactly what she must do. "You are the strong one," her father had told her. "I rely on you to take care of Zoë and Leon." She accepted her responsibility for her younger siblings as if it had been a sacred trust.

Over Leon's protests, she insisted that they follow their father's instructions to the letter. They must make for Rouen and take up their lives there. Leon finally gave way when Claire pointed out that, as well as Madame Lambert, there were friends in Rouen waiting to help them. She was far from sure on this point, but she refused to delay. Warrants for their arrest might be sworn out at any moment. It was a common story. Except for young children, whole families were sometimes arrested and sent to the guillotine.

With the exception of Madame Lambert, however, there were no friends waiting to help them in Rouen. As the weeks passed, it became evident to Claire that they must fend for themselves. She had come to accept that they must ride out the storm in France under their assumed identities. Later, when the world returned to sanity, they would take up their lives where they had left off.

It was a vain hope. From the moment Philippe Duhet's eyes had locked on hers, two months before, as he rode into Rouen's market square at the head of his troops, Claire sensed that she would not be left alone to live in peace. That damnable beauty of hers, which she had tried to conceal behind nondescript frocks and plain bonnets, had served her ill, had served them all ill. The last thing they wanted was to come to the notice of the authorities. The last thing she wanted was to come to the notice of a man like Duhet.

His reputation curdled her blood. All Rouen was agog with stories about the new commissioner. It was said that he had murdered all the members of his family one by one. It was known for a fact that he'd had a hand in razing to the ground a convent just outside Paris. Some of the nuns had perished by the guillotine. He was a known debaucher of innocents. Mothers were already warning their young daughters to keep out of his sight.

There were some in Rouen, however, who welcomed Philippe Duhet's appointment. The fanatics were jubilant. Duhet would bring the Terror to their province. He must. He was Robespierre's man. And then the North would be rid of all subversive elements and their spawn.

Before a week was out, she was summoned to the commissioner's office and her false papers examined. Commissioner Duhet made no bones about what he was after. He wanted her for his mistress, and told her so straight out. His crudity inflamed her temper. Before she could stop herself, she was spitting her hatred at him. Far from angering him, her proud defiance only enamored him the more. He let her go, but Claire was sure that the reprieve was to be only temporary.

Before Commissioner Duhet could bend her to his will, duty had intervened. For six weeks, she was given a respite. The commissioner and his soldiers were under orders to track down the remnants of the defeated Grand Army of the Vendée. Six weeks of considering the hopelessness of their position had brought Claire to an about-face.

"You are the strong one, Claire," her father had told her. "I rely on you to take care of Zoë and Leon."

43

Sometimes Claire thought that it was Zoë, for all her gentle manner, who was the strong one in the family. No one would have taken the two girls for sisters. In temperament and in looks, they were complete opposites. Zoë was as dark as Claire was fair. She took after the rest of the Devereux. Claire was reputed to take after her paternal grandmother.

Zoë was younger than Claire by three years. She looked up to her older sister for some reason that Claire could not conceive. Zoë, in her opinion, was by far the finer person.

For the present, Zoë had adopted the role and modes of a thirteen-year-old schoolgirl. But Claire worried about her sister incessantly. How long, she wondered, before some male predator penetrated the disguise? And if and when that happened, what would become of little Zoë?

It was Leon, however, who gave Claire her worst anxieties, and never more so than in the last few days. In an unguarded moment, she had confided the disquieting news that their parents had been transferred from the Abbaye to the prison at Carmes. It was Madame Lambert, the proprietress of the girls' school where Zoë and Claire resided, who had received the report from friends in Paris.

Leon was beside himself. Carmes was one step closer to the impregnable Conciergerie. And as everyone knew, the Conciergerie was the last stop on the way to the scaffold.

Claire, too, was wracked by fears for the fate of her parents. Leon was not the only one to grasp that something must be done for them soon if they were to cheat the guillotine of two of its victims. But Leon's way was reckless. He was threatening to return to Paris and enlist his friends' aid in an attempt to storm the prison. Such foolhardiness was doomed to failure. Claire had a better way, but one that she dared not confide to Leon.

"I rely on you to take care of Zoë and Leon." She

could hear her father's words as if he had just whispered them in her ear.

If it was in her power, she would take care of them all, she resolved—Zoë, Leon, as well as her parents. The beauty she had once despised could be turned into a valuable asset. She would barter it, if Philippe Duhet was willing to meet her price.

The door opened and Philippe Duhet strode into the anteroom. There was no denying that he was a handsome creature. Hair as black as sable was tied back in a queue, accenting the patrician features. Claire found that she was holding her breath. His eyes swept over the crush of people. When he saw her, a look of triumph fleetingly flashed in those extraordinary green eyes. Claire felt her skin begin to crawl. The commissioner always had that effect on her.

He said something in an undertone to one of his subordinates and Claire was not surprised that it was she who was chosen to enter the commissioner's inner sanctum. When she entered, he was seated at his desk, his long fingers idly drumming a tattoo on the blotter. He seemed preoccupied. Not for one moment was Claire deceived by the pose he had adopted. He was toying with her as a cat toys with a mouse.

"Please be seated," he said, indicating a chair pulled close to his desk.

Claire, thankfully, sank into it. Her knees were buckling under her. Her throat was so dry she could barely swallow. She knew that he was staring at her, but she was afraid to lift her head.

The girl was beautiful, startlingly so. Philippe Duhet allowed his eyes to wander at will over her womanly contours and he was struck anew by the thought that never, in his whole life, had he ever encountered a more perfect or delectable specimen of the fairer sex.

Her skin was translucent, like fine parchment

tinted with roses. Her heavily lashed blue eyes were slightly slanted at the corners and gilded by the delicate arch of her brows. And her hair, bathed by the thin wintry sun which streamed through the west windows, seemed to be touched by fire.

He had wanted her since he had first caught sight of her as he had ridden into Rouen. Claire Michelet—not her real name, he surmised—was one of the spectators who, silent and morose, had thronged the market square as his soldiers had set up the guillotine, at his command.

He'd made it his business to find out as much as he could about her. She was one of the schoolmistresses at Madame Lambert's School for Girls. He had not been in Rouen a week, before he had sent his men to fetch her, ostensibly to examine her papers.

He wanted her as he had never before wanted any woman. She was a spitfire. Her defiance stirred him. He would subjugate her just as he had subjugated those rebel peasants of the Grand Army who dared to challenge his authority. The blood lust was still in him. At Angers, they had captured Sillery, one of the rebel leaders. On the morrow, he would ride out and bring the man back in chains. Sillery would be tried and publicly executed. The thought excited his passion for the woman to fever pitch.

He had promised to humble her pride. Claire Michelet would soon learn that he never made idle threats. "How may I serve you, Mademoiselle Michelet?" he murmured, breaking into Claire's train of thought.

She raised her head, and her eloquent blue eyes narrowed unpleasantly. She came directly to the point. "I have two young friends who wish to visit relatives in England. I was hoping, Commissioner Duhet, that you might assist them."

Subduing his annoyance at her barefaced effrontery, he smiled, saying, "What you suggest is treasonable. Our two countries are at war."

46

Silence.

His smile deepened. He decided that Claire Michelet would be suitably chastened by the time he had finished with her. "Two passports," he drawled. "You sell yourself cheaply."

Color came and went under her skin, but she held his gaze steadily. "Passports won't get my friends to England," she said. "As you say, our two countries are at war. I want some assurance that transportation will be arranged for them."

No fool, the beautiful Claire Michelet. "Consider it done. Is there anything more?"

There was one thing more, but Claire was reluctant to mention it until Zoë and Leon were safely away. The instant she introduced the subject of her parents, the name Devereux must be out in the open. She was deathly afraid that to reveal so much might be tantamount to signing a death warrant for them all. And yet, she must say something.

"Well?" His patience was wearing thin.

She inhaled deeply. "There are two people in Carmes Prison who are very dear to me. I want you to use your influence to have them released."

"Their names?"

She shook her head. "Now is not the time to discuss it. Once my young friends have arrived safely in England, I shall give you their names."

"Suit yourself." It made little difference whether she told him now or later. He had no interest in assisting Claire Michelet or any of her friends. The little he would do, would be for appearances' sake only.

He would sign the passports and provide a carriage. Millot, his clerk, would arrange it. But once the coach left Rouen, Claire Michelet's young friends would get no help from him. Nor would her friends at Carmes.

He leaned forward on the desk, his hands clasped loosely in front of him. His charming manner repelled Claire.

"And now, mademoiselle, allow me to tell you exactly what you may expect from the bargain we have struck."

Brutally, graphically, unsparing of her blushes, he described how she would pleasure him when she came to his bed. By the time he had finished, Claire's head was bowed, her cheeks were ashen. Duhet was smiling, well satisfied with the effect he had achieved.

"Tonight," he said. "You will come to me tonight."

At this, her head lifted, but she kept her eyes downcast. Her breath was fluttery; her voice was low. "I shall come to you when my friends have left Rouen and not a moment before."

Without warning, he brought his fist down on the flat of the desk, sending papers and inkwell scattering. Claire's heart leapt to her mouth.

"Millot!" roared Duhet.

The door opened to admit a young man, one of the clerks. "Commissioner?"

Duhet was on his feet, pacing angrily. "Two passports, Millot, for Mademoiselle Michelet. See to it."

Claire forced herself to her feet. "And transportation?" She faltered under the blaze of fury in his eyes. She could hear the rasp of his breath before he brought himself under control.

"Millot, you heard the lady. She desires transportation for two friends."

The clerk waited respectfully. After a moment, he coughed. "What destination, sir?"

Duhet laughed, and the sound of it made Claire flinch. "Tell him, my dear. No need to dissemble. Millot is in my confidence."

She looked at the clerk pleadingly and something in his expression emboldened her to voice the word. "England," she whispered.

A long look passed between the two men. Claire did not notice. Her head was bowed.

"That will be all, Millot. You may wait on Mademoiselle Michelet in the outer office."

"Certainly, sir."

When the door closed behind the clerk, Duhet folded his arms and lounged against the desk. "I ride for Angers at first light," he said.

"Angers?"

He smiled unpleasantly. "Your hopes are misplaced, my dear. The last thing I shall do is instruct Millot to install you here, in my chambers, before he hands over those passports to your friends."

"I'm to be your prisoner, then?"

"Prisoner?" A look of amusement crossed his face. "You have a flair for the melodramatic." He gestured with one hand. "Look around you. Is this a prison? I shall provide you with fine clothes, fine food. You'll be waited on hand and foot. Do you know how many women would give everything they possess to be in your shoes?"

She *was* giving everything she possessed, but not for the rewards Duhet held out. Zoë, Leon, her parents—their safety was paramount. Oh God, she prayed that she could go through with it.

Her silence provoked him to anger.

"I shall be gone for three days—four at the most. When I return, I shall expect to find you here. I advise you not to try to go back on our bargain. Do you understand?"

Claire could not seem to find her voice and signified her assent with a quick nod.

He turned his back on her. "My clerk will write out the passports. I shall sign them before I leave," and he dismissed her with a wave of one hand.

In the anteroom, Claire absently accepted the chair the clerk indicated. She was beginning to have second thoughts about the path she had chosen. Every instinct screamed that Philippe Duhet was not to be trusted.

"For whom are these passports intended?" The clerk's quill was poised over a piece of velum.

Claire licked her lips.

"Mademoiselle?"

She could not know that her beautiful eyes betrayed a tormented spirit. Millot, the clerk, found himself swallowing.

He knew something of the girl's story, having unobtrusively eavesdropped at the door. Fleetingly, he considered the wisdom of meddling in her affairs. She blinked back tears, and in the space of a single heartbeat, Millot was lost.

"Mademoiselle," he said, and Claire detected a thread of urgency in the soft tone. "I, Nicholas Millot, shall personally undertake to see that your friends are conveyed to a place of safety." He smiled encouragingly. "Leave everything to me."

The words had a sobering effect on Claire. She studied the young man closely. He wasn't handsome in the sense that Philippe Duhet was handsome, but Claire supposed that every man's looks must pale into insignificance when compared to the commissioner's. Millot might not possess Duhet's looks, but she infinitely preferred the younger man. He had kind eyes, she decided, and a smile that invited confidence. She had to trust someone. And it was too late to turn back.

Long after Claire had quit the commissioner's headquarters, Nicholas Millot sat hunched over his desk, feigning absorption in the papers he was perusing.

The girl was desperate and he had promised to help her. In two days, three at the most, the substitution would be made and Adam Dillon would be at the helm. There was no doubt in Millot's mind that Adam would sanction the decision he had made respecting the girl.

Their own network was useless for the girl's

purposes. She insisted that her friends' destination be England. Evidently, she thought that America was at the end of the world. It would have been easy to persuade her, but Millot had not the heart. Nor was it necessary. There was a British network with agents in Rouen. One of those agents owed him a favor. It was time to call in the debt.

Chapter Three

Three days later, Claire stood at one of the small windows in the commissioner's private suite of chambers, gazing steadfastly at the scene below. Though tears misted her eyes, a smile was pinned resolutely to her lips. Zoë was about to enter the carriage which was to take her to the coast and freedom. Their eyes caught and held. Claire nodded encouragingly, and Zoë, with one last lingering look, obediently climbed inside the coach.

The temptation to call out, to do something to attract Zoë's attention one last time was almost irresistible. Claire bit down on her lip when the order was called out and men mounted up. As the carriage jostled into motion, with a choked sob she turned back into the room.

It was done. Zoë was on the first lap of a journey that would take her to England. Millot, the commissioner's clerk, had arranged everything. Claire trusted the young man far more than she trusted Philippe Duhet. And, oh God, she must trust someone. If Millot had lied to her, God knows what might become of little Zoë.

As she idled her way to the small table with the remains of the meal she had shared with her sister moments before, Claire clung desperately to the reasons for her confidence in the commissioner's clerk. Millot liked her. He liked her a lot. She suspected that he might even think himself half in love with her. He was considerate of her feelings. He had done everything in his power to reassure her, even going so far as to arrange this last meeting with Zoë.

For all her tender years, Zoë was nobody's fool. She knew! O God, Zoë knew why her elder sister had taken up residence in the commissioner's headquarters! Not that Zoë had said anything. But the knowledge was there in her sad, dark eyes. It was almost more than Claire could bear. Zoë had always looked up to her. Now, she was a fallen woman, or she soon would be, once Duhet returned from Angers.

If it had been in her power, she would have arranged this last meeting with Zoë at the school—anywhere, in fact, except the commissioner's headquarters. Millot, she was sure, would have permitted it. But by ill-luck, or design, Duhet had given the precious passports into the hands of another subordinate, one who was completely indifferent to Claire's feelings. He had his orders. Until the woman was established in Commissioner Duhet's chambers, he refused to hand over the passports. It was no less than she expected. Millot had tried to argue the point with the other man to no purpose.

Millot was a gentleman. It was obvious that he wished to spare her embarrassment. The removal to the hotel had been accomplished under cover of darkness, when the curfew was on. It was almost as if he wished no one to know the identity of Duhet's mistress—a forlorn hope. As she'd walked into the hotel's lobby the night before, a throng of young conscripts had blocked her path. She was recognized, and her name was taken up and bandied about.

"Isn't that one of the teachers at Madame Lambert's?"

"The stuck-up one. Claire something-or-other."

"Michelet," supplied someone, and laughed suggestively. "If I had known that she was for sale, I'd have tried to meet her price."

"Forêt, you couldn't meet the price of the town whore, and what she has, she gives away. This fancy bit of stuff is a rich man's toy."

Laughter drowned out the next remark.

Claire's cheeks burned. Millot's face twisted with fury. He would have put a stop to the coarse talk if Claire had not prevented it. Laying a restraining hand on his sleeve, she shook her head and quickly began to mount the stairs. What did it matter that she had been recognized? It was only a matter of time before the whole of Rouen knew that she was Duhet's mistress. But oh, she had hoped that word would not get out until Zoë and Leon were on their way.

The thought of Leon brought her back to the present. He should have been on the coach with Zoë. He, at least, had been forewarned that he was to leave today.

Millot had tried to delay the departure of the coach until Leon arrived. It was impossible. He'd done the next best thing. He had gone in person to fetch her brother. There was no need for alarm, he had told her, for when he found Leon, they would simply ride after the coach and soon catch it up. Claire's one regret was that the three of them, she, Zoë, and Leon, had not shared one last meal together before they must part.

The word "forever" almost intruded to be quickly banished. One day, she promised herself, they would all be together again. They would sit down at the dinner table with Maman and Papa presiding. Papa would tell his funny stories one after the other, and, as usual, he would ruin the joke by fumbling the ending. And the dining room in their house in Saint-Germain would ring with laughter at Papa's expense. Afterwards, they would retire to the music room, where Zoë would entertain them at the piano, or

Claire would sing one of the old ballads which Papa preferred. Sometimes, Leon would join her and they would sing a duet. Leon had a very fine baritone.

When a tap rattled the door, Claire stiffened. the door rattled again, and Claire went to open it. One of the maids to whom Claire had taken an instant liking, simply because she reminded her of Zoë, shyly proffered a folded note. It was from Millot.

His first words were reassuring. He knew where her brother was to be found. Unfortunately, he went on, to fetch the boy and catch up with the coach would take him longer than he had anticipated. At all events, he expected to return long before nightfall, by which time Commissioner Duhet was expected to arrive from Angers.

Claire lowered her brows. Leon, surely, would not be so foolish as to jeopardize this one chance of leaving France? Where was he? What was he up to? She pressed a hand to her temples. No. She would not believe that he had run off to Paris with some fool notion of helping their parents. He had promised that he had given up that reckless scheme.

But when was Leon not reckless? From the day of his birth, he had been possessed with a spirit of adventure. Their mother had sworn that she never would have had a gray hair in her head had it not been for the antics of her youngest child. And though Maman had spoken in jest, her two daughters had recognized that her words held the substance of truth. Leon would dare the devil just for the fun of it.

It was that same recklessness which had once saved Claire's life, and she never forgot it. There had been a fire at the inn where they were staying. Claire's room was in the attics and the stairs were impassable. Leon had somehow managed to get to her window and had coaxed her to safety over the inn's roof.

Recalling that incident filled her with foreboding. It was entirely possible that Leon had run off with some harebrained scheme of saving their parents. She quickly scanned Millot's note for a second time, and gradually Millot's words restored her confidence. He knew where Leon was to be found and expected to return before nightfall.

But when dark descended, and Millot had not returned, Claire's misgivings came back in full force. At every sound in the street below, she gave a little start of dread. It might be Millot. On the other hand, the sound of horses' hooves might signal the arrival of Philippe Duhet. She hardly knew what she hoped for.

The hours passed slowly. Eventually, the candles were lit. To pass the time, Claire investigated every nook and cranny in the commissioner's suite of rooms. In one of the *bureaux*, she came across a decanter of brandy. To steady her nerves, she imbibed a little. She was on her second glass when the maid, Blanche, entered to inquire whether or not she should draw Mademoiselle's bath.

Claire must have given her consent, for some time later, the maid called her into the adjoining room. Averting her eyes from the huge tester bed, Claire allowed herself to be led to the steaming wooden tub which was placed strategically before the hearth.

With the maid's assistance, Claire began to disrobe. For no reason that she could fathom, she began to giggle. Naked, Claire stepped into the tub still clutching the glass of brandy to her breast. She frowned, observing that the glass was almost empty. The maid obligingly fetched the decanter and replenished Mademoiselle's glass.

Claire sank into the fragrant water with a deep sigh of contentment. Her fears, she decided, were completely unfounded. Leon was, in all probability, safely on his way to England. And as for Philippe Duhet . . . She smiled. These were uncertain times. Between Angers and Rouen, anything might have happened to the commissioner. In all conscience, she could not wish for something fatal, but there were lesser evils that she had no hesitation in wishing upon him. His horse might have stumbled and thrown him, or he might have sustained an injury from another quarter. Perhaps he was wounded, or he might have broken a leg, or been captured by the rebels, or . . . Her pleasant thoughts droned on.

It was after midnight before Adam rode into Rouen at the head of a small band of men. Having been well briefed, he knew exactly where the commissioner's headquarters were to be found. And even if he were foolish enough to mistake the way in the dark, his two companions, Bernay and Granville, who rode on either side of him, were there to keep him right.

When they entered the arch leading to the hotel's courtyard, Adam snapped out orders and the men quickly dismounted. Stableboys came running to lead the horses away. With a show of supreme confidence, Adam led the way into the back entrance of the timber and wattle building.

Once in the hotel's cramped foyer, he shouted a name. "Domfrey!" and then, in an undertone to his two companions, "Where the devil is Millot?"

They shrugged with an assumed indifference. Millot's absence was the one small wrinkle in an enterprise which had gone off like clockwork. They had delayed for two hours at the rendezvous, waiting for their fellow conspirator to show. Millot had never appeared. It was his task to report on anything of significance which had transpired in Rouen in the last little while, anything that might jeopardize their mission.

"Domfrey!"

The word was scarcely out of Adam's mouth when a door to the left of the narrow staircase opened. "Sir!"

The young captain who stumbled into the hallway

adjusting the tunic of his uniform was flushed. A woman's voice languidly called an endearment from the room he had quit and the captain's cheeks burned scarlet before he made haste to shut the door at his back. *A clear case of dereliction of duty if ever I saw it*, Adam was thinking. He felt like laughing. Recalling himself to the role he was playing, he smiled unpleasantly.

"Captain Domfrey," he said, and gestured to his companions, "these envoys are from Deputy Robespierre. They are to be my aides. See that they and their men are comfortably quartered in the hotel."

There was a silence and Adam began to wish that he had listened to his friends' advice. They should have waited for Millot. For all he knew, Robespierre, himself, might have descended on the hotel in the last day or two. Or perhaps John Burke was right. There was more to impersonating a man than showing his face to the world and donning his clothes.

Imperceptibly, Adam's hand moved to the hilt of his short sword.

The captain cleared his throat. "What news of Sillery, sir?" He was referring to the rebel leader whom the commissioner had promised to bring back in chains from Angers.

Adam's hand fell to his side. Assuming an attitude compounded of dignity and suppressed rage, through his teeth, he gritted, "Evidently, he is not here."

"A bad business, a bad business," commiserated Granville, looking at nobody in particular.

Bernay clucked his tongue and shook his head. "The commissioner was fortunate to escape with his life."

The captain gasped and looked incredulously from one gentleman to the other.

Adam made a growling sound deep in his throat. "Gentlemen," he said, "you may assure Deputy Robespierre that it is only a matter of time before we

58

catch up with Sillery, yes, and with those misguided peasants who sprung him from my trap. You may depend upon it, every available man will be set to track down the outlaws."

The captain wasn't to know it, but there were several "Sillerys" in the area whose mission it would be to keep the commissioner's troops busy and out of Rouen. The presence of soldiers in the city had curtailed the work of the escape route. In the last number of weeks, the house-to-house searches had led to a spate of arrests and subsequent executions. For as long as Adam could maintain his disguise, the citizens of Rouen could expect an improvement in living conditions.

"I believe I gave you an order," said Adam softly, looking directly at the captain.

"Sir." Domfrey's heels clicked together. "This way, gentlemen." He pivoted and had taken no more than three steps, when the commissioner's voice halted him.

"Captain!"

"Sir?"

"I'd like a word with Millot. See to it."

"He hasn't returned, sir."

"He hasn't . . . returned," repeated Adam noncommittally.

"No, sir. Not since Mademoiselle Michelet sent him on an errand."

There was a pause. Bernay and Granville chanced a quick look at each other. Adam's expression was inscrutable.

"Carry on, Captain."

"Sir!"

Adam delayed until his companions had turned the corner in the long corridor before he began to mount the stairs. Mademoiselle Michelet. The name meant nothing to him *Nicholas, you sly dog!* he was thinking, and laughed.

The commissioner had his suite of rooms—an

office, a parlor, and two bedchambers—one floor up. Millot had drawn a map of the hotel for Adam so that there could be no careless gaffes. Without hesitation, Adam pushed into the room that he knew was Philippe's private parlor.

He saw at a glance that the candles had been lit for some time. The embers of a fire glowed a welcome in the grate. After removing his cloak, Adam made straight for the bureau where Philippe kept his brandy. He found a fresh bottle and opened it. The thought that he was depriving Philippe of his best cognac put Adam in a more congenial frame of mind,

The first small glass, he bolted. The second, he savored, imbibing slowly, having settled himself in one of the armchairs flanking the hearth.

He had one regret, he decided, and that was that his fellow conspirators had not allowed him to come face-to-face with Philippe. He had anticipated that moment with relish. It was not to be. Everything had happened so quickly.

Philippe, all unsuspecting, had walked into the hut where they were holding "Sillery." His two faithful bodyguards were dispatched instantly. They had no choice here. Since Remy and Savarin were Philippe's intimates, Adam could never, for one moment, hope to maintain his role with the likes of those two. Philippe suffered only a bump on the head, but severe enough to render him unconscious.

He was stripped, and Adam had donned his clothes. A moment later, "Sillery," with a knife to Adam's throat, exited the hut, and while all eyes were on the rebel leader and his "hostage," Philippe was safely spirited away out the back door. At this very moment, he was under lock and key in the real Sillery's stronghold in the Forest of Verte.

Adam cocked his head. For a moment, he imagined that he'd heard a woman's laughter, low-pitched and melodious. He listened, but there was nothing but the soft hiss of the dying embers in the grate.

He was about to replenish his empty glass when it came again. There could be no mistake, the laughter was definitely feminine, and coming from one of the bedchambers.

Adam set down his glass. Without haste, he rose to his feet. Two strides took him to the door. With the press of one hand, he slowly pushed it open.

The girl in the tub had her profile to him. Like a waterfall of liquid fire, her gold-red hair cascaded over her shoulders and breasts. She was gurgling with laughter.

Adam recognized her at once. In the weeks before he had removed to Angers to await Duhet's arrival, from an upstairs window in a safe house hard by the cathedral, he'd watched her come and go. Something about the girl had intrigued him.

She was more beautiful than was good for her, a truth she seemed to grasp. She'd done her best to conceal her loveliness beneath a nondescript disguise. Much good it had done her. It had amused him to note that every man and boy over the age of thirteen summers, like himself, trailed her with ravenous eyes. A few of the bolder ones approached her, attempting to get up a flirtation. She repelled every overture with a cool, distancing stare. For the most part, her ploy was successful, but there were always gentlemen who would not take no for an answer. It was then that the girl betrayed her temper. With eyes flashing fire, and head and shoulders thrown back, she flayed them with her tongue. And the men, more fools they, let her get away with it, slinking away with their tails between their legs.

Beneath the haughty facade, the girl was a spitfire, a veritable tigress. To Adam, she was the ultimate challenge to his masculinity, arousing the hunter in him.

He might have forgotten her very existence, if she had not betrayed another side of her character. The boy was evidently her brother, or a close relative, though there was nothing in their resemblance to suggest such a thing. Her manner with the boy, the way she smiled at him, the way she clung to him, and scolded him and laughed with him, touched Adam in a way he would not have believed possible. He looked more closely at the boy. Did he know how fortunate he was to have someone lavish him with such affection? He thought of his own boyhood, and Adam envied him.

The boy said something to the girl and he stalked off in a sulk. Adam felt like going after him to administer a thrashing. The girl was close to tears.

"Ah, tigress, don't cry! Don't cry!" He'd said the words out loud.

As if she'd heard him, she felt in her reticule and withdrew a lace-edged handkerchief. She blew her nose, squared her shoulders, and proceeded purposefully on her way.

"Good girl," he'd said, and smiled, touched by her hard-won control, knowing intuitively that she carried burdens too heavy for one slip of a girl. He'd wished, quite seriously, that he was in a position to shoulder some of those burdens. But he dared not show his face in the streets of Rouen, not until Philippe was safely locked away.

If Adam was intrigued with the girl before, by this time, he was fascinated. Who was she? What was her relationship to the boy? Why did she try to conceal her beauty behind a dowd's disguise? Such a girl did not belong in a backwater like Rouen. It was inevitable that she must belong to some powerful man. Who was her husband and where was he? And what, if anything, would he, Adam Dillon, do about this shadowy figure should he ever meet him face-to-face? The question was a serious one, and Adam did not care for the farfetched solutions which came to his mind. That he would go after the girl once his hands were free was no longer debatable.

The questions had teemed inside his head. And

now he had his answer. It was evident that the woman was the property of his half-brother, Philippe. Millot had never as much as hinted that Philippe had taken a mistress. There were women, yes, but no one of any significance. That this woman would be significant to the man who possessed her, Adam never doubted.

His eyes swept over her beautiful body, and the cynical twist to his mouth became more pronounced. He felt, in some strange way, that she had betrayed him.

Claire was absorbed in hunting for the bar of rose-scented soap which seemed to have developed a mind of its own. It kept slipping away from her hand. Her fingers closed around it, and she held it aloft with a crow of triumph.

"Good evening."

At the quiet salutation, Claire froze. She closed her eyes, then opened them wide. It was some time before she could regulate her breathing.

As Duhet came further into the room, she was not aware that she counted each soft footfall under her breath. Before he halted, facing her, she had forced herself to a tenuous calm.

Slowly, her head lifted, her eyes fastened on him, absorbing the finely etched features, the well-shaped mouth, the thick pelt of dark hair tied back with a ribbon. But it was the promise in those glittering green eyes which made her shiver. "It's you," she breathed hoarsely. "It's you."

He was studying her silently. Where his eyes touched, her skin grew cold. Her hands clenched around the rim of the tub. "Oh God, it's you," she repeated.

The words scarcely registered on Adam's brain. He was staring at the woman as if he were seeing a vision. He had known, intimately, many beautiful women, he was thinking. Never, *never*, had any woman had such a profound effect on him. If it had been only her beauty, only the pull on his senses, he would have discounted it, but this girl's attraction went deeper than anything he had ever known.

Without conscious thought, he captured her hands and drew her from the bath. The scent of roses filled his nostrils. With any other woman, he would have openly appraised her naked loveliness. Her eyes held his and he could not seem to look away.

"It's all right," he soothed, and the words surprised him. Slowly, inexorably, he pulled her into his arms.

His lips found hers and sank into their softness. She did not respond, but she did not resist him either. Adam pulled back and studied her wide-eyed expression. There was feminine wariness in her eyes. Every instinct told him that she was coming to him reluctantly.

He wasn't a complete scoundrel. Her reluctance should have mattered to him. It didn't. Something primitive, something savage and totally masculine seemed to have entered his bloodstream. His skin was fever hot, his breathing was difficult. He seemed to have lost his grip on reality. Philippe Duhet was forgotten, as was the elaborate charade that had brought him into Rouen. The only thing that Adam was conscious of was the woman in his arms and the driving compulsion which urged him to prove to her that she belonged to him.

He kissed her again, and this time her lips softened beneath the fierce pressure of his. It was all the encouragement he needed.

"It's all right," he repeated, soothing away the panic that flashed in her eyes. He swept her up in his arms and carried her to the bed.

Chapter Four

Adam felt as though he had been hit by a bolt of lightning. If he were not struck so dumb, he was thinking, he would have laughed out loud. He had discovered something about himself that both staggered and amused him. He had discovered that Adam Dillon, cynic, dilettante, connoisseur of fine women, was as green as grass. Where women were concerned, it seemed that he was as gullible as the next man. He did laugh, but muted, so as not to waken the sleeping girl by his side.

Virgins. How had he ever imagined he had taken a virgin to his bed? He'd had his first virgin—his first and last virgin, he amended—and now he knew the difference. Shuddering, he resolved that he *never* wished to repeat the experience.

She'd been so small, so tight. As soon as he'd pressed into her, he'd felt the delicate barrier protecting her innocence from his masculine invasion. For a moment, a very fleeting moment, he'd almost had second thoughts, had almost heeded the incipient stirrings of his tardy conscience. But the lust to possess this particular woman and no other was driving him relentlessly. He was her first lover. The knowledge acted like a spur to the ardor he was barely holding in check. He could not help himself. He'd tried to gentle her with words, to no effect. And

65

though her nails flayed him without mercy, slowly, surely, he had penetrated till he was deeply embedded in her body.

To his knowledge, it was the first time he had failed to bring pleasure to his bed partner. He was a skillful, careful lover. He'd never hurt a woman in his life. But this experience was profoundly different, as he had known it would be. It was as though he wished to impress his stamp of ownership upon the woman. She was his. He would prove it to her.

He had never considered relations with a female in such terms. It was laughable, only he wasn't laughing. Where this woman was concerned, he felt barely civilized. If she ever belonged to him and betrayed him, he knew that he would not be able to contain his violence.

The girl stirred restlessly, and Adam turned into her. He smoothed one swatch of satin-soft hair across his throat. The faint fragrance of roses clung to her skin. He'd already tasted the brandy on her lips and had wondered at it, but idly. There were things of far more significance on his mind.

She was, without doubt, the most beautiful woman he had ever set eyes on. No man could fail to be affected. Everything about her, from her glorious flame red hair to her shapely feminine contours, tempted a man to handle her possessively.

Yet, it wasn't her beauty that pulled at him so ceaselessly. Adam had known many beautiful women. He could take them or leave them. This girl's appeal was different. There was something here, something he could not name, that drew him inexorably.

He rolled to his side, away from the girl. She was just a woman, he told himself. Her appeal was all to his senses, nothing more. No woman had ever held Adam Dillon in thrall. No woman ever would.

There came to him a fragment of conversation with a former mistress whose name he'd long since forgotten—a possessive woman whose incessant jealousies had bored him to tears. Their liaison had been stormy and mercifully brief. Her parting shot came back to him.

"One day," she'd flung at him, "one day the glove will be on the other hand. Some woman is going to wrap Adam Dillon around her little finger. I hope I'm there to see it!"

The day when Adam Dillon would make a fool of himself over a woman would arrive when hell froze over. Desire was a fickle mistress, here today, gone on the morrow. He had only to sate himself with the girl, and her hold on him would be broken. Even as the words registered in his brain, he knew that they were a lie. He cursed derisively, and he damned himself for a fool. It had been a mistake to take this woman, perhaps the biggest mistake of his life. He'd broken one of his own cardinal rules. At the moment of climax, he'd spilled his seed into her. But in that moment, rules had been the furthest thing from his mind.

Mother Nature, he thought, was cunning. She played a waiting game. He was overconfident. For years he'd kept one step ahead of that devious old dame. He'd never lost his head over any woman. He'd never spilled his seed inside a woman's body—until this woman had fallen in his way. Even now, the girl might have conceived his child.

Again he swore, but this time more luridly. God, he could hardly credit it—that he, Adam Dillon, having deftly evaded the coils of worldly, experienced women in a long life of dissipation, should be caught finally in a trap as old as time! It was galling, all the more so because he knew that the girl at his side would be less thrilled with the notion that she might be pregnant than even he was! He knew a score of women who would give everything they possessed to be in her place. A child would hold him as nothing else could. Why the hell did it have to happen with her?

If the girl was pregnant, he would marry her, whatever her sentiments on the subject. By and large, in his dealings with women, Adam Dillon was a rogue. But there was one thing he had long since resolved. He would never father a bastard child.

He knew what it was to be a bastard, to be raised by people who never wanted him. No child of his would suffer the indignities, the agonies he had been made to suffer. If the girl was pregnant, he would accept the consequences.

Already, he wanted to take her again. The thought appalled him. He scowled into the darkness. Though the girl was willing, she had suffered his caresses in silence. At the last, when the pain of his possession had frightened her, she had fought him like a tigress. No sane man wished to take an unwilling woman to his bed. Then what the devil was the matter with him?

If he had any sense of self-preservation, he would get up and walk away from her. He knew almost nothing about the girl except that she was an innocent, she was here by choice, and that his half-brother had some claim to her. He couldn't begin to speculate on what was going on.

God, what a fiasco he had blundered into. He felt like an actor who had stumbled on stage without knowing his lines or which drama was in progress. Millot had much to answer for. It was his responsibility to supply the missing gaps. But Millot had gone off on some fool errand for a woman. Something must have happened to him. There could be no other explanation for his absence at such a critical time. And he, Adam, was hardly in a position to order out his guards to track down his errant clerk until he had more information.

If Millot didn't put in an appearance soon, he did not know what tack he was going to take with the girl. What was her relationship to Philippe? What-

ever it might have been, he had changed it irrevocably. It was that thought which led to another.
He might as well be hanged for a sheep as a lamb.

He turned the softly sleeping girl into his arms.
His mouth pressed gently against her throat, savoring the lingering scent of roses. He tasted the brandy
on her lips and his blood began to heat.

"Chèrie?" he murmured. *"Chèrie?"*

His hands roamed over her naked form, tracing the
soft swell of her breasts, the sleek waist and hips, the
taut flat of her stomach. *"Chèrie?"* he repeated, his
voice thick with desire.

She came awake by degrees, then suddenly she was
fighting him. "Ah, no! Commissioner! No! I beg of
you."

His arms wrapped around her like bands of steel,
easily subduing her resistance. Her strength was no
match for his.

"I want you," he said, "and this time, I won't hurt
you."

His mouth closed over hers, stifling her whimpers
of protest, following her relentlessly as she tried to
avert her head. When he positioned her beneath him,
her struggles became more frantic.

"Be still," he gritted.

The girl could not know that it was passion that
hardened his voice. Beneath him, she stilled. Her
submission was not what Adam wanted. He wanted
her to respond to him, he wanted her to writhe with
the same need that drove him.

He stroked her softly, then more voluptuously as
he felt desire rise in her. His mouth touched the peak
of one breast, his breath heating the engorged crest
before his tongue and lips sucked gently, then hard.

She jerked, and tried to pull away. He parried her
movements. This time, he was determined to bring
her to completion. Gradually, it dawned on him that
the girl was fighting to remain passive in his arms.
The passion was there, but she refused to give in to it.

Ruthlessly banking his own fires, he set himself to destroy her defenses. The contest became a battle of wills. There was never any doubt in Adam's mind who would carry off the victory. His experience, his skill, his patience, outmatched the girl's.

And then he felt it—the quivering, deep in her belly, and the erratic, agonized shortness of breath.

"Ah no!" she panted. "No! I won't . . . ah . . ."

"Yes," he said fiercely. "Let it happen. *Chèrie*, give in to me."

She began to shudder to her first climax, Adam's control snapped. He sheathed himself in her moist woman's core. As his own violent release convulsed him, he smothered her face and mouth with kisses, exulting in the response he had won from her. At the last, she held nothing in reserve.

In the gentle wash of spent passion, Adam smiled. He'd never felt more complete in his life. The soft words of praise died on his lips when the girl tore herself out of his arms and curled away from him. Her piteous sobs scourged him like the flick of the lash. Adam's teeth clenched.

The woman did not know when she was well off. If it had been Philippe who had taken her innocence, she would really have had something to cry about. Good God! He hadn't forced her! She was here of her own volition. Unlike Philippe, Adam Dillon had never forced a woman in his life.

There was something about his logic that didn't bear too close a scrutiny. He shifted restlessly. The girl's weeping continued unabated. For several minutes, he stewed in silence. Finally relenting, he dragged her into the protection of his powerful body. "It's all right," he soothed. *"Chèrie*, it's all right. Everything will seem different in the morning." He wished that he knew her name.

Gradually, she quieted. Finally, she drifted into sleep. Adam lay wide-eyed. Before long—he groaned in disbelief—the need for her was tearing his control to shreds. Where this woman was concerned, he seemed to have no willpower. He fought himself for as long as he was able.

"*Chérie*," he said urgently, shaking her awake. "Don't fight me. Please! Don't fight me." And then the seduction began all over again.

Adam came awake instantly. The soft scratching at the door came again. Disentangling himself from the woman in his arms, he lit a candle and reached for a dark brocade dressing gown which was draped over a chair. He looked at the timepiece on the table beside the bed and saw that it was five o'clock.

He found Millot in the bookroom. One arm was in a sling and an ugly welt stood out redly across one cheekbone.

"Commissioner?" Millot rose from his chair and swayed unsteadily. Adam's first rush of relief at seeing the young man quickly subsided.

"Nicholas?" In two strides, he reached him. He pushed him into the chair. "For God's sake, sit down before you fall down."

Millot grinned painfully. "So it is you! Thank God! For a moment there, I wondered."

Adam sliced his companion a warning stare before moving to the door. He closed it gently. "What's going on?" he asked. "What on earth made you desert your post at such a time? Captain Domfrey said something about a woman."

"Claire Michelet. Have you met her?"

"What?"

"Claire Michelet. You *must* have met her."

"Is she the girl with the mane of red-gold hair?" Adam lounged against the desk in a posture of indolence. Only his eyes betrayed his alertness.

Millot pressed a hand to his temples. At length he murmured, "Yes. That's her. Oh God. What am I going to tell her?"

71

"Look," said Adam, searching for his patience, "why don't you begin at the beginning. For God's sake, tell me what's going on! How did you come to sustain those injuries?"

"I was set upon by common footpads," answered Millot, grimacing in self-disgust. "Can you believe it? Don't alarm yourself, I've taken only a few bumps and scratches."

Adam curbed the string of questions that were gathering on his tongue, and Millot, making an effort to pull himself together, embarked on a recitation of the events which had led to the attack upon him.

The girl, he told Adam, had struck a bargain with Philippe Duhet. He explained about the passports and his own intervention to ensure that her young friends got safely away. The boy, he said, had other plans, as he had discovered when he'd gone to the school to fetch him. The boy had run away.

Late of the afternoon, he'd picked up his trail in a local hostelry. As he left the building, he was attacked by two footpads. When he'd come to himself, he was in a quarry, outside the city, and minus his horse and purse.

Adam heard him out in silence, except for the odd question to clarify some point or other.

"I suppose," he struck in at length, "that these so-called 'friends' for whom the girl bartered herself are related to her?"

"It's my guess that they are her brother and sister, though, to be sure, there's no family resemblance. They are as dark as she is fair."

Adam was remembering the youth he'd seen with the girl outside the cathedral. "I wonder what happened to the boy?"

"To be perfectly frank, I have a suspicion that it was the boy, himself, who arranged to have me waylaid."

"What makes you say so?"

"Mmm? Oh, those footpads—they had knives and pistols. They might easily have killed me. They merely mishandled me a little, and before I lost consciousness I heard a voice ordering them to stop— a young voice."

"Strange, that the boy doesn't wish to leave France. There are thousands who would do anything to have the chance he was offered."

"God knows what he hopes to accomplish!"

"You've no idea?"

"None whatsoever. I don't like to think how Claire will take the news of the boy's disappearance."

Adam's eyebrows rose. "Put your fears to rest, Nicholas. The girl . . . Claire . . . must know nothing about the boy's disappearance." He knew that the news would devastate her, and he wasn't going to permit it. One way or another he would find the boy for her.

"Then what are we going to tell her?"

"We shall tell her what she wishes to hear, namely, that you found her young friend and saw him safely on board the coach."

"In the long run, I don't think that's a kindness," objected Millot. "When she gets to England, she's bound to find out. Then think of the agonies she will endure wondering why I concealed the truth from her."

"When . . . she gets . . . to England?" repeated Adam cautiously. "I understood from what you said that she struck a bargain with the commissioner— her person for safe-conduct passes for her young friends?"

"That's true. But under the circumstances, with you now acting as commissioner, there's no point in her remaining here." A thought struck him. "Good God! You don't suppose that I permitted her to go through with the bargain?" He laughed. "No, no! There has not been the opportunity. I made sure of it."

Adam came away from the desk. Millot's expression became arrested as he sensed something new, something unexpected in his companion's stance.

"You're enamored of the chit," said Adam, so softly, so quietly, that Millot felt the hair on the back of his neck begin to rise.

He cleared his throat. "No . . . I mean to say . . . what difference does it make?"

Adam deliberately returned to his relaxed pose. "Only this," he said. "The girl stays here in her role as Duhet's mistress." With an impatient gesture of one hand, he stayed the spate of his companion's objections. "Don't let your feelings for the girl run away with you. Duhet wanted the woman for his mistress. To send her away now would be totally out of character for the commissioner."

Millot shook his head. "You're mistaken. It's not generally known that the girl means anything to Duhet. There's still . . ."

"Think man, think!" Adam interrupted. "Who's to say with any confidence how many people know about the girl? Who's to say what transpired between my half-brother and Claire, or what promises he made to her? Just for argument's sake, let's suppose we arrange for the girl to get to England. Can you swear to me that she won't jeopardize our enterprise *here* by revealing something only she knows?"

There was an obstinate set to Millot's features. "What can she know?"

"That's what I mean to find out. And that takes time. If she proves to be harmless, we'll soon convey her to a place of safety, and that's a promise."

Adam believed every word he uttered. He was involved in a dangerous game. The stakes were too high to take needless chances. As a soldier on active service, his judgment must not be impaired by sentiment or emotion, and least of all, by the leap of his senses for one slip of a girl.

74

Millot's reflections ran on similar lines. He had known Adam Dillon for a very short while, but in that time they had become friends. He admired the American. He handled himself well. His military training stood him in good stead, as had his subsequent career as a man of business. The mantle of authority rested easily on his shoulders. He made decisions quickly, but not without forethought. The risks he took were never ill-advised.

There were other aspects to Adam Dillon, however, which the young Frenchman remembered with unease. Though he himself never suffered from a lack of female companionship, the American attracted women in droves. He had a way with him to which few women were indifferent. Belatedly, Millot remembered something else. In his dealings with women, Adam Dillon tended to be unscrupulous.

Ignoring the pain from the wound in his arm, he leaned forward in his chair. "Where is Claire now?" he demanded. "What happened last night when you met her?"

Adam had been expecting the question. Though he might have lied to spare Millot's feelings, he chose not to do so. If there was one thing he meant to nip in the bud, it was Millot's obvious *tendresse* for the girl. His green eyes blazing dangerously, he said, "What a singularly stupid thing to ask! She is a beautiful woman. I am a man. What do you think happened? Nature took its course."

The blood rushed out of Millot's face. He tried to rise to his feet, but Adam forestalled him, pressing him back with both hands on his shoulders.

"I'll get you a brandy," said Adam, and began to rifle the drawers in the commissioner's desk. A moment later, he curled Millot's fingers around a small glass and ordered him to down the contents.

When Millot could find his voice, he gritted, "I shall kill you for this."

"It's I who should be saying those words to you," retorted Adam, and he began to pace furiously about the room.

"What?"

Pausing to pin his companion with a look, Adam went on, "You deserted your post. No, don't interrupt me. Who gave you permission to involve yourself in the affairs of this girl—and at such a time, for God's sake? You allowed sentiment to cloud your judgment. Your thoughtless actions might have proved catastrophic for our mission. Our lives were in your hands. Didn't you know that, man? Didn't you care?"

Adam came to tower over Millot, and the younger man shrank into himself. "So," said Adam, a faint sneer in his inflection, "who was here to warn me about the girl? I was playing a role. I was Philippe Duhet. What would you have had me do?"

By degrees, the belligerence faded from Millot's ashen face. He closed his eyes momentarily, and let out a groan. To some extent, he knew himself to be culpable. But he wasn't willing to shoulder all the blame. If it were only that! He felt as though he had sustained a mortal injury. The wounds in his flesh were far less real to him than the wound he had taken to his heart.

Painfully, his throat working, he got out, "But you must have known that she was different from your other women? Who could see her, converse with her, and not know what she is? You could have spared her."

"I didn't know," said Adam, and he knew, as soon as the words were out, that he wasn't being completely honest. The truth was that he had been in such a fever of impatience to make the woman his that he hadn't given more than a cursory thought to who and what she was. And later, when he'd known better, he hadn't wanted to pursue the matter.

"Recriminations are useless, as is this conversation," he said abruptly. Seating himself behind the large leather-topped desk, he leaned his weight on the palms of both hands. "We have a job to do. Shall we get on with it?"

Millot looked at him blankly.

"Your report," said Adam. He seemed to be completely relaxed and quite unmoved by what he had done to the girl. Millot's blood began to boil.

"What happens to Claire now?" he asked, trying to appear as calm as Adam.

Adam toyed with a pencil he had absently picked up. At length, he said mildly, "I've already told you what will happen to the girl. If she knows nothing, she will be free to go."

"Yes, yes! But in the meantime, what do you propose to do with her?" And to make sure that the other man got his point, Millot added for good measure, "I want some assurance that there will be no repetition of what took place last night."

Green eyes locked on brown, and it seemed as if a silent battle of wills was fought in that small room. The pencil in Adam's hands suddenly snapped. His eyes dropped to the two halves.

Millot looked away, and let out the breath he had been holding. Quietly, doggedly, he continued, "Let her go, Adam. Claire is not for you. She's led a sheltered life—don't ask me how I know, I just do. You can't know what it did to her to sell herself to someone like Duhet for the sake of the people she loves. She has no experience of men of your stamp. She is an innocent. She's . . . sensitive, fragile. She doesn't stand a chance. You'll only destroy her."

The aggression that had been building in Adam from the moment he'd deduced that Millot had a proprietary interest in the girl, suddenly disintegrated. He saw the whole situation as ludicrous. He'd never felt this sense of possession for any

77

woman and this woman he did not even know.

But some things he should have known. Millot was right about that. Though she was an innocent, he had persuaded himself that she had come to him willingly, because it suited him to think so. He must have been mad to force her to experience passion in his arms. Thankfully, he'd recovered his sanity. Henceforth, he determined, he would keep his distance from the girl.

And as for Mother Nature . . . His lips curved slightly, cynically. He was giving that Old Harridan fair warning that the battle was joined. He'd fight the girl's attraction with every weapon in his arsenal.

As Millot watched the play of emotions on Adam's face, he found himself beginning to relax. Intuitively, he grasped that his companion had found his control. The menace which had seemed to radiate from Adam since the girl had become a bone of contention was no longer apparent.

"Well?" ventured Millot cautiously.

Returning his companion's steady regard, coolly, casually, Adam said, "The girl is beautiful, certainly. But as we both know, the world is full of beautiful women." He paused, and when next he spoke the amusement in his tone was edged with acid. "And from this day forward, I promise you, I'm making it a rule to steer clear of innocent young girls."

In other circumstances, if the woman in question were not Claire, Millot might have laughed. But he was still laboring under the blow he had received when he'd discovered that Adam had taken Claire to his bed. His emotions were cut to ribbons. He wanted to do *someone* a violence, himself most of all. In all conscience, he could not lay the entire blame for what had happened at Adam's door. He might as well rage at a tiger for pouncing on an antelope that had blundered into its lair. He knew this, but it could not relieve the storm that raged inside him.

More than anything, he wanted to see Claire,

question her, if only to assure himself that she was all right. He half toyed with the idea of putting his questions to Adam. He gave him a searching look and decided against it. But there was one question that must be resolved if he was to have any peace of mind.

"What I don't understand is this. If you are determined to keep Claire with you until you discover whether or not she poses some kind of threat to our mission," (and Millot's tone demonstrated how farfetched he judged that piece of logic) "how can you possibly . . . ?" He frowned as he groped for words.

"Yes?"

". . . how can you possibly maintain the fiction that she is your mistress?"

"I don't think I follow you."

"By your own admission, she *won't* be your mistress. Then how are you going to explain to Claire the necessity for her to remain here? Won't that arouse her suspicions?"

Adam's smile was anything but pleasant. "I am Philippe Duhet," he said. "I don't have to explain myself to anyone, least of all to a neglected mistress."

"Neglected?"

"As I said, the world is full of beautiful women. The girl will know what to think. And now, if you please, Nicholas, I should like that report before the hotel comes to life. As you may understand, I've no wish to stumble into another little drama without knowing my lines."

"What about Claire?" persisted Millot. He observed his friend's mouth harden and hastily elaborated, "She'll wish to know the fate of her young friend."

Coolly, Adam answered, "I'm in command here. Anything that touches upon the girl is my business. Do I make myself clear?"

Absently, Millot nodded his assent before it

79

occurred to him that there was a wealth of meaning in those few terse words.

"I shall tell her the story we agreed upon," said Adam in a more softened tone. "All right?"

"All right," answered Millot. But he knew in his heart of hearts that things would never be right again.

Chapter Five

It was midmorning before Claire came to herself, slowly at first, and then with a start. She closed her eyes tightly, hardly daring to draw breath. The muted sounds from the courtyard below and from other parts of the building gradually reassured her. She was alone.

With a sudden sob, she pulled herself to a sitting position and looked about her. She noted the fire in the grate and the closed windows. Not unnaturally, the room was stifling hot. Worst of all, however, was the scent of the man on her skin, forcing her to remember what she wished fervently to forget.

Oh God, how could she have been so naive! In her ignorance, she had thought that when he possessed her she would suffer him in silence, and that it would be soon finished. How could she have known that he would take her again and again, that he would prolong the agony and force her to meet his passion till she thought that she could die from pleasure?

For just a moment, her head swam, and she could no longer hold back the succession of images that swamped her senses—those powerful masculine muscles clenching under the sensitive pads of her fingertips, that smooth warm skin, those burning kisses and demanding, intimate caresses. He had made her weak with wanting him.

81

She hated him. But not half as much as she hated herself. She had thought herself immune to the frailties of the flesh. To give her body coldly, as a calculated act, was one thing. To find pleasure in the experience was intolerable. For the first time in her life she had met a man who had made her give in to him. Only a woman of the streets would succumb to a man for whom she felt nothing but contempt. Philippe Duhet made her skin crawl! Hadn't she known it from the moment she had first set eyes on him? Then why, in the name of heaven, had everything changed last night?

Like a drowning man clutches at straws, she thought of the two small glasses of brandy she had consumed before Philippe Duhet had walked into her room. She'd been inebriated. She must have been. There was no other explanation to account for her subsequent behavior.

Another reason instantly came to mind. Claire tried to suppress it, but the thought was tenacious, defying her will to set it aside. Her worst fears had been realized. There was a fatal flaw in her character. She was no better than that poor, weak-willed creature who had been her mother, Juliette Devereux.

She closed her eyes against the remembered shock of that day when she had discovered the truth about her parentage. Her grandmother had told her, not deliberately, not maliciously, but when she was in the last stages of the illness that had taken her life. Grandmère's mind was confused, Maman had told her. But Claire was not convinced. Grandmère's words stirred a host of half-remembered conversations between her parents that had faltered in midsentence as soon as they had become aware of her presence. She had worried at it like a dog with a bone until she had the truth. And the truth had destroyed her safe world.

At fifteen she had learned that Zoë and Leon were

not her sister and brother, but her cousins. The man she had always regarded as her father was, in point of fact, her uncle. And Maman was no relation at all, except through marriage.

At first, she was shocked, and then she was bitter. She hated the woman who had given her birth. Papa had tried to soothe her. Her natural mother was to be pitied, he'd told her. Juliette Devereux had been a good girl and too young to know what she was doing. The scoundrel who had seduced her was older and more experienced. He had a wife and children waiting for him in America.

On her natural father's identity, Leon Devereux was adamantly silent. No good could be served, so he had told Claire, by revealing the man's name. It was enough for her to know that he was an adventurer and completely without scruples. Claire did not doubt it. Only a black-hearted knave would stoop to seducing an innocent girl.

As she grew to womanhood, the specter of her birth cast a shadow on Claire's life. Though they tried to conceal it, it was borne in upon her that her parents watched her anxiously. She knew that, apart from her blue eyes, she closely resembled her natural mother. Were Maman and Papa afraid that she resembled her mother in other ways? Were they afraid that she, too, might prove to be susceptible to the blandishments of some unscrupulous degenerate who was cut from the same cloth as her natural father? Their fears were groundless. She would prove it to them. There wasn't the man born who could get around Claire Devereux.

There were two kinds of men, she had discovered—good ones, like Leon Devereux, and the other sort. She could be charming to men, she could be nice—when she wanted to be. But she had only to smell the scent of a predator, someone who brought to mind the image of the man who had fathered her, and she would annihilate him with her barbed tongue or freeze him out with her ice.

She had proved her immunity to the male of the species to such a degree that, far from setting her parents' fears to rest, their anxiety increased tenfold. It was unnatural, her mother gently remonstrated. But Claire could not help herself. Her contempt for men was immutable. She could not even bear the touch of a man . . . until last night.

In a flurry of motion, she threw herself from the bed. Clutching the coverlet around her, she stalked to the windows and flung them wide, savoring the frigid air that assaulted her. She breathed deeply. The man's scent disgusted her. She would clear him from her nostrils, then she would scrub him from her skin.

The water in the pitcher on the washstand was cold. Claire was glad of it. Now was not the time to pamper herself with warm water and the rose-scented soap which had pleasured her senses the night before. With a coarse washcloth and lye soap, she attacked herself furiously, relishing the punishment to her sensitive skin. She deserved to be punished for her iniquitous conduct.

Her hand stilled as she noted the purplish bruises against the white of one shoulder. There were others on her thighs. Oh God, what sort of man would inflict pain on a helpless female? He was a fiend! Her entreaties, her tears, her shame—nothing had moved him, not even the bite of her sharp teeth when she had clamped them on his shoulder. He had laughed softly in sheer masculine triumph. There was a recklessness in Philippe Duhet that she would not have believed.

"Tigress," he had called her, but that was later, much later, when he had swept away every vestige of modesty, every remnant of resistance. The scratches and bites she had inflicted, then, were not the result of panic. It was passion that had moved her.

She almost gave in to the tears of self-pity that threatened to spill over. It was the thought of the man's return that sobered her. How could she face him after last night? What would she say to him? What would he say to her?

With trembling fingers, she quickly dressed herself. Only then did she turn her attention to the bed. She had one thought in her mind—to make up the bed as though it had never been slept in, as though what had happened the night before was only a figment of her imagination. She pulled back the covers and froze.

Adam walked in when Claire was on her knees in front of the fire. In her arms, she clutched a bloodstained sheet. With a comprehensive glance, he took in the opened windows and the made-up bed. He tried to bite back the chortle of laughter and almost choked.

One look from those brimming half-guilty, half-reproachful blue eyes and everything inside Adam melted. Sternly, he reminded himself that he must never relax his guard. He was Philippe Duhet, a cold and unfeeling monster.

Only, he wasn't his half-brother. He was Adam Dillon. And he had just spent the most memorable night of his life with the woman who was kneeling on the floor. Henceforth, all women must be compared to her, to their detriment. She was too inexperienced to know it. She should be gloating. She looked as though one unkind word would shatter her into a thousand pieces. He could no more have stopped himself than he could have turned back the tide.

"Tigress," he said under his breath, and crossing to her he fell on his knees beside her. The smile in his eyes was reflected in his voice. "What are you trying to do? Destroy the evidence?"

Pride stiffened Claire's spine. "I have no wish to become the object of gossip belowstairs," she retorted, and there began a tussle as each tried to wrest the sheet away from the other.

It was Adam who won the battle. Holding the sheet aloft like a trophy, he said gently, "I can't let you do this, Claire."

She pulled herself to her feet and stalked to one of the windows. With her back to him, she flung over her shoulder, "If you think for a moment that I shall stand idly by while you blaze your—your—your virility to the world, you'd better think again."

The girl didn't have red hair for nothing, thought Adam, not for the first time, and was delighted that she had not disappointed him. Like a man marooned in the desert dying for water, he thirsted to know more about her.

"Blaze my—virility—to the world?" He preserved a grave face. "How might I do that, may I ask?" He gave a cursory glance at the sheet in his hands, then looked innocently at Claire.

Claire had a horrible vision of the sheet flying from the flagpole or flapping on the washing line in the hotel's courtyard. The amusement reflected in those glittering green eyes told her that the commissioner had correctly read her mind and judged it fanciful.

In a more subdued tone, she asked, "Then what are you going to do with it?"

A slow, wicked grin touched his lips. "I thought I might keep it as a memento, you know, paste it in my scrapbook for future reference."

Her cheeks flamed scarlet. She would have run from the room if she'd had anywhere to go.

"Claire!" He flung the balled sheet into a corner and crossed to her in two swift strides. With both hands he framed her face, bringing her head up. There was not a trace of the amusement he'd barely kept in check moments before, but Claire wasn't to know that. Her gaze was deliberately averted.

"Look at me!" He exerted enough pressure with his long fingers to arch her head back. Softly, he said, "I won't let you burn it because you'll set the chimney on fire. Leave it for the maid. She'll launder it. It's what she's paid to do."

Her blue eyes were as cold as an arctic ocean.

"Claire, what is it? What's wrong?" he murmured.

She tried to shake free of his grasp, but his fingers only tightened, biting into her flesh. "I have no wish to reveal my shame to anyone," she said.

"Shame?" Adam felt the faint stirrings of annoyance. His hands dropped away and he took a step back. Millot's words came back to him. She was an innocent with no experience of men, let alone men of his stamp. She was fragile and he could easily break her.

What Millot had neglected to mention, thought Adam irritably, was that he had no experience of girls of *her* stamp. To his utter confusion, he'd discovered that what he knew about innocent young girls could be written on the head of a thimble. And if his performance last night was anything to go by, it was *he* who stood in some jeopardy, not the girl.

Shame. He tested the word gingerly and decided he didn't like it. Women found pleasure in his arms, not shame. And he'd made damn sure that this woman was no exception. She should be thanking him, not testing the limits of his patience.

"You enjoyed what happened between us last night." He couldn't believe the tone of voice he had employed. He sounded like a sulky schoolboy.

She gave him one of her haughty stares. "You hurt me." She didn't know why she was trying to make this man squirm. As she well knew, men of his kidney didn't have a conscience.

A tide of color rose in Adam's neck. "Only the first time," he said. God, why was he justifying himself? "It was inevitable. But later . . ."

Not wishing to think about what had happened later, she quickly cut in, "I'm covered with the bruises *you* inflicted."

His voice rose. "And my back and shoulders are a mass of bites and scratches *you* inflicted. It will be a wonder if I don't come down with a case of blood poisoning."

She bit down on her bottom lip and hurriedly looked away. "Perhaps you should . . ."

"What?" He was bristling with masculine outrage.

She looked fearfully at him. "Perhaps you should send for the physician?"

Her suggestion floored him. He knew he had behaved like a crazy man when she had finally given in to him, but, oh God, surely he hadn't hurt her that badly? "Physician?" He said the word cautiously.

"Those . . . ," she had to search for the right words, " . . . injuries you sustained? Someone ought to have a look at them."

At her tremulous words, the tension went out of him. Smiling whimsically, he said, "It's too embarrassing. How should I explain my . . . injuries . . . to anyone?"

She hung her head. Adam knew he was a knave. He was playing on her innocence but he couldn't seem to help himself.

He flexed one shoulder and let out a muffled groan. When her eyes flew to his, he gave her a pained smile. Massaging his shoulder, he said, "I've managed pretty well to doctor myself. But there are few scratches I can't quite reach."

It was a moment before she took the hint and offered diffidently, "Would you . . . that is . . . I could help you, if you would permit it?"

If he would permit it? The thought of those soft, lily white hands moving over his body acted on Adam powerfully. He swiftly found a jar of sweet-smelling salve and thrust it into her hands. His coat and shirt were quickly discarded. A moment later, he was seated on a chair.

"If you would be so kind?" he said lazily, smiling at her over his shoulder.

He was going to stand by his word to Millot, he promised himself. He wasn't going to bed the girl

88

again. He hadn't made any promises about a light flirtation.

He smelled the roses on her skin as she bent over him.

"Hell and damnation!" he bellowed. He started to his feet and glared down at her. The jar of sweet-smelling salve was nowhere in evidence. In one hand she held a decanter of brandy and in the other a coarse linen washcloth.

"What the devil do you think you're doing?" he roared.

She might have been a nurse addressing one of her small charges. "There, there," she said consolingly, "that wasn't so bad, was it?"

Claire replaced the decanter on a small side table against the wall. Her back was to Adam. As she fiddled with bottles and glasses, Adam pulled on his shirt. He looked up and caught sight of Claire's reflection in the looking glass. Something was different about the girl, some small change that he could not put his finger on. Her head moved slightly, bringing her chin up. And then he saw them—dimples, winking at him like lights on a ship out at sea.

At that moment, their eyes met in the mirror and held. There was an odd silence.

"Oh!" said Claire. The dimples faded and she expelled a long, ragged breath.

Laughing, Adam crossed to her. "Tigress!" he said, but tenderly, and cupped her face with both hands. This girl was truly a delight to him. His lips sank into hers. "Was it so very bad last night, Claire?" he asked softly.

Her hands closed around his wrists. "You know it was!"

"It was good. I pleasured you." He kissed her again. "Tell me! I want to hear you say it."

"No! You made me!"

"What's this?" Tears were standing on her lashes.

"You made me! I didn't want it. You know I didn't

want it!"

"Yes, I made you." He studied her set face. "So you found pleasure in my arms. Why is that so bad?"

Blue fire flashed in her eyes. "It wasn't part of our bargain."

Bargain. Adam was beginning to detest the sound of that word. It reminded him that the woman had not given herself to *him*, but to Philippe. Adam Dillon meant nothing to her.

But in their coming together, there had been . . . something different, something extraordinary. The pity of it was the girl was too inexperienced to know it. He smiled ironically. No. The pity of it was there could be no repetition of what they had shared. Not only had he given Millot his word on it, but his affairs were too desperate at present to allow for distractions. And this girl would be more than a simple distraction. No, thought Adam, there must be no repetition of what had happened last night, else he might find himself truly caught.

Releasing her, he picked up his coat and shrugged into it. "Millot returned early this morning," he said. His eyes were watchful. "You'll be happy to know that he found your young friend and sent him on his way."

A light leapt to life in her eyes. "Leon is safe?" she murmured. "Nicholas found him?"

"Leon? That's not the name on the boy's passport. Who is he, Claire? And who are you?"

It was as though a curtain of ice came down on those expressive blue eyes. "You know who I am. I'm Claire Michelet, one of the teachers at Madame Lambert's."

"But the boy, Leon—he *is* your brother?" When she remained frozen in silence, he said softly, "Why won't you trust me?"

Her gaze wavered, then steadied. "I trust you to hold to our bargain. As I told you, when I'm satisfied—that is—when the time is right, I shall give

90

you the names of my friends in Carmes." Something in his expression brought the words spilling from her lips, "You promised to help them! Don't say you are going back on your word!"

He answered her curtly. "When you know me better, you will know that I never go back on my word." Hearing himself, he almost grinned. It was Adam Dillon who had taken umbrage at the girl's slur on his character. Philippe Duhet would have laughed in her face, or he would promise her the world, and forget about it in his next breath.

With Claire Michelet, he was discovering, he could not sustain the part he was supposed to be playing. It was more than that. With this girl, he didn't want to play a role. He wanted to be himself. He wanted her to know the man. Whether he went by the name of Adam Dillon or Philippe Duhet was immaterial. And he wanted to know *her* more than he had ever wanted to know any woman.

At the thought, a modicum of caution returned. Given their circumstances the notion was ludicrous. He would wager his last groat that the girl was no more who she pretended to be than he was. She could be anyone. In all probability, she was an innocent victim of the Revolution. As soon as may be, she would wish to follow her young friends to England. It was her bargain with his half-brother that held her in Rouen—that and some promise Philippe had given her respecting her "friends" at Carmes.

He'd been right to defer making a decision about the girl. There might be more still to discover about this bargain she'd struck with Philippe. To send her away before he'd learned everything there was to know was sheer folly.

There was another reason to keep the girl with him. He was not forgetting that she might be pregnant with his child. He could not say with any conviction how many times he had taken her the night before. One thing, however, he did remember—not once had he made the slightest effort to prevent conception.

Claire lowered her brows, suddenly wary of the inexplicably foolish grin which touched the man's lips. "What is it?" she asked.

He kissed her swiftly, and laughed. Having conveniently furnished some foundation to explain his reluctance to part with the girl, Adam felt more like his old self. He turned his mind to the problem of discovering who and what she was.

"Hungry?" he asked.

After a moment's hesitation, she nodded.

"I'll have something sent up, and while we are waiting, we'll talk." Something came and went in her eyes, and Adam offered reassuringly, "You'll wish to know about your young friend—Leon, I believe is his name?" To this comment, the girl made no response, and Adam went on in the same reassuring tone, "Sit down, Claire, and I shall tell you where and how Millot found him. No, don't look like that! Leon is safe. Really! It's Millot who deserves our sympathies."

Much later, when she was alone, Claire gazed absently into space, reflecting on the story she had just been told. Leon had run away from school because he was involved with some girl or other. Millot had gone after him. When he'd found him, he'd persuaded the boy to return with him. Having ridden after Zoë's coach and caught up with it, Millot had seen Leon safely on his way. On his way back to Rouen, Millot was set upon by footpads. It was this which accounted for his tardiness in making a report to Claire.

It all sounded so plausible. Even at fifteen, Leon attracted his share of feminine attention. What she found difficult to swallow was that, having set his course, Leon would be so easily deflected from it. That was out of character for her brother. Yet, why should Philippe Duhet lie to her?

Deliberately, she forced herself to think about Philippe. The images that came and went in her mind were so contradictory that she could form no clear impression. She was sure of one thing. Since she had given herself to him, he seemed like a different man. He even looked like a different man.

She shivered and hugged herself in a protective gesture. By giving herself to him, she had softened something in him. She could see it in his eyes, hear it in his voice. He was susceptible to her. And in some way she did not understand, she had changed, too.

A faint smile curved her lips as she thought of the trick she had played on him. By substituting brandy for the salve, she had turned the tables on him. And she still did not know how she had come by the confidence to mock him so.

It was as though they were no longer the same two people. Before last night, one touch, one look from Philippe Duhet was enough to make her skin crawl. Today . . . But Claire could not bear to contemplate that thought.

Her eyes fell on the balled sheet which had been carelessly discarded on the floor, and her thoughts took a new direction. Within moments, she had the sheet between her hands and was ferociously ripping it to shreds. The task was harder than she had imagined. Piece by small piece, she patiently fed the small scraps of material to the fire till there was nothing left of it but ashes. It made no difference. Nothing could burn away the reality of what had happened to her the night before in Philippe Duhet's arms.

Chapter Six

In the following weeks, Claire saw very little of Adam. There was unrest in the provinces, and the commissioner and his troops were hard-pressed to impose law and order. Gangs of bandits roamed the countryside, leaving a wake of terror wherever they appeared. Sillery, the defeated rebel leader, seemed to be everywhere at once. There was a price on his head, but no one was surprised when the reward lay unclaimed. No man trusted his neighbor, and to inform against the rebel leader might mean instant reprisal.

In the city itself, the commissioner's frequent absences were deemed, at least by the populace at large, beneficial. There were fewer arrests. Discipline was less severe. The guillotine in the old market square was relatively idle. As is the way of things, however, these unexpected benefits were soon taken for granted by the citizens. They turned their minds to other grievances. Food was scarce and rationed. Prices were astronomical. And the refugees who flocked to the city placed an intolerable burden on its already overstrained resources. The new year was ushered in with little in the way of celebration. Only the news of the lifting of the English blockade at Toulon brought a measure of hope for the future. When the war with England was over, things must get better.

Claire, as much as anyone, regarded the commissioner's absences as an unmitigated blessing. He was too preoccupied to spare much time for a mere mistress, so he'd abruptly informed her on one of those rare occasions when he'd dined with her before riding out on yet another mission. When in Rouen, he was often closeted behind closed doors. Where he spent his nights, Claire did not inquire, nor did she care. She had her own bedchamber with a door which gave on to Philippe Duhet's room. He rarely came through that door, and never at night when she was in bed. Claire could hardly trust her good fortune. She suspected that a voluptuary such as Duhet would never be satisfied with only one woman. There must be others. Millot had hinted as much. She sincerely hoped that there were.

In many respects, she felt like a prisoner. For the most part, through choice, she kept to Duhet's suite of rooms, fearing to show her face in the hotel. Occasionally, from sheer boredom, she forced herself to go as far as the kitchens on some pretended errand. The ordeal left her shaken. The looks that were slanted her way were avidly curious. She could almost feel the eyes of Duhet's men move over her person in slow and appreciative perusal. With the ladies, those women who had braved the commissioner's headquarters to plead for information on loved ones, it was otherwise. Their looks were hostile, as were their snide remarks. It was then that Claire adopted her haughty pose. She looked through all of them as though they were transparent. They could not know that behind the cool, intimidating facade she concealed all the hurt she suffered from their barbs.

Millot was one of the few people with whom Claire felt any degree of comfort. That first day, after Duhet's return from Angers, she'd been afraid to look him in the eye. His matter-of-fact manner had gradually restored her confidence. They'd conversed on the safe topic of Leon. Only then was Claire satisfied that the commissioner had not misled her. She trusted Millot implicitly.

In other ways, Millot proved himself indispensable. He made it his business to see to Claire's comfort. Nothing was too much trouble for him. And when he discerned that Claire was almost going out of her mind from boredom, he arranged a distraction. Blanche, the maid who reminded Claire so forcibly of Zoë, was freed of her other duties to spend each afternoon as a companion to Claire.

Blanche was a godsend and a cut above the regular run of domestics. Not only could the girl read and write, but her speech was refined. She possessed a lively intelligence and she was eager to better herself. It was natural for Claire to fall into the role of mentor. Sometimes, when she looked up and caught sight of Blanche's dark head bent over a piece of needlework, she could almost imagine that she still had Zoë with her. In just such a manner they had whiled away the hours in their mother's yellow *salle* in their house in Paris.

It did not take Claire long to perceive, however, that Blanche's resemblance to Zoë was only superficial. Blanche was older than first impressions indicated. Claire was halfway persuaded that the maid might even be her senior by a year or two. Moreover, the Devereux girls had led a very sheltered existence. Blanche had been raised by an older sister, an actress with the Comédie Française, and had witnessed a side of life that was foreign to Claire. Her acceptance of Claire's position as Duhet's mistress was so matter-of-fact as to be almost shocking. On the other hand, the girl's lack of censure broke through the wall of protective reserve which Claire had carefully established.

"You had no ambitions to follow your sister's profession?" asked Claire.

The two ladies were involved in a quiet game of cards. On this occasion, it was the maid who was the teacher. Claire had never cared much for card games. In her present circumstances anything which relieved the tedium of her self-imposed captivity was to be welcomed.

Blanche carefully scrutinized the cards in her hand before replying, "My sister wouldn't permit it."

There was a pause. "What does that mean?" asked Claire.

Blanche absently shrugged her shoulders. "She wanted me to have a normal life, you know, a husband, children. When I was fourteen she sent me away."

"Oh? Where?"

"A convent."

Claire digested this in silence. That explained Blanche's ability to read and write. In other respects, however, it was puzzling. A girl with a convent education would be less worldly than Blanche.

As if reading Claire's thoughts, Blanche flashed a little smile and said confidingly, "I hated it. I ran away. Eventually, they refused to accept me at the convent. I was very naughty. The nuns could do nothing with me. In the end, Verity relented and decided to keep me with her."

"Verity. That's a nice name. Where is she now?" Claire plucked two cards from her hand and placed them on the table. In the ensuing silence her gaze lifted indifferently, then held. Blanche's slender figure was so still, so rigid as to be almost frozen in ice.

"Blanche!" Claire stretched out one hand, but something in the other girl's pose made her hesitate, and her hand dropped away.

And then, as though the change had never taken place, Blanche placed her cards on the table and said, "My trick, I believe?"

"What?" Claire looked down in some confusion.

Blanche smiled. "My trick!" In a mock commiserating tone, she went on, "My trick in more ways than one. When playing cards you must never become so involved in what's going on around you that your concentration is broken. You'll do better the next time."

Claire sat back in her chair and watched Blanche's nimble fingers scoop up the cards and shuffle them in a practiced manner. She had been put in her place, and she had deserved it. As much as anyone, she should have known better than to pry into someone else's affairs. Her own affairs could not bear a close scrutiny either.

Smiling, at her most charming, Claire embarked on a flow of small talk to smooth over the awkwardness. But behind her carefully composed features, she could not help speculating on the other girl and her former life. The whisper of something awful, something tragic had been introduced. That thought put her in mind of her own family. She wondered what Leon and Zoë were doing at that very moment. Soon, her thoughts drifted to her parents.

It was one of those nights when Claire wrenched herself free of her nightmare a split second before the blade of the guillotine hurtled down to finish off one of its victims. When she came to herself, she was bent over, one hand pressed to her mouth as if to smother her screams. Her shoulders were heaving; her night rail was drenched with perspiration.

She cried out when Adam came storming into the room. "Claire? What is it?" he demanded, and quickly strode to the bed.

For a moment, Claire shrank from him. With the only light to illuminate her room coming from the open door, at first she did not recognize him. He said her name again, and there was something in his tone that calmed her. She knew that he was the commissioner, and that she should fear him, but instinct proved stronger than reason. "It was a nightmare," she whimpered brokenly. "Philippe, please, hold me," and she held out her arms to him like a child.

"Claire!" He reached for her and with a rough tenderness, he dragged her into his arms, cradling her against his broad chest. "Don't take on so! It was only a dream. This isn't like you. Where is my little tigress?"

The sound of his voice far more than his words soothed her fears, washing over her, freeing her from the vestiges of her terrors. She savored the lean strength of him, the hard muscles beneath the pads of her fingers. His heartbeat was strong and regular, its slow rhythm steadying her own erratic pulse. Even the masculine scent of him was comforting. It was a long time before she lifted her head.

Sudden awareness held her immobile. She was in her nightclothes and Philippe was only half-dressed in breeches and shirt. He wore no neckcloth and his hair was loose about his shoulders.

"Better?"

She nodded, but stark fear was reflected in her eyes.

Seeing it, Adam mistook its source. "I know the cure for nightmares," he said, his tone emulating the one he had often heard Sarah Burke employ to calm a frightened child. "We talk about it. But first, you must slip into another gown. This one is soaking. I shall wait for you in the other room. All right?"

He left the door halfway open so that the light from the parlor filtered through to Claire's chamber. As soon as he moved to the other room, Claire's demons returned to plague her. Trembling, quickly donning a fresh gown and robe, she went after him.

"Sit down, Claire," he said, indicating the stuffed armchair closest to the grate. "Here, drink this, and not one word of argument if you please."

A small glass of brandy was thrust into her hand. She was reluctant to drink it, remembering the last time she had imbibed too freely. One look at the determined set of his mouth was enough to persuade her. Obedient to his command, she brought the glass to her lips.

Only then did Adam seat himself. "Tell me about the dream, Claire. Was it so very bad?"

His avuncular manner hit just the right note. Once again, she was struck with the difference in him since he had returned from Angers.

"Well?"

"I don't wish to remember my nightmare. It's too . . . too . . ." Her voice faded, then died away altogether.

"I know. But it's best to face our fears."

She tilted her head back to get a better look at him. "What would you know about fears?"

Her words amused him. "I'm human. In my time, I've had my fair share. Now tell me about the dream, Claire."

She took a few healthy sips of her brandy before complying. "It's always the same dream," she said, and shivered. "What else should it be but arrests and executions and the screams of the victims?" She frowned, wondering if her words were incautious.

"Ah, I think I understand. Are you the victim, Claire?"

"One of the victims." The others were the members of her family, but she feared to mention them lest the commissioner press her to give him the names of her "friends" at Carmes. Until she knew for a certainty that Zoë and Leon were settled in England, it was safer to preserve her silence.

"Then your fears are groundless. I am your protector, Claire. No possible harm can come to you. If you remember that, and really believe it, I promise, your sleep won't be disturbed by troublesome dreams."

All her life, Claire had known a father's protection. In the normal way of things, she would have passed from her father's protection to that of her husband. She heard Philippe's words and she wanted to weep an ocean of tears. She was only a slip of a girl. Her burdens were too heavy for her shoulders, yet, she must carry them, for all their sakes. If Philippe had been a different sort of man, if she could really trust him, she would gladly surrender her burdens to him. She dared not trust him, in spite of his show of solicitude. The kind of protection he offered was no protection at all. She must never forget that it was Philippe and men like him who had brought disaster to France and ruin on herself.

His eyes were watching her intently. Shaking his head, as though reading her mind, he said roughly, "I'm not the man you think me . . . that is . . . you are safe with me. You can trust me. Don't you know that?"

The words were out before she could stop them. "Why should I believe you? You are notorious, do you know?" This time her words were more than incautious. They were downright inflammatory. She glanced at her empty glass and set it down sharply. When she chanced a quick look at the commissioner she was relieved to note that her taunt had made little impression on him.

"So I believe," he said. "But things are not always what they appear to be. Claire, is it fair to judge a man on hearsay alone?" He angled her a smile that had been known to break a few hearts. "I promise you, I am not the ogre I've been made out to be."

The awful thing was, she almost believed him. But some things were a matter of record. There was no getting round them. Philippe Duhet was Robespierre's protégé, and the scourge of the Convention.

"Claire, what is it? What's really troubling you?"

She was afraid that she was weakening, afraid of saying too much. He didn't look like a monster. In some respects he resembled her brother. But there was nothing boyish about this man. He was so supremely confident, so patently a man who was used to getting his own way. She couldn't match wits with him and win.

Abruptly rising to her feet, she stammered out, "Thank you for the brandy and . . . and everything. You have been more than kind."

He was on his feet before she could slip past him. "No, don't go," he said. "I thought you might wish to tell me about your friends at Carmes."

Her whole body went rigid with shock.

"Claire?"

"No! That is . . . as I told you, when the time is right, then I shall reveal the names of my friends."

Adam was thinking that Philippe's promises to the girl were empty ones. His half-brother would not have lifted a finger to help her friends. Unfortunately, he was in no position to help either. It was an impossible situation. He wanted to prepare her for the worst, but decided that in her present state of mind it was better to leave her with some hope. As Millot had said, the girl was fragile.

When he reached for her, he had only one thought in his mind. He was going to comfort her. As his hands cupped her shoulders, Claire jerked away.

"Don't touch me!"

She saw at once that she had made a fatal blunder. Until that moment, Philippe's manner had been almost fatherly. By that one injudicious act, she had reminded him that they were male and female and that she was his for the taking. "I don't like it when you touch me," she said, hardly knowing what she was saying.

Her taunt rankled, not only because it challenged everything that was masculine in Adam's nature, but also because he'd been applauding himself on his prodigious restraint. From the moment he had gathered her in his arms when she had awakened from her nightmare, he'd had the fight of his life on his hands. He'd wanted to take her. He'd wanted to push her back into the bedclothes and cover her with his body. He'd wanted to come into her and ride her till she was mindless with pleasure, mindless with wanting him. Instead, he had heeded the dictates of his better nature, more fool he.

"You don't like it when I touch you?" His hands circled her waist.

Swallowing, Claire shook her head, but already in her mind she knew that she must yield to him. Philippe had kept his part of the bargain and so must she. But this time she was resolved to take no pleasure in the giving of herself.

"You don't like it when I do this?" One hand molded itself to her breast beneath the wrapper, and Claire gasped. "Or this?" With finger and thumb, he plucked at her nipple, squeezing gently, then hard.

"Philippe," she breathed, the moment before his mouth crushed the word against her lips.

It was all so familiar—the weakening, the dizziness, and that leap of the senses that robbed her of reason. The rights and wrongs of what she was doing lost focus, submerged in the rising tide of pleasure and the instinct to yield everything to him.

When he pulled back, his breathing was harsh and uneven. "Little hypocrite," he said. "Tell me now that you don't like my touch."

Claire felt bereft. "No," she protested, and twining one arm around his neck, she pulled his head down and took his lips in an open-mouthed kiss. He tensed, then in an explosion of passion, he lifted the hem of her nightdress, sweeping aside its folds. She whimpered when his hands moved over her, urgently cupping the soft swell of her bottom, lifting her, grinding her against his aroused flesh in a blatantly erotic rhythm.

Claire teetered on the brink of total capitulation. It was only a sop to her conscience, but she said the words anyway, "Commissioner ... please ... no." And even as she said the words, she reveled in the violence of his passion, returning kiss for kiss.

Commissioner. A blinding light penetrated the fog in Adam's brain. He was forgetting the part he was supposed to be playing. If he wasn't careful, he would not only break his promise to Millot, but he would find himself truly caught.

"Claire!" he said hoarsely, and his hands moved to her shoulders, his fingers biting into her soft flesh as he tried to disengage himself. "Claire!" The words had all the force of an oath, and in the next moment, she was thrust roughly at arm's length.

Panting, dazed, she gazed up at him.

Adam's fingers combed through his hair in a distracted gesture. It took a moment or two before he could find his control. When she swayed toward him, he took a quick step back. Adam Dillon retreating from a willing woman, and one, moreover, whom he wanted as he had never wanted any woman? The picture was ludicrous. He could not help shaking his head at the absurdity of it all, and then he laughed. "I haven't got time for this," he said.

He didn't wait for her answer, but made a great show of putting on his coat and neckcloth. Finally, he found his black ribbon and tied back his hair. It was the instinct for self-preservation which forced the next words from Adam's lips. "I assure you, Claire, I enjoy nothing more than to take a beautiful woman to my bed. Unhappily, time is wasting and duty calls. The commissioner's time is never his own." At the door, he turned back. In a different tone, he said, "And Claire? Sweet dreams."

When he left his suite of rooms, he was whistling. Halfway down the stairs, he let out a shaky breath. He was thinking that Claire Michelet was a dangerous woman. When he was with her, it was almost impossible to sustain his role as Philippe. He had

had a very close call indeed.

Upstairs, Claire climbed into bed and drew the covers under her chin. She was thinking that she had had a very close call indeed. Her guardian angel must have been looking out for her. On that happy note, she tumbled into sleep. Her dreams were all of Philippe Duhet, but when she awakened, refreshed, she had no knowledge of it.

When Millot quietly informed Claire that her young friends had safely crossed the English Channel, her heart gave a great leap of gladness. With Zoë and Leon beyond reach of retribution, the impediment to revealing the name of 'Devereux' was removed. The time had come for her to approach the commissioner about her parents.

This was easier said than done. She seldom saw the commissioner, and when she did, his mood was anything but mellow. Time was slipping away, and it seemed that her influence with Duhet was completely eclipsed. For whatever reason, Philippe Duhet had lost interest in her. He could barely spare her the time of day. When she was with him, she sensed a wariness in him that was completely baffling. She had the strangest feeling that those green eyes which narrowed on her with such intensity were seeing her as if *she* posed some kind of threat.

The notion was absurd. She and Philippe Duhet had struck a bargain. She was his for the taking. Evidently she had not pleased him. Evidently, he had come to regret their bargain. Yet, he kept her as his mistress. Claire did not know what to make of it.

For more than a week after she had received Millot's assurances respecting Zoë and Leon, Claire suffered agonies as she tried to summon the courage to approach Duhet. And then, something happened which completely reversed her purpose. She discovered that she must never reveal her true identity to the commissioner.

It was to be Claire's first venture outside the hotel since she'd taken up residence. She was dreading the prospect and, at the same time, she was desperate to leave her prison. The suggestion had come from Blanche.

"You're cooped up here like a broody hen," she'd scolded. "It's not good for you. Why won't you leave the hotel? The streets are quite safe. The military are policing them. No one will molest us."

"That's not it," said Claire, and could do nothing to prevent the pink that stole across her cheekbones.

Blanche's expression altered, and Claire's cheeks bloomed.

"You're ashamed?" The maid's observation was more in the nature of a statement.

Claire looked up and she had the curious feeling that she was not seeing the Blanche she knew but a different person altogether. Her mind grappled with confused images, trying to determine the difference.

The maid's outward appearance was much as it always was. The habitual black gown was relieved at the neck by a white lacy fichu. Her luxurious dark hair was coiled in a sleek chignon, and adorned with the ubiquitous white cap. Her features were pleasant to look upon, but far from remarkable, with the exception, perhaps, of those compelling dark eyes.

"Why won't you leave the hotel?" asked Blanche.

Claire's eyes dropped away. "I hate it when people stare at me in that way," she said.

"What way?"

"You know." Claire moistened her lips. "As though I'm beneath contempt."

"And are you beneath contempt?"

Claire's eyes were caught and held. She could not

have looked away even if she had wanted to. "I . . . I did what I had to do," she said.

There was a silence. Blanche nodded. "You're too sensitive for your own good. You're wrong, you know. The gentlemen all admire you and the ladies are green with envy."

"Envy?"

"What did you expect?" Blanche absently smoothed out the lace cover on the table. "You have a powerful protector. He's very handsome . . . like a dream lover." She sighed and shot Claire one of her shy smiles. "If the commissioner belonged to me, I wouldn't give a straw for the stares of those vindictive old dragons who secretly would give anything to be in my shoes."

Claire was aghast. Blanche was once again the little maid who reminded her of Zoë. She needed some sisterly advice, whether or not she wished for it.

"Philippe Duhet is not a dream lover," denied Claire hotly. "He has only one use for women. You'd better remember that and stay clear of him."

"Oh I wouldn't poach on your preserves," said Blanche, eyes downcast, "not even if he noticed me."

Claire gave her a startled look. "Poach? I wish some lady *would* poach on my preserves. But not *you*, Blanche. One day you'll meet a nice man, one who will wish to marry you. Just remember, no man wants another man's leavings."

"Isn't the commissioner a nice man?"

"He's a libertine, Blanche, a rake. He's unscrupulous. Oh, he can be very charming when he wants to be. But it's just an act. Men like him don't care what happens to women like us."

"Don't you even like him a little?"

"I . . ." Belatedly, Claire became conscious that she had allowed her unruly tongue to run away with her. She groped in her mind for a way of softening her scathing remarks. "Perhaps a little," she allowed, smiling. "But I mean what I said, Blanche. You don't

107

have the experience to manage a man like Duhet. Keep your distance from him, for your own sake."

Blanche laughed. "You sound just like my mother," she said.

"Your mother?" Claire's brows knit together.

"And my sister," answered Blanche easily, then went on in the same tone, "but we have wandered far from the point. I suggested that you should get out for a breath of fresh air, and you have yet to give me your answer."

"I don't know . . . I'm not sure."

"Think about it. It can only do you good."

Claire did think about it. In the end, hesitantly, she gave way to her maid's persuasions. She dressed herself with as much care as she had ever taken for any of the elegant parties she had attended in Paris. Where formerly she had wished to appear at her best, on this occasion she hoped to melt into her surroundings. She did not wish to attract attention. Her threadbare cloak was of a nondescript gray, as was the unadorned bonnet which concealed the soft cloud of silky red hair.

Philippe had taken umbrage at her meager store of possessions. He'd offered to rectify the situation by supplying a whole new wardrobe as befitted one in her position. Her polite refusal had startled him. He'd insisted. She had turned stubborn. It wasn't part of their bargain, she had told him. In tight-lipped silence, he had left her. The door had hardly closed behind him when she regretted her stand. If she had only been more conciliatory, she might have introduced the subject of her parents.

Blanche ran a practiced eye over Claire and shook her head ruefully.

"What is it?" asked Claire.

"It's not working," she said. "In point of fact, you've only made yourself more alluring. My dear, I've known actresses who would kill just to have your bone structure. And as for that cloak, any man worth his salt is going to go mad trying to imagine what you're concealing beneath its folds." Suddenly conscious of Claire's sharp look, she said more brightly, "But I will say one thing—in that getup, no one could possibly mistake you for the commissioner's lady."

"I'm counting on it," said Claire, and both girls laughed.

They descended the narrow staircase in single file, Claire in the rear. In the foyer, they stepped to the side as the front doors opened. Three men entered with the cold blast of January air, two dragoons flanking a young man in civilian garb. He looked to be no more than a boy.

Claire's eyes traveled over him, absorbing his unkempt appearance and his torn coat. It was very evident that he had been manhandled. Perhaps his papers were not in order. More probably, he'd been discovered in one of the house-to-house searches. Suddenly, all her anticipation for the afternoon's outing evaporated, leaving the taste of ashes in her mouth. How was it possible for anyone to be happy when there was so much misery in the world? How could she let herself forget that it was Philippe Duhet who held the power of life and death over all Rouen's citizens? He was responsible for this.

The young man's chin drooped on his chest. He could hardly stand on his own feet. Claire looked at the callously indifferent expressions of the dragoons who held him up and her temper began to simmer. And then a name was called out by one of the clerks, and Claire's throat closed on her next breath.

"Devereux! Jules Devereux!"

The young man's head was jerked back by one of the dragoons. His eyes were closed. His mouth was bleeding. "It's him all right," said the dragoon. "Leastways, that's what he told us before we arrested him."

"What happened to him?" asked the clerk.

"He resisted arrest. We were forced to subdue him."

The clerk clucked like an irate hen. "Commissioner Duhet won't like it. You heard his orders. Anyone by the name of Devereux was to be taken in for questioning. That means he wants them alive."

The soldier laughed. "He's only half dead. Why should the commissioner care? If we don't finish him off, the guillotine will. What's he done then? Is he one of them aristos or what?"

"I am not in the commissioner's confidence," answered the clerk coldly.

Claire was avid to hear more, but Blanche was holding the door for her. As she stumbled down the front stairs, her legs threatened to buckle under her. She was sure that she must have betrayed herself.

"Try to put it out of your mind," said Blanche.

"What?" Claire looked quickly at her companion. She wondered if her own face was as colorless as Blanche's.

"Don't think about it," said Blanche. "There's nothing we can do to help that poor devil unless, of course, you wish to use your influence with the commissioner."

"What influence?" asked Claire without thinking.

Blanche darted a quick look at Claire, then looked away. After an interval, she asked, "Do you know the boy?"

"I've never seen him in my life," answered Claire truthfully. "Why do you ask?"

"Oh, no reason. You were shocked, I suppose, as I was also."

It was hearing the name Devereux that had shocked Claire, that and the brutality of the commissioner's soldiers. Nor had the subsequent conversation done anything to alleviate her panic. She wondered if the authorities were on to her, or if it was a coincidence that Philippe Duhet was hounding

110

anyone who had the misfortune to go by the name of Devereux.

Jules Devereux, the young man who was under arrest, was a complete stranger to her. She knew without a doubt that he had no connection to her own family. Devereux was not so uncommon a name. She remembered the clerk's words, that anyone who went by that name was to be taken in for questioning, and she began to tremble.

"Cold?" asked Blanche, and immediately quickened her footsteps.

They gave the Vieux Marchè, where the guillotine had been set up, a wide berth, and struck out, uphill, toward the old Abbey of St. Ouen. No one gave them a second stare. It was bitterly cold. Snow was in the air. And no one wished to loiter unless he had business that could not be avoided.

Neither girl had much to say for herself. Near the summit of the hill, they turned to survey the old Medieval city. Floes of ice floated downstream on the Seine. In her mind's eye, Claire followed their progress. They would pass through Caudebec and then Le Havre on their way to the English Channel.

The scene looked so dreary. She wondered if spring would ever come, and if it did, who would be there to see it.

"Let's go back," she said. "I want to speak to Millot about that young man."

Chapter Seven

The only light in the commissioner's office came from two tallow candles on the oak mantle. Millot squinted at the level of brandy he had just poured into the glass in his hand. He shot a quick look at his companion, then tipped up the decanter and poured a more liberal measure.

"Here, Commissioner," he said, setting the glass down in front of Adam. "Get that down you. You look as though you haven't slept for a week."

"You're right. I haven't." Adam lifted the glass to his lips and took a long swallow. "I had no idea that my duties as commissioner would be so onerous. Think yourself lucky, Nicholas. You have a soft life. In the last number of days, I've scarcely been out of the saddle."

Adam rarely relaxed his guard. That he was doing so now was partly the result of fatigue, and partly because he knew that in this inner sanctum his words could not be overheard. At the door to the outer office, one of his own men stood on watch. Sometimes it was necessary to talk freely with his fellow conspirators. Even so, Adam was circumspect to a degree. He was the commissioner, and must always be addressed as such.

Millot lowered himself into the chair facing Adam, thinking that his admiration for the American and the way he had pulled off their masquerade was boundless. No one questioned the commissioner's identity. To all appearances, he was exactly as he appeared to be. Sometimes Millot had to remind himself that it was not Philippe Duhet who was barking out orders, but his friend, Adam Dillon.

It could never have worked, thought Millot, if they had not struck at the right moment. Duhet was not well known in Rouen. His appointment was so recent that there had not been the time for him to establish himself. His colleagues and his subordinates had not had the opportunity to form a clear impression of the man. To them, Adam *was* the commissioner. If the real Philippe Duhet were suddenly to take over, it was *he* who would be taken for the impostor, not Adam. The thought made Millot smile.

"A bath and a bed," said Adam, grinning. "It's all I can seem to think about." He leaned back in his chair and stretched out his long booted legs, resting them upon the flat of the desk. "How is Claire?" he murmured.

The half-smile on Millot's lips withered. "So," he said, "a bath and a bed is all you can think about, is it?"

The unrepentant grin on Adam's face intensified. "More or less," he allowed. "How is she?"

Under his breath, Millot muttered indistinctly.

"I didn't quite catch that," murmured Adam.

"I said that's she's as well as can be expected under the circumstances."

"What does that mean, precisely?"

"It means that the poor girl is so ashamed she's afraid to show her face. She's made a virtual prisoner of herself, always moping in her room. Today was the first time she ventured outside this building. Her maid finally persuaded her to go for a walk."

Adam carefully raised his glass to his lips. "This is excellent brandy," he observed, and took another long swallow. 'I'm not sure that I approve of her wandering all over Rouen. Anything might happen. These are dangerous times. And Claire is too beautiful for her own good.''

Again, Millot muttered something under his breath.

"I must be going deaf," said Adam. "I swear I saw your lips move, but I didn't hear a sound.''

"I'm glad that you find me amusing," said Millot truculently.

Adam's brows rose. "I'm not laughing," he said. After a moment, he sighed and continued in an altered tone, "Say what you have to say, man, and be done with it."

Millot's truculence began to soften. "Let the girl go," he said. "She doesn't know anything. She never did. You know that as well as I do. What point is there in keeping her here? Send her away. It's the only decent thing to do."

Adam took a moment or two to adjust his long length. Finally, he said, "The girl doesn't want to leave." At the surprise which registered on Millot's face, he smiled. "I assure you, Nicholas, Claire has no desire to leave France. No, I did not offer her the choice. However, I made an oblique reference to that eventual possibility. She was evasive. There's something keeping her here. I wish I knew what it was."

"What about these friends in Carmes?"

"That could be it. I shall raise the subject again when next I see her."

"Perhaps that problem has been resolved."

Both men fell silent as they considered the import of Millot's words. The guillotine in Paris was never idle.

Abruptly, Adam asked, "Is it possible that she knows we lied to her about the boy?"

"The boy?"

"Louis Reubel, his papers say. The one she refers to as 'Leon.'"

"I shouldn't think so," answered Millot thoughtfully, then with more confidence, "No. She trusts me. I'm sure of it. Did you pick up his trail?"

Adam's tone suddenly turned curt. "Yes, I picked up his trail. The young fool has joined up with the rebels, or he's been press-ganged into service. Either way, we've lost him."

Millot thought of Claire. "There must be something we can do."

"What, for instance?"

"How should I know? I'm not a military man. You're the commissioner. You're the law in this neck of the woods."

Adam took exception to something in the other man's tone. His frustration showed. "Look," he said, "we have a job to do. The boy doesn't wish to be found. And to divert my energies and men to discovering what has become of him is not only a waste of time, but it might also raise questions in some quarters that we don't wish to raise. Let sleeping dogs lie, Nicholas. That's our safest course, our *only* course."

The next impulsive thought was voiced before Millot could prevent it. "God, you're a hard man!"

Adam's head came up. "And you're too soft for your own good."

After an interval, Millot's lips became unsteady. "My mother used to say that about me," he said, and grinned sheepishly. "Coming from her, it was something of a compliment."

Adam shook his head. Before he could deliver some caustic retort, Millot quickly intervened, "Speaking of letting sleeping dogs lie, I have a suggestion to make."

"About what?"

"About those Devereux you are anxious to trace."

"What about them?"

"Today, two of your dragoons caught another one in their net. When they brought him in, he wasn't a pretty sight. I questioned him personally. It turns out that, though he has no connection to the branch of Devereux in whom you are interested, his name is on the proscribed lists."

"Oh God!" groaned Adam. "Poor devil!" Wearily, he pressed a hand to his eyes. "Then he'll be tried and executed."

This was one part of the enterprise that Adam heartily detested. Not everybody could be saved. In point of fact, there were many whom Adam was happy to see go to the guillotine, men who in their time had vigorously persecuted their political opponents including their innocent wives and children. But the Revolution was a fickle mistress. Shifts in power were unpredictable. Those same persecutors sometimes woke up to find themselves on the wrong end of justice. With such as these, Adam was almost merciless.

There were others, however, whom Adam pitied. These were the men and women whose only crime was the misfortune of their exalted birth or that, in an unguarded moment, they had criticized the conduct of the new masters of France. If their names were on the proscribed lists and they were caught, Adam seldom intervened. It was a policy that had been decided upon from the first, before he'd displaced his half-brother as commissioner. The wheels of justice could not simply grind to a halt, else everyone must know that something extraordinary was going on.

And something extraordinary was going on. In the few weeks since Adam had assumed his role as commissioner, hundreds of refugees had been issued with false papers and conveyed to harbors where safe ships were docked. Adam himself did not deal directly with the refugees. His part in the enterprise was, in that respect, a passive one. He signed *carnets* by the score and left them to the discretion of Millot. But Adam's role was crucial. In the provinces, he represented the Convention. He implemented or disregarded policies. He deployed his troops as he saw fit. Though in one sense he was the law, there were others who administered the law for him. To interfere with the established process might jeopardize all their endeavors.

The judges were jealous of any interference in their domain. They met in the law courts where they tried the cases which came before them. It was from the law courts that the tumbrils set out in the afternoon with their human cargo for the guillotine in the market square.

"Oh God!" said Adam. "I should have anticipated something like this. From now on, spread the word that I am no longer interested in anyone who goes by the name of Devereux."

"That is what I was about to suggest," said Millot gravely.

Adam gave no evidence that he had heard Millot's words. Removing his booted feet from his desk, he straightened in his chair. He finished his drink quickly and silently indicated that he wished for another.

"Who is he?" he asked at length.

"Jules Devereux," answered Millot. "He's no more than a boy really."

"How old?"

"Eighteen."

"Why is his name on the proscribed lists?"

"He proposed a toast to the House of Bourbon. There are affidavits signed by several witnesses."

"When does his case come up?"

"Tomorrow, or the day after."

Adam let out a frustrated sigh. "Sometimes I think I've wandered into an asylum for the insane. How can men in their right minds condemn a callow youth for proposing a toast?"

"That's just it. These days, men are not in their right minds. And any show of support for the Bourbons, however slight, is considered treasonable.

Men have been condemned for less."

"He must have known the risk he was taking?"

Millot was silent.

Adam's annoyance grew. "Did he or did he not know the consequences of his actions?"

"You know that he did."

"Well?"

"Well what?"

"What do you suggest I do?"

Millot shifted restlessly under Adam's hard stare. "You're in charge," he said. "It's up to you to decide."

"Thank you. Your sage advice almost overwhelms me," retorted Adam savagely.

Some time elapsed before Millot gently interjected, "What have you decided?"

Adam's fingers were idly playing with a letter opener. He threw it aside. "I dare not intervene. We both know it. To do so might jeopardize our mission."

Millot helped himself to a small brandy. He felt the need of it. "He's only a boy," he said.

"No!"

For a moment or two, nothing more was said, then Millot cleared his throat before continuing, "So, what happens to your search for members of the Devereux family?"

"A search? That word connotes positive action on my part. I was never involved in a search for the Devereux."

"Oh? What then?"

"Mmm? Oh merely this. I promised someone that if any member of that family chanced to fall in my way, I would lend my assistance if it was necessary. The likelihood of that happening, however, seems very remote. And after what you have related to me, I've decided to forget about the Devereux altogether. At all events, they seem to have disappeared off the face of the earth."

"I'm sorry," said Millot, for something to say.

Adam's smile was not reflected in his eyes. "To be perfectly frank, Nicholas, if I never hear the name Devereux again, it will be too soon for my liking. And now, if you wouldn't mind, I'd like to have that bath before I fall asleep on my feet."

Millot was in the anteroom when Claire was announced. Adam was still in his office, looking over the report on Jules Devereux.

One look at Claire's beautiful blue eyes and Millot knew that something was very far amiss. "Claire," he said, crossing to her, "my dear, what is it?"

"Nicholas, I've been looking for you everywhere. Thank God I have found you. That boy? What are they going to do to him?"

He reached for her hand and patted it comfortingly. "What boy?"

"Jules Devereux. They brought him in this afternoon. If only . . ."

Adam's laconic tones cut across Claire's impetuous words. "What is Jules Devereux to you, Claire?"

Her head swiveled sharply and the hiss of her breath was clearly audible. She hadn't counted on Philippe being here. He wasn't due back until tomorrow. From the look of his mired boots and breeches and the stubble on his chin, it registered that he was newly arrived. "Philippe," she said feebly, "I did not know you were here."

Millot was still clutching Claire's hand. There was something in the look that his friend directed at him that made him quickly release it. "Commissioner," he blustered, "I shall be more than happy . . ."

"That will be all, Millot." Adam's tone brooked no argument, and Millot, with one reassuring glance at Claire, turned on his heel and quit the room.

"In here, Claire, if you please."

He held the door to his inner sanctum and Claire suppressed a shudder of apprehension as she obediently slipped by him. "It was only an idle . . ."

"Please be seated."

Inclining her head, she accepted the chair he indicated. Calm. Composure. She had to fight herself to find them.

From the other side of the desk, Adam said, "Now, Claire, I should like to know why you are in such a tempest."

There was only one way to deflect him. She must brazen it out. No sooner had she decided on her course than her panic subsided. She was still alive to every threat and danger, but now she met it head-on. So must a soldier feel, she supposed, when the battle was finally joined.

"I'll tell you why I am in such a tempest. I was there, you see, when they brought in that poor boy."

"Not a pretty sight, as I hear."

Her eyes flashed daggers at him. "Your troops are an affront to all decent people. That poor boy had taken a beating."

With both hands on the flat of his desk, Adam pushed himself back in his chair, stretching his cramped muscles. "According to reports, the boy resisted arrest," he said mildly.

"Why was he arrested?" She took a quick breath before continuing. "The clerk made mention of the fact that it was merely because his name was Devereux."

Adam nodded. "He was the wrong Devereux," he said.

Her performance, she judged, was masterly. Feigning incredulity, she demanded, "Are you saying that anyone with the name of Devereux is subject to arrest and execution?"

"Don't be ridiculous!" he snapped. "Besides, the Devereux I am interested in are the Devereux banking family. This boy . . ." Suddenly his eyes narrowed on her.

Alive to her danger, she exerted herself to throw

him off the scent. Eyes snapping, voice spitting fire, she bit out, "Why am I surprised? I should have known what manner of man you are. *Claire*, she mimicked, *is it fair to judge a man on hearsay alone? I am not the ogre I've been made out to be.* Liar!" she raged at him. "Monster! This is a personal vendetta, isn't it? The rumors about you are true. If anyone falls foul of you, they might as well sign their own death warrant." She was trembling in her shoes, almost sure that she had gone too far.

His anger was equal to hers. Through set teeth, he said, "This is not a personal vendetta. If that boy's name had not been on the proscribed lists, he would be a free man at this very moment. Furthermore, I am the commissioner here. You would do well to remember it, Claire."

It was no idle threat. Claire paused, marshaling her thoughts. For some reason, on his own admission, this man was searching for the members of her family. Her father had made many enemies in his time. Was Philippe one of them? She did not know what to think, but of one thing she was certain. She would never reveal her identity now. Through sheer force of will, she let that thought go and concentrated on the fate of Jules Devereux. The boy was not much older than her own brother.

She wasn't acting now. "Philippe," she said, her voice hoarse and breathless with emotion, "what will happen to the boy?"

A muscle clenched in his cheek. "His case comes up tomorrow or the next day. It's out of my hands."

"But why? As you say, you are the commissioner. If you really wanted to, you could save him."

"No."

It dawned on her that she wasn't merely pleading for the boy, or her family, nor even for all the victims of this senseless persecution. She was pleading for Philippe as much as anyone. He wasn't completely bad. There was something there, a core of good, if only she could reach it. No man who had comforted a hysterical girl in the throes of a nightmare as if she were a hurt child could be without some redeeming virtue.

Reasoning with him, she began, "Philippe, surely you must see that this wholesale slaughter is wrong? To cheat the guillotine of even one of its victims is a worthy ambition. You are so placed that you could do so much good." He gave a start at her words and she was encouraged to continue. "Save the life of this one boy, I beg of you."

Abruptly he rose to his feet and glared down at her. "I warn you, Claire, those words are treasonable. If you had said them to anyone but me, it would be *you* who would be facing arrest and execution. Don't meddle in what does not concern you! This is a man's business! Go work on your embroidery or whatever it is ladies do to keep out of mischief."

Her cheeks were ashen as she rose to face him. "Man!" she scorned, her lips curling. "What makes you think you are a man? I say you are no man because you do not share in the sufferings of other men. Only a monster or a devil may stand aside and remain indifferent to the plight of the persecuted. If this is what we have all come to, we might as well be dead." Her voice broke on the last word.

"Claire, that's enough!" He was yelling at her, his eyes leaping with violence. God, he did not deserve this. It was Philippe who was the monster, not Adam Dillon. And he was helpless to defend himself. She didn't understand and he could not, would not explain it. But it infuriated him to think that their time together had made so little impression on her. She must see that he was not the man she had just described.

Another thought came to him, one that he was in no mood to entertain. There was a germ of truth in everything she had just said.

"Philippe, I beg of you . . ."

"No!" he roared.

For a long moment, stricken, she stared at him. Then, with a choked sob, she picked up her skirts and fled the room.

Long after she had left him, Adam stared into space, hating himself, hating Claire, but most of all hating the caprice that had brought him to this pass. He must not interfere with the wheels of justice, he reminded himself. To do so might easily range the judges of the Tribunal against him. The success of their enterprise might well be in jeopardy if that were to happen.

Millot found Adam still at his desk a good hour later. "Commissioner, shall I order your bath to be drawn?" he asked quietly, his eyes taking in the droop of his friend's shoulders and the lines of weariness etched deeply into his face.

Pressing a hand to his temples, Adam said, "Yes. No, wait."

Millot waited patiently, thanking his lucky stars a hundred times over that he was not the leader of their mission.

Sighing, Adam looked up. "I have made up my mind, Nicholas. I shall speak to the judges first thing tomorrow. That boy—Jules Devereux? I want him released. See to it at once."

"You mean . . . now? This instant?"

"At once, I said." To Millot's questioning look, Adam responded, "If it were not for me, he would still be a free man. That is the only reason I have decided to involve myself in his case. But this is an exception, my friend. Make a note of that."

The look of relief on Millot's face was almost comical, but Adam wasn't smiling. He was thinking that he must be mad to allow a mere female to influence him like this.

A few minutes later, Millot returned. "It's done," he said. "The boy can't believe his luck."

Adam nodded. "And now for my bath."

Having ordered that a bath should be drawn for the commissioner, Millot solicitously walked him to his suite of rooms.

"Where is Claire now?" asked Adam.

"She retired to her chamber some time ago."

"Then I won't disturb her."

Millot made no comment, but the fact that he passed the door to Claire's bedchamber with alacrity in order to enter the door to the commissioner's bedchamber was a telling gesture.

With a soft sound of derision, Adam crossed the threshold.

"Is there anything else you require, Commissioner?" inquired Millot softly.

Two young conscripts were setting a wooden tub before the fire. A maid was laying out towels on a rack.

"Thank you, no, Millot," said Adam politely. His look was pointed and conveyed a wealth of meaning.

Millot's gaze faltered before that blighting stare. He interpreted Adam's look perfectly. He'd made the error once before of anticipating his friend's needs. On that occasion, Adam had walked into his chamber to find Carmen in his bed.

Carmen was the drawing card of Madame Latour's establishment just off the Rue de la Pie. The girl did not come cheaply. She knew the value of her hot-house beauty and a form that would drive any man crazy to possess it. Millot had counted on the girl's attributes and acknowledged skills to prevent Adam's mind from straying to the innocent beauty who was asleep in the next room.

Whether or not he had succeeded in his design, he was never to find out. Knowing Adam and knowing Carmen, he was almost sure that he must have been successful. Nevertheless, the following morning, Adam had displayed the sharp edge of his temper. He was perfectly capable of finding his own women, he had tersely informed him. And in a tone soft with menace he'd reminded Millot that he had already given his word respecting Claire Michelet. There was not the least necessity to throw other women at his head. Millot had nothing to fear on that score.

Millot was almost persuaded, but not quite. He knew of Adam's reputation in New York. He'd seen him in action. No woman was safe from him if he happened to take a fancy to her, not even the innocent ones. Not that Adam did all the chasing. He had a whole repertoire of special smiles, knowing looks, and soft seductive words, all of which were calculated to lure his prey into his net with the least amount of effort. Women didn't stand a chance with him.

One part of Millot admired Adam's way with women. Another part was scandalized. As the children of gentle, unworldly parents, Millot and his two brothers had been raised to revere womanhood. Women, especially women like Claire Michelet, were to be placed on a pedestal. There were others, of course, women of a different class, who were fair game. Adam did not play by the rules. To him, all women were fair game.

"That will be all, Millot. Good night."

Adam's dismissal barely brought Millot out of his reveries. He absently stepped out of the way as conscripts shouldered past him bearing wooden buckets of hot water for the commissioner's bath.

"Good night, Commissioner," he murmured in reply. Deep in thought, he descended the stairs to his own chambers. He was reflecting that Adam was no monk. There must be a woman somewhere. He wondered who she was and where Adam was hiding her.

In his chamber, Adam quickly shed his travel-stained clothes and stepped into the bath water. He reached for the soap to scrub the smell of horseflesh from his skin.

"Damn!" The soap was highly scented. He put it

125

to his nose. Roses! He looked about him. The block of lye soap was on the washstand. As he made to pull himself from the tub, the door from the corridor opened, and Adam sank back into the bathwater.

"Fetch me the soap over there," he said, gesturing with one hand.

He looked up expecting to see one of the conscripts with a bucket of water for his bath. A young woman came into his line of vision. In her arms, she clutched a bundle of coarse linen towels. Adam recognized her as the maid who had set towels on the rack to warm at the fire.

At once Adam's suspicions were aroused. There were plenty of towels on the rack. There was no need for the maid to return with more. Was Nicholas taking a hand in things again, trying to supply him with a warm, willing female to take his mind off Claire Michelet? But Nicholas was well aware that any repetition of the Carmen incident would lead to an instant and savage reprisal. Then what, wondered Adam, was the woman doing here, and why was she lingering?

He stretched both arms along the edge of the tub, flexing his powerful shoulders. The woman walked slowly, sinuously, toward him, one arm holding the towels, the other extended, proffering the soap. With blatant provocation, her eyes swept over his naked torso.

The soap wasn't the only thing she was offering him. Adam recognized a siren when he saw one. And this dark-eyed lovely was the original Circe. Unhappily, she was not Claire.

"What's your name?" he asked.

"Blanche," she replied, smiling invitingly.

Adam wasn't interested in what she was offering. He wasn't a boor, however. As he had done with Carmen, he tried to let the girl down lightly.

"I only wish it were possible," he murmured. "But you see, my mistress would *kill* me if I dared." He relieved her of the soap and pressed a kiss to her fingers. "She's a veritable tigress!"

The girl stiffened. Someone on the threshold gasped. Adam jerked his head round in time to see Claire stalk into the room. He dropped Blanche's hand as though he were holding a red hot poker.

"Claire!" He cleared his throat. "Claire," he said, "I thought you were asleep."

Claire's arms went around her maid's shoulders as if she were comforting a child. With a venomous look at Adam, she said, "Blanche, you are not to enter this room again, do you understand? Now wait for me outside until I have a word in private with the commissioner."

"I was only fetching fresh towels for the commissioner's bath," replied Blanche. The towels in question were still clasped to her bosom.

The change in the maid, noted Adam dourly, was something to behold. Before his very eyes, the siren turned into a little girl. She might be able to fool an innocent like Claire, but Adam Dillon was wise to her, on all counts. The girl was a consummate actress.

The maid departed. Eyes flashing, Claire approached the tub. Resignedly, Adam folded his arms across his chest and waited.

"What kind of monster would seduce an innocent like Blanche? She's just a child."

There was no point in defending himself. If he were to swear his innocence on a stack of Bibles, Claire would not believe him. "I cannot abide jealous women," said Adam, going on the attack.

"Jealous?" When she could find her breath, she laughed. "You think I'm jealous?"

"It's as plain as the nose on your face."

Her bosom began to heave. Adam began to soap himself as if he had not a care in the world. He chanced a quick look at Claire. Her eyes were moving over him, absorbing the breadth of his powerful arms and shoulders, the muscular chest with its dark mat of coarse hair. Claire's perusal was nothing like the maid's. Adam sensed her fear.

"Claire," he said softly. "Don't look at me like that."

Startled, she looked up at him.

In the same unthreatening tone, he said, "I am not a brute. I would never hurt you."

Her expression altered. The blue fire was back in her eyes. "Liar!" she hissed. "You enjoy torturing people."

As she made to flounce from the room, Adam called her back. "About that boy," he said, "Jules Devereux? I ordered his release." He was sure she would be overcome with tears of gratitude and was taken aback by the furious look she threw at him.

Shoulders heaving, eyes snapping, she raged, "You are the most perverse creature it has ever been my misfortune to encounter." She stomped to the door.

Adam's face was thunderous. Before he could give her the set-down she so richly deserved, she pivoted to face him.

"Thank you," she said, then her voice broke. "Oh, Philippe, I do thank you," and she slipped through the door.

Adam shook his head. After a moment, his glower dissolved and became a smile.

"Tigress!" he said and began to whistle. A moment later, he frowned. He'd done it again. He'd forgotten that he was Philippe Duhet, a cold and unfeeling monster. Shaking his head, sighing, he began to soap himself.

In a room that was no bigger than a cubicle, just off the kitchens, Blanche slowly began to disrobe till she was down to her underthings. Methodically, she folded her clothes and placed them in a tiny closet in

128

the wall. Formerly, Blanche's room had been used as a pantry and the closet had been a lift, a dumbwaiter which conveyed hot food from the kitchens to the floor above. Directly above was the commissioner's office. When the rooms on the upper floor were rearranged years before, a new pantry was installed on the other side of the kitchens, with a bigger, more efficient dumbwaiter.

In time, the existence of the old shaft was forgotten. In the commissioner's office, the door to the lift was papered over. Blanche would never have realized the significance of the tiny closet in her wall, if she had not by accident heard the commissioner in conference with some important dignitary. The sound of their voices which carried down the shaft was muffled, but she was able to pick up enough to get the gist of their conversation. From time-to-time, she had deliberately eavesdropped, but there was never much of interest to her.

She had listened in tonight and had made little sense of the tail end of what she had heard, except that the commissioner intended to have a bath. She had been given her chance and she had seized upon it.

Seating herself on the narrow cot, she felt in the folds of the bedcovers and withdrew the knife she had hurriedly concealed when Claire had seen her to her door moments before. Slowly, thoughtfully, she turned it over in her hands. She was thinking that she had been given her chance and she had fumbled it. It didn't make sense.

She shivered. There was no fire in the room, nor even a fireplace. During the day the heat from the ovens in the kitchens was adequate to take the chill off her tiny cubicle. At night, the water in the slop pail formed icicles.

Quickly slipping between the sheets, she carefully replaced the borrowed knife under her pillow. She must return it at first light, before Cook discovered that it was missing. She blew out her candle and

129

stared up at the ceiling. Why, she asked herself, had she hesitated to use the knife on Philippe Duhet? It was not the girl's sudden appearance on the scene which had prevented her. Before Claire Michelet stepped into that room Blanche knew that her resolve had begun to waver. Why?

For a moment there, in spite of her changed appearance, she'd thought that Duhet might have recognized her. She should have known better. A man such as Duhet must have lost count of all the women he had known. And she had never been one of his women. He had looked into her eyes without suspicion. He had allowed her to approach within striking distance. And she had hesitated. Again, she asked herself why.

She let the question revolve in her mind. The answer came to her in dribs and drabs, stirring impressions and fragments that resolved themselves into a whole. She had set the stage so that suspicion would fall on Duhet's mistress. When it came to that point, however, she could not go through with it. Claire Michelet was not the hardened harlot she had anticipated. She genuinely liked the girl. Claire stirred something in her, some hidden center where the emptiness had failed to penetrate.

When she found her thoughts drifting to her sister Verity she ruthlessly brought them round. Philippe Duhet would be served his just desserts. She would find a way to destroy him without implicating the girl. She must not lose patience now. The thought soothed her. She closed her eyes. But still sleep eluded her.

Chapter Eight

Adam's intervention in the trial of Jules Devereux had repercussions as he suspected might be the case. The majority of the judges and lawyers tamely accepted his suggestions and acted on them as if they were commands. They were intimidated by the power the commissioner wielded. There were others among them, however, the fanatics, who stewed in outrage. Jules Devereux was only one small provocation in a long list of grievances they nursed against the commissioner.

In short, they had come to view Philippe Duhet's appointment to their city as a grave error in judgment on Robespierre's part. While commissioners in other cities, notably Lyons and Nantes, were zealous in bringing the Terror to the provinces, Rouen was relatively undisturbed. Duhet had not fulfilled his promise.

Before long, secret letters were passing between the law courts in Rouen and the Committee of Public Safety in Paris. Adam soon got wind of it. He called a meeting of his associates. They met during the dinner hour, when the day's business had been transacted and the offices were vacant. A guard was posted at the door to the hallway.

Adam's eyes touched briefly on each of his companions. Millot, Bernay, and Granville, young

131

men all, were the only other occupants of the room. Adam was thinking that he knew very little about them except that these young men had known each other from before. They were the sons of professional men, lawyers, and doctors. Of the three, Millot was the youngest, Granville was the handsomest, and Bernay, though the most unprepossessing, the one who attracted the most feminine attention.

"Women like to mother me," Adam had once overheard Bernay remark, laughing off his success with women.

"And you take advantage of it," Granville had shot back.

They were good men; they were moderates; and they were passionately devoted to ending the Terror in France. As for himself, thought Adam, his purpose in coming to France had altered. At one time, he'd hoped merely to make things awkward for his half-brother. When this was over, Philippe would know that he'd taken another bloody nose from his father's bastard son. It was all a game.

It was Claire who had shamed him, Claire who had opened his eyes and had revealed the pettiness of his ambition. God, would he ever forget how she had chastened him, right here, in his own office? Would he ever forget those words that she had flung at him? *You are no man because you do not share in the sufferings of other men. Only a monster or a devil may stand aside and remain indifferent to the plight of the persecuted. If this is what we have all come to, we might as well be dead.*

Though it was Philippe she was judging, Adam was forced to admit that his own motives were anything but pure. It was not true to say that he was indifferent. But that was a far cry from sharing in the sufferings of other men. Claire didn't understand. His hands were tied. Yet . . . it was not for saving lives that he had come to France, but to pay off an old score.

Her words had scourged him, not least because he admired her. She possessed a rare courage that must command respect. To save her friends she had sacrificed her honor and her peace of mind to become the mistress of a man she feared and hated. And though believing him to be Philippe, and knowing what Philippe was, she had dared to upbraid him. Did she know the risks she ran? Did she understand the consequences she might bring down upon her head? She must have.

It was insane. He should have been doing his utmost to convince her that he really was his half-brother, a man without conscience, a man who would exact a quick retribution on anyone who flaunted his authority. Instead of which he had allowed a mere woman to divert him from his set purpose. He had intervened in the case of Jules Devereux, persuading himself that the only reason he had done so was because he owed it to the boy. It was part of the reason, but it wasn't the whole of it. He had done it to please Claire.

He could no longer deceive himself. He wanted Claire to think well of him. He wanted her to see that he was not the depraved monster his brother was. The thought irritated him, not least because her influence had led to this. The masquerade was coming to an end, and hence his ability to direct events.

"Commissioner?"

Coming to himself, Adam briefly outlined the secret report he had received from one of their agents in Paris. He ended by saying, "Gentlemen, we've had a good run, longer than we anticipated. But the writing is on the wall. In a matter of weeks, perhaps sooner, I may expect to be recalled to the Convention to answer charges of corruption. As I said, an investigation is already underway. I suggest that each of you take stock of your position. It goes without saying that those closest to the commissioner will also come under suspicion."

There was a silence as each man absorbed the shock of Adam's words.

"Bloody hell!" The expletive came from Bernay. "This could not have come at a worse time." To Adam's questioning look, Bernay said simply, "General Theot."

"Ah!" Adam sat back in his chair.

In America, General Theot had many influential friends. Like Adam, as a young man he had served with Lafayette in the Revolutionary War. On his return to France, Theot had meddled in politics. He'd chosen the wrong side. At that moment, the general was lauguishing in the Abbaye Prison in Paris.

"As I understand," said Adam, "there have been official overtures from the American government on Theot's behalf?"

It was Granville who answered. "Unfortunately, highly incriminating letters from General Theot to the Comte d'Artois were intercepted. All entreaties on his behalf have since fallen on deaf ears."

"Theot was ever a hothead," observed Adam. He could well imagine the contents of Theot's letters. Theot, in later years, had become a Royalist and made no bones of the fact that he regarded the present regime in France as contrary to the laws of both God and man. In normal circumstances, Theot would have been summarily executed for professing such views. But the Convention was sensitive to American opinion. France had few friends. America, at least officially, was one of them.

"I take it," said Adam, "that Theot's friends are preparing to subvert the course of justice?"

"Our agents are working on it," said Bernay.

No one asked Bernay to elaborate on this simple statement. The less each man knew, the safer for all concerned. Their part in the enterprise was self-evident. If and when Theot escaped his jailers, he must be smuggled out of France.

"We can do it," said Adam finally, "as long as I am still in command here. But the sooner it's done, the better."

Millot took a more cautious approach. "Ours is not the only network. Let someone else get him out."

"Who, for instance?" asked Adam.

"The English."

Adam shook his head. "Theot is no friend to the English. They wouldn't lift a finger to save him. Besides, the English network is no longer in existence. If we don't do it, it won't be done."

Millot was not convinced. "What if the Convention sends out deputies with warrants for your arrest? Once you are in custody, your chances of getting away will be very slim. You must think of yourself, Commissioner."

"According to our man in Paris, that is not likely to happen," answered Adam. "As I told you, I shall be recalled and will be given an opportunity to defend myself before my peers."

The irony behind Adam's words was not lost on his companions. It was the real Philippe Duhet who would be conveyed to Paris to face the charges against the commissioner. By that time, Adam would be safely on his way to America. In that event, each man there had laid his own plans to evade capture.

"Gentlemen," said Adam, his gaze moving between Granville and Bernay, "I don't need to tell you that events could move very swiftly. I shall delay as long as possible. If General Theot is to be got out, it must be soon. That is all I wish to say."

When Bernay and Granville had quit Adam's office, Millot lingered. "I don't like it," he said. "We knew something like this would happen sooner or later. We agreed that, of us all, you are in the most vulnerable position. You should get out now, while you still have the chance."

"There's very little danger," said Adam, "at least,

not more than usual. And I know General Theot personally. He's a good man. The risks are worth it."

Millot did not continue to debate the point. He was coming to know Adam too well to hope that he could be persuaded of something once his mind was made up. In some respects, Adam Dillon was a man of iron. In his own milieu, his friends and associates did not realize it. They were deceived by his easy charm and open, natural manners, none of which had been evident in the last number of weeks when, of necessity, Adam had adopted his half-brother's role. Millot was beginning to wonder how much of it had been playacting and how much of it was the real Adam Dillon.

Millot thought of Claire, but almost at once, he decided not to mention her name. Adam knew as well as he that, as things stood, the girl was also in a vulnerable position. If the Convention's deputies arrested the commissioner, it was almost certain that they would also arrest his mistress. Millot dared not voice what he was thinking. Claire had become one subject on which Adam Dillon was extremely sensitive.

Millot would have been surprised to know to what degree Claire had come to occupy Adam's mind of late and how reluctant he was to come to a decision about her future. Within minutes of Millot's quitting the room, Adam's thoughts had turned inevitably to Claire.

With the threat of recall hanging over him, he could no longer defer making a decision. He must make up his mind to part with her forever, or take her to America with him. And in that moment, Adam knew that he was a victim of his own duplicity. The decision had been made weeks, no, months ago. He would never give up this girl. He'd known it before he had ever taken over as commissioner. He'd known it as he watched from an upstairs window as she came and went in front of the cathedral, a girl who squared her slight shoulders under the weight of her burdens. He frowned, remembering that he'd wished, then, to take the weight of those burdens on his own shoulders. Instead, he had only added to them. Millot was right. The decent thing to have done would have been to let her go. He had made her his mistress and in so doing he had shamed her.

In the former pantry, directly below the commissioner's office, Blanche quietly closed the doors to her closet. Her hand was trembling. Her eyes were glowing. She could not believe her good fortune. It wasn't the first time she'd noted the guard outside the commissioner's office, indicating that something of significance was taking place. It wasn't the first time she'd stolen downstairs to her own room to listen in by way of the disused dumbwaiter. But it was the first time she had heard anything to her advantage.

Philippe Duhet's days as commissioner were numbered. He was to be recalled on charges of corruption. She had no doubt that in the normal course of events, Duhet would get off scot-free. Men like Duhet had influence. He had powerful friends. He also had powerful enemies. And now, she had learned something that could help those enemies. She had enough on Duhet to send him to the scaffold and not only Duhet, but General Theot also.

Blanche knew of this man, and what she knew, she did not like. He was an aristocrat and a rabid Royalist. Duhet was one of the same breed. She'd never accepted his professions of loyalty to the Revolutionary cause. Not that Blanche cared a jot for the Revolution. What she loved no longer existed. Duhet had seen to that. And now the fates had put into her hand the means of repaying an old debt.

Men like Duhet did not deserve to live. Born to a life of wealth and privilege, he could not conceive of denying himself whatever struck his fancy. He had taken one look at Verity, and he had reached out to take her—Verity with her mischievous smiles and her laughing eyes; Verity who had a child's mind in a woman's body. She would never grow up, never assume an adult's cares. Her simplemindedness evoked the tender feelings of everyone who knew her. At the Comédie Française, where Blanche had been one of the leading actresses, Verity was as cherished as a delicate piece of porcelain. She had no experience, no conception of men of Duhet's stamp.

But Blanche understood Duhet. She had recognized the look that came into his eyes whenever they came to rest on her beautiful young sister. What she had not known was the man's capacity to persevere until he had grasped what he wanted.

Oh God, how clever she had thought herself when she'd taken Verity out of his orbit. The theater was no place for a young girl, she'd told Verity, and she had taken her in person to live with the nuns. If she closed her eyes, she could still see the nuns in their black habits as they strolled in the sun-dappled cloisters. Peace. Godliness. Sanctuary. She had sensed all of those things—and how wrong she had been. And in her abysmal stupidity, she had returned to Paris, secure in the knowledge that Verity was safe.

Duhet had plucked Verity from the convent as easily as he would pluck a rose from his own garden. And when the nuns had protested, he'd dealt with them, too. The convent was razed to the ground. The nuns were dispersed, or butchered. No one dared reproach him openly. He was following official policy. Under the new regime, religion was severely proscribed. And Verity . . . It had taken Blanche nearly a year to find her, and when she did, Verity had not known her. She was in an asylum for the insane. Her profession was recorded as "prostitute." She was only fifteen years old.

Blanche had taken her to their former home in Rouen. A month later, Verity died in childbed, giving birth to a stillborn son. And something inside Blanche died with her.

She had no thought of taking revenge on Duhet. Their paths no longer crossed. He was a powerful figure in French politics. She hated him, but there was nothing she could do about it. Until Fate had taken a hand in things.

Though she was sorry that necessity had forced her to lie to Claire, she knew that she dared not, under any circumstance, confide in her. Claire despised Duhet. But in an unguarded moment, if she knew Blanche's circumstances, she might let something slip.

She must protect Claire. But how was it to be done? For the rest of the evening as she went about her duties she pondered that thought. On retiring for the night, she had determined her course of action.

It was Claire who must denounce Duhet. It must be Claire's signature on the letter that informed against him. When Duhet was arrested, Claire would be exonerated.

For the rest of the day, Adam was fully occupied. When he thought of Claire it was with the conviction that he was going to take her to America with him. Adam thought no further than that till he was in the privacy of his own chamber and readying himself for bed.

In the act of undoing his neckcloth, his hands stilled as the thought that had been hovering on the periphery of his consciousness throughout the day finally came into focus. He would take Claire to America with him, but in what capacity? Wife or mistress—it must be one or the other.

Marriage. Adam approached the word gingerly. With Claire, it had to be marriage. Given his druthers, so he told himself, he would have leapt at the chance of carrying her off to America and making

139

her his mistress. In that event, she could have commanded her own price. He would have paid it without batting an eyelash. He would have set her up in grand style. Claire was worth it. Regretfully, Claire was not cut out to be a man's mistress. Claire was not like other women.

In his dealings with women, Adam was charming but cautious. A man had to be. Women, he had discovered, had a whole arsenal of weapons that they ruthlessly employed in order to lead some unsuspecting male to the altar. In Adam's opinion, he was more scrupulous than the women who tried to trap him. He never concealed what he was after. He wanted a *liaison*. At the outset, he made it clear that Adam Dillon was not a marrying man. No woman ever listened to him. Each woman thought that she would be the one to make him change his mind. Claire Michelet was the first who had succeeded and this girl wasn't even trying.

In the beginning, he'd resented what she was doing to him. He'd been as wary as a wily fish with a baited hook. If she was playing hard to get, he was on to her. When it was obvious that she wasn't playing a part and that she really was hard to get, he'd resented that, too.

This girl wasn't predictable. Nothing in his previous experience with women had prepared him for Claire Michelet. She wasn't vain. She wasn't avaricious. And the last thing she wanted, by all appearances, was Adam Dillon within a mile of her. It was entirely possible that Claire would be no more gratified by his offer of marriage than she was with their present arrangement.

He wasn't going to let a refusal deter him, Adam decided. He knew how to change Claire's mind. As of that moment, his promise to Millot counted for nothing, and he was going to tell him so the first chance he got. This was too important a matter to let trifles stand in his way. He must take Claire with him

140

to America or lose her forever.

Adam quickly shed his garments and slipped into bed. With his hands laced behind his neck, he stared at the blue velvet hangings on one of the bedposts. If he were a gentleman, he was thinking, he would settle Claire with some suitable family in New York and give her the freedom to decide her own future. He snorted, knowing full well that he wasn't going to take the chance of some other gentleman snatching Claire from under his nose.

Not that he was unprincipled, Adam quickly convinced himself. It was not as though the girl was indifferent to him. In spite of appearances, Claire was as susceptible to him as he was to her. That cool composure could not deceive him. He knew how to shatter her control. In his arms, she turned wanton. She could not say no to him. She was all female, and so sweetly, passionately giving. But she didn't want to be; that much was evident.

"You made me," she'd flung at him, as though accusing him of some abomination.

Yes. He'd made her, and if she made things difficult for him, he would not hesitate to unleash her own capacity for passion against her.

The thought brought him up short. Good God, this was Claire, not some woman who knew how to play the game. He wasn't about to do anything to bring further shame on her head. He respected her scruples. He was offering marriage. A fine opinion she would have of him if he forced her to lie with him. And she would lie with him because she'd made a bargain with Philippe Duhet. But it was Adam Dillon who would reap what he had sown once she knew the truth about him. She would hate him for taking advantage of her. That was no way to start a marriage.

Marriage. The more he thought of it, the more appeal the idea gained. Conversely, the more he thought of making Claire his mistress, the more

141

ridiculous he knew the notion to be. Nothing was more certain than, in very short order, he would have fathered his child on her. Then his own principles would come into play. He would marry her. How much simpler, how much wiser, to marry her at the outset? That thought led to another. Was it possible that Claire was already pregnant with his child? It seemed unlikely. A woman must naturally turn to the father of her child for protection. Claire had said nothing to him. Again, the thought occurred to him that Claire was not like other women.

Claire, the mother of his children. The thought, surprisingly, was . . . erotic. His seed impregnating her body. Claire, nurturing his child under her heart. A rush of tenderness swept through him. He felt . . . unworthy, and, at the same time, elated. Adam Dillon, husband and father. The reverie was a pleasant one. He would cherish Claire and the children she gave him as they deserved.

He did not want her to have a baby every other year, he decided, as was the way with most married women. That was too hard on a woman's health. Some women were old before their time. He wasn't going to let that happen to Claire. He would find the control to protect her. In the last several weeks, he had exercised more control than he'd ever dreamed he possessed. He could do it again, for Claire. Marriage. There were compensations to this arrangement, Adam allowed. Once he put his ring on Claire's finger, his claims would be indisputable. Formerly, Adam had been something of a careless lover. He'd lost mistresses to the encroachments of other gentlemen, accepting his losses with more indifference than regret. There were plenty more pebbles on the beach. If he were Claire's husband, he would take a different view. As his private possession, Claire would be his alone to enjoy.

He savored the thought. Then all the passion she carefully hoarded behind that cool facade would belong to him; all that beauty, so sweetly accessible. When they were married, he could take her anytime he wanted. Those little cries of surrender she made just before she turned into him, offering him the freedom of her body, would never be heard by any other male. He was the one who would push her over the edge of that rigidly imposed control until she could deny him nothing. It was in his arms that she would turn tigress. He was the one who would bear the marks of her passion, those little bites and scratches that made him go crazy for her.

His body tightened, his blood began to throb. Vehemently cursing his stupidity in letting his imagination run away with him, Adam forced the return of more sober thoughts.

Time was of the essence. One way or another, Claire must be persuaded to go with him to America. With women, when he set his mind to it, he was a master of getting what he wanted. It had never mattered to him before. It mattered now, and for the first time he was unsure how to approach the woman he wanted above all others.

There were two things in his favor, decided Adam. The first was Claire's susceptibility to him. The second was her evident desire to give him the benefit of the doubt. From something Millot had told him, it would seem that, in Claire's eyes, the commissioner was no longer a man to be feared. In point of fact, Millot was quite anxious about Claire's softening toward the commissioner. He did not want to see the girl get hurt.

It was something to think about. Claire would not trust herself to an unprincipled scoundrel such as Philippe, unless she was persuaded that she had misjudged him. For a long time, Adam played with that thought. Before sleep claimed him, he was devising ways and means of taking advantage of Claire's naïveté. Once he had won her trust, he would have her in the palm of his hand.

*　　　*　　　*

There was a time when Claire considered herself a shrewd judge of character. But that was before she had met Philippe Duhet. The commissioner was a complete enigma to her. For the life of her, she could not make up her mind about him. He was no saint, but neither was he the brute she had been led to expect.

After his surprising change of heart over the business of Jules Devereux, she had made a point of seeking out Millot, trying to find out more about Philippe without giving the appearance of doing so. What Millot had revealed completely mystified her. The commissioner's administration of Rouen was a humane one. Jules Devereux was not the only man who had reason to be grateful for the commissioner's timely intervention on his behalf. Though the judges on the Tribunal mistrusted Philippe, by and large, he had the confidence of Rouen's citizens.

"In point of fact," said Claire, "there is no foundation to the rumors that have circulated about the commissioner? He is a far better man than his reputation would suggest?" She was holding her breath in anticipation of Millot's answer. If only it were so! Oh, if only it were so!

Millot's eyes went curiously blank. He shrugged negligently, and laughed. "Oh, I would not go so far as to say that," he demurred. "You know how it is with great men. They are a law unto themselves."

"Yet you admire him," said Claire stubbornly.

"Did I say so?"

"No, but . . ."

"My dear Claire, with men of Duhet's stamp, one never knows what to expect. I may admire him as a soldier, but I am careful to watch my step, and so must you."

The warning was unmistakable, and still Claire was unconvinced. In many respects, Philippe Duhet

144

had failed to live up to his reputation. There was no evidence that he was a debaucher of innocents. True, he had made Claire his mistress, but the suggestion had been as much hers as his. She had wanted safe-conduct passes for Zoë and Leon, and would have done almost anything to acquire them. It hardly seemed fair to cry "outrage" when the commissioner accepted what she was offering. And he had kept to his part of the bargain. He had done more. After that first night, he had left her in peace.

If he had gone to other women as Claire supposed he must, Blanche was not one of them. The maid had completely absolved him of all blame the night that Claire walked into his chamber and surprised them together. No one had sent for her, Blanche protested. It was her duty to see that there were towels in the commissioner's room. She was merely handing him a bar of soap.

Claire believed her. There was no reason not to. She was not a wife who had any claim on Philippe Duhet. She was a mistress, and *that* in name only. If Duhet wished to replace her, there was nothing to stop him. She should be overjoyed at the prospect. Instead, she was oddly . . . disturbed.

In the act of running a comb through her long hair, Claire's hand stilled. Startled, she stared at the reflection in her dressing-table mirror. Why should the thought of Philippe replacing her disturb her composure? She could not possibly be attracted to the man, could she?

"Jealous," he had called her.

Her first impulse was to deny it. She had wished only to protect her maid, she told herself. But Claire was too honest not to admit that she had felt a pang of something when she'd walked in and had surprised him with Blanche.

She snorted indelicately. The man could not help himself. Young, old, beautiful, ugly—no woman was safe from the play of his charm. He knew

145

precisely what he was doing. And so did the women, those few she had observed with him, and who had come to the commissioner's headquarters on some errand or other. God only knew what they were thinking! They simpered and giggled and batted their eyelashes. The spectacle made her positively . . . jealous.

Claire threw down her comb in disgust. For almost a week, she had come under the full force of the man's charm. She thought she was immune to it. Now she knew better. He was courting her. There was no other way to describe it. He escorted her on long walks. He took her driving in his carriage. Every evening, he dined with her. And every night, when she thought that *now* she must pay the piper, he walked her to her door, pressed a kiss to her hand and wished her good night.

Good night? If only he knew it! In sleep, her thoughts defied her. They summoned Philippe to her dreams. She welcomed him eagerly. Every kiss, every touch of his hands made her on fire for him. When she wakened in the mornings, she ached from head to toe with unsated desire. She could have wept in frustration.

She resented his charm. It was too practiced, too calculated, too studied by half. And she was an idiot, Claire admitted, for allowing herself to be swayed by it. As Millot said, Philippe was a law unto himself. She must watch her step with him. Then why did her heart try to persuade her otherwise?

She could not answer herself, and she came at the question from all sides. In the beginning, the man had terrified her, and it was not only because of the stories she'd heard about him. He made her skin crawl. Not for the first time she reflected that his effect on her had changed drastically from the night he'd returned from Angers. He'd seemed like a different man. Either she had misjudged him from the very beginning or something had happened to him in Angers, some experience that had exerted a profound effect on him. But what? Millot would know. She would ask him about it first thing in the morning.

The answer to that question suddenly became overwhelmingly important to her. She could not wait till morning to have her answer. Besides, she told herself, these days, Millot was so preoccupied, so taken up with his duties, that she scarcely saw him. It was ten o'clock of an evening. Claire did not think that he would be abed. He'd told her once that he could never sleep until he'd filled his mind with beauty. He liked to read from the classics, or from the English poet, Milton, before retiring. Claire understood him perfectly. Music had the same effect on her. There was so much ugliness in the world. To reach for beauty was a form of escape.

She fastened her wrapper high at the throat. It was voluminous, like a tent, and more concealing than her walking coat. It took her only a few minutes to descend the stairs and cross the corridor that led to Millot's rooms. The house was relatively quiet. Guards were posted, but no one bothered her.

She rapped on Millot's door. "Nicholas," she said urgently. There was no answer. She tried again with the same result and was just about to turn away, when she recognized Philippe's voice. He was in conversation with someone, and ascending the stairs. In another minute, he would take the turn in the stairs and she would be in full view.

Claire did not think about the wisdom of what she was doing. She opened the door to Millot's chamber and whipped inside. She closed the door gently and waited. The voices grew louder and slowly faded till all she could hear was the rasp of her own uneven breathing. Gradually, her confidence returned.

"Nicholas," she said softly, and looked about her with interest. She was in a small parlor with a door to the right which she surmised must lead to a bedchamber. The candles were still lit. On a small table close to the dying fire were the remains of a supper that evidently two people had shared.

She would give Philippe a few minutes to get to his own chamber, she decided, and then, when the coast was clear, she would make her way upstairs. Without conscious thought Claire moved about the room, inspecting first one object, then another. On top of a small writing table, she came across a piece of paper. She smiled when she observed the pen marks along the border. It seemed that Millot shared one of her idiosyncrasies. When deep in thought, without being aware of it, she would decorate any sheet of paper that lay to hand with the most intricate designs. For some reason, her designs were always based on the letter "S." She wondered what Millot's might be. She picked up the scrap of paper and examined it closely. It took her some time to decipher it. Not a letter of the alphabet, she observed, but someone's name. General Theot. Now where had she heard that name before?

Hearing a sound outside the door, Claire jerked round sharply. The wide sleeve of her wrapper caught on the inkstand and toppled it. Claire gave a little cry and righted it before any harm was done.

The door to the hallway opened. Adam stood on the threshold. In one comprehensive glance, he absorbed the table set for two and the woman with unbound hair and in her nightclothes. His eyes blazed with sudden savagery. "I thought it was you," he said. "You had better have a good reason for being here, Claire, else I think I shall kill you."

She was frozen with fear. Adam took one stride toward her, and in her panic, she said the first thing that came into her head. "Who is General Theot?"

If anything, Adam's expression became more murderous. Like a great dark panther, he pounced on her. His fingers bit into the soft flesh of her shoulders. "What do you know about General Theot?" he demanded, shaking her to loosen her

148

tongue. "Damn you, Claire, have you been spying on me?"

"N-no! I swear it! I-I read his name on a piece of paper not minutes ago," and she gestured to the writing table.

It took a few minutes before the commissioner would accept her story. But she could see that he was far from satisfied. His fury was under control, but by no means spent. Claire hardly dared swallow she was so afraid of the threat she read in every tensed muscle of his powerful body.

"Where is Millot," he asked softly, "and what do you want with him?"

She shook her head, but her gaze strayed guiltily to the closed door to the bedchamber.

With a savage oath, Adam sprang to the door. It was locked. With one powerful thrust, he kicked it in. The sight that met his eyes shocked him into immobility. Millot bolted up in bed and reached for the pistol he kept primed and ready on the nightstand. His voluptuous companion emitted a soft cry of alarm, and turned into him.

"What the . . . ? Commissioner!" Stunned, Millot stared at Adam, then quickly recovering, he pulled up the sheet to cover the nakedness of the woman beside him.

Carmen, coming to herself, sat up in bed.

Adam felt like laughing. To Millot he said, "Remember to thank Carmen for saving your life." He turned to face Claire. "Come here," he said, smiling, and he extended his arm, palm up.

He knew that what he was about to do was not the act of a gentleman. Millot had been caught in a very awkward position. The proper thing for Adam to do was to shut the door quickly before Claire was aware of what was going on. But something more powerful than the obligations of noblesse oblige was at work in Adam.

Claire was his woman. She was partial to Millot.

149

The younger man was far more in her confidence than Adam was. This was a situation which Adam would not tolerate. Anything which led to an awkwardness between Claire and Millot was to be looked upon with favor, if not actively promoted.

"Come here." This time his words were brusque.

Dragging her steps, Claire approached the open door. She put her hand in Adam's and gave him a searching look. She'd seen cats with that same expression, she thought, shuddering, *after* they had eaten a mouse whole.

It was Millot's shocked exclamation which drew her eyes to the bed. She had one horrified glimpse before Adam quickly shut the door in her face.

Color ran from her throat to her hairline. She did not know where to look. She knew that she was angry, but whether that anger was directed more at Millot than the man with the infuriating smile, was debatable.

She snatched her hand from his and stalked to the door which gave onto the hallway. Adam was hard at her heels. He allowed her to precede him up the stairs. When they came to his suite of rooms, he captured her wrist and drew her into the parlor.

"And now we talk," he said.

Chapter Nine

It was more like an interrogation than a conversation, thought Claire. She was wishing that she had never picked up that scrap of paper on Millot's writing table, had never deciphered the name the letters formed, had never been so stupid as to mention the name General Theot to Philippe Duhet. But most of all, she wished she had never had the insane notion of going to Millot's rooms in the first place. Then she would not have been subjected to this tiresome interview, nor would she be embarrassed to face Millot in the morning.

"That's all I know," she said, and she was tired of repeating herself.

"I believe you," said Adam. He had the paper in his hand. And from such small slips, he was thinking, disaster might easily overtake them. He would tear a strip off Millot in the morning. Balling the paper, he threw it in the fire and watched as the flames consumed it.

He gave Claire a very direct look. "You must forget that you ever heard that name, do you understand? To even breathe a word of what you know would put the lives of many good men in jeopardy—not to mention my own," he ended ironically.

Her eyes went wide. "I promise you, I know nothing."

And just when she thought he was going to let her go, he started over, demanding an explanation for her presence in Millot's rooms so late at night.

"Ten o'clock isn't so very late," she prevaricated.

"Claire," he said warningly, "You are in your nightclothes. You'd better have a good explanation or I may yet lay my whip to your bare backside."

Fuming at this high-handed approach, sighing audibly, looking pointedly at the clock, yawning hugely, she gave in. "I wanted Nicholas to tell me about Angers," she said.

His stare was long and searching. "What about Angers?" he asked.

Though she felt like a fool, she told him what had been going through her head. "So you see, when you came back from Angers, it seemed to me as if you were a different man. I can't explain it, but either instinct or womanly intuition told me that you had changed."

"A female should always trust her instincts or her womanly intuition."

Her eyebrows lowered when she observed the foolish grin on his face.

"You thought I was different somehow," he murmured.

"Yes." What had she said that was so amusing?

"Don't you know what happened?"

"What?"

His voice was little more than a husky whisper. Her very pores seemed to open and drink in the sound of it. "I walked into a room," he said, "and saw the most beautiful woman I'd ever seen in my life. It was like seeing you for the first time. Claire, my world turned upside-down. And it's never been the same since. How was it for you?"

"I told you. You seemed different."

"How was I different? Tell me, Claire, I want to know."

With the tip of her tongue she moistened her lips.

She couldn't tell him the truth. It would enrage him.

"I want the truth," he said, reading her expression. "Tell me, Claire."

And as though mesmerized by the low husky rasp of his voice, she told him what he wished to know. "My skin didn't crawl." To his blank look she elaborated, "I was still afraid of you. But it was different. I wasn't sick to my stomach."

There was a moment of silence, and Claire cursed herself for going too far.

"I am grateful," Adam murmured and smiled.

She felt her own lips begin to turn up. Something very strange was going on if only she had the wit to see it.

Her next words took them both by surprise. "You are not the man you pretend to be, are you, Philippe?" Observing his start, she went on hurriedly, "What I mean to say is this. You have a reputation for brutality, yet you are not a brutal man. If you were, I would have known it. Oh, I am not saying that you are a saint . . ."

"Thank God for that!"

". . . but all the same, you are not as black as you are made out to be." She looked away. "I'm sorry I said what I did. You are not a monster . . . at least . . . not with me."

She could see that her words had pleased him inordinately. A question sprang to her lips, but before she could voice it, Adam interposed, "And I'm sorry about Millot."

Claire looked down at her clasped hands, then looked up at him. "Why did you want me to see Nicholas with that woman?" she asked.

His eyes mocked her. "You know why."

The words seemed to hang between them.

After a moment, Claire said, "What you did was unkind and not necessary. I don't think of Nicholas in that way."

"What way is that, Claire?"

153

The amusement in his eyes, his whole demeanor was deceptively casual. Claire was not deceived. He was jealous. Fleetingly, she savored that knowledge. Then she thought of possible consequences, and flicked him a quick glance before looking away. She groped for words, but whether she wished to save Millot's skin or her own was not clear to her. In either case, the truth would serve. "He's just a friend, nothing more," she replied.

The complacency in his grin spoke volumes. "Poor Nicholas! Those words would annihilate him if he could hear you say them."

She bore his scrutiny without a flicker of expression. But when he abruptly sat forward in his chair, she jumped.

"Do I still frighten you?" he asked, watching her with a passionate intensity that brought an unwelcome heat to Claire's cheeks. Before she could frame a reply, he captured her hands and went on, "You look fevered. Claire, you would tell me, would you not, if you were . . . sickening of something?"

She frowned. They'd had this conversation before. "I'm not sickening of anything," she protested.

"You're not . . . nauseated? And I don't mean only first thing in the morning. It can happen any time."

"What makes you think I'm not well?" She was beginning to lose patience with the same old questions.

"Claire," he said, "sweetheart . . ." He shook his head at the innocent look she returned. Hints weren't working. "Are you or are you not pregnant?" he demanded bluntly.

She mouthed the last word, but no sound came.

"Yes, pregnant. Did I put a baby inside you? You do know how babies are made, don't you, Claire?" His eyes brimmed with masculine enjoyment. "Sweetheart, I want to know, when did you last have your woman's courses?"

She shut her teeth with a snap and tried to pull her

154

hands away. This seemed to amuse him even more. He reached for her and captured her in a bear hug, setting her down in his lap.

"Well?"

She gave up the unequal struggle. Ignoring her blushes, she glared doggedly into his face. "I'm not stupid," she said. "Do you really suppose that I would become any man's mistress without knowing how to prevent conception? Let me set your mind at rest, Commissioner. I am not pregnant."

She had not had her woman's courses since she had become Philippe's mistress, and long before that, they were irregular. Madame Lambert had explained it all to her. It was a common phenomenon in times of stress. Lots of women suffered from her symptoms. But there was nothing to worry about. She had protected herself. She could not possibly be pregnant.

He did not believe her and wanted to know what steps she had taken to prevent the inevitable happening. Claire thought of the small pieces of sponge and string hidden in the bottom drawer of her dresser. He could boil her in oil or break her body on the wheel before she would divulge her secrets, and she told him so.

He was not so fainthearted as she. In quick order, he described several ways of preventing conception. His frankness made her cheeks burn and her mouth gape open.

"Did you employ any of those methods?" he asked. Nothing seemed to embarrass the man.

Claire nodded.

"They're not worth a damn," he told her succinctly. "We have been fortunate this time around, but after this, you'll leave such things to me."

Wonderingly, she looked into his face. "What are you saying?" she asked.

He inhaled deeply. "What I am saying is this. There comes a time in every man's life when he wants children. I've discovered that I'm no different from other men."

Baffled, she stared at him.

The word was not one that Adam ever used in a woman's hearing. He said it now and could not believe how easily it tripped off his tongue. *"Matrimony*, Claire, and children born in holy wedlock."

"Marriage? With me?" Her astonishment was almost insulting.

"Why not? No woman has ever pleased me as much as you." He searched for a reason that would be acceptable to her and discovered that he was not above professing adherence to a code that he held to be a joke. "I took your innocence, Claire. It's a matter of honor. The least I can do is offer you the protection of my name."

"Honor? This . . . from you? A man who is known far and wide as a debaucher of innocents?"

He was not quite sure if her words were meant to be humorous or chastening. Frowning, he said, "I told you once, Claire, not to trust to hearsay. I may not be a paragon of virtue, but I am no satyr either."

After several false starts, she managed, "You *can't* wish to marry me."

"I assure you I do." This wasn't precisely true. If things had been different, or if Claire were less scrupulous, so Adam told himself, he would have carried her off as his mistress without a ripple of conscience.

"But why? And don't give me that nonsense about honor. You never thought of that before. You knew I had never known a man before I became your mistress. You didn't ask me to marry you then. Why have you changed your mind?"

No fool, Claire Michelet, thought Adam, and he took his time to set his thoughts in order. His voice was low and earnest. "There's something special between us Claire. You feel it, too. I was your first

156

lover. That means something to a woman. You'll never forget me." He rubbed her knuckles against his cheek. "I'd kill to keep you. It was touch and go tonight with Millot. If Carmen had not been in that bed with him, poor Nicholas would be nursing a broken jaw right now, or worse."

She didn't smile or laugh, but Adam caught the slight change of expression. Her dimples were winking at him. He touched a finger to one, then the other. He was thinking that Claire Michelet had her fair share of fatal charm.

"Who was your first lover?" she suddenly quizzed.

He answered curtly. "Nobody important. It's different for a man."

"Is it?" she murmured.

He sliced her a sharp look. "You know it is."

She gave him back stare for stare. "If and when I marry, I shall expect the same rules to apply equally. One man. One woman. Fidelity."

One man. One woman. Fidelity. It was all Adam could do to suppress his shudder of revulsion. Naturally, he expected fidelity in a wife. His own conduct was another matter. No woman was going to dictate terms to Adam Dillon.

That he had been celibate since the night he had taken Claire's innocence, did not strike him as particularly significant. He'd been fully occupied with his role as commissioner. He was scarcely a man of leisure, and when he had found himself with an hour or two to spare, it was not surprising that he had sought Claire out. The girl intrigued him. She was a novelty. That would not last forever. And when the novelty faded, Claire would have her children and he would have his amusements. To Adam's way of thinking, the arrangement seemed entirely equitable.

It was on the tip of his tongue to tell her what she wanted to hear. In his previous relationships with women, Adam had never balked at palming them off

157

with a tissue of lies. If women were naïve enough to believe everything a man told them, so much the worse for them. With Claire, it was different. He did not wish to lie to her. On the other hand, he would be a fool to tell her exactly what was on his mind.

He was still pondering his dilemma when she said, very gently, "Commissioner, your reputation preceded you. You've had legions of women."

She was going to refuse him, and Adam wasn't going to permit it. Smiling easily, he said, "Would you prefer an untried boy for your husband?"

The question was rhetorical, and Claire, wisely, made no attempt to answer it. But her dimples flashed, mocking him.

Adam laughed, thinking as he often did, that this girl was truly a delight to him. "Claire," he said, and his tone was so gentle that Claire felt a frisson of alarm, "you will marry me. I insist."

Strangely, his offer of marriage moved her. There was something about this man that touched her, called to her, appealed to her. It took every ounce of willpower to resist.

"Your destiny lies here in France," she said. "I can't live here. You must have realized that eventually I would wish to follow my young friends to England."

"Claire," he said softly, persuasively, "anything is possible. And things are not always what they seem to be. I'll take care of everything."

She studied him frankly, curiously. "Are you saying that you would be willing to leave France?"

"I may have to," he answered simply.

"Does this have anything to do with General Theot?"

His expression became shuttered, closing her out. "I told you to forget that name."

"It makes no difference. I can't marry you."

"Why?"

She was thinking of her parents. Though she

158

longed to confide in him, she was afraid to take the chance. The commissioner hated the name of Devereux, or so she had inferred from his comments.

At present, her parents were relatively safe. On one of her rare walks with Blanche, she'd dropped in at the school. Madame Lambert had sent her a note inviting her to do so. Her parents were well and were still being held at Carmes. That was good news. To draw Philippe's attention to them now might prove disastrous.

"Marry me, Claire!"

Claire was almost shattered by the impulse to give in to him. There was nothing she wanted more than to lay her head on that broad chest and be held close in the protection of those strong arms. She felt so weary of it all, and so uncertain.

"I can't," she said. "Please, don't say more."

He expelled his breath on a long sigh. "Very well," he said, "you leave me no choice. Mistress it is. Remove your robe, Claire. I want to see you naked."

"What?" Her eyes went wide with shock.

"You heard me. You are my mistress. Is that not so, Claire?"

"But . . ."

"Remove your robe.'

When his lips brushed her throat, she gasped. "Philippe," she cried out, pleading with him.

His green eyes locked on hers. "Mistress or wife, Claire. I promise you, you will be one or the other. Which is it to be?"

She looked at him in despair. "Philippe, try to understand. I can't marry you. I can't."

For a moment, Adam hesitated, but only for a moment. With heart-stopping slowness, his fingers began to undo the tiny row of buttons from her throat to her waist. Claire could hardly breathe. His hands brushed over her shoulders, freeing her from her nightclothes, baring the top part of her body to his view. She shivered.

Instantly, he stopped what he was doing. "It's up to you," he said. "We don't have to go on with this. Say yes, Claire, and you can go to your own chaste bed."

If he had once mentioned their bargain, Claire would have braced herself to yield to him. The bargain was the furthest thing from her mind. In the last number of weeks, he had won her confidence. She had come to believe that there was some good in him, and that she held a special place in his affections. A man who cared about a woman did not try to coerce her to his will.

"I was wrong about you," she flung at him. "You *are* a monster." He laughed, and the sound of it set her teeth on edge. With no clear idea of what she was saying, intent only on wiping the grin from his face, she gritted. "How many other unwilling females have you forced into your bed?"

One eyebrow arched. "Unwilling? You deceive yourself if you think that you will come to me unwillingly. Claire, I know you better than you know yourself." His voice turned husky, persuasive. "Give me the answer I want, sweetheart, and I promise I shall go no further."

"I have no confidence in your promises," she rashly taunted.

His laugh verged on the triumphant. "I was hoping you would say something of the sort," and he bent to her.

She braced herself for the smothering pressure of his kiss. The lips that took hers were devastatingly gentle. She was hoping that he would hurt her, then she would have a reason to hate him. He was wooing her, and this man was a master of seduction. In a matter of minutes, her senses were spinning, she was losing her grip on reality. Her fingers curled into the fabric of his shirt, clenching and unclenching. When he released her lips, she rested her head on his chest, deliberately avoiding his astute stare.

He lifted her chin with one hand, his gaze searching, assessing. "Are you unwilling, Claire?"

"You know I am," she said, trying to inject contempt into her words, wincing at the betraying tremor.

His gaze dropped to her breasts and Claire could feel them begin to swell.

"I haven't laid a finger on you," he said, "and already your body is telling me that you want me to."

Claire looked down. Before her eyes, she watched the pink crests darken to crimson as blood engorged them. She gasped when he bent his head and his warm breath blew across first one nipple and then the other.

"Put your arms around my neck," he said, and Claire unthinkingly obeyed. "Do you know what your response does to me?" he asked thickly. "Do you know what it does to me to know that you are like an iceberg for other men but an inferno for me? Do you know what it does to me knowing that I can make you give in to me even when you don't want to? You're mine, Claire. I was telling you the truth when I said I would kill to keep you. Don't make the mistake of thinking I shall ever let you go."

He was serious. She could see it in those burning eyes. He would never let her go. The thought should have panicked her. Instead, to her utter confusion, a strange exhilaration seemed to take possession of her. She didn't have to fight against his magnetism. It was out of her hands.

His mouth closed over one ripe nipple, his teeth gently clamping. A hot surge of sensation burst through her. He moved to the other breast. She cried out as he began a gentle sucking. His teeth bit down, and fire raced through her. Her bones were melting. She was suffocating. Her movements became restless. "Yes," she said. "Yes."

He didn't seem to hear her. With a groan, he pulled back and quickly stripped her nightclothes from her.

161

"Like this," he said, and adjusted her naked limbs to the fit of his body. She was kneeling over him, straddling his lap. She began to struggle, not because she was afraid, but because she was embarrassed.

"I said yes," she said, "what more should I say?"

He stilled. After a moment, with head thrown back, he closed his eyes and made a sound that was halfway between a groan and a laugh. "Claire, please don't tell me to stop, not now. I promise, I won't take you to bed, but I don't think I can go on without something from you."

"What do you want from me? I don't understand?"

His eyes locked on hers. One hand brushed lightly from her throat to her wrist. "I want you to trust me. I want you to give me the license to do whatever I wish, not because of any bargain we struck, not because I'm forcing you to give in to me, but because you choose to."

"I . . . I think I do trust you."

Adam inhaled sharply. His gaze dropped and made a sweep of her nakedness. Were all men like this? she wondered. Didn't they possess a shred of modesty? And then those green eyes looked into hers, and the blaze from them burned all thoughts of modesty to a cinder. She was trembling with a desire she wouldn't have believed possible. She wanted him with a hunger that stole her breath.

She moaned as his hands molded themselves to her breasts. "Lean back," he said, and he shifted her till he had positioned her just as he wanted.

"It's all right. It's all right," he murmured. "Ah God, Claire, your skin . . . so smooth . . . so soft."

His hands brushed over her, slowly, endlessly, sensitizing her skin, building the pleasure in her till she felt her blood leaping in her veins. And all the while that golden voice drew pictures for her, seducing her senses with blatantly erotic words.

"I can feel the shudders begin deep in your belly," he said, and she could hear the rasp in his voice as he

162

tried to control his breathing. "Feel them." He detached one of her hands from around his neck and pressed it against the flat of her stomach. "You can't hide it from me, Claire."

Her head sagged against his shoulder. The pleasure was torture. If he didn't stop, she knew she would disgrace herself.

"Don't," she panted. "I can't bear it. It's too much."

"I think I understand." She heard the smile in his voice. "I don't want you to fight what's happening. Let go. Trust yourself to me. Will you do that?"

"Yes," she said, but not very convincingly.

Chuckling, he answered the unspoken question in her dazed eyes. "I promise I won't do anything to shock you, at least, not this time. When you are more comfortable with me, things will be different. Don't worry. I'll make you want it."

She blushed at his directness. And then hot color flared into her face as she absorbed his meaning. What more could he do to her? Just thinking about it made her writhe in anticipation.

"Keep still," he warned. "I want to feel the heat of you. I want your scent on me, all right?"

His words created pictures inside her head that made the heat between her legs burn like a furnace. As his hands slipped up the inside of her thighs, moving her legs farther apart, Claire made a soft sound of protest. She could feel the moisture pooling between her legs. She didn't want him to know about it. She flashed him a pleading look but his eyes were closed, and those beautifully sculpted bones looked as though they were carved in marble.

He slipped one finger inside her. Claire gasped and jerked her hips away, at the same time flinging her head back. The protest was automatic. "Don't!"

His chest lifted and fell with the harshness of his breathing. "You want me to, Claire. You know you want me to. Come back to me," and he eased her down, giving her a moment before his hand gently cupped her. Sweat broke out on his forehead. He opened his eyes and gave a half-amused, half-painful groan. "My imagination is running riot. Next time, I'm going to have you spread-eagle on my bed, and I'm going to feast on every last inch of you. Now kiss me, Claire."

One arm locked around her hips holding her steady. Obediently, Claire lowered her lips to his. His tongue invaded, taking intimate possession, plunging, thrusting, withdrawing. His breath was coming hard and fast. Claire felt light-headed and clung to him.

His fingers slid and dipped, opening her body to him. Feverishly, he whispered, "So soft . . . so wet for me, my Claire?"

She arched and cried out, breaking the contact. Adam brought her back, taking her lips in a searing kiss. When he sheathed his fingers inside her, Claire bucked wildly. She could not get away from him. The arm clamping her down was like a vice. Deeply, rhythmically, his fingers penetrated her body. Writhing, fighting him, Claire tried to break his hold. The pleasure was too intense. It was ripping her apart. She pleaded. She begged. This wasn't what she wanted. It wasn't enough. She wanted him deep inside her. She wanted what they had shared before. He tried to soothe her with words, but still he refused to give her what she wanted, what she needed. When the crisis came, she went wild. A cry tore from her throat. She curled her nails into his shoulders and nipped at his neck with her sharp teeth.

"Tigress!" he groaned.

Gradually, her convulsions ceased. She collapsed against him as if her bones had turned to water. His strong arms crushed her to him, and he covered her face and mouth with kisses. The leaping of her pulse quieted.

His voice was rich with masculine satisfaction.

"Didn't I tell you how it would be? Claire, when are you going to admit that you want me as much as I want you?"

The words lapped the edges of Claire's consciousness. She had pleased him, and she was glad. Her eyelids drooped.

She was as limp as a rag doll when Adam drew her nightgown over her head, and already drifting into sleep when he settled her beneath the covers of her bed. He kissed her softly, before retiring to his own bedchamber.

It took him some time to get himself under control. His loins were still throbbing. He'd never put such restraints on himself before. He was beginning to wonder if he was insane. He could have taken her. Why was it necessary to put himself through such torment?

By the time he'd found his balance, he remembered why he had deemed it necessary to exercise such formidable control. He'd wanted to prove something to Claire. He'd given her his word that if she promised to marry him he would let her go to her chaste bed.

He grimaced at the convolutions in his logic that made an odd sense. Strictly speaking he had not broken his promise. On the other hand, he hadn't exactly kept it either. Yet . . . he was reasonably satisfied that Claire would not feel that her trust had been misplaced. For his purposes, that was paramount. Claire must come to believe that he was to be trusted.

He couldn't put himself through that again, he decided. It was sheer agony for him: to taste her, but not to take her; to sample, but not to enjoy fully what was his for the asking. He was more saintly than he would ever have suspected. Not that Claire had noticed. It would have shocked the Brussels lace off her drawers if he had taken her the way he wanted to. And if he had as much as hinted that there was a way to relieve the ache in his loins without consummation, he was sure she would have had a fit of hysterics. Claire Michelet had a lot to learn about men, he reflected, and he would permit no man to be her teacher but himself.

That thought led to another. In her own inimitable way, Claire Michelet was teaching Adam Dillon a thing or two. Not all women were alike. He'd had his share of women. But he never made the mistake of thinking that it was Adam Dillon, the man, they were interested in, except superficially. They were attracted by his wealth and position. Women were always drawn to powerful men. He'd learned that lesson very early in life. His half-brother had taught him well.

With Claire it was different. She knew nothing about his wealth or position. To her, he was Philippe Duhet, a man for whom she felt nothing but contempt, a man who, according to her own words, made her skin crawl.

Yet, in spite of her aversion to Duhet, in spite of her shame at becoming the mistress of such a man, she had accepted his claims to her tonight. It was Adam Dillon who had won her over. It was to Adam Dillon, the man, that she had trusted herself. At the very thought, Adam felt his blood sing.

Maybe, just maybe, he was thinking, Adam Dillon had known all the wrong women. If there were others like Claire out there in the world, he had yet to meet them. He knew that Claire was too good for him. If he were a better man, he would stand aside and let her go to someone else, someone less worldly-wise, someone nearer her own age, someone who had led a different kind of life from Adam Dillon. Someone like Millot.

The thought wasn't a serious one. Millot had had his chance and had been too fainthearted to grasp it. Second chances seldom came a man's way. From the very first, Adam had known that he was going to reach for Claire, no matter what stood in his way. Only one thing could have stopped him.

Claire. If she could say no and make him believe it, he would let her go. *Past tense*, added Adam on further reflection. Having tasted her surrender tonight nothing now could compel him to give her up, not even Claire. She wanted him as much as he wanted her.

There had been no mention between them of the word love. It surprised him that Claire had not demanded the words from him. He'd said them to dozens of women in his time. It was expected, and meant less than nothing.

He poured himself a small shot of brandy and sipped it slowly as he tried to analyze what he was feeling. Pique, he thought, and could not believe that he was so small-minded. Dozens of women had told him that they loved him. He hadn't wanted to know it. What perversity in his nature made him want to hear those words from Claire?

Frowning in concentration, he stretched out on top of his bed. His thoughts drifted to home. There was a ship, one of his own line, waiting for him off La Rochelle. He and Claire would be married by the captain and spend their honeymoon on the long ocean voyage to New York. Soon, he would make love to Claire the way he wanted to, without holding back. By degrees his dour humor lifted. The next hour was spent in pleasurable reverie.

Chapter Ten

Adam had lost count of the number of times he had scanned the letter in his hand. He scanned it again, as though *this* time the words would rearrange themselves into something more acceptable. He was seething. He was shaking. Sweat beaded his forehead. He fought to regain a small part of his balance. It was hopeless. His sense of betrayal was too searing for anything but the most murderous thoughts to prevail. He knew that if Claire Michelet had been anywhere in the building, he would have tracked her down and strangled her with his bare hands. But when the messenger from Paris had put the evidence damning her into his hands, Claire had the good fortune to be out walking with her maid. She had escaped the first surge of violence that had erupted inside him like a tidal wave.

The bitch had betrayed him. And not only him. She had also informed against Theot. The general had been moved to the Conciergerie, that most infamous of all prisons, and the holding pen for those who were fated for the guillotine. At this very moment, representatives from the Convention were secretly on their way to Rouen with warrants for the commissioner's arrest. And lest he doubt the seriousness of the situation, his source in the Office of Public Safety had enclosed a copy of the letter and

168

handwriting which had denounced the commissioner. Claire's signature on the bottom of the one page epistle leaped up to strike him like a blow to the face.

The anger in Adam suddenly boiled over. He picked up a paperweight from his desk and flung it from his hand. It shattered the glass in one of the windows. The buzz of conversation in the anteroom abruptly died. Moments later, there was a knock on the commissioner's door and one of the clerks stood hesitating on the threshold.

"Commissioner?" Fleuriot, the young clerk, trembled in his boots. He had been left in charge when Millot and two of the commissioner's aides had absented themselves on some unspecified business earlier that afternoon. It was he who had shown the messenger from Paris into the commissioner's office not thirty minutes before, and he who had seen that same messenger depart as though the hounds of hell were after him. It did not take a sage to know that the news from Paris was not good. He prayed fervently that the commissioner's fury would not fall on his head.

Adam stared at the clerk with barely restrained ferocity. "When Millot returns, I want to see him in my office at once."

"Yes, Commissioner," stammered the clerk.

"Find Captain Domfrey, and tell him to report to me in one hour, no more, no less."

"Yes, Commissioner." Fleuriot kept his eyes steadfastly on his boots.

"And as for Mademoiselle Michelet . . ." There was a significant pause before Adam went on with soft menace, "under no circumstance is she to be admitted to my presence. Do you understand, Fleuriot?"

"Yes, sir."

Fleuriot threw one half-fearful, half-questioning look at the shattered windowpane, and swallowed the question that trembled on his tongue. After a quick glance at the commissioner's bent head, he shuffled out, closing the door softly behind him.

Adam stared into space. After a moment, he shook his head and emitted a low laugh. The sound in that small room was chilling. Adam Dillon, he was thinking, had made a royal fool of himself over a woman. He, of all men, should have known better. He *did* know. He'd learned his lessons in the cradle. His mother had been his first teacher. But she was by no means the only one. He had a grasp of the female psyche that few men could hope to equal. Before he reached his years of discretion, his experience was extensive. He wasn't thinking of women as lovers, but in their other roles, as wives, mothers, sisters, sweethearts. All of the significant women in his life had betrayed him.

"Trust your instincts, trust your womanly intuition," he had told the deceiving bitch, or words to that effect. Good God! The irony was consummate. The only instincts women possessed were entirely centered on themselves. There was no such thing as mother love. Women were strangers to the softer emotions. Self-interest was their guiding principle. Hadn't he always known it?

She had completely taken him in—Claire Michelet with her challenging hard-to-get air. She was no harder to get than any other woman. If the price was right, she would sell herself to the devil. She'd sold her delectable body to Philippe Duhet for a couple of safe-conduct passes. Knowing all that, he should have expected treachery if the price was right. The rewards for selling him and General Theot must have bettered his offer of marriage and vague promises for the future. How could he doubt it?

Cursing violently, he pushed himself to his feet and stalked to one of the windows. His chest burned with the acid of self-contempt. What a blind fool he had been to let himself be taken in by her. What

170

colossal conceit on his part to think that Claire Michelet wanted him for himself, that in spite of believing him to be Duhet, she had responded to Adam Dillon, the man. It was all an act to keep him off-guard.

And she had succeeded. God, how she had succeeded! He had thought that Claire was too good for him, that she deserved someone of less tarnished virtue. Because of her, he was coming to think that he might have misjudged the whole race of women. He would never make that mistake again.

His pride had taken a beating. But there was more at stake than his pride. She had placed the lives of innocent men in danger. No, Adam quickly amended. The fault was his. General Theot was paying the price for Adam Dillon's criminal negligence. He'd discovered her in Millot's rooms going through his desk. And the only action he had taken was to swear her to secrecy. He should be shot for dereliction of duty! He'd put personal considerations before devotion to his mission. His one hope was that French authorities were so sensitive to American opinion that no real harm would come to Theot. If he was tried and executed, diplomatic relations between their two countries would almost certainly be broken off. Adam did not think the French would risk such a thing.

Thank God he'd had the sense not to take her fully into his confidence. He had wanted to. God, how he had wanted to! To continue with the pretense that he was Philippe Duhet was almost more than he could endure. More than anything, he'd wanted to approach her as himself, as Adam Dillon. He thanked his lucky stars for the innate sense of self-preservation that had protected him from complete catastrophe. Claire Michelet knew nothing of Adam Dillon. After this, she never would.

He should be thanking his lucky stars ten times over, he reflected savagely. He might have made the bitch pregnant. In point of fact, he had hoped that he had made her pregnant. Then she must turn to him to take care of her. Then she must give in to his persuasions to go with him to America. He should have known what kind of woman she was. She knew how to take care of herself. Hadn't she told him so? God, what a lucky escape he'd had, for if she had conceived his child, she would have had a terrible power over him.

From this day forward, Adam bitterly vowed, he would revert to his old ways. Women were his playthings. They would service his body, nothing more. He would play their game, but he would play it by his own rules.

All memory, every trace of Claire Michelet, must be effaced. He knew of only one sure method of achieving his goal. As soon as possible he must sate himself with another woman, a dozen other women if it became necessary. Only then would he be free of her. It shouldn't be too difficult to accomplish. Of all the women he had ever wanted, she was the only one from whom he had deliberately kept himself out of some misguided notion of chivalry. His first and last attempt at chivalry had been the saving of him. There was that much less to forget and regret. In the last few months, he had led the life of a monk. His self-imposed celibacy was coming to an end.

Even as he told himself that it would be easy to forget her, the memories started to intrude. She was so sweetly giving, she could not say no to him. It was to him that she had surrendered her virginity.

No, not to him, to Duhet, Adam viciously reminded himself. And it would have been any man's for the taking if he had met her price. White hot anger boiled inside him. She was a scheming bitch. She had betrayed him. She had betrayed Theot. It was only by the sheerest good fortune that she had not the knowledge to betray the whole network.

But she would pay for it. As God was his witness he

swore that he would make her pay for it. She was an informer. She deserved a swift death. And that he was too weak-willed, too much still in her thrall to order her arrest and immediate execution only exacerbated his feelings of self-revulsion. As a man, he had experienced the final humiliation. He was pathetic. She had done her best to send him to the scaffold, and he could not bear to think of her getting her just desserts.

Slowly, he forced himself to relax. For his own peace of mind, he could not permit any real harm to come to the girl. But on one thing he was resolved. Claire Michelet would not get off scot-free.

When Millot entered the commissioner's office, he knew at once that disaster had struck. Wordlessly, Adam indicated the letter on his desk, then stood with his back to Millot.

Millot read in silence. "Oh God, no!" he exclaimed. "Not Claire! I can't believe it!"

Adam did not try to keep the sneer from his voice. "Your first thoughts naturally would be for Claire Michelet! Don't you understand anything, man? We've blown our chance to get Theot out!"

Millot shifted uneasily. "You're right, of course. Even so, Theot is in no real danger, surely?"

Adam's tone was scathing. "Who can say with any certainty what may become of Theot? The girl has tried to do her worst. Isn't that enough?

Millot was silent.

Adam spoke through his teeth. "If not Claire, then who? This letter is in her writing. You, yourself, know that she went to your rooms. She knows about Theot. She has the run of the place. Who knows how she came by her knowledge? We should think ourselves fortunate that she doesn't know enough to have the lot of us arrested on the spot."

"What are you going to do?" asked Millot, every fine hair on the back of his neck rising as he grasped the danger Claire had brought on herself.

173

"I know what I should do," said Adam savagely, and smashed his balled fist into his open palm. After an interval, he seemed to regain his control. "Our mission in Rouen is over," he said quietly. "Pass the word along. In one hour, two at the most, I leave for the Forest of Verte. I shall follow our original plan to the letter. If all goes well, Duhet should be returned to Rouen at almost the same moment as deputies arrive with warrants for his arrest."

Millot was almost too afraid to voice the next thought. "And what of Claire?" he asked.

Adam smiled unpleasantly. "Rest easy, Nicholas. No real harm will come to her. How should it? She is responsible for informing against me. No doubt, she will be suitably rewarded. However . . . ," Adam's face twisted bitterly, "she won't get off scot-free. I shall warn Duhet about her."

"What are you going to say to Claire?"

"Nothing. I never want to set eyes on the bitch again." Suddenly, pain sliced through him. He turned from Millot before his expression gave him away. He would never see Claire again. Something precious, something priceless had been lost. And something that was entirely counterfeit, he furiously reminded himself.

"Then this is goodbye," said Millot.

Adam blinked rapidly to clear the sudden haze in his eyes. He grasped the hand Millot proffered. "Not goodbye," he said, "merely *à bientôt*. You know where to find me." What he was thinking was that soon an ocean would separate him from Claire. It was over. It was for the best.

Having newly returned from the walk with Blanche, Claire was in her room removing her coat when she heard the clatter of horses' hooves in the courtyard. From the window, she watched as the commissioner rode out at the head of a troop of dragoons. Later, on applying to Millot, she was told curtly that the commissioner was acting on information received. He was leading a surprise attack on Sillery, the rebel leader.

The following morning the whole building buzzed with the report that Commissioner Duhet had walked into an ambush. His troop of dragoons was decimated, and the commissioner was either captured or left for dead.

Captain Domfrey had explicit orders. He marshaled the remnants of his forces. Every able-bodied man in Rouen was pressed into service. That same day, more than thirty dragoons and twice that number of civilians set out for the Forest of Verte.

Claire was in a state of shock. No one would tell her anything. Millot, when he finally condescended to see her, was evasive, and there was something in his eyes which chilled her to the marrow.

Numb with grief, she retired to her own chamber where she sat in abject misery, contemplating her clasped hands. From time-to-time, she cried out to a God in whom she had long since lost confidence.

In the Forest of Verte, in the cellar of a forester's stone cottage, Adam sat facing his half-brother across the width of a trestle table. They were alone. There was murder in Philippe's eyes. The first shock of Adam's arrival was long past. For twenty minutes, Philippe had simmered in silence as Adam related a summary of events which had taken place in Rouen since Philippe's capture by the rebels. In the space of three months, Adam told him, hundreds of lives had been saved by a joint Franco-American escape network. He went on to tell Philippe of General Theot, and of the letter from Claire Michelet which had informed against him, and which had precipitated an investigation and the subsequent warrants for the commissioner's arrest.

175

As each word fell from Adam's lips, Philippe's expression became more vicious. Adam ignored the killing looks. He knew that if Philippe were to act on his feelings and launch himself at him, the manacle which chained Philippe to the wall would bring him up short.

"So you see," said Adam calmly, "I leave forthwith for greener pastures, while you shall be taken in chains to Paris to face the music."

Philippe looked down at his manacled hand. Though it almost choked him, he swallowed the string of obscenities which he longed to fling in the other man's teeth. Adam was as cool as ice. To appear any less in control was to lose face. Above all, Philippe hated to lose face.

"What I cannot understand," said Philippe, "is why you don't simply kill me. Wouldn't that be more expedient?"

Adam said nothing.

"Ah! You always were too fainthearted for your own good."

"If you mean that I cavil at fratricide and the like, then convict me, I confess."

Philippe laughed. In a conversational tone, he said, "I'm not complaining, you understand. But it's fair to warn you that that attitude may very well be the death of you."

"Point taken," said Adam, matching Philippe's tone exactly. "I only wish our father could hear you say so."

"I was not responsible for our father's murder," answered Philippe coolly.

"Perhaps not," allowed Adam, "but you were quick to make capital of his death and fabricate evidence against me."

Philippe's smile was genuine, and deliberately gave the lie to his words. "I had no reason to wish you harm."

"Nor yet your two sisters," retorted Adam, "but as I

hear tell, they met their ends in far from innocent circumstances, and their fortunes passed to you."

One eyebrow rose. "Malicious rumor," drawled Philippe. "Nothing was proved. Nothing can be proved. I had nothing to do with it."

Adam snorted, but Philippe was struck with the odd sensation that Adam accepted his assurances. It seemed that he could not conceive of so heinous a crime when it touched so close to home.

Before that thought had caused more than a ripple of interest in Philippe's mind, Adam went on, "All this is beside the point. I am here with the express purpose of offering you a way out of the trap that is about to be sprung on you."

"A trap of your making!" said Philippe, and his eyes flashed dangerously.

Adam shrugged.

"So," said Philippe. "I'm to be given a sporting chance?"

"That's one way of looking at it," agreed Adam amicably. "Frankly, that's the naive view. At this stage of the affair, what helps you, also helps me."

"At last, you are making sense. Pray continue."

"If it becomes known that Philippe Duhet was played by an impostor for an interval of three months, indiscriminate arrests and executions are bound to follow in Rouen. In short, heads will roll."

"Your co-conspirators are nothing to me," was the instant rejoinder.

"My colleagues don't come into it. They will be long gone," answered Adam.

Philippe's smile verged on a sneer. "Your anxiety for the innocent is touching. For my part, as you must know, I should like to see every man, woman, and child who was duped by your little charade go hang from the nearest lamppost."

Adam's smile conveyed nothing but amused tolerance. "In that event, you would be condemning the entire population of Rouen."

With a sudden show of anger, Philippe brought his manacled hand hard down on the flat of the table. Adam's eyebrows shot up.

"You always had a vicious temper," he remarked mildly. He made a show of looking at his watch. "Time is wasting. I really must be on my way. May I be allowed to continue?"

The other man was silent. The only evidence of the storm of his emotions was the muscle which pulsed in one cheek.

"Thank you," said Adam. "As I see it, your best hope is to go along with the charade. For three months, you have been fully occupied fighting rebels. General Theot means nothing to you. If I were you, I would attack the girl's evidence, you know what I mean. Let them think it's the work of a scorned woman. It's her word against yours."

At the mention of Claire, like a wolf scenting its quarry, Philippe's head came up. "Claire Michelet," he said, and his eyes narrowed as Adam's shoulders tensed imperceptibly. "She's very beautiful, wouldn't you say?"

"Very," answered Adam, carefully neutral.

"Is she . . . my mistress?"

By a supreme act of will, Adam managed to convey indifference. "She is, and an extremely jealous one. She sees rivals everywhere. I would have rid myself of her long since, but I could not be sure how much she was in your confidence. If I were you, I would refuse to see her. She, more than anyone, will recognize that you are not the man she knew in Rouen." Adam did not wish to tip his hand by belaboring the point, but he was determined to keep Claire out of Philippe's orbit. "If she suspects that there are two of us, it could be all up with you."

Philippe's eyelids drooped, concealing his expression.

Adam rose to his feet and Philippe rose with him.

"You still have not give me one good reason why I

should do as you suggest," said Philippe.

"There are two reasons. In the first place, Franco-American relations are delicately balanced at present. Think what might happen if you decide to tell the truth. It's quite possible that your own people will silence you—permanently—if only to save them embarrassment."

The color in Philippe's cheeks heightened. "And the second reason?" he asked.

Adam grinned lazily. "To save *yourself* embarrassment." He lowered his voice. "Publish the truth, Philippe, and you'll make yourself a laughingstock, whilst I, naturally, will make capital of the whole affair. I shall dine out for months on the stories of how I impersonated my wicked half-brother, and no one the wiser. Think about it."

It was far from the truth but Philippe wasn't to know it. If the truth ever became known in American diplomatic circles, there would be hell to pay. Adam could weather the storm with impunity. It was John Burke and men like him, diplomats and public figures, who had the most to lose. The American government knew perfectly well that American money, men, and ships were committed to getting refugees out of France. The presence of twenty thousand and more French nationals on American soil was a clear indication of that fact. Diplomats turned a blind eye to it. What they would not tolerate was an international incident of the first magnitude.

Adam hoped that he had averted the likelihood of that eventuality, if only for John Burke's sake. Knowing Philippe, he was almost sure that he had. One way or the other, it made little difference to him. But the people of Rouen—that was a different matter. He was quite serious when he had told Philippe that he was afraid of reprisals. He could not live with himself if such a thing happened.

"Why did you come here?" asked Philippe abruptly.

179

"I beg your pardon."

"It wasn't necessary for you to come in person to tell me all this. You could have sent one of your underlings. You came to gloat! That's it, isn't it?"

"No," said Adam, and wondered if he was being completely honest. "No," he repeated with more assurance. "I came out of curiosity."

They stared at each other in silence. They were half-brothers. The resemblance between them was striking. They held in common certain gestures, a way of looking and speaking. And they were as different as chalk from cheese. A shudder passed over Adam. Seeing Philippe was like unveiling the dark side of himself. He turned on his heel and ascended the stepladder.

Once outside, Adam quickly mounted up. Granville and Bernay were already in the saddle and waiting for him.

Sillery came forward and extended his right hand. The rebel leader had the build of a gladiator, thought Adam. No one admiring the breadth of that powerful physique would credit that the man had once been a lawyer's clerk.

"Good luck," said Sillery, grasping Adam's gloved hand. "Leave everything to me. When they come to fetch me, we'll make it look good."

Adam saluted and wheeled his horse to face the setting sun. "Home," he said, and he dug in his spurs and shot forward. Granville and Bernay followed suit.

Hands on hips, Sillery stared after them for a long moment. He was thinking that although the half-brothers might be taken for twins, he could never mistake one man for the other. Duhet was too much the aristocrat. Blue blood ran in his veins and he never forgot it. It showed in a certain way he had of looking at people, a certain note in the tone of voice he employed. It had nothing to do with the fact that he despised his captors. Sillery had occasion to meet

Duhet in the early days of the Revolution. The man was an egoist. How he had managed to ingratiate himself with the Revolutionaries was more than Sillery could fathom. But there was one thing of which he was certain. If Duhet and his half-brother had changed places, Duhet would have ordered the younger man's execution without a ripple of conscience.

From the very beginning, Sillery had tried to convince the American that their wisest course was to slit Duhet's throat. It was no less than he deserved. The man was a known butcher of innocents. His meteoric rise to power was accomplished over the broken bodies of his political adversaries. And the most cogent reason of all for sending him to meet his Maker was the safety of their enterprise. Prisoners were sometimes known to escape their captors. Should Duhet escape before time, the consequences were bound to be dire.

The American was adamant. If anything happened to Duhet, they could count him out. And though at first Sillery saw this scrupulousness as a fatal weakness on the American's part, it was one which he had grudgingly come to admire. The American was no weakling. In some respects he was harder than the stone walls of the medieval keep which towered above the Seine at Gaillard. There were many unpleasant decisions which were forced upon the young American, decisions which would have turned the stomach of a weaker man.

Sillery turned away. For a moment the thought occurred to him that, with their mission over, he could slit Duhet's throat and the American would be none the wiser. He could not do it, though every instinct warned him that it would be the wisest course, not only for himself, but for the American also. To act on that impulse, however, would make him no better than the beasts of the jungle. It would make him no better than Philippe Duhet.

181

He was joined by one of his lieutenants, St. Roch, a boy of no more than sixteen or seventeen summers. "What now?" asked St. Roch.

Sillery clapped him on the shoulder. "Now we build up the fire so that Captain Domfrey can't miss us. They should be here by nightfall."

The boy was transparently eager to see action. The thought twisted something deep inside Sillery. The boy's mind should be filled with poetry, or the beauties of nature, or a dawning awareness of his opposite gender. His own generation had served the children of France ill. On Judgment Day, he wondered how he was going to give an account of himself.

In the cellar of the forester's cottage, Philippe gave way to the temper which he had barely held in check during the interview with Adam. Cursing fluently, he slammed his manacled hand against the stone wall. His chest rose and fell with the violence of his emotions. It was as though the old resentments rose in his throat like bile to choke him.

Adam Dillon had usurped his rightful place from the time they were youths, from the moment, in fact, that his father's eyes had observed the boy at the Court of Versailles. From that day forward, it was Adam whom their father incessantly extolled in Philippe's presence till he thought that he would go mad with hearing that name. It was Adam who had stolen the spotlight as they grew to manhood. And now, at Rouen, history had repeated itself. The bastard son had robbed the heir of his destiny. Power had been in his grasp. Absolute power was on his horizon—until Adam Dillon came on the scene.

He would lose face if the truth ever got out. He gnashed his teeth in impotent fury. A laughingstock! His enemies in the Convention would not restrain their mirth at his expense. In his mind's eye, he could see their leering faces when they heard how he had been impersonated. He could not, would not endure

182

the public humiliation. Far better to die a traitor's death ten times over than suffer their catcalls and sneers.

It took Philippe a good ten minutes to get himself in hand. By degrees, he forced himself to be calm, to think, and above all, to plan his future conduct. His mind weighed every word, every nuance that Adam had let slip. Claire Michelet, Philippe calculated, was of far more significance to his half-brother than Adam wished him to know. It was something to remember. One day, in the future, if he managed to survive his present perils, he might make use of what he knew.

Having considered the significance of the woman, Philippe turned his attention to the rest of his exchange with Adam. His mind was still assessing, still adding and subtracting, when he settled himself on his pallet for the night.

Hours later, he came to himself with a start. In the distance he could hear men shouting mingled with the sound of sporadic gunfire. The rebel camp was under attack. It was not only that which had wakened him, thought Philippe, but the sudden blinding conviction which had come to him in his sleep. The years had made little impression on Adam Dillon. In spite of everything, he still allowed his conduct to be guided by the old codes.

To Adam Dillon, blood was thicker than water, even the blood of a half-brother whom he had every reason to fear and hate. It was for this reason alone that Adam had spared his life. And even if Philippe had confessed that he had indeed murdered his sisters in cold blood, Adam Dillon did not have it in him to exact a fitting retribution on their murderer. The ties of blood constrained him.

The thought was almost laughable. For the first time, Philippe saw Adam as an insignificant creature bound by convention. In the pursuit of his own destiny, Philippe had set aside every other considera-

183

tion. He was fated to be a giant among men. The rules applying to lesser mortals did not apply to him.

Outside, a sudden silence descended. The moment of his release was at hand. His confidence was restored. A pewter tankard lay to hand. He grasped it and began to beat out a tattoo against the table.

Chapter Eleven

The commissioner returned to Rouen in a state of
collapse. Physicians were summoned to his bedside.
They were able to assure Captain Domfrey, his
second-in-command, that they had every hope of the
commissioner's speedy recovery. Duhet had suffered
a concussion. He slipped in and out of consciousness. Naturally, he was confused. They expected that
with a period of unremitting rest, the commissioner
would be fully restored to health.

Claire waited to be summoned to Philippe's
bedside with barely contained impatience. She
regarded his deliverance from the rebels as nothing
short of a miracle. She was so full of happiness that
she easily forgave Millot his unnatural silences and
stern looks. Millot, she conjectured, had suffered almost as much as she when it seemed that
Philippe must be lost to them forever. With that
threat removed, her heart soared. She felt light-
headed. Evidently, Millot had yet to throw off his
melancholy.

Even the arrival of deputies from Paris could not
dim her happiness. She met them on the stairs. Millot
made the introductions. The gentlemen were all
politeness. Claire was all charm. She could not know
how each gentleman interpreted the sparkle in her
eyes, and the smile which lit up her face.

She was in love and supposed that everyone must know it. She wanted to shout it from the rooftops. But most of all, she wanted to whisper the words in her lover's ear. She had no doubt that Philippe returned her sentiments.

It seemed to her as though she had been reborn. She could never now regret the hours she had spent in her chamber in the deepest travail, not knowing what had become of Philippe, for when she emerged from that room she had known that she loved him without reservation.

For a whole day, she drifted in a state of euphoria. Her troubles seemed less frightening when there was someone to share them. She would confide in Philippe. She trusted him absolutely. It was her newfound love for him and her almost certain conviction that he loved her too which buoyed her hopes. When two people loved each other as they did, they were as one person. The marriage of her own parents followed that pattern. It was an example Claire meant to emulate.

Her love for Philippe resolved all her former doubts. The rumors respecting the commissioner's vices and the atrocities which were attributed to him were just that—rumors. She knew him too well. It had nothing to do with the sifting and weighing of evidence. Her knowledge was intuitive and bone deep. If a hundred witnesses came forward with evidence to convict him, she would not believe them.

She said as much to her maid when Blanche, referring to the deputies, voiced the hope that the commissioner's sins had come home to roost.

"I don't believe a particle of what I've heard," retorted Claire. "The commissioner is not the villain he's been painted, and I shall tell the deputies so."

The color washed out of Blanche's cheeks. "You told me you cared nothing for him," she said.

"I . . . I was mistaken."

Claire was smiling and that seemed to infuriate the

186

other girl. "Don't be a fool, Claire! You don't know Duhet."

"And you do, I suppose?"

"More than I care to! If you would only listen to me! Claire, there is something I must tell you—"

But Claire refused to listen. Nor did she invite Blanche to return to her chamber. No one needed to tell her that Philippe was no saint. Where women were concerned he was no novice, nor did he pretend to be. If the choice had been hers to make, she would have given her heart to a different sort of man. Someone like Nicholas. She had not forgotten that her most scathing vituperation had once been reserved for men of Philippe's stamp. Those former animadversions now appeared mean-spirited. Love did not keep a record of wrongs.

Blanche's remarks about the deputies, however, was the first shaft to penetrate Claire's euphoria. She half expected Millot to say something to her on the subject. When he made no move to approach her, she presumed that her fears were groundless.

On the second day of the commissioner's return, Claire was greeted by the news that he was almost fully recovered. She lost no time in seeking him out. The adjoining door to their bedchambers had been locked from the moment Philippe had returned to Rouen. Claire never gave it a thought. It seemed to her that his men were taking no chances, and she was glad of it. She approached the door that gave onto the corridor. There was a guard on duty. She was given to understand that the commissioner had explicitly ordered that she not be admitted.

She turned away thoughtful but not unduly alarmed. The guard must have mistaken the matter. On applying to Millot, however, she was told that there was no mistake. Philippe did not wish to see her.

Something was amiss, but nothing to set her into a panic. There had been a misunderstanding, thought

Claire. Or perhaps Philippe was fatigued with the press of business. The deputies from Paris were in conference with him. This was not the time or place for matters of a personal nature to intrude. Soon, Philippe would send for her, and everything would be settled between them.

She slept restlessly and was awakened in the morning by her maid. Outside it was still dark.

"What?" Claire saw by the timepiece on the bedside table that it was not quite six o'clock.

The tension in Blanche communicated itself to Claire. "I'm to help you dress and pack. You are to accompany the deputies to Paris."

Claire came fully awake. She reached for her wrapper. "Where is Philippe? I must go to him."

With a strength that Claire would not have believed possible, Blanche wrenched her round by the shoulders and held her fast. "Claire, there is something I must tell you."

"Where is Philippe?" demanded Claire, fighting to free herself.

Blanche's expression hardened. "Duhet is in chains. Even now, he may have left for Paris. Listen to me! Claire! You must save yourself! You must convince the deputies that you hate the bastard, else—"

Claire gasped and her struggles increased. All that registered in her mind was that Philippe was in chains. Like a madwoman, she flung out of Blanche's grasp and without benefit of her wrapper went tearing along the corridor to his chamber. It was empty. Fear lent urgency to her steps. She hared down the stairs and pushed outside.

The courtyard was lit by several pitch torches. A fine drizzle was falling. Men were mounting up. Claire was insensible of the picture she presented. The rain plastered her fine lawn night rail to her body, shielding nothing. Her unbound hair streamed over her shoulders like liquid fire. Men, seeing her, found it easy to condone the commissioner's infatuation.

"Philippe?" she called brokenly, her eyes anxiously scanning each shadowy face and form.

A horse and rider detached themselves from the main group and slowly approached her. She squinted up, but tears and rain made it impossible for her to see clearly.

"Lying whore!" snarled Philippe, and men gasped as he leaned down from the saddle to strike at her with his bound fists.

The blow caught her across the face. Claire sagged to her knees and grasped instinctively for his stirrup. She was living through a nightmare and she did not know how to reach him. "I love you," she cried out. "I love you."

He would have struck her again if Millot had not come between them. Claire's fingers had to be pried off the stirrup, and Millot had to forcibly restrain her as men and mounts cantered through the archway into the twilight.

There was nothing to keep Millot in Rouen. Their network had been disbanded. Bernay and Granville, so it was presumed by the authorities, were either captured or killed by Sillery's forces. The plan was that Millot, after a suitable interval and without rousing suspicion, should resign from his post on grounds of family obligations. It was no less than the truth. His parents were long gone. Millot thanked God that they had not lived to see the Revolution. But he had two older brothers, both of whom had, at one time, thriving law practices in the city of Bordeaux. The last he had heard, their names were on the proscribed lists. He had it in his mind to try and find them or, at the very least, to discover what had become of them.

Yet he had lingered in Rouen. The reason was not

hard to find. From the moment he had set eyes on Claire Michelet he had placed her on a pedestal. She was the epitome of everything he admired in a woman, so he'd thought then. She was a deceiving bitch. Adam had said so. The proof against her was incontrovertible. Millot had accepted it. But he knew in his heart of hearts that until he heard Claire admit to it with her own lips, he would always carry with him a small, niggling doubt.

Her jubilation when the deputies arrived from Paris was enough to convince him of her guilt. He set things in motion. He would leave for Bordeaux just as soon as the deputies removed Claire and Duhet to Paris. Having witnessed that awful scene in the courtyard, he knew that Adam Dillon had made the worst mistake of his life. Whoever had betrayed him, it was not Claire.

It was in her best interests to disassociate herself from Duhet. Yet in the interview with the deputies which had followed the commissioner's departure, she had been unshakable. She knew nothing of a letter informing against the commissioner. She knew nothing of an attempt to rescue General Theot. In the end, the deputies were forced to accept her word. Formerly, they had proposed to convey her to Paris with all the respect due a material witness. Instead, she was treated like a common criminal. She was Duhet's whore. That alone made her suspect.

One of the deputies, younger than his colleagues by a number of years, had taken pity on her. Millot had sensed that the man was *willing* Claire to save herself. So much beauty, so much grace and dignity, his eyes said, must not be allowed to end on the scaffold.

"Admit to writing the letter denouncing Duhet," he'd said, "and I give you my solemn promise that no harm shall come to you. Deny it, and you will almost certainly suffer the same fate as Duhet."

And Claire had answered dully that she wished she

190

could save herself, but she could not, in all conscience, accuse the commissioner. The letter was not in her hand. The deputy had shrugged and turned away. By her own words she had condemned herself.

In that moment, Millot cursed Adam a hundred times over. Adam Dillon was not forced to watch as Claire was led out to the waiting carriage that would take her to the Conciergerie in Paris. He was not there to witness the vacant look on her face as though she understood nothing. And that face—no longer beautiful but grotesquely swollen on one side where Duhet had struck her. But worst of all, thought Millot, were the jeers of the spectators, women all, who had congregated outside the doors of the hotel to enjoy Claire's shame.

The Conciergerie. The very name was enough to make all sane men shudder in revulsion. Claire was there now. Millot knew that her chances of survival were now closely tied to Duhet's fate. If he was condemned, as his loyal mistress, Claire would be condemned also. If Duhet escaped the guillotine, so would Claire. Adam was sure that Duhet could save himself. Millot prayed that Adam's confidence was not misplaced.

Whatever the outcome, Claire was in need of friends. Bordeaux was forgotten. His destination was Paris. Adam Dillon had much to answer for, thought Millot. He hoped that he would be spared so that one day he could tell him so to his face.

Adam watched through narrowed lids as the woman undressed for him. He lay full-length on the bunk, one knee slightly bent. His coat was discarded, as was his neckcloth and the ribbon that tied back his hair. His white lawn shirt was open at the throat.

Desire was slow in coming. He put it down to fatigue. It had taken him more than a week to reach

191

La Rochelle, detouring around checkpoints and hiding out in farmers' fields. There was no longer any need for subterfuge. He was aboard his own ship.

In the morning, the *Mariner* would weigh anchor and set sail for New York. The voyage would take six or seven weeks, possibly more. The woman was to accompany him. She had been well paid for her time.

"You like what you see?" murmured Yvette, and she threw a fall of jet black hair over her shoulders.

Yvette had the look of a gypsy. There was something wild and untamed about her. She was the kind of bed partner that Adam preferred. The exchange was basic. Money for her favors. In his experience, whores were more honest than most women. There was no need for pretense.

With practiced sensuality, she ran her hands over her naked body, brushing the pads of her fingers against the dark aureole of her nipples, bringing them to hard peaks. Her fingers moved on, caressing the valley of her waist, the rounded swell of her hips. She moaned softly as she wound her fingers into the thatch of dark hair between her white thighs.

Desire began to stir in Adam. He almost groaned in relief. The first woman who had been brought to him had Claire's coloring. She left him cold. He could not have touched her if his life depended on it. He'd sent her on her way with a fat purse and a charming if lame apology, wondering all the while if every woman was going to produce the same effect in him.

Yvette tilted her head and slanted him a long, smoldering look. Her red lips parted invitingly. She repeated her former question. "American, you like what you see?"

Yvette was obvious. Too obvious. He squelched the last thought. "I like what I see." He tried to smile, but the muscles in his face refused to obey the commands of his brain. Even his charm seemed to have deserted him. God, he'd felt more desire for a woman in the heat of battle. What the hell was the matter with him? He was a healthy male animal. He had been celibate for three months. His pulse should be leaping at the sight of the woman's ripe beauty. Again, he thought of Claire, and furiously tried to shut her out of his mind.

He extended one hand. "Come here," he said.

Yvette moved toward the bunk with feline stealth. Her eyes dropped to the American's flat stomach and groin then flew to his face. Her lips pouted.

Adam ran his hands over her spine, urging her closer. He laughed softly. "I'm trying," he said. "Believe me, I'm trying. There's a woman I want to forget. Please, make me forget her. Can you do that for me?"

For a moment, Yvette was almost insulted. Men fought each other to possess her. She had the favor of Commissioner Thiers. Even his liaison with Louise Riverol had not put a stop to his visits to la Maison des Rêves. There was only one woman he asked for, only one woman who could satisfy him and that was she, Yvette Gouverner. By the time she made the trip to and from America, all her regulars would be desperate to have her back.

She looked into those incredibly green eyes, and her pique dissolved. The American was a winsome devil. Raven dark hair fell loose about his shoulders and framed the most beautifully carved masculine features. That well-formed mouth was smiling faintly. A strong pulse beat at his throat. Yvette rarely felt desire for a man. She experienced it now.

Over his shirt, she allowed her hands to wander from his heavily muscled chest to his trim waist. She fiddled with the waistband of his breeches. When his breathing altered slightly, Yvette smiled. Catlike, she rubbed herself against him.

"Don't worry, American," she said and laughed deep in her throat. "Yvette knows how to make you forget."

"God, I hope so!"

She pushed him into the mattress and began to

unbutton his shirt. Adam eagerly helped her till every article of clothing was dropped in a heap on the floor. She wouldn't allow him to touch her.

"Let me," she said, scattering kisses along his powerful shoulders. Slowly, slowly, her lips traced the path of coarse hair from his chest to his groin.

Yvette knew her business. No man could long withstand her art. Adam lowered his lashes and gritted his teeth. Her mouth closed over his aroused flesh, and desire rose in him, hot and fast. With tongue and lips she pleasured him. He would never have asked as much from Claire.

Furious with himself for allowing Claire's image to spoil the moment, he reared up and flipped Yvette onto her back. His hands were almost desperate as they rushed over her soft curves. Her breasts were heavy, the nipples were like pebbles against his palms. He sucked greedily on one. The woman was heaving and panting. He buried his face between her breasts, inhaling the musky scent of stale perspiration. He thought of roses, and cursed himself for remembering.

He entered her with such violence that Yvette cried out. Powerfully, rhythmically, he set the pace. His thrusts became frenzied. He shut his mind to everything but the feel of her woman's flesh enveloping his hard shaft. She was female. He was male. That's all there was to it. That's all he wanted.

Yvette writhed beneath him. She had never experienced such intense pleasure. For the first time in her life, she knew that she was going to come to climax. Whimpering incoherently, she wrapped her legs around his waist and ground herself against him. When release came, she screamed. The American pulled himself from her body. As he spilled his seed over her belly, he cried out a woman's name.

Long minutes were to pass before Adam raised himself from the woman. He rolled from the bunk. With quick economy, he dressed himself. "I'm sorry," he said. "That was unforgivable."

His voice was unnaturally hoarse. He cleared his throat and moved to the small window, staring out blindly.

At his back, Yvette raised to her elbows. No man had ever taken the trouble to give her pleasure before. No man had ever restrained himself in the throes of his passion. Whores did not expect it. Abortion was a commonplace. She wondered about the woman called Claire, and knew that she envied her.

Swallowing, she said simply, "You gave me great pleasure."

Adam made a noncommittal sound. He did not trust himself to speak. Pleasure was not what he had ultimately experienced. He felt sick inside.

Yvette eyed him thoughtfully. She had a fair idea of which way the wind was blowing. She had already been paid generously to be the American's woman on the long voyage to New York. The sum was so substantial, so excessive, that she could not refuse it. But it wasn't only the money she was thinking of at that moment.

The American was the kind of lover all women must secretly desire. He wanted the woman called Claire but could not have her. He was male. He must have some woman. She did not see why that woman should not be she.

Yvette knew how to arouse a man. A certain tone of voice, a look, a gesture—when the need arose, she employed all the tools of her profession with consummate skill. The American had his back to her.

Her voice was husky and faintly teasing. "Come back to bed, American. I can pleasure you in ways this Claire could not imagine in a hundred years. By the time we reach New York, she won't even be a memory, I promise you."

Adam didn't want Claire's name on this woman's lips. He felt sordid. It wasn't Yvette's fault. He'd had many encounters similar to this one. But he'd never

195

taken one woman to his bed and been haunted by another.

With a supreme effort of will, he made himself turn to face her. He summoned the remnants of the old charm. With a smile that made Yvette's heart leap in her throat, he said, "It's not going to work, Yvette. I can't think what made me hope that it would. It's not your fault. The fault lies in me."

"You love her." She voiced the stray thought without thinking. She saw at once that she had made a fatal blunder.

The smile left Adam's face. A dark tide of color rose in his throat. "I'll leave you to get dressed," he said. "Peters will see you safely to shore." He cut off her protests. "The money means nothing to me. Keep it. You earned it. You were not the one to break our bargain."

Again, thoughts of Claire intruded. He was beginning to think himself demented. Every chance word seemed to start a train of thought that led straight back to her.

Cursing under his breath, he slammed out of the cabin. He spent hours tramping the decks. He didn't want to return to the cabin. Whether or not the woman still occupied it made no difference. Something obscene had happened there. If he entered it, he knew he would feel like a murderer returning to the scene of the crime.

The thought that this was to be his future pattern with women took hold of him. Like some malevolent spirit from his past, Claire was going to haunt him. He had known that no woman could ever compare to Claire. Poor Yvette. She thought to seduce him with her promise of sensual delights. Claire was a complete novice. He burned for her.

His hands clenched convulsively around the ship's rail. Claire. She was a scheming jade. He waited for the predictable rush of fury to rise in him. It was there, but muted. The fever had burned itself out.

He had come to a crossroads. Tomorrow he must either set sail for America or return to fetch Claire. His pride had been driving him hard. It spurred him to leave her. His heart was wiser. It knew that he could never be happy without Claire. His one attempt to forget her with another woman had left him feeling . . . polluted. In some strange way he felt as though he had defiled not only himself and the woman he had tried to use as Claire's substitute, but also Claire.

He still wanted her. He'd finally admitted it, and a strange calm possessed him. He wanted Claire. Even knowing what she was, he wanted her. And he refused to leave France without her.

By the time he caught up with her it would be all of three weeks since they had last seen each other. She would be in Paris. He hoped she had the sense to keep out of the public eye. She was so damnably beautiful that some male or other was bound to covet her. His face twisted in a bitterly self-mocking smile. He was that male, and he was bound and determined that he was the one who was going to walk off with the prize.

If Philippe had played his cards right, Claire's motives for writing the letter would be suspect. In that event, she would find herself in Paris alone and friendless. It's what he had hoped would happen to her. At the height of his rage he had imagined all sorts of dire calamities overtaking her—but not too dire. She would be known as Duhet's cast-off whore. Decent women would shun her. She'd be forced to earn her bread by becoming a laundress or a kitchen menial or some such thing. If all else failed, she could sell her sexual favors to keep herself from starvation. He had told himself that he did not care if she sank to that level. He lied.

When he found her, he could not simply overlook her perfidy. At the very least, he would give her a good tongue lashing. She deserved a beating. If it was necessary he would administer it. It's what he should have done in the first place. He was going to give her such a fright that she would never forget it. One way or another, he would have her submission. He would take her to America with him. If she proved to be a truculent wife, he would saddle her with a baby every year. That would tame her.

In the morning, Adam went in search of Bernay and Granville. He found them in the dockside tavern where they had parted company the day before. They were bound for Spain. When he told them what he meant to do, they were incredulous.

"You can't go back," they exclaimed in horror.

"It's too dangerous," added Bernay.

Adam could not be swayed from his purpose. He was not surprised when they threw in their lot with him. They were good fellows and he had need of them. It only wanted Millot to complete their little circle.

Chapter Twelve

They said that she was in the infirmary. Claire knew better. She was in purgatory, or she was in hell. Everywhere she looked there were iron bars and grilles. But she had found a way to escape them. By directing her gaze upwards, deviating to neither left nor right, she concentrated on the great Gothic arches. She was in a convent, she told herself, or she was worshiping in Rouen's ancient cathedral.

Sometimes the word Conciergerie penetrated the numbing fog. She grew restless on her straw pallet. No. She refused to allow that word into her consciousness, 'else she would be forced to admit that the footsteps she heard were those of the condemned as they trod the path to the tumbrils which awaited them in the Cour du Mai. Then she would be forced to admit that her turn was coming. She would be taken to *la salle de la toilette*. Her hair would be shorn, her hands tied behind her back, and her collar ripped from her throat to make the work of the guillotine that much easier.

Purgatory was a strange place. There was frivolity, there was despair. Few clung to hope. Somehow, that seemed wrong. God was merciful. Why did no one believe it? She tried to pray.

"Philippe," she said. "Oh God, Philippe."

A cool cloth bathed her hot cheeks. "It's all right.

It's all right," soothed someone.

"Blanche?" Claire's brows knit together. Blanche was in Rouen.

"I'm here," said Blanche.

And then the fog began to lift, and Claire did not think she could bear it. "I didn't write the letter," she whispered brokenly. "Oh God, why won't he believe me?"

"He believes you."

"Yes." It was coming back to her. The letter was not in her hand. In that first interview with her interrogators, when she was shown the original, she had proved that it was a forgery. The writing was similar, but not close enough. They had accepted that the letter was a piece of mischief-making on someone's part. But they had not released her. She was Duhet's acknowledged mistress. Her fate was tied to his. Claire resigned herself to death. If Philippe was condemned, she would not wish to live.

"Philippe!" Her body began to shake. "Where—?" What—?"

Blanche gritted her teeth, but she concealed her murderous thoughts behind a composed facade. "He's safe," she said. "He is to be given the opportunity to defend himself on the floor of the Convention."

Claire quieted. "He's free?"

"Until the Convention decides whether or not he is guilty of corruption. Don't worry, Claire. Duhet has powerful friends. They won't see anything happen to him." And it galled Blanche past bearing that, for Claire's sake, she must pray that Duhet would get off scot-free.

She had considered confessing that she was the one who had written the letter, but saw, almost at once, that no good would be served by it. By signing Claire's name, she had hoped to disassociate Claire from Duhet. Claire, herself, would not permit it. In that event, any evidence that damned Duhet also damned Claire. Though she could not explain it to herself, Claire's welfare had become paramount to Blanche.

"How are you feeling?"

Claire turned her head to face the wall. They had told her that she had lost her baby. She knew that they lied. She had hemorrhaged. That much she did remember. "They said I miscarried," she whispered.

"Yes."

Claire's head whipped round. "No! I couldn't! I would have known if I was with child."

"Don't think about it. Just think about getting well."

"Tell me!" Claire's hand grasped the other girl's wrist with extraordinary force.

Blanche hesitated for only a moment. In a matter-of-fact tone, she said, "You were three months along."

"I would have known!"

"These things happen. Don't think about it, Claire. Look, I have to go. I shall be back tomorrow. I'll bring a change of clothes with me. All right?"

Claire had once more slipped away into unreality. Blanche's throat tightened. Claire looked so pale and thin and so forlorn. And she felt so helpless.

"How is your friend?"

The question came from the woman on the next pallet. Her belly was swollen with child. Because of it, she had been given a reprieve. Until her child was born, she was safe from Madame Guillotine.

The rumor was that on the floors above, where the aristocrats and those with money were incarcerated in their tiny cells, love affairs of an unlikely sort flourished. Pregnancy could bring a stay of execution. Claire's misfortune was greater than she realized.

"Not good," said Blanche. The air was foul with the stench of latrine buckets and unwashed bodies. Blanche fought down a surge of nausea.

"I haven't seen you before," remarked an older

201

lady with a friendly smile. She was dressed in gray, without ornamentation.

"I arrived today from Rouen," said Blanche, "and came at once to see my friend."

"Poor child!" said the older woman, coming to stand by Claire's cot. "She lost the baby. It's not to be wondered at. I hear that for three days she was penned in the paupers' gallery?"

Blanche did not know if she could bear to hear what had happened to Claire since she'd been lodged in the Conciergerie. "The paupers' gallery?" she repeated faintly.

In view of the girl's ignorance, Madame Lamont decided it was kinder not to enlighten her. "Now that you are here," she said, "if you can manage it, ask to have her moved upstairs. They won't allow her to remain in the infirmary indefinitely."

"I'll see what I can do," said Blanche. What she was thinking was that she had no money to spare. The little she had was reserved for bribing her way in to seeing Claire.

Someone began to moan and wail as if her heart were breaking. Others cursed her and shouted for her to be quiet. Blanche had to get out of there before she was sick. She stumbled her way past closely packed pallets and latrine buckets to the iron grille. A guard opened it for her. Once on the other side, she pressed a coin into his palm. Corruption, even in the Conciergerie, was rife. The only thing that money could not buy was freedom.

A few steps took her to the most public section of the prison, the Couloir des Prisonniers. The corridor was like a marketplace as lawyers, prisoners, jailers, police, and the odd visitor jostled each other. Blanche kept her head well down. But someone saw her and gave a start of recognition. Blanche scarcely drew breath until she was outside. She struck out toward the Pont Neuf. She looked to neither left nor right. Had she done so, she would have recognized the

202

gentleman who was pacing his steps to hers. It was Millot, Duhet's head clerk.

The room that Blanche had rented for herself was up three flights of stairs. It was almost bare of furniture. She seated herself at a broken-down table and stared into space. She did not know how to begin to help Claire. At one time there were friends in Paris she might have turned to. Robespierre, however, had closed down a number of theaters. Many of her fraternity had gone to the guillotine. She knew of one way of earning money. She did not think she could bring herself to do it.

The door suddenly burst inward. Blanche leaped to her feet with a cry of alarm. The gentleman who advanced upon her was so threatening that at first Blanche did not recognize him. She saw only a deranged man.

"You filthy bitch," he raved at her. "It was you! All the time, it was you! You forged the letter and signed Claire's name to it! By God, I should kill you! I think I will kill you! If you have made more trouble for Claire, tell me at once, or I shall take great delight in throttling the life out of you."

"Millot!" cried Blanche. Relief swamped her. Millot had a *tendresse* for Claire. She backed away from him, and held out both hands in a pleading gesture. "I'll tell you everything," she said. "Calm down, all right? Oh Millot, if only you knew what I've suffered, what Claire has suffered." Her face crumpled and she covered her eyes with both hands. "Oh Millot," she sobbed. "Thank God you are here."

On the first floor of the Convention, Robespierre held every eye. He was in one of his more frenzied humors. Several of the deputies came under a scathing attack. Sane men trembled in their boots. Commissioner Duhet was particularly singled out. Robespierre castigated Duhet with a vengeance. It was evident he felt betrayed. He had regarded Duhet as his protégé. He spoke darkly of aristocrats who, despite their protestations of revolutionary zeal, were suspected of coming under the influence of moderates, or worse, petticoat government. He had before him a long litany of complaints from the judges of Rouen's Tribunal. Claire Michelet was mentioned by name. The judges argued that since taking this woman as his mistress, the commissioner had grown soft. Robespierre hinted at those responsible for military affairs having dealings with the enemy. By the time he sat down, he was practically foaming at the mouth.

His words, which had been heard without interruption, were met with polite applause. Only Danton and his followers were seen to refrain, and of course, those deputies and commissioners who had come under Robespierre's vituperation.

Before the applause had died down, Philippe Duhet strode to the rostrum. His defense of the charges against him was impassioned. He was a soldier, he informed his peers. While Robespierre and his ilk were enjoying a life of relative ease in Paris, he had spent the last three months on active duty, subduing the rebels in the north. If he had a mistress, he would never have known it. His most constant companion was his horse. (Laughter greeted this sally.) To indict him for dereliction of duty was not only to sully his honor, but also the honor of the brave soldiers who had fallen while fighting to secure France's borders.

The silence was eloquent.

The choice, said Duhet, had been thrust upon him. He must either direct all his energies to subduing the rebels or to looking under beds or in closets for so-called enemies of the Revolution. (The laughter this time was less subdued.) He concluded by saying that he was sure that the judges in Rouen's Tribunal who had brought him to this pass were fair-minded men.

Their opinions meant nothing to him.

His voice trembled with emotion. "But if any of my loyal troops were to say one word against me, I would gladly embrace a verdict of death."

When he returned to his place, the applause was thunderous. There was no doubt that the commissioner cut a glamorous figure. He was a man's man. In comparison, Robespierre, with his moralism, made a very poor show.

Danton was next to speak. There was no love lost between Danton and Robespierre. Each man had a sizable following in the Convention. Each man knew that one day soon there must be a final confrontation with only one of them the clear victor. Danton did not think that that day had arrived. In this he was mistaken.

He spoke in defense of Duhet. But his speech was restrained. He was careful to give Robespierre his due. Danton was not to know it, but already Robespierre was setting things in motion to discredit him. In less than a month, Danton and his supporters would be denounced, tried, and summarily executed.

When Philippe Duhet left the chamber, he was a free man. In deference to Robespierre, however, his peers had voted to relieve him of his office.

The Cour des Femmes, where female prisoners took their exercise, was in the very heart of the Conciergerie. It was open to the elements, but very little sun penetrated to this small courtyard. In the center was a pathetic patch of grass, and a deformed tree. On every side, the walls of the Conciergerie rose up, its windows with their iron bars a grim reminder that the former palace of the kings of France was now a prison.

Claire had been persuaded to take the air. She leaned heavily on her companion, a woman who was old enough to be her grandmother. Since her release from the infirmary, Claire had shared a cell with Madame Lamont. Claire supposed that Blanche must be footing the bill for this luxury. She, herself, had no money. If it were not for Blanche, she would be forced to endure the hardships of the overcrowded paupers' gallery.

From time to time, Claire rested. At the fountain, in one corner of the yard, some women were washing their linen. Adjacent to the fountain, with only a grille separating them, male and female prisoners were conversing. The younger ones were flirting.

Claire's companion urged her forward. "You must exercise your limbs," she upbraided gently, "else you will lose the use of them. Don't give way to self-pity, Claire. You have everything to live for. Did you not hear your friend tell you that your husband had been set free? You will be too. I'm sure of it."

It took a moment for Claire to sort everything out in her mind. Madame Lamont had naturally jumped to the conclusion that Philippe was Claire's husband. Claire said nothing to correct that misapprehension. She could not seem to care.

It was not ill-health which robbed her of the energy to obey Madame's pleadings, thought Claire. It was inertia. She was losing hope, just as surely as she had lost her unborn child. She thought it must be a punishment from God for all her sins. She had been too proud, holding herself aloof from the follies of lesser mortals. Her pride had been humbled with a vengeance. She had fallen in love. She would have prostrated herself before Philippe if only he had given her a chance to defend herself.

The news of Philippe's release had given her new heart. But in the three days since Blanche had told her that he had walked out of the Convention a free man, he had made no move to approach her, either by letter or in person. It seemed that he wanted nothing to do with her.

She needed him. No one understood what she had suffered when she was told that she had lost her baby. The guilt was like a leaden weight across her shoulders. She had not wanted a child. She'd deliberately taken steps to prevent conception. It seemed to her that her baby had known that no one would mourn its loss. It was all her fault. Only Philippe had the power to comfort her. It was his child too. If he forgave her, perhaps she could forgive herself.

"My dear," said Madame Lamont, "forgive me for adding to your burdens, but there's something I must tell you."

Claire heard the note of sorrow and turned her face up to study her companion. "What is it?" she asked.

As gently as she could, Madame Lamont said, "I am to go before the Tribunal tomorrow."

Claire inhaled sharply. She looked into those untroubled gray eyes and her own self-pity seemed like a sacrilege. She said the first words that came into her head. "Madame, what makes you so brave?"

Madame thought for a moment and said, "Contempt for life. No! Don't look like that, child. You have everything to live for. I am an old woman. My life is over. You must not mourn for me if I do not return tomorrow. Agreed?"

"But . . ." They had known each other for only a short while. They had traded no secrets. But a bond had been established between them. Claire supposed that soldiers on the field of battle must form these instant friendships.

Guards were calling out, telling the women to get inside. Claire became aware that it had started to rain. At the gate, the guards turned her aside. Madame Lamont protested, and was shoved none too gently through the wicket. Women darted sideways looks at Claire from beneath their lashes as they hurried to obey the guards' orders. Within moments, Claire was alone in the Cour des Femmes. She wandered about, not knowing what to do with herself, not knowing what to expect.

The grate of metal on metal brought her head round. A man had been admitted to the small, railed-off corner where male prisoners were permitted. Claire's eyes narrowed on him.

Her heart lifted. "Philippe?" she whispered, not daring to believe the evidence of her own eyes.

Like a sleepwalker, she approached the iron grille. Her hands curled around the railing. Philippe stood well back from her, close to one of the arches.

"Philippe," she said. "I did not write that letter. I did not betray you."

"I know," he said.

Claire's eyes drank in the sight of him. He looked so handsome. He looked so fresh and neat. Her own clothes were stained and creased beyond redemption. Her hair was sorely in need of a wash.

For long minutes she simply stared at him. And then she began to experience the familiar unease. It started with goose bumps and a faint tremor of revulsion. It built till she could almost feel her skin begin to crawl. Philippe moved closer to the grille.

Her eyes moved slowly over him. Every feature was familiar. Yet everything about this man was unknown to her. But he was not a total stranger. This was the man who had gone to Angers. It was a different man who had returned.

With piercing clarity, she had the answer to the question which had long puzzled her. "Who are you?" Her words were barely audible.

"Philippe Duhet at your service, mademoiselle," he said, and made her an elegant bow.

The blood rushed from Claire's face. She gave a little cry. "You are not Philippe. You can't be!"

"I assure you that I am."

"No." The denial was torn from her.

"I suspect you are confusing me with my half-brother."

She closed her eyes, assimilating his words. It was the only explanation that made sense. Philippe Duhet must have a brother. A twin.

She felt sick with premonition. "What have you done to him?" she asked hoarsely.

He made a show of surprise. "I have done nothing. You should ask rather what he has done to us."

"I don't understand." Had she said the words aloud?

His smile twisted, became ugly. "My half-brother has used us as pawns in his own elaborate game. And now that we have served our usefulness, he has left us to our fate. We shall be fortunate to come out of this alive."

Half-formed sentences whirled in her head. She couldn't seem to find her voice. She didn't believe him. The Philippe she knew would never have allowed her to go through the nightmare of the past days. She'd been sick with terror, not only for herself, but also for him. She'd been lodged in the dread Conciergerie. She had lost her baby. She had almost lost her will to live. No, the Philippe she knew would have moved heaven and earth to save her.

She must have voiced something of what she was thinking, or her tormentor was able to read her mind.

"He hates me," said Philippe. "He always has. He always will. He did it to discredit me. You may have heard that I have been relieved of my command?"

She pressed a hand to her eyes. "What did he do? I don't understand."

Philippe spoke quickly. In a matter of minutes Claire was apprised of the masquerade which had duped not only her, but the whole of Rouen for three months.

She made an inarticulate sound, then burst out, "But I have done nothing to earn his hatred. Why has he abandoned me? Why didn't he warn me?"

"You just happened to get in his way. And then, of course, there was the letter. I think it annoyed him."

It was too horrible to contemplate, too horrible to be believed. Yet everything was beginning to fall into place. "Why are you here?" she asked. "Why are you telling me all this?"

Philippe had been asking himself the very same questions. Unlike Adam, he had not come out of curiosity or to gloat. There was danger in revealing himself to the girl. Adam had warned him of it. But that was before they knew she had not written the letter.

Philippe was persuaded that, like himself, Claire must hate Adam when she knew the truth about him. That gave them something in common. No one had ever understood his hatred for his brother. Claire must be as enraged as he.

And Adam wanted this woman. He would writhe if Claire ever became Philippe's mistress. It was something to think about. And the woman was worth having. Even her soiled clothes and bedraggled hair could not dim her beauty.

The indolent pose had fallen away. His mouth hardened into a grim line, but no grimmer than the expression in his voice. "He has wronged us both," he said. "You must hate him too. We could work together—find him—punish him." When she said nothing, he went on in a softened tone, "Claire, you must know that I still want you. You will be released soon. Where will you go? What will become of you? Come to me, Claire. I shall take care of you."

She understood the hatred that moved him. His pride had been lacerated. She sensed that he felt something genuine for her, pity or desire, she could not say which. It did not matter. Nothing mattered.

"I don't care what happens to me," she said.

The jailer rattled his keys, warning them that their time was up. "If you change your mind," Philippe said, "you may find me at this address."

He held out a piece of paper. Claire made no move to accept it. It slipped from his fingers to flutter close to her skirts. With one last look Philippe was gone. Only then did Claire retrieve the paper.

When she was returned to her cell, her face was as white as the paper she clutched in her hand. She was wet through. Her teeth were chattering.

Madame Lamont helped undress her and put her to bed. She summoned one of the jailers, calling out through the bars of their door. She ordered dinner. With Madame Lamont, there was no shortage of funds. The food supplied by the prison was inedible swill, not fit for pigs. The rich did not care. They had the means to send out for something to tempt the appetite.

Madame Lamont forced the hot soup past the girl's frozen lips. Claire did not have the energy to refuse. She drank the red wine sparingly. Madame, however, was not satisfied until Claire had drained the glass to the dregs. She poured her another.

"Now," said Madame. "I want to hear all about it. Child, whom else should you trust? I shall take your secrets with me to the grave. You have nothing to fear from me."

At Madame's words, tears sprang to Claire's eyes. In that moment, all she could think about was what awaited her companion on the morrow. Once the tears started, however, she seemed to be crying for the cares of the whole world. She cried for France. She cried for her parents. She cried for Philippe. She cried for her lost child. And finally, she cried for herself. She cried till there were no tears left.

"Start at the beginning," said Madame soothingly. "Tell me about your family."

And Claire did. She told Madame about the golden days of her childhood as she grew to womanhood in the Devereux household. She spoke about her parents' arrest and the flight to Rouen. She told her about Philippe and how she had come to be his mistress. And she told her about the interview she'd had with his twin, the other Philippe, in the Cour des Femmes.

211

Madame cradled the girl in her arms, one hand ceaselessly patting her on the back in a comforting gesture. When the story was told and the hiccups and sobs had finally subsided, Madame held Claire away from her.

"There is something I must say to you," she said gravely, "something I think your parents would wish me to say. Claire, their case is hopeless. You know it in your heart of hearts. No, don't interrupt, my dear. Answer this question. What is the worst thing that can happen to them?"

Claire winced. "The guillotine," she whispered.

"Think again."

Claire's eyelids fluttered. "Zoë and Leon are safe," she said.

"And what about you? You told me of your despair when you lost your child. How do you think losing *you* would affect your parents? My dear, nothing will compensate them for the loss of a child, not even the gift of their own lives. I know. I speak from experience. You must get well. You must leave this place. Leave France, Claire. That is the best gift you can give your parents—to be safe and live well."

Claire's eyes searched the older woman's face. "Oh, madame, I'm so sorry," she said.

Madame smiled. "I told you that I had nothing to live for. I see now that I was wrong. You need someone to take care of you. I wish that I could be that person. Since I am unlikely to have my wish, I will leave you with what I may. A few words of wisdom, Claire. That is all I can offer. Join your brother and sister in England. It's what your parents would wish. Forget about the Duhet brothers. Such men are not for you. You have told me that you love your Philippe, and I believe you. You must ask yourself whether or not you would ever find happiness with such a man."

Madame sighed. "I have given you all that I have to give. Now, you must excuse an old woman as she

212

makes her peace with God."

Claire lay back on the pallet. Madame went down on her knees. A rosary was in her hands. Her lips began to move. Claire was past praying. Nevertheless, she felt as though she too shared in Madame's ritual. The pain became a little easier to bear.

Long after Claire was asleep, Madame stared at the faint light coming from the barred window high in the wall. It was too bad of the Lord God, she was thinking, to disturb her peace with the plight of this poor child so late in the day. She could do nothing to help her. And she wanted to. It made her unsettled, reluctant to depart this life when someone still needed her.

Perhaps she should have said nothing. She was not God after all. Sighing, she turned her face toward Claire. Everything was in God's hands. She wished she could believe it.

She closed her eyes and drew on the memories of those she had loved best in the world. One face, one presence, never failed her. "Ah, Robert, my heart," she whispered. "Soon, my love . . . very soon. But I am so afraid. Stay with me."

In the morning, Madame kissed Claire on both cheeks and pressed a velvet *pochette* into her hands. "This is farewell, my dear. We both know it. I have no one to whom I may leave my mementos. Perhaps you will find a use for these."

Claire did not refuse the gift that Madame pressed upon her. Every trinket, every sous of the condemned would be taken from them in the *salle de la toilette* to become the property of the nation.

"God go with you," said Claire, wishing she could say so much more.

"And with you."

Madame did not return.

On the following day, Claire was released.

Chapter Thirteen

Outside the doors of the Conciergerie, Claire was met by Blanche. She was led to a waiting carriage and showed no surprise when Millot reached down to help her inside. On the short drive to Blanche's lodgings, Claire was silent. Millot and Blanche kept up a flow of small talk until they too fell silent. Their eyes kept darting to the unnaturally composed features of their companion.

Once in Blanche's room, Millot pressed a glass of wine upon Claire. As she obediently sipped it, he embarked on an explanation for his presence in Paris. She interrupted him once to say that the real Philippe had been to see her and that there was not the least necessity to conceal the truth from her. She knew all that there was to know about the fraud that had been perpetrated in Rouen. Slightly taken aback, Millot stumbled his way through his explanation.

"So you see, Claire," he said in conclusion, "when it was borne in upon me that you were not the writer of that letter, I knew that things would go very badly for you."

"You came to help me."

"Yes. If it was possible."

"Am I supposed to be grateful?"

"What?"

"Both you and Philippe abandoned me without

giving me a chance to defend myself."

"No! That is . . . the evidence against you was overwhelming."

Claire looked down at her clasped hands and Millot blushed like a guilty schoolboy.

Blanche pulled her chair closer to Claire's. In a tortured, earnest tone, she said, "It was I who wrote the letter and signed your name to it. I thought you despised Duhet. I did it to protect you. I did not know that there were two Duhets. Oh God, Claire, can you ever find it in your heart to forgive me?"

Claire did not answer. She turned her eyes upon Millot. Such beautiful, cold eyes, he thought, and nervously touched a hand to his cravat.

"I want to get one thing absolutely clear in my mind," she said. "Is Philippe safe?"

Millot was glad to reassure her on that point. "Perfectly safe, Claire. He's no longer in France."

She recoiled as though from a blow. Before his horrified eyes, the frozen mask on her beautiful face cracked. Pain such as he had never seen before and never wished to see again was patently transparent on every feature.

"I see," she said. "He saved his own skin and . . . and abandoned his brother and me to the dogs."

"No!" exclaimed Millot. "Claire, you've got it all wrong. No harm was supposed to come to you. A . . . that is, Philippe did a very fine thing by impersonating his brother. Hundreds of lives were saved. We always knew that sooner or later it would end and that he would have to leave France. He was simply following our plan. You were released. Duhet has been rendered harmless. All things considered, we have come out of it quite well."

He could not know his words damned Adam all the more in Claire's eyes. He was simply following a plan. But in its execution, she had become an innocent victim. He had made her his mistress. He

215

had given her a baby. He had asked her to marry him. He had abandoned her. She would not allow that Blanche's letter informing against him mitigated his guilt. If he had felt anything for her, he could not have dealt with her so cruelly, whatever the provocation.

There was a lump in her throat that made speech impossible. She fought to regain her control. After a moment she managed, "I should like to know his name."

Millot was expecting the question and was ready for it. "It's better if you don't know," he said. "What I mean is, no one must suspect that he was ever in France."

She did not argue with him, but turned her attention to the cold collation which was set out on the table. In the same colorless tone, she said, "After we have eaten, I shall tell you my plans for the future."

Millot darted Claire a quick, uneasy glance. The subject of Claire's future was one that he had already considered. He had hoped that he had found a way to send her to Adam. He was sure that when Adam knew the truth about the letter, he would be conscience stricken, as indeed, he himself was. Before the whole thing had blown up in their faces, Adam had told Millot that he meant to marry Claire. Millot heartily approved. It was the only solution for a man of honor. Adam's credit had risen by several notches.

In Claire's eyes, it was evident that Adam's credit had never been lower. Claire was not thinking straight. She had been through too much in too short a time. When she had a chance to put things in their proper perspective, as he had done, she must see that no one could have foreseen how events would fall out.

The glibness of his thinking arrested him. He saw that he was attempting to vindicate conduct that was inexcusable. No sooner had that thought occurred

than he became impatient. No one was infallible, not Blanche, not Adam, and certainly not himself. He was trying to make amends. God, in the great scheme of things, the wrong that they had done to Claire was scarcely worth so much remorse. She had survived where thousands had perished. He was doing the best he could. It would have to suffice.

During the meal, the conversation was desultory. Once or twice, Millot tried to broach the subject of Claire's sufferings in the Conciergerie. He knew that Claire had been ill. But that was all he knew. Blanche did not think it was her place to tell him the nature of Claire's illness. Claire was polite but noncommittal. The Conciergerie was a subject she wished to avoid.

The future was something Claire did not want to think about either, but she knew she must. The future would be empty without Philippe. Nothing could change that. She didn't wish to change it. She just wished she could accept it. It didn't help to know that in time the pain would become more manageable. Only one thing held her together. She must not disappoint those who loved her. She clung to that thought. It gave her a reason to go through the motions of living when all she wanted to do was curl into a ball and die.

"You are the strong one," her father had told her. It seemed inconceivable that her father, who had known her all her life, could be so mistaken in her character.

The table was cleared. Millot replenished the wine glasses. "Now, Claire," he said, "tell us about your plans for the future."

"First," she said, "I shall visit Carmes to say farewell to my parents. Then I shall find a way to join my brother and sister in England."

As it turned out, Claire did not visit her parents in Carmes Prison. Millot absolutely forbade it.

217

"Blanche visited me in the Conciergerie," pointed out Claire stubbornly.

"That's different," said Millot. "Blanche is not related to you. Good God! If the authorities thought that you were your parents' daughter, they would incarcerate you, too."

"I could pretend that I was merely a friend," insisted Claire.

"You would never pull it off. You would start bawling your head off. Then where would you be? Would that make your parents feel better?"

Once more, she retreated into silence. Millot was becoming more and more alarmed by her withdrawal. If she were to cry or rage at the fates, he would have felt better. He saw his own consternation mirrored in Blanche's set face.

"I'll go," she quickly offered.

"No!"

In the end, it was Millot who had taken that office upon himself, though he'd thought himself insane to take such chances, especially when he learned Claire's true identity. She was a Devereux of the great Devereux banking family.

Christ Jesus! He and Adam had suspected that Claire Michelet was an assumed name, but they had never imagined that she had such exalted connections. The Devereux were almost a legend in France. It was said that the king of France bowed down to God and only one man, Devereux—his banker. Any visitor to Leon Devereux was bound to come under a great deal of speculation. It was Blanche who offered the suggestion that Millot should pass himself off as a lawyer or a lawyer's clerk.

The whole enterprise had been so easy to pull off that it was almost laughable. Millot did not feel in the mood for laughter, not after what he had witnessed in Carmes. There was enough at Carmes to make a brave man weep. With no exaggeration, the prison was described as an Augean stable. The stench of row upon row of latrine buckets along every corridor fouled the air. The inmates were crowded as many as fourteen into a single cell. He didn't know what he was going to tell Claire. And then he remembered that she had been an inmate of the Conciergerie. There would be no need to describe Carmes to her.

He'd met with Devereux in a small cell reserved for lawyers and their clients. They'd had only five minutes to transact their business. In few words, Millot had told the older man exactly what Claire had asked him to say. Leon and Zoë had made it safely to England. Soon, Claire would join them. They were all well. She wanted her parents' blessing.

Leon Devereux did not believe him. He became agitated. He seemed to suspect a trick to trap him, and nothing that Millot said could convince him otherwise. Millot had been on the point of departure when Devereux appeared to have a change of heart.

"Every afternoon at three, the prisoners are allowed to walk in the gardens," he said. "There's a window above the wicket. I shall be there at three." As an afterthought he added, "I took it upon myself to tell Madame Devereux some time since that all our children reached England safely. It would only upset her if she were to see Claire still here."

By the time he returned to Blanche's lodgings, Millot had made up his mind to lie in his teeth. *Your parents look well*, he was going to tell Claire. *They are in fine fettle and have every hope that the charges against them will be dropped*. The words stuck in his throat. She would not believe him. He told her the truth and she accepted it stoically.

Just before three the following afternoon outside Carmes prison he assisted Claire to alight from their hired carriage. They walked slowly along the opposite side of the street. When they came to the wicket gate, they halted. True to his word, Leon Devereux appeared at the small landing window.

Claire let out a little cry and grasped Millot's coat sleeve. For a long moment, father and daughter stared at each other somberly. Then Devereux touched his fingers to his lips and moved away.

For the next few days, Claire retreated into a place by herself where no one could reach her. When she emerged, she had only one thought on her mind. She must be reunited with her brother and sister.

The task of persuading her to go to America was more easily accomplished than Millot could have hoped. He simply told her the truth. He did not know how he was to get her to England. The escape routes of which he had knowledge had ceased to exist.

They were, however, in luck. An item in the newspaper indicated that American ships were now free to leave French ports. There were a number of American ships in the harbor at Bordeaux. He had friends there who could help them. Once Claire reached America, passage to England was easily arranged.

He was counting on the fact that without funds, Claire would be stranded in New York where he was sure Adam would soon set things to rights between them. His consternation was great when Claire produced a velvet pochette which contained a small fortune in precious jewels. He'd quickly invented a pretext to take it away from her. The bribes necessary to arrange transportation to Bordeaux and thence to America were astronomical, so he told her.

Later, when Claire had retired to bed, Blanche tackled him about it.

"There was no mention of money changing hands before you discovered that Claire had funds. What are you up to, Nicholas?"

"Nothing, nothing at all!" he snapped. God, he was not cut out for this, to have the care of two women, one of whom seemed to have regressed to infancy and the other who was as pugnacious as a shrew.

Blanche sniffed. She folded her arms across her breasts and surveyed Millot from beneath lowered brows.

"Look," said Millot. "It's some time since I was in Bordeaux. For all I know, my friends may no longer be there." He tossed Claire's *pochette* from one hand to the other. "I am hopeful that I won't require all of this. In that event, I shall return the balance to Claire. Does that meet with your approval?"

"We can't simply arrive in America as paupers," Blanche argued. "I have a little, but not nearly sufficient for two people."

"I have friends in New York," replied Millot. "I shall give you letters of introduction. They will help you get established."

One small foot tapped rhythmically as her dark eyes openly assessed him. "Why aren't you coming with us?" she asked at length.

Millot felt on surer ground. "I have family . . . friends. I'm going to try to find them."

She nodded and turned away. That was something she could understand. Millot retired to his own room which he had rented on the floor below.

He would have liked to take Blanche fully into his confidence, but he had decided that he could not take that risk. Blanche's antipathy to Adam almost equaled her hatred of Duhet. By her lights, both men were abusers of women. When he thought about it, Blanche seemed to view all men in that light, even himself—preposterous woman! And such a waste! He had not noticed her much in the commissioner's headquarters in Rouen. To him she had been merely one of the maids, a soft-spoken, retiring girl. He'd since learned that she'd been playing a part. Released from the constrictions of that role, Blanche became a virago. Such a woman must always wear the breeches.

On further reflection, he allowed that that wasn't precisely true. The day he had burst in upon her and threatened to murder her, Blanche had been something of a clinging vine. Her relief at seeing him was stunning, to say the least. She had wept copiously. Millot could never withstand a woman's tears.

His rage had dissolved. He'd taken her into his arms and comforted her as though she were a child. When she was sufficiently recovered, between broken sobs, she had related the events which had driven her to write the letter and sign Claire's name to it.

After that, he could not be angry with her. If Verity had been his sister, he would have found a way to punish Duhet. Women should leave such things to men, and so he had told Blanche. She had accepted his words meekly.

More sternly, he had reproached her for meddling in an affair she knew nothing about. He had not meant to say so much, only to impress upon her that she had almost brought catastrophe on the head of a very fine man.

"There were two Duhets?" she asked incredulously.

He had answered in the affirmative.

Blanche's tears dried. Her chin came up. She had no more respect for the one than she had for the other, she told Millot. Stung, Millot elaborated a little. Without revealing Adam's identity, he told her of the many lives which had been saved since the real Duhet's brother had taken command in Rouen.

Blanche was unimpressed. Claire was enduring unspeakable hardships. In her eyes, that damned both brothers equally. Millot gave up the argument. He had already revealed too much.

Since then, he did not know what to make of Blanche. For the most part, she reminded him of a mythical Greek heroine, the kind of woman to be found in the dramas of Euripides. At other times, especially after one of her visits to the Conciergerie, she was like a child, looking to him for support and advice. Women, he had decided, wanted things both ways. When it suited them, they insisted on ordering their own lives. When their troubles became too much for them, they expected some strong male to step in and assume them.

Women were not the same docile creatures they once were. The Revolution and the rhetoric of the new French philosophers had put strange ideas into their heads. They demanded the same freedoms as men. They did not know when they were well off. He didn't understand Blanche and all women like her. He was horrified. At the same time, he was fascinated.

Very soon, they must part company. Blanche refused to be separated from Claire. Claire needed her. Millot was grateful for the way things had fallen out. He did not wish to leave France at present, and someone must look after Claire till Adam assumed his responsibilities.

Millot would see both ladies take ship for America with a letter of introduction to his good friend John Burke, and then he would wash his hands of the whole affair. Surely, then, he would have atoned for the wrong he had done Claire?

He contemplated that moment when Adam came face-to-face with Claire. He almost wished that he could be there to see it. The fireworks would be spectacular. When he discovered the truth, Adam would be properly chastened. Millot hoped, quite sincerely, that Claire would give Adam a hard time. It was a damn sight less than he deserved.

Armed with false papers and disguised in peasants' clothes, they made the perilous journey to Bordeaux. With the help of a shipping agent, an old friend of his father, Millot was able to obtain places for Claire and Blanche aboard the first American ship to leave Bordeaux harbor in over a year. The *Diana* was bound for Boston. He impressed on both ladies the urgency of reaching New York where he had friends who would assist them. Blanche did not need persuading. What she knew of Boston, she did not like. She had heard that there were no theaters there. Boston was too staid for her taste. New York was more cosmopolitan.

A small boat was to row them downstream to the ship. They said their farewells on the jetty of the Quai des Chartrons. Claire was first to step into the boat.

Millot turned to face Blanche. He felt elated. Laughing, sweeping her into his arms, he kissed her soundly. Her struggles soon ceased and she kissed him back.

"Wait for me in New York," he said. "Then I shall know where to find you."

She tossed her head, "Men are always telling women to wait for them," she retorted. "I wait for no man."

He gave her a sharp swat on the posterior and laughed. "You'll wait for me," he said, and kissed her again.

Smiling, Millot watched the boat till it was well downstream. He turned back into the town. Bordeaux was agog with the news of Commissioner Tallien's recall to the Convention. A new commissioner was to replace him. It seemed that Commissioner Tallien had been too lenient. The Terror was to be stepped up.

While Claire and Blanche embarked on the long sea voyage that would take them to America, Adam reached Paris. He arrived to chaos. The capital was used to bloodletting but never more so than in the following weeks. In quick succession, various factions in the Convention were denounced and followed each other to the guillotine. Adam was sickened by what he saw. In his drive to become dictator, Robespierre's passion knew no limits.

The prisons were packed to the rafters. It was almost impossible to discover who had passed through them, so irregular were their records. The name of Philippe Duhet was entered in the Conciergerie, but no one seemed to know what had become of him. There was no record of his release. Adam did not know why he mentioned the name of Claire Michelet. The clerk was happy to inform him that that particular prisoner's records were complete. She had been released two weeks before.

Adam was stunned. Claire had been incarcerated in the Conciergerie! He could not believe it. He did not wish to believe it. The very thought made his flesh crawl. Something in his calculations had gone very far wrong. He could not begin to speculate on what had happened.

Demented, desperate, he searched for her everywhere. He went to Rouen, uncaring of the risks he ran. Claire was nowhere to be found.

Book II

The Unmasking

Chapter Fourteen

If she closed her eyes, for a few minutes at a time, Claire could almost imagine that she was in the house in Saint-Germain. There was a sense of belonging. The servants were kind to her. She was an honored member of the family. Her garments were of the finest materials. Her body was pampered. Her skin was faintly perfumed. And her host, John Burke, unfailingly addressed her in her native tongue.

But when she opened her eyes, the dream faded. She was in the lavender room. The servants were mostly black slaves. The furniture was after the English style, rich mahoganies and walnuts, polished to a mirror perfection. Her gowns were too elegant for her mother's modest taste, high-waisted with a dearth of ornamentation, after the latest fashions from Paris. Even her hair was cut and styled in the current mode. Small curls framed her face. Ringlets fell to her shoulders. And she had only to step outside the door of John Burke's great red-bricked mansion on Broadway, and the dream faded to oblivion.

The noise was remarkable, even to one who was inured to the hustle and bustle of Paris. New York was a seaport, and therein lay the difference. At every crossroads one might glimpse water and sails. The wharves were a hive of activity. An army of drivers and their carts were engaged in moving goods to and from warehouses to destinations all over Manhattan. Their raucous calls were intermingled with the cries of street vendors pushing handcarts filled with every kind of mouth-watering comestible for sale to eat on the spot.

The city itself was an odd mixture. There were steep-roofed Dutch houses of a former era, and there were stately Georgian mansions complete with white plaster porticoes. In Paris, Claire was used to a magnificence which was not evident here. But it was the cold magnificence of white marble. She infinitely preferred the yellow and red-bricked buildings of New York. The architecture suited the residents. Warm. Friendly. Informal.

Yet passions smoldered beneath the surface. The gentlemen fought duels at the drop of a hat. The ladies were spared most of the gory details. As is the way of things the world over, however, women soon wormed the scandals out of their menfolk. To Claire, having recently escaped the Terror in France, the quarrels between gentlemen seemed nonsensical as well as frightening. By her lights, Americans enjoyed the most just form of government in the world. For a man to risk his life for a small point of honor seemed almost blasphemous. The gentlemen did not agree with her. Scarcely a week went by when the dread word "Weehawken" was not bandied about in some assembly or other. Weehawken was just across the river in New Jersey. It was there that the gentlemen settled their differences with pistols at twenty paces. Claire's nightmares took a new twist.

That thought engaged her mind as she readied herself for the assembly which regularly took place every Friday evening in the ballroom of the City Tavern. In New York, every tenth building was a tavern. Most were exactly as the name indicated, a public inn where travelers might put up for the night, or where gentlemen could enjoy a tipple in convivial company. The City Tavern was exceptional. It was the former mansion of the Delancey family. Only the crème de la crème of New York society entered its magnificent portals. Its stables could house, at a pinch, up to two hundred horses.

As was to be expected, for these assemblies, the patrons were decked out in their most elegant finery. The mature matrons continued to adopt the regal fashions from London. Not for them the simple sheaths of silk or satin, *à la Grecque,* which their daughters had ordered from the influx of Parisian modistes who proliferated in New York. The gentlemen, in matters of fashion, followed the ladies' lead. The younger generation had taken up the new vogue for dark, more restrained garments and unpowdered hair. Even here, there was no uniformity, for some grew their hair long and tied it in back with a black ribbon, while others sheared their locks to the collar.

Claire critically assessed her reflection in the looking glass. She was fortunate to have fallen heir to any number of fine gowns which Sarah Burke's youngest daughter had left behind on the occasion of her marriage the year before. Jane had subsequently removed to her husband's home in Connecticut. Sarah's youngest daughter, Claire deduced, was up to the mark on the latest fashions. The sheath of pale blue silk would have passed muster in Paris.

A little black maid draped a matching silk shawl around Claire's shoulders. There was no need for anything heavier, for the temperature was comfortably warm. Claire picked up her fan, warned her maid, Dulcie, not to make herself sick on the bonbons she had left for her, and slowly made her way to her hostess's drawing room on the ground floor.

Besides herself and the Burkes there were two others making up their party—Betsy Fulton, the eldest daughter, who was visiting with her children from Hanover, and David Burke, John Burke's brother, and younger than he by a good twenty years.

When she entered the room, all conversation died. Claire's first thought was that she must have been the topic of conversation. It troubled her not one whit. The Burkes were not malicious. They had adopted her as though she were a daughter of the house. John Burke had given her to understand that he had made her father's acquaintance years before, when he had traveled in France to trace his Huguenot forbears. A friendship had developed. For a time, he and Leon Devereux had kept up a correspondence. Claire thought it a marvelous coincidence that of all the people in America to whom Millot might have sent her, he chanced upon the one who was intimately acquainted with a member of her family.

Sarah came forward and crooned appreciatively over Claire's borrowed finery. John pressed a glass of lemonade into her hand, and the conversation resumed where it had left off when Claire entered the room. She sipped her drink slowly. Adam Dillon. She had heard the name before but could not remember in what connection. His ship had docked that very afternoon, and the whole of society, it seemed, was eager to renew his acquaintance. Claire listened in silence. Evidently, Adam Dillon was a great favorite with the Burkes.

"Poor Adam," said Sarah, "to be holed up for months in a French port. No wonder public opinion is turning against the French. What right have they to interfere with American merchant ships?"

"None whatsoever," agreed her husband amicably. "But the British are no better. Were it not for a most fortuitous fog blanketing the coast of France, the *Diana* might very easily have fallen prey to a British frigate, as Claire can testify."

Truth to tell, Claire remembered very little of the voyage from Bordeaux to Boston. As soon as the

French coast had faded from view, that strange inertia had returned to claim her. She could not seem to summon more than a passing interest in past, present, or future. It was Blanche who had bullied her into writing a letter to her sister and brother in England, and Blanche who had secured a promise from the captain that on landing in Boston, he would undertake to see that the letter was conveyed to England.

The New World had gradually worked a change in Claire. She saw that here, of all places, was the possibility of a fresh start. Her sufferings were not so unique. Others had fared far worse. They had not wallowed in self-pity. America had been the making of them. They had made fortunes, established dynasties. Claire deemed that she was more fortunate than most. She was young. She was healthy. And she had landed on the doorstep of a family who accepted her without qualification.

She knew that she could not remain as a guest with the Burkes indefinitely. Her pride spurred her to make a push for independence, as Blanche had done. Blanche had hired herself on as an actress. New York, unfortunately, did not support a resident drama company as did the major cities of Europe. Blanche had been obliged to go on tour. The girls had talked in general terms of opening a school of deportment for young ladies when Blanche returned at the end of the season. Until such time, Claire was content to drift.

She became conscious that she had come in for some good-natured cajolery. Betsy's blue eyes, so like her father's, danced mischievously.

"I can scarcely wait to see Claire's effect on him. As we all know, Adam has an eye for a pretty face, and Claire's beauty is breathtaking." Claire's brows winged upward, and Betsy laughed. "Oh very good, Claire! That look would freeze live coals! Do practice it on Adam. It's about time some female cut Adam

233

Dillon down to size!"

"Betsy!" protested her mother. "Anyone would think that you did not like Adam."

"Nonsense, Mama. Like every other female who hasn't quite reached her dotage, I'm a fool for Adam. All the ladies love him." She wagged her finger playfully. "But I warn you, Claire, he's a heartbreaker. Keep your distance or you'll rue the day."

"Betsy," said her father dryly, "you are a young matron of three-and-thirty. You have young children in your care. Kindly try to conduct yourself in a more mature fashion, else I shall advise Alex that he should swat you more regularly."

"Yes, Papa," answered Betsy irrepressibly, and winked at Claire.

Claire had met Betsy's husband, Alex Fulton, only once, when he had delivered his wife and children to her parents' home some weeks before. Alex Fulton, like his in-laws the Burkes, was of a gentle disposition. Claire could not imagine him swatting a fly.

David Burke took Claire's empty glass from her hand. He smiled into her eyes. "I'll stick to you like a limpet," he promised. "No one will trouble you, else I shall make myself very disagreeable."

At these faintly loverlike words, mother and daughter exchanged a startled look. Over the rim of her glass, Sarah surreptitiously contemplated her young brother-in-law.

David Burke, at five-and-thirty, was a fine-looking man. His thick dark hair was tied in back with a black ribbon. His garments, though sober, were exquisitely tailored. David had presence. He was less serious than the rest of the Burke clan. But Sarah did not find fault with the young man on that score. In her opinion all the Burkes wanted a little leavening. In her own small way, she considered herself the spice that added a little flavor to her husband's life. David Burke had no need of spice.

He was presumed to be a confirmed bachelor. What was not generally known was that David had formed an ineligible connection with a married lady some years before. The complacent husband, like himself, was a member of Congress. Many ladies in Philadelphia had set their caps for David Burke. He had deigned to notice nary a one.

On settling down at the Burke household two weeks before, he had apologized for having only a day or two to spare to catch up on family gossip. That was before he met Claire. There was no talk now of rushing back to Philadelphia to attend to his numerous duties.

Sarah smiled a secret smile to herself. Betsy, recognizing that smile, looked a question at her father. John Burke, thinking only of Adam, frowned. His tone was uncharacteristically testy when he said, "Stuff and nonsense! Claire is too young for flirtations and such like. She is hardly more than a child. Adam is like a member of the family. It would never enter his head to offer insult to a lady who is under my protection."

Claire was becoming bored to tears with the topic of Adam Dillon. It was not necessary for her to make his acquaintance to grasp the gentleman's character. She'd met his like in the salons of Paris. Her dimples flashing, she said demurely, "I am not so young as you think me, John. I'm one-and-twenty. I'm French. I've long since outgrown the practiced flatteries of charming flirts, be they ever so handsome."

Everyone laughed.

As it turned out, Adam Dillon did not make an appearance at the assembly that evening. Nevertheless, his presence was felt. From the moment Claire walked into the ladies' cloakroom to deposit her wrap, till the moment she retrieved it after supper, the name of Adam Dillon was on everyone's lips.

Claire had the pleasure of recognizing many of the ladies to whom Sarah had introduced her in the previous weeks. The pattern of their lives was almost identical to the one Claire had followed in Paris before the Revolution had become a Terror. There were afternoon calls where the ladies conversed over tea and plum cake; there were shopping expeditions to William Street where the most fashionable mantua makers displayed their wares. There were long carriage drives in the country. There were both private parties and public balls, such as the present agreeable affair. And on Sundays, there were church services.

In religious matters, the citizens of New York, so Claire was given to understand, were more tolerant than most. There were twenty-two churches representing thirteen denominations, some of which Claire had never even heard of before. Claire was a Catholic. In France, there had been religious persecutions. It was years since she had attended Mass. In New York, she followed the Burkes' example. John Burke was a church warden at Trinity, the prestigious Episcopalian church. Every Sunday, Claire sat with the Burkes in their family pew. Occasionally, she idly debated with herself whether or not she should make herself known to a priest of her own faith. The matter hardly seemed pressing. Time passed, and she did nothing about it.

The first person who met them as they stepped into the cloakroom was Sarah's contemporary and very best friend, Mrs. Martha Armstrong. Her opening remarks were to be the model for everything which followed that evening. Adam Dillon was the subject of her conversation.

"Lily's nose is out of joint," she told Sarah gleefully.

Claire affected an interest in arranging her curls at one of the long pier glasses. The two older ladies bent their heads together and dropped their voices, but Claire overheard every word. The rumor was that the beautiful young widow was incensed. Adam had given Lily her walking papers. Scarcely had she welcomed the return of her erstwhile lover when he had declared his intention of taking ship for France as soon as he had cleared the press of business which had accumulated in his absence.

Later in the evening, Claire had the privilege of being introduced to Lily Randolph. It was Betsy who did the honors. Naturally, Claire was curious. In one comprehensive glance, she took the beauty's measure. The lady was wealthy. She was fashionable, after the French manner. And for some inexplicable reason, she was also hostile. Claire was dismissed with a deliberate flick of the eyelashes before the lady moved away.

The exchange delighted Betsy. "She's jealous," she said. "I never thought I'd see the day, but Lily Randolph is positively green with envy. You're a potential rival, you see."

Claire looked sideways at her companion. "Why do you dislike Mrs. Randolph?"

"I? Dislike Lily Randolph? I'll have you know that we were at school together." After a moment Betsy grinned sheepishly. "When I was a young girl, she stole all my beaux," she confessed.

Claire laughed and in the next breath refused several young bucks who descended upon her to secure the next dance. Her manners were charming. Her smile was sincere. These young men posed no threat to her. They reminded her of eager young puppies bent on mischief.

Couples were taking the floor for a stately cotillion. "A dowager's dance," disparaged Betsy. "Let's sit this one out."

They watched from the sidelines. David Burke joined them for a moment or two, but was soon called away to converse with a number of the gentlemen. He threw Claire a pained look of apology.

"I'm glad that affair is over," observed Betsy idly. Claire had no difficulty in deducing that they had returned to the boring topic of Adam Dillon and his notorious liaison with the lady who had dismissed her with a flick of her long lashes.

Betsy sighed. "Adam ought to get married, settle down, set up his nursery. He would make a wonderful father. He has a way with children." She sighed again. "Unhappily," she went on, "he also has a way with women. His interest never fixes on one girl for long."

Claire, thinking of the poor girl who must one day sacrifice herself on the altar of his dynastic ambitions, suppressed a shudder. As the evening wore on, everything she heard about Adam Dillon only reinforced her first impression. The man was a libertine of the first order. Conversely, he was also the biggest prize on the matrimonial market. The more she heard, the more cynical Claire's smile became. Fond mamas looked as eagerly to the glass entrance doors as did their fledglings. Lily Randolph, however, was taking no chances. Like a sentry on duty, she patrolled the area. By the time David Burke led Claire into supper, one interesting fact had emerged. Adam Dillon, in spite of his unsavory reputation, was universally liked.

Claire dismissed the libertine from her thoughts, and gave her attention to her partner. For some time, they talked in generalities about Philadelphia, and David's work as a congressman. To the Burkes, public service was a family tradition. The Devereux at one time had held an equally estimable position in France, but of a different character.

"The king was absolute monarch," explained Claire. "The only way for a man who was not an aristocrat to advance himself was through commerce or, more recently, the army."

"Did your father ever mention my brother's name?"

"Not to my knowledge." This was something which had puzzled Claire. After reading Millot's letter of introduction, John Burke had greeted her as a long-lost relative. It seemed odd that her father had made no mention of such close friends in America.

"Tell me about your family," David prompted.

She told him about the early days, when it had seemed to her that her parents were demigods. A sparkle crept into her eyes. Her dimples were flashing. It would have surprised Claire to know that her own name figured in conversations almost as often as did Adam Dillon's. Her companion knew it. Like others in that ballroom, he was captivated by Claire Devereux.

"Now it's your turn," she teased. "How is it that you are so much younger than your brother?"

"I," he said gravely, "was an afterthought, or rather, no thought at all. My parents, like Abraham and Sarah, believed that they were too old to be fruitful."

"Did you have no brothers or sisters apart from John?"

"Several," he answered, making a face. "But thankfully, the last of them left the nest soon after I was born. And so I reigned in solitary splendor."

She laughed. "I'll wager you were spoiled."

"Do I seem spoiled to you?"

"No. But then, I scarcely know you."

"You may have observed that I am doing my best to rectify that omission." His mouth curved.

They fell silent for a moment. He made a gesture with one hand. "I've been fighting off the competition all evening. You don't seem to notice the hordes of young blades who are panting to be introduced to you. Most young ladies would be highly gratified.

239

You are a most unusual specimen, Miss Devereux."

Her eyes danced. "They remind me of my younger scapegrace brother. I am more partial to mature gentlemen, such as John Burke, or yourself, for instance."

He laughed. "What news of your brother and sister?"

Claire looked down at her plate. She selected a sweet biscuit and nibbled daintily before replying, "I should like them to come here to be with me." She gave him a steady look. "I like America. I think they will like it too. I've written asking them to join me, if only my letter will find them."

"It will," he said, and gently squeezed the hand in her lap.

Claire was no fool. David Burke was clearly demonstrating a partiality toward her. She gently withdrew her hand. To distract him, she said the first thing that came into her head. "Tell me about Adam Dillon." Inwardly, she groaned.

That night, for the first time in weeks, sleep eluded her. A fierce sadness had taken hold. She was thinking of the old days, the old places and the old faces. It seemed to her, then, that the best and the finest part of her life was over. Nothing that came in the future could ever hope to match those magical days of her young life when she had been supremely happy without being aware of it. Everything worthwhile was gone. The flower of France had perished in a tide of blood—those carefree young men and beautiful young girls who had graced her mother's ballroom in Saint-Germain. Where, oh God, where were they now? In desperation, she forced herself to think of the present.

David Burke. He was pleasant to look upon, of medium height, well built, and with eyes as clear and as blue as a mountain lake. When he smiled, which he did often, those eyes crinkled at the corners. He was John's youngest brother, but Claire would never have guessed that they were related. David was too much the gallant. He was more fashionable, more worldly, less serious than John. Still, when she was with him, she felt safe.

The next thought struck at her before she could prevent it. Philippe. She did not know his real name. She hoped she never would. He had used her and discarded her like so much refuse. He had nearly destroyed her. The pain almost shattered her. A confusion of thoughts spilled into her mind.

Of a sudden, she had a recollection of something she had said to John Burke about the whole tribe of Devereux. The name of Devereux stood for something. She'd had those lessons drummed into her along with her catechism at her grandmother's knee.

The Devereux had risen from nothing to make their mark on France, Grandmère had told her. They had suffered crushing defeats only to rise again. The blood of generals ran in their veins, as did the blood of felons. In each generation, there was a Devereux who pulled himself up by his bootstraps and set about rebuilding the family fortunes.

Claire had no memory of names, had no memory of each personal history. In those days, the stories her grandmother had passed on had seemed to resemble the myths and legends of ancient Greece. Her father made light of Grandmère's revelations. They were an embarrassment to him. Those days were gone forever. The Devereux were firmly established in French society. They had the king's favor. Events proved that he was not so farseeing as Grandmère.

The name of Devereux stood for something, if only she could remember it. Claire let her thoughts drift. Grandmère's soft tones seemed to echo in her head. Honor, duty, valor—many noble houses claimed these virtues as their own. The Devereux claimed something unique. Resurrection.

241

It was the wrong word, but the thought was exactly right. Resurrection. The dogma of the church had become inextricably tangled in her child's mind with the dogma of the Devereux. And she would be damned by all former generations of Devereux if she allowed herself to sink under the weight of her misfortunes. The thought was vaguely comforting. By degrees, she drifted into sleep.

In another part of the house, John and Sarah Burke readied themselves for bed. Sarah was brushing out her long hair. "Did you hear what Claire said before we left for the assembly?" she asked.

John's face was averted. He was removing odds and ends from his pockets. His movements stilled. "What did she say?"

"She said that she was one-and-twenty. I understood that Leon Devereux was a single man when you met him first in '72?"

"I don't know what gave you that idea," answered John, and he carefully set down an enamel snuff box on the flat of a walnut dresser. He traced the pattern on the lid with his eyes.

"It's so long ago," said Sarah, quite unaware of the tension emanating from her husband. "I suppose I made an error." She laughed softly. "At the time, I was taken up with my own woes. I had just been delivered of our fifth daughter and was sunk in despair. I did not know how I was to greet you with the sad news when you returned from France." She twisted on her dressing-table stool to face him. "You've never reproached me for failing to give you a son. Yet, you are a man. You must have felt that lack."

Gradually his harsh features relaxed into a smile. "I would not exchange one of my daughters for a dozen sons. Besides, now that they are all married, our girls have brought five very presentable young men into the family."

"Not to mention grandsons," added Sarah.

"I like my granddaughters equally as well."

"Still . . ." Sarah turned back to watch herself in the mirror. "You must sometimes wish that your name could continue."

"There are plenty of Burkes to carry on the name. I have never held with that foolishness as you well know, Sarah. Our blood continues, by whatever name."

Sarah's next observation grated on John's ears. "David seems quite taken with Claire. Did you see the way he looked at her? She's very beautiful, of course. She draws men's eyes like a magnet."

"What nonsense is this? David and Claire? It's impossible!"

Sarah's hand stilled. "Why is it impossible?"

John struggled out of his coat and began to undo the buttons of his waistcoat. "My brother is too old for her," he said gruffly.

"Is he?" Sarah seemed to consider the matter. At length, she observed, "I don't think David would agree with you. I suppose Adam is quite out of the picture?"

"I thought you liked the girl?"

"I do."

"Then why this unseemly haste to marry her off?"

"Unseemly haste?" Sarah laughed. "Your own daughters were all married by the time they reached Claire's age. Good God, John, you yourself were that very age when you married me. Have you forgotten that I was barely sixteen?"

His answer was indistinct. Sarah's brows knit together. After a moment, she returned to her task, and said in a more thoughtful tone, "My dear, marriage is the only solution that presents itself. Claire is too proud to stay on with us indefinitely.

She won't want to accept our charity. Then where will she be? And with the prospect of no dowry, a suitable marriage may be difficult to arrange. Adam wouldn't care a fig whether or not a girl was well dowered, and David, I'm sure, shares his sentiments."

John had nothing to say to these moot points. When Sarah slipped into bed beside him, his arms went round her, pulling her close. "Do you love me?" he whispered.

"I love you," she answered, pressing herself to his length.

"You are my heart," he told her. "Without you . . . ah Sarah, show me how much you love me."

Later, sleepy and sated, he listened to his wife's even breathing. He had loved Sarah from the moment he had first caught a glimpse of her on his way to classes as a student of law at King's College. He was barely twenty years old. Sarah was fifteen. He was inexperienced, and totally unprepared for the passions which overwhelmed him. He could not keep his hands off her. He was terrified that he would dishonor her.

A year later, he asked for her hand in marriage. Both sets of parents were aghast. It was not that they opposed the match. The Burkes and Schullers were leading families in New York. Such an alliance could only find favor. But not yet. John had years to go before he was established. They were both so young. Love did not enter into the calculations of their parents.

John chose his weapons with care. To his own religious father, he quoted scripture. To Sarah's worldly parents, he prophesied scandal. He would have her with or without benefit of marriage. Finally, their elders relented. John took Sarah to wife. She filled his whole soul.

Almost fifteen years were to pass before he was

tested. Juliette Devereux was breathtakingly beautiful. From the moment she had come into his line of vision, he was smitten with the girl. She was an innocent. She was barely twenty. He was five-and-thirty years old.

He was missing his Sarah. That much he remembered. And then all thoughts of Sarah were ruthlessly suppressed when he walked into his bedchamber to find Juliette Devereux waiting for him. God! In her own father's house with her brother in the next room! For more than two months he indulged in this insanity before he put a stop to it. The girl would not listen to reason. She went to her brother.

He'd tried to make amends. But what amends could he make? The Devereux did not want for money. He was a married man with a wife and children waiting for him at home. It was a matter of honor. Leon Devereux would be happy with nothing less than his blood. He had betrayed their friendship. He had dishonored his sister.

There was a duel. Leon Devereux had aimed to kill him. John had stood there like a target and was only sorry when the bullet hit the fleshy part of his shoulder and not his heart. His own honor lay in ruins.

Life must go on. Sarah was waiting for him in America. He had not known how well he could act, how easily he could pretend that nothing of any significance had occurred while he was away. But it wasn't acting. Because as soon as Sarah's arms closed around him he knew that whatever he'd had with Juliette Devereux was as a shadow compared to this. Sarah was his heart, his life. She was dearer to him than honor.

It was that poor girl who was forced to pay the penalty for his sin. More than ten years were to pass before he discovered it. He and Sarah were on an

245

extended tour. They were in France as the guests of Benjamin Franklin. God forgive him, but he had scarcely spared a thought for Juliette Devereux in the intervening years. He'd fought in a war. He had become a statesman. He'd raised a brood of children. In France, his thoughts had naturally turned to the girl. He wished merely to assure himself that things went well with her. His letters to Leon Devereux were returned unopened. It was Benjamin Franklin who had satisfied John's curiosity. The Devereux were well known in France. There was a sister who had died a number of years before. Her name had slipped his mind.

John was conscience-stricken. He'd come down with a fever. When he recovered, he'd hired men to ferret out what had become of Juliette Devereux. In his heart, he knew what they would uncover before their findings were put into his hand. Juliette Devereux had died in childbirth. She had been delivered of a girl-child. No one knew what had become of her baby.

Always, he had wondered, half fearful, half hopeful, until Juliette's daughter had walked into his study some weeks ago with a letter of introduction from Nicholas Millot. John did not believe in coincidence. In everything, he saw the hand of God.

He would have recognized her anywhere. Those finely sculpted features! That halo of red-gold hair! Only the eyes were different. His eyes, a true blue without a trace of either gray or green. Claire Devereux was his daughter. He would stake his life on it.

He did not know what he was going to do about it. Sarah's words had disturbed him. Claire would not wish to exist on the charity of strangers for long. Marriage was the only solution that presented itself.

But not with his brother! David was Claire's uncle. If the worst came to the worst David must be told.

John did not think it would come to that. David was thoroughly enamored of Mrs. Baynard of Philadelphia.

Marriage was the easiest solution. Adam's name came to mind and was instantly rejected. Adam Dillon was not a marrying man. There were others who would fall over themselves to claim the girl's hand, if she were well dowered. John's mind sifted through the names of those young gentlemen of his acquaintance who would meet with his approval. His last thoughts were of Sarah and his newfound daughter. Whatever happened, he did not want Sarah or Claire to be hurt. Oh God, they must not be hurt.

Chapter Fifteen

Claire was upstairs in the nursery helping Betsy ready the children for bed when the sound of Sarah's voice carried to them from the front hall.

"Adam! It's Adam! John, come quickly!"

Doors opened and slammed. "Adam!" John's words became muffled, but there was no mistaking the welcome in his voice.

Betsy was up to her elbows in bathwater. Her infant son gurgled as his small fists sent a stream of water in every direction. "Adam is downstairs!" exclaimed Betsy, and looked helplessly at Claire.

Claire and Dulcie were pulling nightclothes on two squirming infants. "Go on down," said Claire, moving to Betsy's side. "Dulcie and I will manage the children."

"You don't mind?" Betsy's look was hopeful.

"I don't mind."

It was all the encouragement Betsy needed. She smiled brilliantly at Claire. "You are a dear!" she said, and deftly slipped her precious burden into Claire's outstretched arms.

Master Paul, at nine months, was not quite sure that he approved this sudden change of nurses. His lower lip trembled. His eyes searched for his mother, but Betsy was already halfway to the door. She rushed to the stair rail and leaned over. "Adam!" she called out. "Adam!"

A masculine voice laughed and called out in reply, "Betsy! How's my best girl?"

Betsy picked up her skirts and dashed toward the head of the stairs. The air of rapture was contagious. Claire and Dulcie laughed together.

"Dat Mr. Adam some mighty fine man," observed Dulcie wisely.

"I'm sure." Claire became involved in distracting Master Paul from venting his displeasure at his mama's sudden desertion. She tickled his ribs. He frowned. She splashed him with bathwater. He glowered. She was saved from complete ignominy by the superior knowledge of Master Paul's two older sisters. Mary and Lizzie had a whole repertoire of animal sounds which sent their young brother into convulsions of giggles.

The sounds of homecoming gradually faded. Claire presumed that everyone must have removed to Sarah's little parlor where only members of the family were invited or their intimates. Adam Dillon must certainly be counted as such.

David Burke had related something of the gentleman's history to Claire at the City Tavern when she had impulsively invited him to do so. She must give credit where credit was due. Adam Dillon had made the most of his opportunities.

His early years, David had told her, were something of an enigma. He was Irish with a dash of French thrown in for good measure. He had arrived in America as a penniless youth. He'd fought in the Revolutionary War. He had engaged in the fur trade. On retiring from that business, his rise had been nothing short of meteoric.

"John had hopes that Adam would enter law," said David. "But Adam wasn't interested in a career in public service. John made him a small loan, Adam put it to good use."

For the first time Claire experienced some fellow feeling for Adam Dillon. She thought she understood what motivated him. Her own father and his father before him had made their mark and their money in commerce. For the next generation of Devereux commerce was not good enough. Leon Devereux did not wish his son to follow in his footsteps. Young Leon was to be a gentleman and live a life of indolence. Others would manage his business interests for him.

In America, indolence was frowned upon. To devote one's time and energies to the service of one's country was the highest good a man could aim for. Only a man of property could indulge his interest in politics. Evidently, Adam Dillon aimed to make himself a man of property. Succeeding generations of Dillons would have the means and the freedom to choose their own course.

Claire had just settled Master Paul in his crib when she received a summons to join the company in the green room. She wasn't interested in Adam Dillon. But she was a female. She detoured to her own chamber where she made a quick inventory in the looking glass. Her white spotted-muslin was passable, though she felt only half dressed with so few petticoats. Her fashionably short hair was more to her taste. It was easily managed. She quickly ran a comb through it.

Adam Dillon was held in the highest esteem and affection in the Burke household, she reminded herself as she descended the stairs. She was a guest in that house. It behooved her to be at her most agreeable. Pinning a smile on her lips, she pushed into Sarah's green parlor.

Claire glanced idly across the room at the gentleman who was the center of attention, and all the color seeped out of her face. She was staring at Philippe

250

Duhet or his double. Her thoughts were chaotic; her breathing was not quite regular. She thought she might be on the point of fainting. Adam Dillon must be—who? He was either Philippe Duhet, the former Comte de Blaise, or his half-brother, the man she had known in Rouen. Which one? her mind screamed.

On becoming aware of her entrance, the gentlemen all rose. John brought her forward and made the introductions. Claire was trembling like a leaf. She did not know what account she gave of herself. She chanced a glance into those green eyes, but not a flicker of recognition registered. She accepted a chair but declined the proffered tea. She was shaking so badly that managing a cup and saucer was beyond her.

She struggled to pull herself together and was aware of David Burke's narrowed glance. No one else seemed to observe her agitation. Thankfully, they were all intent on Philippe, hanging on his every word. David's brows knit together and Claire flashed him what she hoped was a reassuring smile before turning her attention to the guest of honor.

What she observed both quieted her nerves and, at the same time, plunged her into despair. She was almost sure that Adam Dillon was the real Philippe, though he was leaner. His face was gaunt. Worry lines were etched into his forehead. His hair was different, shorter, just brushing his collar.

A glass of sherry was thrust into her hand and she looked up into David's searching stare.

"Drink it," he said softly, and she obeyed.

He nudged his chair closer to Claire's and seated himself. There was an odd silence. Everyone was looking at Claire. She had missed something, and did not know how to respond. John Burke took it upon himself to answer for her.

"Claire arrived in New York some three weeks ago. A most interesting coincidence, Adam! Claire's father is an old friend, Leon Devereux. I may have mentioned his name to you? Unhappily, Claire's parents were arrested. She is most anxious to hear news of them, as you may understand."

Adam and John exchanged a long look. The younger man nodded. "Leon Devereux. Yes. The name sounds familiar. I regret to say, however, that I know nothing of his fate."

At this point, Sarah, meaning only to direct the conversation into happier channels interposed, "Adam, do say you can delay your departure. I am giving a ball to introduce Claire to society. Your presence can only guarantee its success."

"Claire is her own guarantee." The curt words came from David Burke.

"Of course, I did not mean to suggest . . ."

"You heard Adam, Sarah," David said, as though there had been no interruption. "His business in France is urgent. He cannot afford to waste time on frivolity."

Adam smiled easily. "You misunderstood, David. Perhaps I did not explain myself clearly. Let me do so now. There is a warehouse in La Rochelle with my name on it. I have contracted to have it filled with French silks and cognacs in a month or so. At present, all my ships are in American ports. To delay may cost me my cargo. It is not necessary for me to go to France in person to supervise things. My captains are good fellows. Naturally, I should be delighted to accept an invitation to Miss Devereux's ball."

Sarah crowed with delight. Betsy looked merely amused. Claire was still struggling to regain her calm. She was scarcely aware when David left her side to replenish his glass from a decanter on the sideboard.

A number of things were jogging her memory. Adam Dillon's early years were shrouded in mystery. He was of French extraction. And he had been holed up in France for the last number of months.

There were other things of more significance. There was a certain inflection in his voice, a way of concealing his expression with the sweep of his lashes, certain betraying gestures which had slipped her mind until the present moment. And that smile . . .

Their glances brushed and locked. Claire sucked in her breath. *You* her eyes blazed at him. A muscle in Adam's cheek tensed. Claire started to her feet. The room spun crazily around her head.

She was conscious of several cries of alarm, and then she was enfolded in arms of iron and carried up the stairs. A woman's voice made soft crooning sounds in her ear. Claire was gently deposited on top of the covers on her bed.

"Betsy, fetch some brandy," Adam said, "and if you can manage it, keep the others out of here for a moment or two. Miss Devereux and I are known to each other. I should like a word with her in private."

Claire moaned weakly. She made a feeble attempt to come to herself. She didn't want to be left alone with him. She didn't want brandy. She wanted a pistol. She was going to kill him.

"I'll send Dulcie for the brandy," said Betsy, "and I'll stand watch outside the door."

Claire heard the soft click of the latch. She flinched when Adam's hands closed around her shoulders.

"Darling, get a hold of yourself," he said. "Do you want the others to know about us? God, when you walked into that room, I thought I was seeing a ghost."

The effort was almost beyond her, but she managed to open her eyes. She made no attempt to shade what she was feeling. Hatred, pure and unadulterated.

"Don't look at me like that," he said harshly. "You brought everything on your own head. I never

253

intended that you should go to the Conciergerie. Something went amiss. If only you hadn't written that letter, we would be together under far different circumstances. Sweetheart, I've been going crazy with worry. I've been searching for you everywhere."

She started to weep.

"Darling, don't! Ah, don't cry! Everything will come right, now that I am here." He kissed her hand passionately. "Claire!" he said, "Claire! How did you find me? Was it Nicholas? Did he send you to me?"

She struggled to free herself, but her movements were weak. She was tired to the marrow. "I shall never forgive you for this," she whimpered.

There was a silence. "So you did not know that I was Adam Dillon?" His hands cupped her shoulders. He gave her a rough shake. "Answer me, Claire!"

"Go away," she whispered brokenly. "Go away. Go away." She kept repeating it till tears clogged her throat.

The door opened to admit Betsy. She flashed Adam a warning look. Raised voices were heard approaching the door. David Burke's tones were strident. "There is something going on and I aim to find out what it is."

"We shall talk later," said Adam, and went to stand at the end of the bed.

The others entered and hovered around helplessly, not knowing what to do. Betsy held Claire's head and urged her to drink from a glass of brandy.

"Claire," said David, throwing a look of pure dislike at Adam, "What on earth came over you?"

It was Adam who answered for her. "Miss Devereux and I met in Paris," he said. "She thought I was dead. It took her a moment or two to recognize me. The shock has been too much for her, poor girl."

David looked as though he was going to be difficult. Betsy, very much in the manner of her

254

mother, took charge and soon cleared the room in the interests of her patient.

She returned to Claire's side and forced her to finish the glass of brandy. Her blue eyes anxiously searched Claire's face. "Sometimes I think I could *kill* Adam," she said.

Claire managed a watery smile. "I'm sure he has that effect on many ladies."

Betsy smiled. "That's better. No man is worth more than a tear or two." She looked away. "You must talk to him, you know."

"No," said Claire. She was too drained to invent a plausible lie to explain her aversion to Adam Dillon. "It's over."

Betsy said nothing. She was thinking that Claire did not know Adam very well if she believed that.

In John Burke's bookroom, Adam sat sprawled in a chair, nursing a glass of whiskey. David Burke had quit the room moments before. Whether or not he was satisfied with the story Adam had concocted to explain his relationship to Claire was debatable. Adam did not care one way or the other. With John Burke, it was different. Adam did not wish to cause his good friend a moment's unrest. John was quite convinced that Claire Devereux was his natural daughter. For Adam to reveal all the circumstances of his relationship with Claire was unthinkable.

"I presume," said John, "that when Claire walked into that room and saw you, she took you for Philippe Duhet?"

"She had no notion that I was Adam Dillon," said Adam.

John nodded. "How did you find her? And what news of the rest of the Devereux? My dear boy, I am impatient to hear the whole story."

Adam embarked on a highly expurgated account

255

of the events in Rouen which had propelled Claire into his life. "She was a schoolteacher. I knew her as Claire Michelet. She came to my notice when Nicholas arranged for her brother and sister to find safe passage to England." He sketched in as many details as seemed appropriate, carefully adhering to the truth as far as possible.

"And Leon Devereux and his wife?" said John. "There is nothing that can be done for them?"

"As I told you, Robespierre and his gang of cutthroats have gone mad. He means to clear all the prisons. No one will escape him." Adam's hand balled into a hard fist, a sure sign of his raging impotence.

"Poor Claire. And who knows what has become of the boy!"

"I saw no reason to disabuse her of the notion that he had reached England. It would have been too cruel."

"I understand. But what I don't understand is this: why did Claire not wish to go to England with them?"

Adam shrugged. "Claire is the only one who can answer that question."

"But you arranged to send her to me?"

"Not I," said Adam. "I did not know that she was Claire Devereux. Nicholas must have discovered her identity after I left Rouen. No, John, I did not reveal your interest in the Devereux to Nicholas, though I may have mentioned something to the effect that there were friends at home who were anxious to help any member of Leon Devereux's family." He hesitated. "You are quite sure, John, that the girl is who she claims to be?"

"I knew before I read a word of Millot's letter."

A silence descended as both gentlemen considered the gaps in their knowledge of the events which had overtaken Claire. Adam considered whether or not he should reveal that Claire had spent some time in the Conciergerie, and decided against it. It would raise questions he did not wish to answer, did not know how to answer.

Finally, he said, "I must be allowed some time to speak with her in private. She knew me only as Philippe Duhet. I must take her into my confidence, or she may make things very awkward for me."

John allowed himself a small smile. "I did my best to give you a few minutes alone with her when you carried her upstairs. David was quite scandalized. Even Sarah looked askance at me."

Adam took a long swallow from his glass. "Your brother seems to have developed quite a proprietary interest in the girl," he said casually.

John's brows came down. "David," he said, "has business in Philadelphia that needs his immediate attention. He does not know it yet, but a letter will arrive for him on the morrow from President Washington with an invitation he may not decline."

Adam laughed. "John," he said, "you wily old fox!"

"I was once a diplomat. One never forgets one's training."

"He'll be back," said Adam.

"Yes. But by that time I hope to have Claire safely married off."

Adam bolted his drink.

In the morning, as John had predicted, a letter was delivered for David Burke's hand. After reading it, he went in search of Claire. He found her in his sister-in-law's cheerful parlor. She was working on a piece of embroidery. Sarah was soliciting her advice on menus.

"Sarah, I should like to speak with Claire," he said.

Sarah could not conceal her delight. She was fond of her young brother-in-law. She had nothing but admiration for Claire. The girl's accomplishments in all the domestic arts was prodigious. Even Sarah's daughters could not match her. Sarah's esteem for the mother of such a paragon knew no bounds. Elise Devereux had fitted her daughter to be the worthy consort of a great man. It was time and enough that David Burke severed his connection with a woman who could never openly be his consort. Claire and David. In Sarah's mind, the two just naturally came together. She left them with a smile.

Drawing a chair closer to Claire's, David seated himself and said without preamble, "What is Adam Dillon to you, Claire?"

Without breaking her concentration, she took a small stitch. "He is nothing to me. Why do you ask?"

After a moment's hesitation, David said, "You were distraught when you saw him yesterday."

Claire knew what Adam had told David. There had been a curt note from him which he had left with Betsy before he had quit the house the night before.

"He arranged for me to leave France. He was arrested. I understood that he had been executed. When I recognized him, the shock was too much for me."

It was evident that David wished to pursue the matter, but Claire's expression was discouraging. "I do not ask out of idle curiosity," he said quietly.

"Oh?" Claire looked about for her scissors as though she had lost interest in the conversation.

"Claire, look at me!" He grasped her wrist. "I . . . I think I may be in love with you."

The shock of his words was evident in her face. He gave her a moment to come to herself before he pushed on. "You will say that we hardly know each other. God, don't you think that I know that? But from the very first there was something between us. It

258

was as though like was calling to like. I feel as though I have known you half my life.

"If there were only more time!" Abruptly, he rose to his feet and began to pace in front of her. "I must return to Philadelphia at once," he said. He turned to face her. "But not for long, Claire, not if you give me the slightest encouragement that my addresses may be received favorably by you."

Claire's brow knit in perplexity. "Are you asking me to marry you?"

"I . . ." He came to sit beside her. Looking intently into her eyes, he said, "There are things I must do before I am free to ask for your hand. Claire, you are not a green girl. I am no callow youth. There is a lady to whom I owe some explanation of my conduct. Once I have spoken to her, I may then speak more freely to you."

Claire did not have to debate her answer. "I wish you would not. It's too soon. We scarcely know each other."

"I had intended to say nothing to you until my return from Philadelphia. But that was before last night. Claire, I ask you again—what does Adam Dillon mean to you?"

Her expression became closed. "As I have already told you, that gentleman means nothing to me."

"I am relieved to hear it."

"But understand this, David. As you say, you are no callow youth. I am no green girl. I do not ask you for explanations of what is no concern of mine. I do not permit any man to question me on what is no concern of his."

She had as much as confessed that she was a woman of experience. They both knew it.

In the silence, David's breathing sounded thick and strained. "I see," he said.

Claire gathered her needlework together, and made to rise. David's grasp on her wrist tightened,

259

preventing her. "And what of a husband, Claire?" he said savagely. "Does a husband merit an explanation?"

"No!" she said coldly.

He released her.

They did not see each other again until David was about to enter the coach that was to take him to Philadelphia. Everyone came out to wave him off, even the slaves and servants.

He bent over Claire's hand. "I shall be back in good time for your ball," he said, and gave her a straight look.

Claire said nothing. John Burke was in fine fettle. Sarah was smirking. Only Betsy looked troubled.

Chapter Sixteen

When the Burkes invited Claire to spend the summer months with them at their country house in New Jersey, she knew that the time was coming when she must chart her future. The social season was wending to a close. Sarah's ball in Claire's honor was only weeks away. By that time, David Burke would have returned from Philadelphia and Blanche's stint with her traveling troupe of actors would be over.

There had been an understanding between the two girls. On Blanche's return to New York they were to set up classes for young ladies in dancing and deportment. There were many such schools in the city. It seemed that New Yorkers were eager to acquire that polish which would distinguish them as ladies and gentleman of some refinement.

There was little doubt in Claire's mind that she and Blanche could quite easily make their living by giving classes to the daughters of the rich. But her heart wasn't in it. And she was perfectly sure that Blanche's heart wasn't in it either. Blanche was laboring under a sense of guilt. The more Claire thought about it, the more she saw the truth of it. Blanche had written the letter which had precipitated the chain of events that had led Claire to the Conciergerie. Blanche was doing her best to make amends. She would stay with Claire as long as she felt she was needed. Freed from the constrictions of her conscience, Blanche might choose to return to France.

Claire was settled in the New World. She had written twice to her brother and sister in England charging them to come to her. Through his bankers in England, John Burke had arranged a loan to pay for their passage. With events in Europe so unsettled, however, and a virtual trade war going on, delays were impossibly long. Moreover, Zoë and Leon could be anywhere in England. It might be months before her letters caught up to them. She had no way of knowing. She must remain in New York to await events. She must find a way to support herself. She toyed with the idea of marrying David Burke. But every time she thought of David, another man's image haunted her.

Adam Dillon was like a specter from her past. He was hounding her. Not a day went by when he did not appear at the Burke's dining table to share some meal or other. And all Claire's carefully constructed defenses began to crumble.

She had hoped to find a fresh start in the New World. She would get over him, she had told herself time without number in the months since she had left France. She had made a good beginning, until an unkind fate had brought them face-to-face in Sarah's small parlor. And all the suppressed memories, all the suppressed emotion, broke through Claire's resolve to tear at her heart.

Night after night, she cried herself to sleep. In the daylight hours, she forced herself to go through the motions of living. No one guessed how fragile was her hard-won control. And always he was there, in the background, waiting to pounce on her.

He wished to speak to her privately. Claire demurred. She felt things too deeply. She was afraid she would disgrace herself. Her thoughts were chaotic.

She did not trust herself. There was a side to herself

she would never have believed existed. There was a girl hiding inside her who did not care for pride or honor or any of the things Claire Devereux valued. That girl would forgive Adam Dillon anything, so long as he wanted her. Claire carefully, deliberately, smothered that girl.

But Adam outmaneuvered her. At the end of a week, his patience ran out. He sent John Burke as his emissary.

"Adam is in my bookroom," said John, watching her gravely. "He's told me a little of your story, Claire. You must not confuse him with Philippe Duhet, you know. Adam is a fine young man. For my sake, I want you to hear him out."

There could be no refusing John's kindly meant request. This time, when she left the children in Dulcie's care to do her host's bidding, she made no detour to her own chamber to check her appearance. The Adam Dillon she knew did not merit such a compliment.

"Shut the door, Claire," he said softly.

Her eyebrows arched but she made no protest. Adam had chosen his ground with forethought. No member of the household would enter John Burke's private sanctum when the door was closed.

She accepted the straight-backed chair he indicated, and laced her fingers together, preserving a stubborn silence. She was not going to make this easy for him. She composed her features into a mask of politeness. Only then did she look at him.

His eyes laughed down at her. "Claire," he said, seating himself within reach of her, "you amaze me! You are the most uncurious female of my acquaintance. I have been in and out of this house for a week and more and you have made no attempt to approach me. Don't you wish to ask me even one question about Rouen and Philippe Duhet? I know that I have a score of questions that I wish to put to you."

There was one question to which no one had given

her a satisfactory answer. "Who are you?" she asked.

Adam breathed deeply. At least she was speaking to him. "My name really is Adam Dillon," he said. "Philippe is my half-brother," and in a few sentences he gave her an account of his early years in France, first with his mother, then with the Comte de Blaise. His tone was noncommittal. He did not want her sympathy, nor did he say anything to arouse that emotion in Claire's breast. She did not ask him to elaborate, but Adam took it upon himself to explain his presence in Rouen.

He said finally, "We saved hundreds of lives, Claire."

She nodded and looked away. Nicholas had told her some of this before. She remembered his words. Duhet's brother was a brave man. He had done a very fine thing. Hundreds of lives had been saved. His conduct with respect to herself, however, had not been so generous. It was the only thing that seemed to matter to her.

"Now tell me about yourself, Claire," he said.

"What do you wish to know?"

"I want to know about Paris, and how you came to be in the Conciergerie."

Her voice was expressionless. "I was Duhet's mistress. He was out of favor. That meant I was out of favor, too."

Adam frowned. "That does not make sense," he said. "You were the one who brought the authorities down on Duhet's head. God, Claire, when I think that you almost sent General Theot to the guillotine, I still want to throttle you! Why in heaven's name did you write that letter? Did you hate me so much?"

This was the moment Claire had been waiting for, the moment when he would discover her innocence and hate himself for everything he had done to her. He would beg her forgiveness, and she would tell him to go to the devil.

"Blanche wrote that letter without my knowledge." She was watching his face intently. "She had a score to settle with Philippe Duhet, you see. At the same time, she wished to protect me from suffering the same fate as he."

Astonishment was the only emotion that crossed his face. "Blanche?" he said. "Wasn't she the little maid who attended you?"

"She was," said Claire. "She came with me on the *Diana*. If you need proof of my innocence, Blanche can vouch for it."

He fired several questions at her in rapid succession. In the space of a few minutes, he had garnered everything there was to know about Blanche's part in writing the letter and their subsequent flight to Bordeaux.

"The little maid wrote the letter denouncing me." He said it as though he still could not believe it.

"Denouncing Duhet," Claire corrected.

"Well . . . I'll be—!" Adam laughed. He felt as if a weight had been lifted from his shoulders. He was thinking that Claire had not hated him. She had not written the letter informing against him. "I should have expected something of the sort. My half-brother had many enemies."

Adam's indifference to the wrong he had done her was like acid on Claire's wounds. She wanted to scream abuse at him. She forced herself to hang on to her control.

His eyes were soft when they came to rest on her. "The Conciergerie?" he prompted, "Was it so very bad, my darling?"

This display of solicitude found no more favor with Claire than his former show of indifference. She knew that this was irrational. She could not help herself. This handsome, smiling man with the ineffably tender light in his eyes had deserted her without a word. He had hurt her past bearing, was still hurting her past bearing. Wild horses could not drag that admission from her.

She focused her attention on her laced fingers. "My friends did not desert me." Though she spoke without anger, she was well aware of the sting in her words. "Blanche and Nicholas were close by. Even Philippe showed some concern for my welfare. He came to visit me."

This last statement stayed the tide of remorse which had begun to rise in Adam's breast. "Philippe visited you?" he asked incredulously. "When was this? What did he say to you? What did he want?"

Claire told him the gist of her conversation with Duhet, ending with, "He offered me his protection. He said that he would take care of me."

The words burst from Adam in a torrent. "God, I should have foreseen it! Philippe must have divined that you were no ordinary woman to me! That devil! Thank God for Nicholas! Let me tell you, Claire, if you had come under Philippe's protection, he would have used you abominably just to make me suffer."

"Yes," said Claire quietly. "Thank God for Nicholas."

For the first time, Adam became conscious that Claire's calm was a pose. Beneath that cool exterior, she was seething. He had known, of course, that she had tried to avoid him all week. He had supposed that it was because, having denounced him to the authorities, she was ashamed to face him. With the revelation of Blanche's part in the affair, he was coming to see that he had misjudged the situation. Claire saw herself as the injured party. By her lights, he was the guilty one.

"Claire," he said, pleading with her, "if you only knew how much I came to regret . . ."

She cut him off without a qualm. "But having some experience of one of the Duhet brothers, you may be sure that I would have cut my own throat before I would have allowed myself to fall into the hands of the other."

"So!" He bristled slightly when it occurred to him

that she judged him to be tarred with the same brush as Philippe. He rose to his feet to tower over her. For a moment, he studied her haughty expression, then he said calmly, "I misjudged you. But I paid for my mistake. It's time now to forgive and forget."

"I shall never forgive you," she said.

He did not believe her. It was only her wounded pride speaking. He remembered how sweetly giving she was, how she would give in to him even when she didn't want to. It might take a little time, but he had every confidence that he would win her over.

For the first time since she had walked into the room, Adam really looked at her. Claire's beauty was so striking that one rarely looked beneath the surface. He noticed things now that he had not noticed before. She was thinner than he remembered. Her skin was parchment white with no hint of roses across the cheekbones. There were no dimples winking at him from the corners of her mouth. He had seen more animation in a marble statue.

"Claire, are you ill?" he asked abruptly. God, if she had been ill and no one had told him . . .

"I'm not ill. May I go now?"

He wasn't sure if he believed her. For the moment, he decided to let it go. Claire was not in the frame of mind to confide in him. There would be time later to pursue the reason for her waxlike complexion and that air of fragility.

"May I go?" she repeated.

"Not until I have had my say."

"Fine." She looked everywhere but at him.

Adam stifled a smile. She looked as though butter wouldn't melt in her mouth. He was sorely tempted to shake her from her pose. He knew how to unleash the tigress in her. Soon, he promised himself, but not before he had set her to rights about a few things.

He folded his arms across his chest and regarded her somberly. "Claire," he said, "I searched for you everywhere. Where do you think I have been these

267

last months? I went to Paris. I went to Rouen. I would have gone to England, only I did not know your sister's name, no, nor even her false name. I tried to find my half-brother, but even he seemed to have vanished off the face of the earth. God, Claire, I've suffered agonies wondering what might have become of you." He paused to steady his breathing. "But all that is behind us now. We have found each other again. We can begin where we left off."

Her voice shook with sudden outrage. "Even *you* could not be so stupid as to suppose that I would wish to resume our . . . friendship."

"Marriage, Claire. It was what we planned to do."

"Thank you, no."

He had heard her refuse a piece of Sarah's prize plum cake in the same polite tone. Adam's patience began to wear thin. "You'd better make up your mind to it. Good grief, girl, don't you understand the seriousness of our situation? You are John's . . . ," he stumbled over the word "daughter" and quickly substituted, "ward. We must marry. We have no choice in the matter. It's the only honorable thing to do."

Adam was well aware that the reason he wanted to marry Claire had nothing to do with what he had just told her. In point of fact, if any of his intimates had overheard that little speech, they would have laughed themselves silly. On more occasions than he cared to remember, women had tried to entrap him into marriage using much the same tactics. Such appeals had not the power to sway him.

He wanted Claire. It was as simple as that.

Her smile was pure malice. "I can't marry you," she said, then hesitated over the untruth. "You see, Mr. Dillon, I am promised to another gentleman."

The silence was electric.

Through his teeth, Adam said, "David Burke!" When Claire neither denied nor admitted the truth of his conjecture, he said in a more driven tone, "You will never marry him! John would not permit it. By damn, I would never permit it! I would tell him the truth first.''

The only truth that Claire knew about was that she had once been Adam's mistress. His venom stunned her. "But why?" she whispered. "Why would you do such a thing to me? Haven't you done enough already?"

She had misunderstood and in one sense Adam was glad of it. At the same time, he was bitterly enraged. She was determined always to think the worst of him. For some moments he merely gazed at her from under his lashes. The seeds of doubt were planted in his mind. In Rouen, Claire had made a bargain with Duhet. Her submission to himself might mean nothing more than that—submission to a powerful male who could be of some use to her. Now that she had no more use for him, it seemed that Adam Dillon did not enter into her calculations.

The hell he didn't!

He swooped down and captured her wrists, dragging her to her feet. Claire tried to fight free of him. When she failed, she stood there, her eyes flashing defiance, glaring up at him. Adam's eyes moved over her. He had forgotten nothing. Every feature, every womanly contour, was scorched into his memory. His senses leapt. His eyes burned into Claire's. She recognized that heated look. Her body answered him. She gave a little cry as she felt her nipples swelling beneath the thin muslin of her gown. Adam's eyes missed nothing.

She struggled in earnest. "You would not dare!"

His arms imprisoned her. His mouth closed over hers with burning urgency, forcing her lips to part. She bent and twisted every way against his hold. His arms were like bonds of iron. She could not breathe. He was hurting her. She was suffocating. She must yield or she would faint.

She stilled, leaning against him for support. The

fierce pressure of Adam's arms relented. "Claire!" he said, and his hands stroked slowly from nape to waist, molding her to his length. "Claire," he said again, and confidently slipped his hand inside her bodice to cup one breast. She cried out softly when his fingers plucked at one sensitive nipple.

He lifted his head, watching her expression as he increased the pressure of his fingers. "You can't hide this from me," he said. When she said nothing, he went on, "For God's sake, Claire, why do you try to deny it when your body tells me everything I want to know without words?"

Her breathing quickened. Her eyes were half closed. She was like warm wax in his hands. Groaning, Adam shifted her, bringing the lower half of her body against his thighs, compelling her to an awareness of his arousal. "Come with me now." His voice was unsteady and thick with desire. "I need to be private with you, where no one can interrupt us. Claire, for pity's sake, if I don't have you soon, I'll go out of my mind. It's been so long, darling, so long."

For a moment, Claire's mind could not adjust to what he was suggesting. She felt drugged. She was trembling. Her body wanted to answer every demand he made upon it. She wanted to submerge herself in him. The feelings were not new to her. It had happened before. This man wielded a terrible power over her.

"Come with me now, Claire," Adam repeated hoarsely.

Everything came together in her head at once. She saw herself as weak-willed, only one among many of all the women Adam Dillon had ever seduced. She burned with shame. Wrenching herself out of his arms, she sent her hand across his face. His head snapped back with the force of her blow.

The silence was broken by their rapid breathing. Adam's eyes were stormy, but no more stormy than Claire's voice.

"I should have expected this from you," she said. "Always, you must take advantage of a woman."

His face twisted cynically. She wanted him, but she wouldn't give in to him until her price had been met. Women were the same the world over. They must count the cost first.

He laughed, and the bitter sound of it mocked himself as much as it mocked Claire. "God, will I never learn? A bargain—that's what we struck in Rouen, wasn't it Claire? Fine. I have no complaints. Some men would think your price was excessive. You'll observe, I don't cavil. I know what I'm getting, you see. You shall have your bargain—my name, my ring, my wealth for your undeniable . . . charms."

If he had not blocked her path to the door, Claire would have made a dignified exit. As it was, she stood her ground, but they could both see that she was shaking.

"Your name," she said scornfully. "I would be ashamed to take your name."

Fury leapt in Adam's eyes. Claire took a quick step back. Adam advanced. His voice dangerously quiet, he said, "Would you care to explain that remark?"

Her tongue seemed to cleave to the roof of her mouth. His hands were on her shoulders, shaking her, and the words spilled out. "I had not been here a week before I was warned to keep away from you. You are dangerous to know. No woman is safe from you. Your indiscretions, your affairs are a scandal to all decent people."

"Is that so?"

Dry-mouthed, Claire nodded and doggedly went on with her catalogue. "Adam Dillon respects neither innocence, nor marriage vows, nor youth, nor . . ."

"I think I get the picture." His hands dropped away. "Dear, dear," he murmured ironically, "I seem to have sunk quite below reproach. So I'm not good enough for you? Why don't you say it straight out, Claire?"

Swallowing, she said, "David Burke . . ."

"Ah! The saintly David! Am I to understand that his *pure* kisses, his *chaste* caresses are acceptable, whereas my embraces are too unclean to be borne?"

She tried to conjure a picture of David Burke kissing her the way Adam kissed her, but she could not. "He has never forced himself upon me," she said defensively.

He smiled without mirth. "Has he touched you, Claire?"

"What?"

"Has he made love to you?"

For a moment, her mouth gaped open. "He respects me!" she burst out. "David would never . . ."

"You don't know the first thing about men," he said viciously.

"I know about David. He isn't like you. He doesn't set out to seduce every woman he meets."

"Must you exaggerate?"

The question had been tormenting her for months. She voiced it as though it had just occurred to her. "Then tell me this," she said. "After you left me in Rouen, how soon was it before you acquired another mistress?"

Something flared in his eyes, and she gave a hollow laugh. "You see," she derided, "it's just as I thought."

For a moment, it seemed that he might refute her assumption. Then he shrugged negligently. "I believe it was all of one week," he drawled. "Certainly no more than two."

"When I was in the Conciergerie." She did not know that she had spoken the thought aloud.

"For God's sake, Claire! I didn't know that you were in the Conciergerie. Must you torture me like this?"

She scarcely heard him. She was thinking that

while she had been delirious on a filthy straw pallet in the infirmary, hemorrhaging away the life of her child, he had been taking his pleasure with some nameless creature between the sheets of a feather bed. She wondered if the sheets were perfumed. She remembered the stench of the Conciergerie.

When he touched her, she sprang back as if she had been scorched by a firebrand. Her face was ashen. Her eyes were wild. "Why won't you listen to me?" she sobbed out. "I don't want you! This isn't Rouen! You can't force me. For God's sake, leave me alone! Don't you understand anything? I would rather have any man than you. I hate you. I hate you."

All the color drained out of Adam's face. With a savage profanity, he turned on his heel and left her.

Adam had been hurt before, but never like this. Claire's parting words had struck at something deep inside him that made him writhe. And before that, her cool disdainful recitation of his iniquities had cut him to the quick. If she had wanted to make him feel small she had succeeded. No woman had ever had such power over him.

He wasn't good enough for her. She had all but said the words. It wasn't the first time he had experienced rejection. But on those other occasions, no one has assassinated his character. He'd been deserted by women, yes, even his own mother, when a better offer had come along. Things were different now. He was a wealthy, powerful man. There was nothing, however, that Adam Dillon had to offer, neither wealth, nor position, nor anything of himself, that was acceptable to Claire Devereux.

Angry and hurt past caring, he flung himself into a round of frenetic pleasure. The flattering attentions of beautiful women who cared not a fig for his notoriety was like balm to a festering sore. To all appearances, he resumed his liaison with Lily

Randolph. He escorted her everywhere. In point of fact, Adam was as celibate as a monk. No one would have believed it. It seemed that he was flaunting his affair in society's face. He knew that Claire was bound to hear of it. They moved in the same circles. His eyes followed her constantly. Claire did not deign to spare him a glance. She was too occupied in fending off the attentions of her own set of admirers.

Adam viewed Claire's suitors with a jaundiced eye. Their private lives did not bear too close a scrutiny any more than his own did. Claire wasn't to know it, and therein lay the difference. She knew more about *his* indiscretions that she had a right to know. It was his own fault. He had never taken any pains to conceal his little affairs. Claire was giving them a significance they did not merit.

He tried to shrug the whole thing off philosophically. Whatever he had thought was between them in Rouen was evidently a figment of his imagination. Claire Devereux was just another fickle woman. Life was too short to waste on regrets. He abandoned himself to gaming and drinking. His temper became explosive. He fought duels at the drop of a hat. No gentleman dared breathe Claire's name in Adam's hearing. Before long, their names became linked. Speculation was beginning to grow.

As was to be expected, Claire's suitors began to fall away. Sarah became quite anxious. When she paid an afternoon call on her great friend Martha Armstrong, she became positively alarmed. Martha had a talent for knowing everyone's business before they knew it themselves.

On her return home, Sarah made straight for her husband's bookroom. "What the devil is this I hear about Adam and Claire?" she asked querulously.

"Adam and Claire?"

"Their names are linked romantically. Adam has been fighting duels over the girl. Don't say you didn't know it?"

"But I didn't know it," protested John in his mild way. He set aside his pen. "Dueling? That doesn't sound like Adam."

"Tell that to Percy Ward and William Quinn! It's a wonder Adam didn't kill them. Percy was lucky. The bullet entered his arm. But as for William, poor boy, he may be left with a permanent limp."

John's brows knit together. "Adam and Claire? The idea is preposterous! Adam has demonstrated no partiality for the girl, and vice versa." What John had immediately grasped was that Adam and Claire had been acquainted in France.

"Poor Claire!" said Sarah crossly. "Poor Claire! She is losing all her beaux. If things go on like this, the only suitor remaining for her hand will be your brother David." Through half-lowered lashes, she surreptitiously observed her husband's reaction to her words.

He grunted, but made no other comment, except to say, "Leave it to me. I shall have a word with Adam."

"I wish you would," said Sarah, "for if Adam refuses to mend his ways, there will be few gentlemen brave enough to dance with Claire at her ball."

Chapter Seventeen

By the time Adam arrived at Claire's ball, he had already fortified himself with several glasses of whiskey. Few would have known it. He was at his most agreeable. Smiles came readily to his lips. His laughter rang out richly as he mingled with the crush of people in Sarah's great ballroom. And if he made frequent forays to the punch bowl, no one thought any the less of him for it. John Burke's rum punch was a great favorite with the gentlemen.

On closer observation, it would have been noted that some of the gentlemen were giving Adam Dillon a wide berth. They had discovered that, latterly, Adam's temper had become unpredictable. He could be charming, or he could be lethal, and there was no explaining it. Sometimes, it took no more than a careless sideways glance to bring his temper to the explosive point. In the last number of weeks, the heights of Weehawken had borne witness to more duels than in the whole of the previous year.

To the ladies, the air of danger that followed Adam only added to his glamour. "And why shouldn't it?" one wit was heard to reply to this moot observation, though not in Adam's hearing. "The ladies stand to lose nothing but their virtue. A gentleman's very life is at stake."

That the ladies were in any danger of losing their

virtue was soon seen to be an absurd fancy. Lily Randolph's unwavering presence at Adam's elbow dashed every feminine hope. The beautiful widow was not slow to unsheath her claws whenever she detected a possible rival. She had not been at the ball an hour before she had a fair idea of who most stood to fill that position.

Claire Devereux was keeping her distance from Adam. The girl made no overt moves. But Adam had only to come into her line of vision and Claire would find some pretext for removing herself from his path. Lily was sure that Adam was aware of what the girl was doing. He betrayed himself in small ways. A muscle would clench in his cheek. He would lose the thread of his conversation. Moments later, he would become flatteringly attentive to his companion.

Lily was no fool. She was a woman of the world and quite adept at reading the little betraying signals that gentlemen gave off. Her own husband had been an expert teacher. At seventeen, Lily had married in opposition to every warning her family had made respecting Larry Randolph. Though he came of good stock, he was a wastrel. He was a womanizer. He was only interested in her fortune.

Though all of her family's predictions had proved true, Lily had never quite come to regret her decision to elope with young Randolph. He was a hell-raiser. He was also exciting and fun to be with. He treated her like a real person, not like a china doll. He introduced her to the pleasures of the flesh. And if, in time, he was faithless, Lily had no real quarrel with him. He was not a jealous husband. She enjoyed freedoms that most married women did not wish to enjoy. With her husband's tacit consent, she took lovers.

In Adam Dillon, Lily felt that she had met her true complement. No man understood her better. In some ways, she was fonder of Adam than she had been of her late husband. There was one major difference.

Time was passing. Lily was no longer in the first bloom of youth. The thought made her quite out-of-sorts. When her beauty faded, as it must, her lovers would look to younger women for their pleasure. For the first time since her husband's untimely death on the field of honor, Lily was seriously considering the possibility of marriage. She thought that she and Adam might do very well together, if only she could persuade him of it. Unfortunately, since his return from France, Adam's ardor had cooled. She suspected that there was another woman. In other circumstances, this would not have troubled Lily overmuch. She understood the necessity for novelty. In the past, she had turned a blind eye to Adam's peccadilloes. But something strange was going on. Adam was not himself, and she was resolved to get to the bottom of it.

Observing Claire Devereux's evasive tactics, Lily's eyes narrowed. She considered the possibility that Adam had taken up with the Devereux girl and almost instantly discarded that notion. John Burke was Adam's friend. Adam would never do anything to offend John Burke. The girl was treated like a daughter of the house. She had a number of suitors. She was destined for marriage. Moreover, Lily recognized the type. Claire Devereux was a very conventional girl. Innocence held no interest for Adam.

That thought stayed with her until David Burke, in full view of Adam, whisked Claire through the doors that gave onto the terraced gardens at the back of the house. With sudden ferocity, Adam set down his glass on the nearest table, sending droplets of liquid flying everywhere. In the next instant, he went after them. After a moment's stunned surprise, Lily ran to catch up with him.

When Adam came abreast of the double doors, his way was barred by a diminutive dark-haired girl with flashing eyes. Lily had a vague recollection that the girl was Claire's particular friend and that there was some talk of them opening a school together.

The girl spoke in French, and though Lily was not conversant in that language, she had no difficulty in making out the tenor of the girl's conversation. She was livid with Adam.

"Haven't you done enough to her?" demanded Blanche. "Let her be! Give her a chance to find some happiness."

Adam's anger was more than equal to Blanche's. "You bitch," he snarled. "If you were a man, I would kill you for writing that letter. And I do want her happiness. But not with David Burke, do you understand? Not with David Burke!"

Blanche fell back, not from the violence of Adam's response, but from the glimpse of something she had caught in his expression. She felt as though she had seen into his soul, and what she had glimpsed made her flinch away.

The gardens were extensive, sweeping down to the river. A number of people were wandering along the various well-lit paths. The air was fragrant with blossom. Adam descended a flight of stone steps and came to a sudden halt, not knowing which way to strike out.

"Adam, this is absurd." Lily laid a restraining hand on his sleeve. "They could be anywhere."

She glanced to her right, to the hedge which sheltered John Burke's private retreat. Behind the hedge, there was a lily pond which John had stocked with carp. A thought came to her.

Her voice took on a suggestive color. "Darling," she said, "do you remember the last time we were at one of Sarah's balls?"

Adam shook off her hand, his eyes and ears straining for sight or sound of Claire. Swallowing her pique, Lily went on, "We slipped away to the lavender room. Don't you remember, darling?"

"Of course I remember," said Adam absently. He

was thinking that it would take him hours to comb the grounds. Where the hell was she? And why wasn't John here to keep an eye on his brother? He must know how things stood with David and Claire.

"You made love to me," said Lily doggedly. "And we agreed that the threat of discovery added unbearably to our pleasure." She paused. "Darling," she purred, "why don't we return to the house and find a quiet nook where we can take off all our clothes and . . ."

A masculine cough followed by a smothered chortle silenced her. David Burke led Claire out from behind the low hedge. Adam remembered, then, that the hedge shielded a lily pond and that there were stone benches placed strategically around it.

"I beg your pardon," said David without a pretense of regret. "We should have made our presence known at once." Fighting back laughter, he went on, "Claire wanted to see if the carp would come to her hand at night, you see."

Adam's mind was grappling with the other man's smirk and the transparent hurt in Claire's beautiful eyes. Lily's conversation finally began to register.

Claire was hurt. That did not make sense. Claire despised him. Lily's words could not possibly have the power to hurt her. Unless . . . "Claire!" he said. "Claire!"

She jerked away from his outstretched hand. Adam took a step forward. David Burke's hand snaked out, manacling Adam's arm. The two gentlemen stood, bristling, eye to eye, like two stags challenging each other over territorial rights.

Before either could voice the irrevocable challenge that would see them at Weehawken at dawn, John Burke's voice cut the silence from the open doors.

"There you are, David." John Burke descended the stairs. "I thought I saw you and Claire slipping away. I want a word with you." He turned to Claire with a smile. "You won't object, my dear, if I steal

David for a few minutes, will you?"

Claire released the breath she had been holding. With patent relief, she said, "No. I don't mind in the least."

It was David who objected. "I was just about to take Claire into supper," he said.

"This is urgent or I would not have sought you out like this." John put his hand on the other man's shoulder.

"Can't it wait till morning? There is something particular I wish to say to Claire." His eyes flicked to Adam.

"I'm afraid not." The gravity in John's expression persuaded the other man that something was seriously amiss.

"What is it, John? Has something happened to Sarah or one of the children?"

John's hand moved from David's shoulder to his elbow. He began to urge him toward the house, "Not Sarah, no. Come along, David. We should have had this conversation a long time ago."

Their voices gradually faded. Claire faced Adam and Lily. Adam could not tear his eyes away from her. He wanted to banish that hurt look from her face. He wanted to comfort her. He wanted to tell her that she had misunderstood Lily's words, that it was all a lie. It was the truth, and he could not get around it. His credit with Claire could not be lower.

As she proudly angled her head back, he thought that he had never seen her look more beautiful. "Don't let me detain you," said Claire. "I believe you were on the point of returning to the house to find a quiet nook."

Adam looked as though he had taken root on the spot. Lily's eyes flashed from Claire to Adam.

"Adam," she said uncertainly, and laid a hand on the sleeve of his dark coat.

The proprietary gesture was not lost on Claire. She picked up her skirts and swept by them. At the top of the little flight of stone steps, she turned to face them. "May I suggest," she said, and cleared her throat before starting over. "May I suggest that you avoid the lavender room this time around? It happens to be *my* room. But don't let that deter you. There are plenty of vacant bedchambers on the floor above."

When Claire slipped through the doors, Lily let out a sound that was halfway between a laugh and a sigh. "I think we shocked the little prude," she said, trying for lightness.

A violent oath exploded from Adam's lips. He moved away to lean one hand against the trunk of a tall oak. His back was rigid. Lily advanced till she was only a step away from him. When she spoke, something hard and ugly seemed to have crept into her voice.

"Claire Devereux is not for you. I know her kind. She could never satisfy a man of your appetites. Good God, Adam, the girl would swoon in sheer horror if she ever suspected how a man and woman could pleasure each other in bed."

"It doesn't signify," he said wearily.

"It doesn't signify?" She forced an arch laugh. "Is this Adam Dillon speaking?" When he did not respond, she went on, "The girl is beautiful. I don't deny it. But you'll get no pleasure of her. Adam, I know you. You could never be satisfied with the likes of Claire Devereux."

Her words died when Adam suddenly swung to face her. His eyes were feverishly hot. The words seemed to be torn from him. "Why the hell does everyone assume that I am a voluptuary? Do you think that the finer feelings are beyond me? I assure you, I feel things just as deeply as the next man. God, what's the use? I could never persuade her!"

Lily recoiled as if he had struck her.

Adam felt a twinge of conscience. Without conscious thought, he put out a hand in a placating gesture. "Forgive me," he said. "That was uncalled for. I don't know what made me turn on you. I have no complaints with our arrangement."

"Our arrangement?" Her bosom began to heave. "What arrangement? Oh I know well enough what the world thinks. But you and I both know better."

A number of things suddenly began to fall into place. Some of the gentlemen with whom Adam had dueled in the last number of weeks had been suitors for Claire Devereux's hand. And while Lily's experienced eye had been trained on the highfliers, Adam had been caught in the coils of an innocent young girl. In tight-lipped silence, she stared at him.

Adam did not notice. He had resumed his stance at the oak tree. He'd been drinking too much. He felt maudlin. He couldn't seem to throw things off with his usual light-hearted banter. He was revealing things that in his saner moments he would die rather than reveal. He knew that he was going to wake up on the morrow and feel like a blithering idiot.

"You're in love with the girl!"

Adam's only answer was a hoarse, curt laugh.

"Oh Adam! You fool! You and I are one of a kind. We could be good together. Claire Devereux will bring you nothing but grief."

When he faced her, she was relieved to see that he was more like his old self. Her pulse skipped a beat when he angled her one of his devastatingly melting smiles. And then his quiet words flayed her.

"I would rather have grief from Claire Devereux," he said, "than pleasure of a thousand other women."

She left him, then, and he could not blame her. His words could not have shocked her more if he had confessed that he had committed a murder. He had shocked himself. He usually kept a close guard on his tongue.

When he finally wandered into the house, he came face-to-face with David Burke in the foyer. David had just quit his brother's bookroom. Twenty paces separated the two men. The symbolism was not lost on Adam. David looked as if he wished to kill him.

With measured steps, Adam closed the distance between them. "I'm sorry," he said simply.

David's smile was bitter. "You should have told me," he said.

"It was not my secret to tell. What will you do now?"

"What can I do but leave this place as soon as may be and save Claire the embarrassment of my presence?"

"That sounds like a capital idea."

David laughed without mirth. "Naturally, you would say so."

From inside the bookroom, Sarah's raised voice was heard. Adam looked a question at the older man.

"My brother," said David with undisguised venom, "has been found out. Oh spare me the murderous looks! I had nothing to do with it. Sarah knows. Don't ask me how. But she knows." His control suddenly shattered. With a vicious oath, he pushed past Adam and made for the stairs. After a moment, Adam turned aside and entered the ballroom.

A country dance was in progress. Claire was partnered by a young man whom Adam recognized as one of William Quinn's younger brothers. The lad was no more than twenty or so. Adam's eyes narrowed as the young man took a daring liberty. His hand surreptitiously brushed the underside of Claire's breast.

At the same moment, Adam's eyes locked with young Quinn's. The boy blushed furiously. His hand fell away from Claire. A look of stark terror crossed his face. With a flick of his long eyelashes, Adam dismissed the youth. Turning on his heel, he made his way to the formal dining room where a lavish supper was set out for Sarah's guests. The long tables which were laden with every sort of delicacy held no interest for him. He wanted coffee, and lots of it. Finding a deserted corner, he turned his back upon the room, daring all but the most foolhardy to approach him. He was on his third cup of coffee when he was joined by Claire's friend, the little maid from Rouen. Now here was a fitting object for his spleen, thought Adam.

He kept his voice low and his smile as pleasant as he could make it. But there was never any doubt about the murder in his mind. "If you had not proved that you were Claire's friend," he said softly, "it would give me great pleasure to tear you limb from limb."

Without waiting for an invitation she knew would never be offered, Blanche seated herself in the empty chair beside Adam's. "Claire is not happy," she said.

Adam made a derisory sound and drained the coffee in his cup. He gestured to the black manservant to refill it for him. This done, he turned his attention to Blanche. "Claire is not happy," he said, mimicking her tone exactly. His mouth contorted in bitterness. "I take leave to doubt that," he said. "She is the belle of the ball. Hell, she is the belle of New York. Suitors beat a path to her door. So, she can't have David Burke. She'll soon get over him. I speak from experience, you'll observe."

Blanche selected a small petit fours from her plate and delicately bit into it. When she finally swallowed, she said softly, "Mr. Dillon, there is so much she has not told you. She suffered dreadfully, you see. She was ready to die for you, whereas you . . ." Adam made a strangled sound, and Blanche looked away. After a moment, she went on, "Perhaps you don't wish to know. Perhaps it's too late."

"It is too late," said Adam, bringing Blanche's dark eyes up to meet his. He inhaled deeply. "It is too late," he repeated, this time with more conviction. "Claire Devereux belongs to me. If she doesn't like it, so much the worse for her."

285

*　　　*　　　*

He wanted his mind to be absolutely clear when he confronted Claire. Blanche had told him things that he could scarcely take in. He saw everything now in sharper focus. His reflections gave him very little comfort. He wavered between hope and despair. It wasn't only his own happiness he was considering. More than anything, he was thinking of Claire.

For three hours, he absented himself from Claire's ball. He went riding. It was a stupid thing to do. New York was not like Paris. There were no extensive public parks laid out for the benefit of its citizens. One must leave the city's environs to find space to exercise one's horses. If his mount threw him or he was attacked by ruffians, no one would know it for days. He would have welcomed an attack. Then the violence inside him would have found a proper direction.

When he returned to the house, he entered it as though he owned it. The ball was long over. John's servants were clearing up. Adam ascended the stairs to Claire's room as if he had every right to do so. Nothing and no one could have stopped him in that moment.

When he pushed into the lavender room, he carefully shut the door and turned the key. Claire was in her cotton night rail, silhouetted against the long window. Several candles around the room were still burning. She turned her head and gave a guilty start of recognition. Adam's eyes fell on the makeshift bed she had contrived from two stuffed armchairs pushed together.

His eyes shifted to the huge tester bed. It was a shambles. Covers, pillows, sheets were all bundled together in the center of the mattress. There were feathers everywhere. Evidently, in a fit of temper, Claire had stabbed the feather mattress with a pair of embroidery scissors. He had a flash of déjà vu, and a picture of Claire, on her knees, on the point of consigning a bloodstained sheet to the flames. As on that occasion, everything inside Adam melted.

He caught back a smile, thinking that the inanimate objects on which his beloved vented her spleen must surely personify himself.

"Tigress," he murmured, but indistinctly.

Coming to herself, Claire dived for her dressing gown and slipped into it. She belted it tightly. "Get out before I scream the house down," she whispered shakily.

"What happened to the bed, Claire?" Adam's tone was conversational.

She said nothing, but her eyes spoke volumes.

Emboldened, Adam took a step forward. "What happened to the bed, Claire?" he repeated, this time in a tone that brooked no evasions.

Through her teeth, she said, "I would not sleep in that bed of iniquity for all the rum in Jamaica."

He looked at her gravely. "You can't bear to think that I have taken another woman in your bed."

Her nostrils quivered. Her chin lifted. A queen could not have looked more haughty, thought Adam, if she had been importuned by a filthy, foul-smelling beggar. There was a tremor in her voice, however, which gave him hope.

"You," she said, "are beneath contempt."

"And not fit to tie the strings of your shoes, or so you think," he added for good measure. "Nevertheless, you don't wish any other woman to have me."

Her brows came down. "You mean nothing to me," she told him. "I scarcely know you."

Adam advanced further into the room until his long legs brushed the edge of the bed. He caught a fistful of feathers and threw them in the air. When they finally settled on the floor, he said, "If I mean nothing to you, Claire, why did you tear up the bed?"

She avoided this moot question by posing one of her own. "Did you and Mrs. Randolph find your

287

quiet little nook? I suppose you must have. Everybody remarked on your absence from my ball."

"Lily and I parted company a long time ago," he said. "You need not concern yourself with her. If you must know, I spent a good half-hour in conversation with Blanche, and then I went riding."

His answer gave her pause. "Blanche?" she said, slanting him an uncertain look. "You spoke with Blanche?"

"I did. And what she told me was most enlightening." Gradually he inched forward until he was within arm's reach of her. "She told me everything," he said. "She told me about the Conciergerie. She told me about the child. She told me that you had a chance to save yourself but that you refused to leave Philippe because you loved him, because you thought that he was I."

It was as though his words had torn the mask from her beautiful face. Everything that had been locked deep inside her, all the pain, all the anguish of betrayed love, was transparently obvious for him to read.

More than anything Adam wanted to pull her into his arms and comfort her. It was too soon. For both their sakes, he must break down every last bulwark she had built against him.

"I see what it is," he said. "You have set yourself up as judge and jury. You must punish me. For how long, Claire? For a year? For two years? And what is my punishment to be?"

She was shaking so hard, she had to steady herself wit one hand against the window ledge. Though she was sure she was screaming at him, her voice was no more than a broken whisper. "You can go to hell for all eternity."

He gave a short bark of laughter. "Hell would be preferable to this. You have sent me into the void." He paused and then went on in a calmer tone. "That I can still want you knowing you for what you are is more than I can comprehend. So—you lost our babe. You suffered unspeakably. Poor, poor Claire Devereux. And now I must be made to suffer. Isn't that so, Claire?"

Her eyes were huge in her face. Her teeth were clamped on her bottom lip.

Adam's voice shook. "You sanctimonious little prude," he said. "What gives you the right to judge me, or anyone else for that matter? I saw how you turned up your nose at Lily Randolph." His tone could not have been more scathing. "Why should you be surprised if I turned to her? Lily knows how to please a man."

He could not go on much longer in this vein. He wanted to fall on his knees and beg her forgiveness. The stakes were too high to take the coward's way out. Soon, she must break, and the poison would come pouring out of her.

"Lily," he said, and got no further.

With a hiss of rage, she launched herself at him. Adam was knocked off balance. Her fists were flying. He swiftly captured her in his powerful arms and bent his head so that her blows struck harmlessly at his back and shoulders.

Claire had never known anger like this. It was as though a dam had burst. In a storm of tears and vituperation, she lashed at him. Everything was flung in his teeth, from the moment Duhet had struck her down in the courtyard of the commissioner's headquarters to her sufferings in the Conciergerie when Adam had been pleasuring himself with another woman. Even his former and subsequent conduct in New York was not overlooked. His scandalous reputation, his dueling, his women—all must be laid to his account.

Adam absorbed her anger in meek silence, occasionally whispering an anguished "forgive me" as the torrent continued unabated. His lips brushed ceaselessly over her hair and wet cheeks. His hands ran over her back, offering a comfort she was not willing to accept from him. All the tears, all the fury and hurt pride poured out of her until there was nothing left to say. It was the moment he had been waiting for.

He dried her eyes and face with his fine lawn handkerchief. Claire was too spent to protest this show of tenderness. Then, keeping her closely held in the shelter of his body, in a voice that was shaking with emotion, he tried to tell her how it had been for him.

He spoke of his fury when he believed that she had been merely using him for her own ends. He told her of his despair when he could not find her. Haltingly, choosing his words with care, he broached the subject of the woman with whom he had tried to supplant her when his ship was anchored off La Rochelle. Adam would have given anything to spare Claire this. But he had stupidly betrayed himself in a fit of temper. She knew about the woman. He must say something.

"It was disastrous," he said. "I hated myself afterwards."

At this, Claire tried feebly to pull out of his arms. Adam would not permit it. When she quieted, he went on in the same low tones, "No mistress, Claire. No other women, I swear it." He gave a shaky laugh. "I learned my lesson, you see. None of them was you."

He was past trying to conceal anything. Everything must be out in the open between them. Many times, words failed him. Always, he returned to the same thing. He was a better man than she gave him credit for. He would prove it to her if she would give him another chance. Finally, he, too, fell silent.

For a long while, they simply held each other, cheeks touching, breath mingling. It was like a moment stolen out of time. The harmony between them was perfect.

Adam was loath to shatter the moment. She was nestled so trustingly against his length, as though his powerful body were her shield and her strength. *Yes,* he thought fiercely. *This* is how it should be between them. As God was his witness, this is how it *would* be in the future. He would protect her as long as he had breath in his body.

He kissed her softly, and she stirred. "Darling," he said, "you are practically falling asleep on your feet. You must get to bed. Tomorrow, I shall return and everything between us will be resolved."

His words brought her out of her lethargy. She gave a little hiccup and sniffed before saying, "N-nothing will induce me to s-sleep in that bed."

Adam had the wisdom not to try to persuade her. Swallowing a smile, he bundled her in a blanket and set her down on one of the stuffed armchairs. He cupped her face with one hand and pressed a chaste kiss to her lips. "Leave it to me, darling," he said. "Until tomorrow then."

When he left her, knowing how easily he could have taken her, he tried to comfort himself with the thought that virtue was its own reward. But all he could think was that the road to nobility was a very rocky course.

The servants were still moving about downstairs. Adam made straight for the back of the house where he found John Burke's steward. If Barbados was surprised to see Adam, he gave no sign of it. He was used to Mr. Adam coming and going at will. Barbados was religiously counting the silver.

Adam explained the problem. A mouse had somehow got into Miss Devereux's feather mattress. Hearing her cries, he had gone to investigate. It was most embarrassing. In her panic, the poor girl had practically demolished the bed with a pair of sewing shears. She did not know how she was going to face the Burkes at the breakfast table.

Barbados, as Adam knew he would, offered to take

care of the matter so that no one was the wiser.

Adam thanked him, and as an afterthought suggested that Miss Devereux might be moved to a different chamber, adding by way of explanation, "She can no longer be comfortable in the lavender room, you see. Like most women, she has a phobia about mice—poor harmless creatures. If I know anything about women, she won't sleep a wink all night."

Barbados displayed a gratifying dismay. For a guest not to be comfortable in his domain was something that he (and his master) would not tolerate. He assured Mr. Adam that he would undertake to move Miss Devereux and her things to a different chamber at once. The rose room came immediately to mind.

"The rose room," said Adam consideringly. "Yes, I think Miss Devereux will be much more comfortable in the rose room."

Barbados's eyes narrowed on the look of bemusement which crossed Mr. Adam's face. He'd known young Adam since the lad had come to live with the Burkes in '84. Barbados's lips turned up at the corners. He was thinking that the poor girl didn't stand a chance.

Coming to himself, Adam let out a long sigh and pressed a coin into Barbados's palm. Moments later, he left the house whistling. Barbados watched him go. He chuckled, wondering if the impossible had finally come to pass. When he ascended the stairs to the lavender room, he, too, was whistling.

Chapter Eighteen

Adam returned the following morning and requested an interview with the master of the house. John was more than a little relieved to escape the gloomy pall which had fallen over the breakfast table. Only the little French girl, Blanche, was civil to him. It seemed that he was in everyone else's black books.

Not only was his wife refusing to sleep with him, but she was also refusing to be in the same room with him. His brother had taken off for Philadelphia as though the hounds of hell were after him, but not before he had said a few choice things in John's ear. Claire could hardly bear to lift her eyes, while Betsy, sensing that all was not right between her parents, looked daggers at her father. In domestic disputes, the girls had always taken their mother's part.

A dram with Adam Dillon might be just the thing to revive his flagging spirits, thought John. Adam was a man of the world. His interests were far-ranging. They would talk politics, or debate philosophy. Anything was preferable to the terse monosyllables which was the only conversation the females in his household were offering.

The first shock hit John when, without preamble, Adam stated unequivocally that he was going to marry Claire. The second shock came when Claire,

293

having been sent for, shyly slipped into the room.

The look in Adam's eyes when they rested on her slender form could have melted a mountain of ice. Adam was in love, and John was staggered. How had it come about? How had Adam come close to Claire without his knowing it? And what of Lily Randolph? He studied Claire, but her face gave very little away.

Before John could voice a single question, Adam took charge. Politely, pointedly, he ushered John through the door. Adam faced Claire across the width of the room. He cleared his throat. "Please," he said, indicating a chair.

Claire duly seated herself and looked at Adam expectantly. There were dimples winking in her cheeks. Adam was too nervous to notice them. Without thinking, he seated himself behind John Burke's massive leather-topped desk. Realizing at once that he had made a blunder, that one did not propose marriage to the lady of one's choice as though one were conducting a business meeting, he shot to his feet and came away from the desk.

"Claire?" he said.

"Yes?" she encouraged.

"Would you . . . that is . . . oh damn, let's go for a walk."

John took a turn in the garden. It was some time before he went in search of Sarah. He found her in her private parlor. She was alone. At the sight of him, Sarah's features hardened into granite.

Recalling the scene which had taken place in his bookroom the night before, John inwardly winced. He still had no notion of how Sarah had put two and two together. When she had first walked in at the end of that painful interview with David, she had seemed in her usual high spirits. But one look at David's stricken face, and she had turned on her husband with a look of loathing.

"Tell me it isn't true," she had said, almost pleading with him.

He had hemmed and hawed, playing for time, as he was sure all husbands must do when confronted with their infidelities. Sarah knew him too well. She had interrupted his evasions with a question which was shocking in its bluntness.

"Is Claire or is she not your natural daughter by Leon Devereux's sister? Don't bother with explanations. A simple 'yes' or 'no' will suffice."

At this, David had unobtrusively slipped from the room.

There was no way to soften the truth. "Yes," said John, "she is. But Claire does not know it, and she must never know it. Nothing must be done to hurt Claire."

He would not have believed that the woman who spat such obscenities at him was the woman he had taken to his bosom for more than thirty years. His Sarah was, above all, a lady. This spitfire used the graphic language of the gutter.

He was in the wrong. He knew it. Having been found out, he did not expect to get off scot-free. But that did not mean he would permit himself to be chastised like some guilty schoolboy. Good God, his fall from grace had taken place more than twenty years before, not yesterday as the excess of Sarah's emotion would have anyone believe. One little slip in over thirty years! Sarah did not know when she was well-off. There was scarcely a gentleman of his acquaintance who had not, at one time or another, dabbled in the petticoat line. And so he had told her.

The scene had become uglier. She would not remain in the same house with his by-blow, Sarah had stormed at him. This incensed him as nothing else could. Claire was innocent. He would not countenance a threat to her peace of mind.

Bristling, he had risen to his feet. He would be

master in his own house, he had informed Sarah. She would obey him or she would suffer some very unpleasant consequences. The matter was closed, and he refused to hear one more word on the subject. Should she disobey him in this, he would pack her off to his estate in New Jersey where she would remain incommunicable until she came to her senses.

Never, in his life, had he addressed Sarah in such terms or in such a tone of voice. It had never been necessary. He and Sarah were friends as much as they were husband and wife. They conversed as equals. Not once had he ever played the part of the heavy-handed husband. It was a role he did not relish. But Sarah had forced him into it.

His words had the desired effect. She had found her control. But having found it, she used it with a vengeance. Whenever he approached her, as at the present moment, she froze like a block of marble.

"I've just left Adam with Claire," he essayed, hesitating beside the stuffed armchair which Sarah invariably invited him to occupy whenever he entered her private sanctum. Wordlessly Sarah picked up her embroidery and took a small stitch. John remained standing. "He wants to marry her," he said.

"Oh?" said Sarah noncommittally. Inwardly, she was teeming with questions. Deliberately, she took another small stitch.

Stifling a sigh, John persisted, "Do you think she will have him?"

Sarah squinted at the stitches she had just executed. "Yes," she said, and folded her lips together.

This time, John's sigh was audible. He gave up waiting for an invitation and seated himself in the chair he regarded as his very own. "Sarah," he said, "this is petty, and not worthy of you."

Her head lifted. In a voice vibrating with scorn, she said, "You are a fine one to talk of what is and what is

296

not worthy. Am I to take you for my model?" She forced a laugh. "You may believe, the idea has merit. Then we would soon see how easily the role of the wronged husband would sit on your shoulders."

A temper he had not known he possessed flared to a white-hot flame. A moment before, he was all guilt and meekness. Sarah's words evoked a picture he would not tolerate. For all her years, Sarah was a handsome, desirable woman. Sarah in the arms of another man? He would kill any man who laid a finger on her. He had to search to find his habitual calm.

"Make no mistake, Sarah," he said, "you are my wife. You have refused me my conjugal rights. So be it. I am free to take my ease where I may. I allow you no such liberty."

Her only answer, before she bent to her needlework, was a slight elevation of one brow. In simmering silence, John left her to it.

No sooner had he quit the room, than Sarah crushed her needlework in a ball and threw it on the floor. She was on her feet, and pacing. The tears that were never far away welled up and spilled over.

She still could not believe that her John was no better than other men. She had placed him on a pedestal, and, oh God, how far the mighty had fallen. Pride was a deadly sin. And she had sinned magnificently. She had looked down her nose at the foibles of lesser mortals. Her John was without equal. He had never so much as looked at another woman. She was the envy of all her friends.

It was one of those friends who had inadvertently put her wise to Claire Devereux.

"The girl is a Burke through and through," Martha Armstrong had reflected sagely. They were at an assembly in the City Tavern and watching Claire converse with a group of young people.

"What makes you say so?" asked Sarah. A number of things were hovering on the periphery of her mind. Martha's observation brought them more sharply into focus, not least the fact that John was opposed to a match between Claire and his brother.

"For one thing," said Martha, "the girl has the Burke eyes, true blue with not a trace of gray or green. And for another thing . . ."

"Yes?"

"It's uncanny."

"What is?"

"Her gestures—the way she employs her hands or tilts her head. You must have noticed. Look at John! Look at your Betsy! They are so similar, one would think they practiced to copy each other. Do you know what I think?"

"What?" asked Sarah.

"I think Claire must be related to the French branch of John's family. Perhaps her mother was a Bourque?"

"It's possible," said Sarah, knowing full well that it wasn't possible. The Bourques in France had all died out. Only the American branch of the family, the Burkes, had survived.

Martha's words planted the seed of suspicion in her mind, not that she admitted to it at once. But she took to watching Claire and John. Martha was right. The similarity in their gestures was uncanny.

Several days were to pass before Sarah thought to look over the letters her husband had written to her over the years. She had kept every last one of them. In short order, she discovered what she was looking for—his correspondence from France in '72.

It was as she remembered. Leon Devereux, John's friend, was a single man. He had a sister, Juliette Devereux. That was something which had slipped Sarah's mind. She wondered at it. As she scanned each letter she soon understood why. Juliette Devereux, the beautiful though precocious daughter of the house, was mentioned by John only once. In his subsequent letters, it was as though the girl had

298

ceased to exist.

Sarah was onto something, and she had known it. But she was far from being ready to admit that this omission on her husband's part was anything but innocent. It was inconceivable that John had betrayed his marriage vows. John was a man of character. Juliette Devereux was his friend's sister. And if that were not enough, there was the tenor of his letters to his wife. Sarah was soon to be delivered of their child. Her husband was all solicitation. He hoped to return home before their child was born. That he would take up with another woman at such a time was too farfetched, too cruel to credit.

In the normal way, Sarah would have confided everything to John. She chose not to do so, and did not care for the reason which came to mind for her reluctance. She was behaving like a suspicious wife.

One thing could have set all her doubts to rest. David wanted to marry Claire. On the night of Claire's ball, so he had confided to Sarah, he was going to propose to the girl. It was a test, and Sarah was on tenterhooks to see if John would permit it.

When she had walked into her husband's bookroom, she knew, oh God, she knew! And his first words were not for her, not begging her forgiveness, but for Claire Devereux. Nothing must be done to hurt Claire.

Until that moment, Sarah had been very fond of the girl. She no longer knew how she could be natural with her. It wasn't Claire's fault. No one needed to tell Sarah that the girl was innocent. But, oh God, she was so beautiful. She did not take after John. She must take after her mother. And to possess such beauty, John had been willing to go against every principle by which he had been raised. And that was saying something.

John's parents were devoutly religious. They were of French Huguenot stock. Sarah's parents had looked askance at such piety. They did not hold with it. Not that they had anything against religion—in its proper place. But there was such a thing as moderation. The Burkes were too saintly, too spiritual for their taste. No good could come of it.

Somehow that thought tickled Sarah's fancy. She began to laugh. When she discerned the thread of hysteria in her voice, she stopped abruptly.

Adam and Claire struck out along Broadway toward the waterfront, to the Battery, the city's favorite promenade, where the breeze was always a little cooler.

"It was here," said Adam, striving to establish naturalness between them, "that the original Dutch colony of New Amsterdam got its start."

There were few promenaders about. In the early hours of the evening, New York's fashionables would flock to the Battery to take the air and take note of each other. Claire's eyes trailed the progress of several sailing ships coming and going from the great harbor. At a rough wooden bench, Adam halted. Claire obediently seated herself. She made an idle comment about young saplings which were set out here and there. Adam thereupon launched into a history of the city. The sun beat down. There was no shade to be had. Claire had no parasol. Adam seemed unaware of her discomfort.

Finally, she broke in on his spate of anecdotes, for Adam had now moved on to describe the Battery's former disposition as a fort. "Adam," she said, "why have you brought me here?"

Adam's nervousness had communicated itself to Claire. An aching uncertainty began to take hold. Had she mistaken his purpose in seeking her out? A declaration of love followed by an offer of marriage—everything that had happened between them the night before had led her to expect nothing less.

Her confidence began to ebb. This was Adam

Dillon. He was not the same man she had known in Rouen. This man was almost a stranger to her. She knew only what she had been told. His affections were fickle. No woman had ever held his interest for long. He was not a marrying man.

Once, an aeon ago it seemed, Claire would have dismissed Adam and all men like him with a snap of her fingers. If she'd had her way, Adam would never have been given the opportunity to get close to her. Circumstances had decreed otherwise. They knew each other as intimately as it was possible for a man and woman to know each other. Once upon a time, she would have said that Adam was the antithesis of everything she admired in a man. Now she was not so sure. She had discovered that there was neither rhyme nor reason to love. For better for worse, she loved Adam Dillon. And she was done with trying to coerce her wayward heart to the opposite persuasion.

Adam looked blindly at Claire then looked away. He was reflecting that he felt as though his fate hung in the balance. This slender slip of a girl could send him to oblivion with one small, annihilating word.

Impatient with himself, he quashed that unacceptable thought. In his mind he marshaled the solid arguments he had been rehearsing to persuade the reluctant lady to his will.

"There's been talk," he began abruptly, then hesitated.

"Talk?" repeated Claire.

"About you," said Adam, unaware that he was frowning.

"What sort of talk?"

"Speculation . . . about us. It's my own fault."

Claire covered her eyes with one hand. "Oh God," she said, "I always feared that this would happen. I've been recognized. Is that what you are trying to tell me, Adam?"

"Recognized?" repeated Adam carefully.

"From Rouen? As Duhet's . . . mistress?"

Adam bit down on a smile. In Rouen, Claire had scarcely set foot outside the door of the commissioner's headquarters. And anyone seeing her in her threadbare garments would scarcely have taken her for a rich man's toy. Besides, this was America. No one was likely to make the connection between Claire Devereux and Claire Michelet. Still, she had given him something to think about.

He sat down beside her. "No," he said. "For the moment, our secret is safe."

"Thank God!"

"However . . . who is to say for how long that happy state of affairs may continue?"

"You think . . . ?"

"It's a remote possibility," he said gravely, "and one I wish you would bear in mind as you listen to what I am going to say to you. Claire, we must marry. You know that as well as I do." He paused before continuing. "I asked you to marry me in Rouen. Nothing has changed. I made all my promises to you then. They still stand. Just for the sake of argument, let's suppose you were to marry some other man. Claire, you would never cease to wonder if your past would not catch up with you. One day it might, then where would you be? I know everything there is to know about you. I was the one who got you into this predicament. It stands to me to get you out of it."

He looked at her then, and she thought that she had never seen eyes so green or so chilling. "Claire, be very sure about one thing before you give me your answer. I've discovered that I don't have it in me to stand aside and let another man take what is mine. I'd see him dead first."

"I see," she said, and she did, more than she wanted to. He did not love her, had never loved her, not even in Rouen. He wanted her. That much was evident. But that was not love. Last night, it had seemed to her that Adam's feelings ran deep and true, as her own did. She saw now what it was. His touching concern was prompted by an odd mixture of lust and remorse.

"Well, Claire, what is my answer to be?"

"I'll marry you, Adam," she said, but there was no joy in her.

The wedding was to take place in a month's time, after the banns had been called. It was the height of the summer, and New York was very thin of company. Every man and his neighbor, it seemed, had removed to his country estate. Adam was glad. He didn't want a big showy wedding with hordes of guests to be entertained. He just wanted Claire.

Claire insisted that she be married by a priest of her own faith. She was a Catholic. No one would have guessed that she cared one way or another. For months, she had happily attended church services at Trinity. Adam understood. He, too, had been born a Catholic, and though no longer a practicing one, he felt the pull of the old and familiar.

The priest wished to see them both, individually, before the marriage was celebrated. Adam was agreeable. Some things, however, had completely slipped his mind. Confession! Adam was aghast. He had no wish to shock the sensibilities of the saintly Father O'Hara. In the privacy of the sacristy, when he fell on his knees before the priest, Adam felt like a felon in the dock. Two hours later, when he lightly descended the stairs of St. Peter's, he was happier and more at peace with himself than he had been in many a long while.

With Claire, it was otherwise. She left Father O'Hara a wiser and more chastened girl.

"How did it go?" asked Adam when he met Claire later. They were feeding the carp in John's lily pond.

"Fine," said Claire. "Father O'Hara thinks I'm a very fortunate girl."

Adam's expression became arrested. "I wonder what he means by that?"

Claire cocked her head as she studied Adam's face. "What he means," said Claire, "is that you will make a very fine husband."

"Did Father O'Hara say that?"

Claire nodded her assent.

Adam grinned. "I expect it was prompted by the rather generous sum I promised to donate to St. Peter's building fund. Which reminds me . . ." and he launched on a description of a number of furnished houses for rent in the heart of Manhattan which he had selected for Claire's inspection.

"Only as a temporary measure, you understand," he told her. "Just tell me what you want, Claire, and you shall have it."

"I hadn't really thought about it," she replied.

"Would you prefer to live in the city or in the country?"

She was too preoccupied to notice the intent look in his eyes. Her thoughts were still with Father O'Hara. She shrugged carelessly.

A sudden coolness entered Adam's voice. "Forgive me," he said. "I see that I am boring you with such trifles."

Claire, realizing that she had been involved in her own reveries, caught hold of Adam's hand as he swung away from her. "Adam! Please!"

His face was carved in forbidding lines, and it came to Claire that she had inadvertently hurt him. She gazed pleadingly into his shuttered face. "I wasn't really listening. I was thinking of Father O'Hara. You see, Adam, unlike you, I don't think I made a very good impression on the priest."

Gradually, Adam's features relaxed. The awkwardness was smoothed over. Not that Adam accepted Claire's interpretation of events. He could not conceive of anyone not being bowled over by Claire. But he could see that Claire was troubled.

"What is it, Claire? What happened?"

She spoke archly, as if the whole thing were a huge

304

joke. "I think Father O'Hara is piqued because I attended services at Trinity for so many months. I'm a Catholic. I should have sought him out sooner."

Adam smiled along with her. "Yes. He had some pithy words to say to me on the same subject. But that isn't it Claire. There's something else. What is it, my love?"

The endearment was almost her undoing. But Blanche, a reluctant chaperone, made a tardy appearance at that moment, and the conversation became diverted to other channels.

On Claire's marriage, Blanche had proposed to find lodgings and establish the school the girls had once talked about. Claire would not hear of it. Blanche was like a sister to her. She must make her home with Adam and her. It was Adam who had settled the argument. There could be no doubt of his sincerity in offering Blanche a home. Her part in precipitating his separation from Claire was no longer of any interest. Blanche had proved a true friend to Claire. Adam would be forever in her debt.

What neither Adam nor Claire was aware of was Blanche's resolve to remain in New York until Millot should come and claim her. *Wait for me*, he had told her. The waiting was killing her. The news from France was not good. She dared not confide her fears to Claire. Claire's anxiety for her parents was too acute and Blanche would say nothing which might add to it. Claire deserved to find a little happiness.

Blanche studied Adam covertly. Their eyes brushed and held. A moment later, over Claire's bent head, they exchanged a smile of complete comprehension.

Throughout the days that followed, Claire's thoughts dwelled more and more on her interview with Father O'Hara. He was like no other priest she had ever known. Though it was years since Claire had made her confession, she knew the ritual. Father

O'Hara made it plain that there was more to confession than mere ritual. Like a doctor with a scalpel, he probed every festering sore. There was no aspect of her life that he did not touch upon. If he was shocked by her account of how she had come to meet Adam, he gave no sign of it. On the contrary, his eyes seemed to bathe her with a mute compassion. Somehow, she found herself relating the circumstances of her birth.

"What do you feel for your natural father?" he asked.

"I despise him," she declared, more passionate than she had meant to be.

"Why?"

"Why? Isn't it obvious? Because he was a scoundrel."

"Perhaps he tried to make amends. Perhaps he has led a godly life. Child, you cannot see into another's soul."

Claire snorted. "Can a leopard change its spots?" she demanded.

"What of Adam?" he said in the same calm tone. "Can he change his spots?"

"That's different," said Claire.

"How is it different?"

Claire began to tremble.

When it was evident that she had nothing to say to this question, the priest said, "Why do you want to marry Adam?"

On a tortured breath, she whispered, "Because I love him, and I can't seem to stop."

"Why should you want to stop? Adam is a good man. He has the makings of a fine husband and father—with the right woman, of course."

Claire had no answer for this either.

The priest sighed. "Tell me, child," he said. "Do you think a man like Adam can be happy with a woman who offers him only a reluctant love?"

"It's more than Adam is offering me," answered

Claire, on the defensive.

Father O'Hara stared at her from under straight bushy brows.

"It's true," said Claire. "Adam does not love me. I told you why he was marrying me."

"He loves you," chided the priest gently.

"He has never said so."

"Child," the priest shook his head, "some things are too deep for words."

"Not with Adam Dillon," retorted Claire. "He has a way with words. Any woman will tell you." She bit down on her lip at the betraying remark.

The priest's eyes probed Claire's. Sighing, he said, "Do you wish me to hear your confession, Claire?"

She rose to her feet, hardly knowing what she thought. "I . . . no . . . that is, I need time to think."

"I shall be here when you are ready," he said, confusing Claire even more with the somber look he gave her.

It was hard to swallow, but it seemed that Adam had sailed through his interview with Father O'Hara without an eyebrow being raised, whereas she had come under the priest's censure. Oh, not that Father O'Hara had said one unkind word to her. But she could sense that he was disappointed in her.

A week was to pass before she could bring herself to return to St. Peter's, a week of unmerciful soul-searching and self-doubt. The shaken girl who met with Father O'Hara was far different than the girl who had met with him the week before, even supposing she managed to greet him with a smile.

"Are you ready to make your confession, Claire?" he asked gravely.

She tried for a laugh. It came out shakily. "This may take some time," she joked.

Father O'Hara smiled. "We have all the time in the world," he replied.

Claire nodded. Sinking to her knees, she made the

sign of the cross and kissed the crucifix he held out to her. Haltingly, she embarked on the customary prayer.

Father O'Hara waited.

"Bless me, Father, for I have sinned," she said and could get no further. There was a sensation of pain in her chest. Her ears were buzzing. She tried to blink away the mist in her eyes. Swallowing, she started over. "Bless me, Father, for I have sinned . . ." She began to weep, softly at first, and then with deep shuddering sobs that wracked her slender frame.

After a while, the priest's hands fell to her shoulders, holding her in a comforting clasp.

"Forgive me," she choked out, "but I can't seem to find the right words."

Father O'Hara forbore to smile. "Some things are too deep for words," he said. "You have a contrite heart. That's a beginning."

Claire wept as though her heart would break.

Before the altar, Claire and Adam went on their knees to receive the sacrament of holy communion. Minutes before they had plighted their troth. They were husband and wife.

In everything, Adam circumspectly followed his bride's lead. He still felt out of place in a church. Claire was familiar with the religious language and ritual. She knew what to expect. Thankfully, Father O'Hara was aware of Adam's plight. With a smile and a nod, the old priest shepherded him through the nerve-taxing ceremony.

As Adam studied Claire's somber profile, he thought that this moment was one that would stay with him for the rest of his life. In the last little while, he had thought of Claire constantly. His thoughts had been mostly of a carnal nature. There was something here that had never remotely entered his calculations, something solemn and sublime that transcended anything he had ever known.

His hands covered Claire's around the silver chalice. Her eyes lifted to meet his. They were soft with emotion. Adam felt as though all the breath had been knocked out of him. Joy burst through him in wave after wave. Long before the priest pronounced the solemn words, he was aware of a benediction in every cell of his body.

Chapter Nineteen

"Adam, this is . . . ," Claire warmed him with one of her own melting smiles, "this is . . . like something out of a fairy tale."

No smile from Adam. "Do you like it, Claire? Do you think you could be happy here? You never did say, you know, whether you wished to live in the heart of the city or in the country."

"So now we have two houses."

"The house in Hanover Square is only rented," pointed out Adam. "We could divide our time between the two. The winters here are harsh. But in the scorching heat of summer, when the city is intolerable, there is nowhere on earth more beautiful, more refreshing, than the Hudson Valley."

He seemed to be hanging on her next words. Adam Dillon unsure of himself? Claire found the picture endearing.

Shading her eyes with one hand she looked back on the meandering river. A flotilla of small boats and sailing ships seemed to bob her a curtsy. The Hudson River, from Albany to the port of New York, was a busy thoroughfare.

It was on one of those small sailing boats that Adam had spirited away his bride, with their wedding guests waving them off from the dock at the bottom of the Burkes' gardens. Some days before, several carriages had set off with baggage and a full complement of servants, traveling by the Albany road. It was how Claire expected to make the journey. Adam had surprised her. The river was the picturesque route, and he wanted Claire to see the Hudson Valley from the best vantage point.

"Adam," she said, matching his gravity, "I adore your country estate."

"Truly?"

"Truly!"

Claire was not exaggerating. A more perfect spot she could not imagine. In the long, uphill climb from the dock, they had passed orchards and fields variegated with grass and grain. The air was rich with the sounds and scents of pasture and woodland, and a welcome relief from the incessant din of New York.

The house and lawns were suddenly before them. Claire's eyes opened wide. The classic elegance of the place took her breath away. She had seen grand houses in New York, but nothing on this scale. Adam's house gave Claire something to think about.

She knew that many of New York's foremost families had country places to which they retired when the season had run its course. The city, as she understood, was not healthy in the sweltering summer months. There were frequent outbreaks of cholera and yellow fever. Those who could afford it moved to where the air was purer and the water sweeter.

In her ignorance, she had assumed that those country retreats were primitive out-of-the-way places. America was a wilderness. It was a young country. It had no history to speak of. Civilization had barely made inroads into the vast interior. Adam's magnificent white stucco house in its fine setting made a powerful impression. Americans were not crude colonials. They could hold their own with anything that was to be found in Europe.

"Adam, it's perfect," she breathed.

Adam captured her hand. Laughing self-consciously, he hurried her to the house.

Everything pleased her—the symmetrical arrangement of the spacious, airy rooms; the mix of elegant English and sturdy Dutch furniture; the wall hangings; the Turkish carpets, and not least, the fine views from the long windows. The sunsets, so Adam assured her, were spectacular.

Over dinner, Adam told her something of the house's history. The house and land for miles around had been confiscated after the war, when the family who owned it had fled to England.

"They were loyal to the crown," said Adam. "The house itself was destroyed by the British. When I bought it, it was a burned-out hulk."

"When was this?" asked Claire.

"In '88," said Adam, "after I had made a little money in the fur trade."

"Why is it," she asked, "that no one told me that you had a place on the Hudson?"

Adam shrugged off her question. "It's no secret," he said, "though I don't advertise the fact. Besides, the house was standing empty. It's only in the last month or two that it has been readied for occupancy." What he did not tell Claire was that since finding her again, he had been in a fever of impatience to get the house furnished and ready for her.

"And you rebuilt the house?"

"As you can see."

"Why?" Claire was thinking that the house spoke volumes about Adam Dillon. It gave the lie to his avowal that he was not a marrying man. Only a man whose mind was set on establishing his dynasty had need of a house like this. She chuckled, reflecting that if Adam's legion of women had known about the house, they would have pursued him even more hotly.

Adam took his time before answering Claire's

312

question. He topped up her glass of wine. "The house is an embodiment of a dream," he said. He glanced at Claire and saw that she was looking at him expectantly.

The impulse to make light of the whole thing was almost more than he could resist. Adam was used to hiding his true feelings behind a bantering charm. To reveal too much was to put a weapon into another's hand. He had learned that lesson from Philippe in the schoolroom at Blaise.

But Claire was different. Together, they must lay a foundation that would endure for the next forty or fifty years. He yearned for intimacy. At the same time, old habits died hard. He wanted to know everything that there was to know about Claire. He was not sure that he had it in him to be as generous with himself.

"I think I told you that I was the bastard son of the Comte de Blaise?" began Adam quietly, and he went on to recount something of his early years.

Claire had heard it all before, and yet, everything was new to her. It was as though a veil had been lifted from her eyes. Adam was the bastard son. Why had she supposed that Adam was any less sensitive than she to the blot of illegitimacy? And his case was worse than hers, for she had been raised in the circle of a loving and devoted family. Adam had had to fend for himself.

As his quiet and dispassionate recitation continued, a pang of something both sweet and sorrowful seemed to pierce Claire's heart. In her mind's eye she could almost see the boy Adam must have been in that small garret when Mara Dillon had handed him over to his natural father. And as he grew to manhood in a household where he had no place, she could almost taste the boy's hurt and bewilderment. Her throat ached from holding back the tears.

Knowing that Adam would be appalled if he could read her mind, that pity was the last thing he wanted, especially from her, Claire became involved in

313

selecting and peeling a peach. But all the while she was thinking that Father O'Hara was right. There was more to Adam Dillon than met the eye.

"So you see, Claire," said Adam in summation, "having not a stick of property to call my own, no legacy, no title to fall heir to, I dreamed of an estate to rival Blaise." There was a touch of irony in his smile. "In retrospect, I see that it was envy that spurred my ambition."

Claire knew, even if Adam did not, that it was so much more than that. She hardly knew how to answer him, and shocked herself as much as Adam by the words that sprang spontaneously to her lips.

"I never knew my real parents. After hearing your story, I begin to think that perhaps it's just as well. My mother was unmarried. My father was an American, an unprincipled adventurer, by some accounts. I shall never know. You see, I was raised by my uncle and his wife as though I was their own. I knew none of the circumstances surrounding my birth until I was fifteen years old. Even so, that kind of thing leaves an indelible mark. You are wrong to say that you had no legacy, Adam. For good, for evil, our parents passed on a legacy. Do you know what I think?"

Adam was still in shock, but he managed a neutral, "What?"

Claire's look was almost pleading. "I think I should like to pass on a different kind of legacy, a legacy of love."

Adam had regained sufficient composure to murmur, "Love?" Then Claire went and blew it all to smithereens.

"To our children, and to our children's children," she said.

Much later, sprawled in his lonely bridal bed, Adam considered the strategy he was employing to win Claire to him. He was making progress, he decided. He felt closer to Claire than he had ever felt to anyone in his life, even closer than when he had made love to her in Rouen. How had it come about?

He rolled to his back and gazed unseeingly at the bed canopy overhead. They were not so very different, Claire had said. They both had a dream. Each wished to pass on something of worth to the next generation. A legacy of love, she had called it. Adam's lips curved.

Claire's mind, Claire's ambitions, were appropriate to the softer sex, he supposed. Her feelings were maternal. She wanted babies. He had known it when he had observed her with Betsy's children. Claire and babies were as natural together as bread pudding and clotted cream. And he would give her babies, lots of them, if it would make her happy.

But children, in themselves, would never serve his ambition. Leastways, he did not think so. He considered the matter carefully, and ended up by laughing. When he thought of babies, he thought of pouncing on Claire and stripping her naked. He thought of penetrating her sweet body and making her give in to him, not in submission, but in passion. He thought of impregnating her, but that thought was an erotic one, as evidenced by his hardening groin.

Groaning, he rolled to his side. In an effort to distract himself, he fastened on something the old priest had told him. Marriage was a sacrament. Adam had no clear idea of what this meant except in general terms. He must put Claire first.

He was trying to. As God was his witness, he was doing his best. He was courting her. He was going to prove to her that there was more to Adam Dillon than brute lust. He was capable of the finer feelings. He had it in him to be as considerate, as forbearing, as patient a husband as any bride could wish, and so he had told her. Surely the torture he was enduring for

315

her sake must count for something?

He felt as though he were skating on thin ice. He wasn't going to do or say anything to alarm Claire. He was going to make her forget the man who had taken her innocence in Rouen. That Adam Dillon was not the same man he was now. The new Adam was resolved to court Claire till she came to him of her own volition.

For some few minutes, he enjoyed the delightful prospect of Claire coming to him willingly. He did not think that day could be far off. She was coming to trust him. That thought opened the door to less pleasant reflections.

He was keeping secrets from Claire. John Burke was her natural father. Adam was not sure that Claire's best interests would be served should she ever learn that fact. Not that he would reveal it. It was not his secret to reveal. Still, it was inevitable that Claire's budding trust in her husband would suffer a setback if and when she learned that he had been party to keeping secrets from her.

But that setback would be as nothing compared to what would happen when Claire discovered that her brother, Leon, had never reached England. In Rouen, Adam had told Claire a blatant untruth. Millot had seen Leon into the carriage that was conveying her sister to the coast, he had told her. And later, in her eyes, it would seem that he had compounded the injury by sanctioning another falsehood. Her young friends had safely crossed the English Channel.

Groaning, Adam threw one arm over his eyes. One day, when the war between France and England was over, perhaps sooner, the truth must come out. Then where would he be? If anything had happened to the boy, and it seemed something must have, Claire would be distraught. She would turn on him. In vain he would plead that his one thought at the time was to ensure the safety of his mission. Nothing must be done that would draw undue attention to the commissioner of Rouen. His search for the boy had been perfunctory at best. But his hands had been tied. Surely Claire would see that?

She wouldn't of course. Because he had told her a lie, and had, indeed, continued to perpetrate the lie when there was no necessity for it. He tried to imagine Claire's response if he went to her now and told her the truth about her brother. She would see it as another betrayal. She would spurn him.

He wasn't going to let that happen. Her trust was a fragile thing. When it was more robust, when she had learned that he had her best interests at heart, he would break the news gently to her. He ran the risk, he supposed, of events overtaking him. There was always the possibility that someone else would get to Claire first. Perhaps Zoë, the little sister. It was a risk he had to take, for every day of grace was a day that worked in his favor. The passage of time strengthened his position. And when he and Claire became lovers, his hold on her would be formidable.

In her chaste bed, Claire was no closer to sleep than Adam. Her thoughts were chaotic. She was bewildered. This was not the wedding night she had dreamed about. To her certain knowledge, Adam was a virile, lusty man. He had an eye for the ladies, and that was putting it politely. Where had she gone wrong?

She pulled herself to a sitting position and glared gloomily into space. No one would believe it if she were to swear it under oath. Adam Dillon, the foremost libertine in the state of New York, had pressed a kiss to his bride's fingers and had thereupon left her. And just when it seemed that they were on the threshold of something new and awesome between them. It did not make sense. What kind of man would treat his bride so shabbily on her wedding night?

317

There was more to Adam Dillon than met the eye, Father O'Hara had told her. Hadn't she always known it? The frown on her brow intensified in concentration. What kind of man had she married?

Impressions came and went in her mind. Fragments of conversations lingered. Finally, her thoughts settled on something inconsequential. She was remembering how John Burke's steward, at Adam's request, had moved her to the rose room on that awful night of her ball when she had stabbed her feather mattress in a fit of hurt pride. *Oh Adam*, she thought, and laughed shakily.

He was a rogue. He was also the most considerate, the most sensitive, and the most generous-hearted gentleman of her acquaintance. Wasn't that why he had married her—to protect her good name from scandal? It was all of a piece with what she knew of Adam Dillon, if only she'd had the wit to scratch the surface long before now. From the moment blind chance had thrown them together, he had proved his sterling worth. He was not perfect, but nor was she.

Unbidden, she had a picture of Adam as he must have been as a boy. Solitary, on the outside looking in, with no place to call his own. Wasn't that what this house and estate were all about? It had little to do with envy as Adam seemed to think, and everything to do with belonging. *That* was Adam's dream. To belong. Suddenly, Claire knew what she must do.

By the time she padded to the adjoining door to Adam's chamber, her courage began to melt away. Her heart was pounding. Her throat was dry. She couldn't go through with it. She did not know the first thing about seducing a man. She would make a fool of herself. Adam was used to worldly women. She was gauche.

The door seemed to open of its own volition. Claire gasped. She was certain that she had not turned the handle. Perhaps she could pull the door shut, and no one the wiser? Holding her breath, she inched forward.

"Claire!" Adam shot bolt upright in bed.

"Hummm," said Claire, her brain cravenly groping for a way out of her dilemma. "I . . . I could not sleep," she offered lamely.

"No more could I."

Claire summoned the remnants of her courage and took a step into the cavernous moonlit interior. "I . . . ," she said, and promptly forgot what she was going to say. Fascinated, she gazed at Adam's naked torso. She had all but forgotten that the man's physique was alarmingly virile. Her very fingertips seemed to quiver with memories—those powerful masculine muscles bunching and rippling as she clung to him in the act of love.

Her eyes closed. Breathing became difficult. She held on to the door for support.

"Claire?" Adam's throat worked. Didn't she know what she was doing to him? The moonlight touched her womanly curves and valleys in all the places his hands itched to cover. Oh God, if this was a test, surely a saint would fail it. And he was only a man.

It was now or never, thought Claire. Her last thought before she blurted out what she had hardly taken time to think about was that Father O'Hara would be proud of her. In fear and trembling and almost inaudibly, she said, "Adam, I did not marry you to save my name from scandal. I love you. That's the reason I married you. I love you. I know you don't love me. But I'm giving you fair warning. I aim to try and make you."

Having said her piece, the next part was easy. She was going to throw herself into his arms. Claire's feet moved, but in the opposite direction. She quickly shut the door and hared back to her bed. She had scarcely pulled the bedclothes over her ears when the door burst open. Her mate gave a roar of triumph and pounced on her. Squirming, squealing, she was swung into his arms and held aloft as if she were the spoils of war.

Adam dropped her on the bed and swiftly covered her with the weight of his body. Though she was breathing hard, she wasn't putting up any resistance. Supporting himself on his forearms, he gazed down at her.

"I did not marry you to save your name from scandal either," he said.

"What? But you said . . ."

"I know what I said. It was the only way I could think to get you to accept me."

Hope shivered through her. "Why did you want me to?"

"Claire," he said, "Claire," and could not find the words to express what was in his heart. To say that he loved her did not do justice to what he was feeling. He had said those words to too many women before Claire. There must be a better way.

He lit several candles around the room before returning to stretch out beside her. As though he were a blind man feeling his way in unfamiliar territory Adam touched his fingertips to Claire's face, reverently tracing over bone and warm skin. One hand slipped to her nape, lifting her to receive his kiss.

"Don't be afraid," he murmured.

Adam had kissed Claire before, but never like this. His lips moved over her without pressure, as though he were afraid she might break. When his lips drifted onto hers, she responded shyly.

He pulled back to gauge her expression.

"I . . . I didn't know it could be like this," she whispered. "This is nice."

Adam smiled. "Nice?" he asked whimsically, and he increased the pressure of his mouth, but only barely. In Rouen, he had behaved like a brute. He was going to make amends. Claire was a novice in the ways of love. He was going to take her with restraint even if it killed him.

His kisses became hotter, deeper, more quickly

than he wanted them to. He left her lips to investigate her cheeks, her throat, her breasts. He was breathing hard. Claire wasn't helping him. Her moans were driving him crazy. She was restless, moving rhythmically beneath him. Her nails were scoring his shoulders. He groaned his frustration. This wasn't what he wanted for her. He was going to cherish her.

Claire was experiencing a desire so intense, so powerful, that restraint was the last thing she wanted. Moreover, she didn't feel like a novice in the ways of love. Pure instinct had taken over. She might know next to nothing about men. But Adam Dillon was no ordinary man. He was the beloved. Her body had understood this truth long before she was willing to accept it. Her mind had loosened all the restraints she normally placed on herself. Her senses were leaping. Adam was too slow for her.

She was whimpering, panting, bucking against him. Modesty had deserted her. Without the pretense of a blush, she told him what she wanted from him. "I want you inside me," she said.

At her words, Adam's good intentions shattered into a thousand shards. He could not help himself. He could not wait to get at her.

When he tried to disrobe her, his fingers became all thumbs. If he was a man of experience, Claire would never have known it. It seemed as if his fingers had never slipped a button from its buttonhole in his life. Claire hastened him along, and finally, in desperation, took over.

He was too close to the edge. He had hungered for her too long. "Claire," he said, trying to explain it all to her. He could not find the breath. He was fighting to pull air into his lungs. There was not the time.

He dragged the hem of her night rail to her waist. His hand was instantly between her thighs. His fingers probed intimately. When he discovered that she was wet for him, Adam's control snapped. *Softly*, he tried to tell himself. Claire wasn't helping. She

321

was kissing and nipping at every exposed inch of his throat and shoulders. His little kitten was turning into a tigress. Slowly, gritting his teeth, he pushed into her. For a moment, they stilled, savoring the wonder of their joining.

"Adam, oh Adam. I feel . . ." Claire laughed. She didn't know what she was feeling. Pleasure. Sweetness. Love. Why wouldn't the man say the words to her? "I love you," she said.

Adam groaned and pressed deeper, lifting her to him. Here, he would show her, with the worship of his body. He began to move, slowly, carefully, nudging Claire into following his rhythm. She obeyed, and Adam was lost. In an instant, the sweetness changed into something quite different. Fever. Their movements became frenzied. The world came to a shattering end.

When their breathing had slowed to normal, Adam pulled to his side, relieving Claire of his weight. He raised to one elbow, watching her through lowered lashes.

Claire stretched like a jungle cat. She turned her head on the pillow. Her mate, she decided, had the look of a hapless lamb that had blundered into the lion's den. Smiling, she pulled herself up to his level.

"Adam Dillon, why won't you say the words to me?" she said, and pressed little kisses to the small scratches she had made on his chest and shoulders.

Adam's hands cupped her shoulders, stilling her movements. Claire lifted her head, her eyes alert.

"Adam, what is it?"

"Don't ask me to say those words," he said. "They don't mean a thing. Claire, I've said those words to countless women in my time. Countless women have repeated them to me. It's all part of the game. It's an empty ritual signifying nothing."

All the joy in their lovemaking seemed to drain out of her. She sank back on her elbows, staring at him with enormous eyes. She swallowed, and felt an ache

322

begin where her heart was supposed to be.

"Damnation," Adam cursed and dragged her back to the shelter of his body. He stroked her soothingly. "Claire," he said, "you're not like those other women. You matter to me. I don't want . . . I won't say . . ." He paused, groping for the words to express himself. His voice gentled. "You know the kind of man I was, Claire. You said it yourself. I was a rogue, a flirt. I know all the right words to persuade a woman into my bed. Hell, those words were my stock-in-trade. I don't even know what they mean.

"You deserve better than that. And I'm going to give it to you, the very best that is in me, Claire. I'll take care of you. I'll be a loyal, faithful husband. I'll be a good father to your children. I'll make you happier than you've ever been in your life. You'll never regret marrying me, I promise you. I don't know what more you could want of me, but whatever it is, I'll give it to you. But I *won't* say those empty words."

Claire stared at him solemnly.

"Claire, say something!"

"I love you," she said, and pressed her fingers to his lips as he opened his mouth to make a protest. "Those words mean something to me," she said. "You see, Adam, I've never said them to another man."

"Claire!" His tone was anguished.

"Don't worry, my love. One day, you'll come to know what those words mean, I promise you. But for the present," she sighed dramatically, "would you be very shocked, my darling, if I seduced you again?"

Adam stared, then smothered her in a ferocious bear hug.

Chapter Twenty

Claire had started something in Adam that slowly gained in momentum. He was more himself than he had ever been. Sometimes, he felt like a young boy again. The world was his oyster, just waiting for him to open it. Everything was possible—as long as he had Claire.

He feasted on her, both physically and emotionally. She was like the bread of life to him, and like a starving man he wanted to hoard her for himself. For years he had existed on half-rations without knowing it. Having tasted Claire, he knew that he had cheated himself.

His appetite was voracious. He must touch her and kiss her and fondle her at every opportunity. And Adam made sure that there were many opportunities. He had been too long alone, too distrustful, too cynical. His cynical turn of mind was not inborn. It had been drummed into him in the hard school of life. With Claire as his teacher, he was gradually learning a better way.

Inevitably, as time passed, he became less reticent about his early years. "I remember when . . . ," Claire would say and start a train of thought that cast them back to the time when they were children. Adam was a fund of funny stories. Claire had never laughed so much in her life. But when the laughter faded, there was a lump in her throat. She did not know why she had laughed in the first place. Adam's early life had not been a happy one. Her mothering instincts came to the fore. Beneath her husband's easy charm, more and more she was coming to see the lost, solitary boy who had been starved of affection. She ached for that boy.

It was only natural that she would take to wondering about Philippe. Why was he so very different from Adam when both boys had been raised in the same household? From what she could gather, Philippe's young life had not been a happy one either. Philippe and Adam might have been friends. Instead they had become bitter enemies, though the hatred was far more on Philippe's part than Adam's.

As she probed deeper, Claire thought she had her answer. Incredible as it seemed, Philippe was insanely jealous of Adam. Philippe had been the heir to the title, to great wealth and estates. Adam's legacy would have been a modest one, but even that had been taken away from him by Philippe. Adam had arrived in America with little more than the clothes on his back. He was lucky to have escaped with his life.

No one knew what had become of Philippe. News from France was sporadic at best. By Adam's account, his half-brother seemed to have disappeared off the face of the earth. Sometimes Claire felt sorry for Philippe. She could not help wondering what kind of man he might have become if the circumstances of his life had been different. Then she remembered their last encounter in the women's courtyard of the Conciergerie and she felt a frisson of foreboding. Even then, Philippe's burning hatred of Adam had seemed like a tangible thing. His mind was set on retribution. Claire did not wish Philippe ill, but she

325

was glad that a whole ocean separated France from America.

The bond between Adam and Claire grew stronger. They were able to speak more easily about their time together in Rouen.

"I don't deserve that you should forgive me," said Adam. He was referring to the night he had taken Claire's innocence. "I behaved with all the finesse of a rutting boar."

They were in Claire's bedchamber. Adam was making love to his wife. He was taking his time about it.

"Hurry," said Claire.

Adam smiled indulgently. "I like making love to you. I don't want it to end."

"But Adam, I can't take much more."

"Then make me give in to you."

Claire propped herself on one elbow. The thought intrigued her. "How?" she asked.

Adam's long lashes lowered to half-mast. "I . . . no . . . it's too soon to initiate you into all the ways a man and his wife can pleasure each other in bed. I'm standing by my promise, Claire. I'm going to be as restrained a lover as a bride could wish."

Claire pulled herself up. She studied Adam's profile. Incredulously she asked, "Are you saying that I have more to learn?"

Adam gave her one of his lazy grins. "You're a mere novice," he teased, and tweaked her nose.

Claire huffed. Her chin came up. "Show me," she said.

"I wouldn't want to shock you," demurred Adam.

"You won't shock me," she promised.

Adam feigned reluctance. Claire lost patience. "You made me give in to you in Rouen when I didn't want to," she remonstrated. "It's only fair that you should teach me how it was done."

"You're sure?"

"Perfectly."

"Like this," said Adam. Holding her eyes with his, he brought her hands to his shoulders. "Touch me," he said softly. "I promise I won't break."

At her first tentative touch, powerful masculine muscles clenched beneath her fingertips. Claire was fascinated. She rose to her knees and became absorbed in the task of forcing Adam to give in to her.

As the lesson progressed, her curiosity faltered.

"I told you it would shock you," said Adam. Smiling reassuringly, he pulled her hands back to the safety of his shoulders.

Claire sat back on her heels. Her brow was furrowed. Without volition, she voiced the stray thought that had entered her head. "I'll wager you've permitted dozens of women to take these liberties with you."

"Claire!" groaned Adam. He hated to be reminded of those other women. More to the point, he hated it when Claire thought of them.

She loomed over him, pressing him back into the pillows. "I'm your wife," she told him. "I should be permitted more liberties than any woman."

"I could not agree with you more. In fact, you have my permission to take as many liberties as you wish," offered Adam generously.

Claire chewed on her bottom lip. The thought that other women had known Adam more intimately than she was something she would not tolerate. Shyness dissolved in the overwhelming desire to stamp her brand of ownership on her mate. But it was the know-it-all twinkle in his eyes that goaded Claire as nothing else could. Her vanity was piqued. She refused to let him be the teacher. With only love and blind instinct to guide her, she taught Adam a lesson he would never forget.

When it was over, he said wonderingly, "God, Claire, I haven't blushed like this since I was a callow youth."

"I thought I would shock you," said Claire, smiling complacently. Her own blushes were still hot upon her cheeks.

Adam fitted her more snugly to his length. "I would never have dreamed of asking so much of you." He pressed tiny kisses to her neck and shoulders. "But now that you have given it to me, hereafter I shall expect it as a matter of course."

Claire turned in to him. Her voice was thick with sleep. "Thank God it was you who came through that door that night and not Philippe."

Adam shook her into wakefulness. "What does that mean?"

Drowsily, she replied, "Even then, I knew you were different."

"But you thought I was Philippe. You were terrified into submission."

Her answer was a huge yawn.

"Claire!"

Something in his voice roused her from drowsiness. She propped herself up on one arm to get a better look at him. "I admit I thought you were Philippe, but at the same time, I knew you were different. It occurred to me that something had happened at Angers which had changed you out of all recognition. I've told you some of this before."

Adam looked to be unconvinced, and Claire roused herself to say, "I assure you Adam, I could never mistake you for your half-brother."

"No?"

"No," and she went on earnestly, "If by some odd chance I came upon you both in a darkened room, I would still be able to tell you apart."

"Now that is too farfetched to be credible."

"You may think so, but it's the truth. I can't explain it adequately. You'll just have to take my word for it."

Claire drifted into sleep. Adam was wakeful. He was thinking of Philippe, wondering where he was and what he was doing, and whether or not they would ever meet again. He prayed that they would not.

They had their first quarrel. Claire started it. It began as an innocent game of dalliance, provoked by Adam's refusal to give her the words she longed to hear. In her heart of hearts, she knew that her husband loved her. But it irked her that he would never give her the words when, by his own admission, he had given them to so many other women. She was going to teach him a lesson. She was going to prove to him that he loved her.

She dressed that evening with particular care, nothing too stylish, but not too dowdy either. She finally settled on a simple sheath of pastel blue silk with puff sleeves and a square neckline. They were going to a public dance in the assembly rooms of the local tavern. Claire loved these informal assemblies. To her knowledge, there was nothing quite like them in France. Her parents would have frowned on such dubious goings-on. Democracy was laudable in principle, but in practice, one did not mix with the lower orders. In America, people did not stand on ceremony. If a man wished to join the assemblies, he was free to do so, providing he had the wherewithal to pay the price of admission.

The ballroom was upstairs, and ran the whole length of the tavern. The music was provided by a couple of fiddlers and an accordion player. The revelers were what Adam called "a mixed crowd," anything from the scion of the largest land-owning family in the district to the three pretty daughters of the local miller and his wife. All the dances were country dances. From time-to-time, someone would sing an old ballad or recite a few verses. The dancers were glad of it. It gave them a respite to recover their breath before throwing themselves into the fray.

"Hello? What have we here?"

Claire smiled a welcome at the young man who had halted by her bench. Adam was at the far end of the room in conversation with the miller.

"I'm Claire Dillon, Adam's wife," said Claire, "and you, I know, are Mark Clay. I was talking to your mother a minute or so ago. She pointed you out to me as you came through the doors."

Mark Clay was in his midtwenties, as near as Claire could judge. His hair was the color of the wheat ripening in the fields just outside the windows. His look was bold but not insulting.

He smiled, just so, and Claire bit back a laugh. She had witnessed that practiced smile on Adam's lips on more occasions than she cared to remember. Young Clay, she conjectured, fancied himself as something of a ladies' man. She took an instant liking to him.

"Lucky Adam," he said, eyeing her with unabashed admiration. "You are the loveliest thing that has ever graced any of our assemblies. Where did he find you?"

Claire, recollecting her first meeting with Adam, lowered her lashes and hoped that she wasn't blushing. "In France," she said, then adroitly changed the subject. "Adam tells me that you are the biggest landowner in these parts, Mr. Clay?"

The music struck up, and before Claire could protest, Mark had led her onto the floor to join one of the sets for a Scottish dance that went by the name of an eightsome reel. This dance was more rambunctious than anything that had gone before, for the gentlemen let out wild yells that sounded like Indian war whoops. Flushed with her exertions, laughing, Claire caught her husband's intensely brooding stare. Adam was in a taking, and Claire could not understand it. Then young Clay spun her round and

330

it all became clear to her. Adam was jealous.

That thought buoyed her hopes. Adam loved her. Why wouldn't he admit it? She would wring an admission from him. She would fan the flames of his jealousy—not enough to hurt him, of course, but just enough to bring him to his senses.

When Mark offered to fetch Claire a glass of lemonade, she suggested that he bring it outside to her. The ballroom was too hot for her comfort. She would slip outside for a breath of fresh air. Mark was too much the gentleman to demur, but Claire caught the uneasy glance he threw in her husband's direction. Adam's look was thunderous. Claire felt a pang of conscience but squashed it. Her motives were pure.

An open veranda surrounded three sides of the tavern. Claire waited for Mark at one secluded corner where she could keep an eye on the stairs. She did not have long to wait. Adam descended as Mark entered the foyer carrying a glass of lemonade. The gentlemen exchanged some few words, then the younger man handed over Claire's drink, and escaped with an alacrity that was comical.

Laughing softly, Claire moved to the rail of the veranda. There were plenty of people about, some of whom had slipped outside to observe the sunset. Adam had made no idle boast. The sunsets were truly magnificent. The sky was a burst of gold.

Claire heard Adam's step behind her. His hand slipped round to cover her breast. She gasped, then giggled. "Sir, you are a bold one!" she exclaimed, spinning to face him. His face was pale and hard. His jaw was clenched. Violence was leaping out at her from his eyes. There was menace in every taut line of him.

"Adam!" she said weakly.

"My God, Claire, I think I shall kill you for this."

She could see at once that he wasn't exaggerating. "A-Adam," she stammered, "I-I knew it was you."

331

There was no softening in him. He dashed the glass in his hand into a flower bed and spun back to face her. Claire's heart seemed to leap to her throat. The deferential lover she had known since her marriage was completely absent in this threatening stranger. This man seemed barely civilized.

She took a step back. Adam advanced and reached for her. Claire didn't think about the wisdom of what she was doing. With a little cry, she picked up her skirts and fled.

She struck out along the only path she knew, the path that wound up to their house, the one they had descended, laughing, arm-in-arm, only an hour or two before. How could the evening have taken such a turn?

She blamed herself. And it was all so pointless. She knew that Adam loved her. Why must she press him like this?

There was a stitch in her side. She was gasping for breath and she had more than a mile to go. She could not outrun Adam. Then why hadn't he caught up with her?

She stopped to listen, half turning to look fearfully over her shoulder. The fading light seemed to dew the tips of the trees and shrubbery with molten gold. The night was alive with sounds, but not the one she was dreading. Adam had not given chase. She let out a shaky laugh. What a fool she had been, blowing the whole thing out of proportion. Adam would never hurt her. She must return to him at once.

"Claire."

She closed her eyes. How had he managed to get ahead of her? "Adam," she whispered.

His powerful hands closed over her shoulders. He turned her to face him. His voice was savage. "Never run from me again. Do you understand? Never!"

Breathing was still painful. She nodded weakly. When he swung her into his arms, she sobbed out in fright. He left the path and carried her into thick underbrush. Beneath the branches of a mature evergreen, he set her down on a cushion of sweet grass and pine needles. There was a clearing in the trees through which she could see out over the river to the dark ridge of the Catskills in the far distance. And then Adam was there before her like a great predatory shadow, blotting out the light.

She put up a hand to fend him off, then thought better of it. He wasn't going to ask. He was going to take. She could read the purpose in his eyes. He had reverted to the old Adam.

The thought both alarmed her and made her ache to comfort him. Alarm won out. He was stripping out of his garments with a speed that left her shivering. He was down to bare skin.

Gulping, Claire hastened into speech. "Adam," she said, pleading abjectly, "It's all a misunderstanding. I knew all the time it was you. I saw you through the veranda window. Oh God, Adam, you must know I would never look at another man."

He believed her, but that did not lessen his sense of outrage. Furiously, he rounded on her. "You weren't *looking* at him. You were making sheep's eyes at him. You were making a spectacle of yourself—simpering, flirting, dimpling!"

It was those dimples that had infuriated him most. They were as scarce as roses in winter and more precious to him than diamonds from Africa. He knew how to read Claire. Those dimples winked only when she was whimsical, or plotting some mischief. He regarded them as his own private possession. That she had bestowed them on another gentleman while ignoring her own husband was tantamount to a betrayal.

"And with Mark Clay of all people," he stormed. In this, Adam was hardly fair. Mark Clay and he were on the best of terms, or they had been until that evening.

"He seemed like a very nice young man," said

Claire mildly, trying to bring the temperature down.

Her defense only aggravated what was already a very volatile situation. *"Nice?"* roared Adam. "That *nice* young man, let me tell you, has been into every pair of drawers between here and Albany, and I don't mean on washing lines either."

"Must you be so crude?" said Claire, turning up her nose. "Besides, that does not signify. Look at you."

Adam was too incensed to realize that Claire had just paid him an artless, though heartfelt compliment. If he had been in a calmer frame of mind he would have seen at once that Claire's few words spoke volumes. She was no longer the young girl who had judged him and found him wanting. Her opinion of Adam had changed irrevocably. Adam could not see it. He saw only that Claire was comparing him to a young jackanapes whose reputation was coming to rival that of Casanova's—or Adam's in his younger, hellion days.

Stung, he ground out, "I've seen more decorum from whores on the docks of New York than I saw in my own wife tonight."

Claire opened her mouth and quickly shut it, swallowing a furious retort. Was that how whores behaved? Adam had said so, and he should know. No sooner had that thought occurred to her, than her anger took a gargantuan leap. "You dare to say that to me?" she sputtered, "you, with your hackneyed Irish charm and your . . . your . . . what do you think you are doing? Get your hands off me!"

With stunning swiftness Adam disposed of Claire's gown. His eyes glittered hotly. His teeth were clenched. There was something at work in him, something primitive that went beyond rational thought. It was as though his rights to Claire had been challenged, not by another male, but by Claire herself. If she did not already know it, he would soon teach her her place.

"Tonight, you have gone your length," he grated harshly. "Let me tell you, madam wife, you have sadly mistaken my character if you think I shall stand tamely by and allow another man to sow his wild oats on my fields."

"Sow his wild . . . !" Claire was affronted. At the same time, her conscience pricked her. She was the guilty party here. She owed Adam an apology, if only he would listen.

"Adam . . ."

She had left it too late. Adam wasn't in the mood to listen. He was in the grip of some powerful emotion. A hand raked through her hair, dragging her face up to meet the fierce pressure of his kiss. She spread her palms against the hard wall of his chest, trying to soothe the savage in him. For a moment, she almost panicked. She felt defenseless, smothered by the press of his body, overwhelmed by his superior strength.

As suddenly as it had come upon her, her fear left her. This was Adam. She loved him. Intuitively, she grasped that he craved reassurance. She wrapped herself around him and gave him what he wanted.

Adam pulled back and stripped Claire's lacy underthings from her. His face was hard with passion.

"I love you," she said.

Her words seemed to make no impression. "Show me," he said, and there was no relenting in him.

Adam was implacable. Claire denied him nothing. He demanded. She submitted. He tested her to the limits of her generosity. She did not fail him. Claire surpassed anything he had ever known in a woman. And still he wanted more.

He wasn't gentle. He was like a storm. She would bend to him or he would break her. Claire yielded herself to his every whim.

The pleasure built in her till it was almost unbearable. "Adam," she panted, "Adam."

He laughed softly, tauntingly, then he was plunging inside her, taking her with a violence and a passion she would not have believed possible. When it was over and she lay shuddering in his arms, she felt as though she had been ravaged by fire.

It was some time before either of them could stir. Adam sat up and reached for his shirt.

"You provoked me," he said moodily. "You know you did."

His back was to her. His spine was rigid and in the dying light she could just make out the muscles clenched in tension. She wanted to put her arms around him, to console him. She could not seem to find the energy to move. But she wasn't going to allow Adam to torment himself like this. And he was tormenting himself. She knew that as well as she knew her own name.

"Lie with me," she said softly.

Adam swiveled to face her. "What did you say?"

Her smile was languorous. She held out one hand. "Lie with me, Adam. It's so lovely here." She giggled. "We could be Adam and Eve. And this could be the Garden of Eden."

Adam knelt down beside her, noting the love-dazed eyes, the sleepy smile, the flush mantling her complexion. "Claire," he said, cupping her face with unsteady fingers, "Sweetheart, are you all right? Did I hurt you? Did I frighten you?" He groaned. "Claire, you bring out the best in me, but you also bring out the worst. For God's sake, darling, say something. Tell me you forgive me."

She hooked one arm around his neck, drawing his head down. Her dimples flashed. "I'll forgive you," she said, "but only if you do it again."

The table was set with silver and fine crystal. The candles were lit, though dusk was hours away. Claire was garbed in her finest—a diaphanous white gauze heavily embroidered in gold satin stitch at the bodice and hem. At Adam's request, she was letting her hair grow. It was undressed, the way he preferred it, and fell in natural waves to her shoulders.

Adam came through the doors and halted. "What the . . . ?" The gilded vision that was his wife took his breath away. He had been missing her all day, and had been wishing his tenants and their troubles at Hades, so impatient was he to get home to his sweet wife.

Claire came forward to greet him. Smiling, she brushed her lips against his cheek and led him to his place at the head of the table. At her signal, the servants began to serve dinner. Claire waited on Adam in person. Every course—the cream of leek soup, the fresh turtle delicately barbecued, the suet pudding with raisin sauce—all were her husband's favorites.

"What's the occasion?" Adam wanted to know.

Claire told him.

"You mean all this," he made a gesture that encompassed the whole room, "is in the nature of an apology?"

"I was grossly at fault," said Claire, as meek as Adam had ever seen her. "It was wicked to deliberately try and make you jealous."

"Why did you want to?"

She shied away from the truth. "It was an impulse. It seemed harmless enough at the time. I'm sorry. It was a stupid thing to do."

Adam was incredulous. "You mean you went to all this trouble just to say you are sorry? Darling, this isn't necessary." It wasn't necessary, but the gesture gratified him. In his memory, no one had ever done as much for him.

"I wanted to do it," said Claire. "In my family, it's a tradition." She poured the coffee, unaware that her dimples were winking.

"A tradition?" murmured Adam. He was mesmerized by those dimples.

337

Claire's eyes sparkled up at him. "This is how my mother makes amends to my father when she has done something very, very naughty."

"It's a tradition of which I heartily approve," said Adam, "and one that I won't let you forget."

His eyes slowly traversed the room, taking in everything. The furniture glowed with a fine patina. Vases of cut flowers made a brilliant splash of color where they were set out here and there around the room. The air was fragrant with the scent of beeswax and lavender.

Something deep inside Adam seemed to expand. He had never felt so cherished in his whole life. Claire knew how to turn a house into a home, and she did it effortlessly. It was a rare gift. How had she come by it?

His eyes came to rest on Claire. She seemed to glow with happiness, reflecting his own state of mind. Smiles and dimples were wickedly flashing at him. The cold beauty he had first set eyes on in the streets of Rouen almost a year before had blossomed into something quite different.

It never occurred to Adam that it was he who had worked this transformation in Claire. He put it down to the change in her circumstances. In France, she had been a fugitive. In America, she was safe. His eyes flared. Nothing must be allowed to disturb Claire's tranquillity.

"What are you thinking?" she asked.

Adam smiled easily. "Tell me more about your family's traditions," he said.

Later, as was their habit, they took a turn around the grounds before retiring for the night. Adam turned Claire into his arms. His lips sought hers. When he pulled back from the kiss, they were both breathless.

"I'm sorry, too," he said. "The other night I behaved like a brute." He stopped her protests with another searing kiss. "I want to make amends," he

338

said. "Tell me how to make amends."

Between melting kisses, Claire made several suggestions. He could give her flowers, or perfume, or something of that nature.

Adam did not care for any of his wife's suggestions. "I know how a man makes amends to his wife," said Adam. He gave a low throaty chuckle and backed Claire against the trunk of a tree. "Lift your skirts," he said.

Claire was aghast. "Adam, what are you doing?"

His hands were moving over her, avidly seeking out all the pleasure points that only he knew. "I'm making amends," he said, "male-fashion. I'm going to pleasure you as you've never been pleasured before, then I'm going to take you to our bed and pleasure you some more. Now lift your skirts."

Hours later, in the afterglow of love, Claire whispered drowsily in her husband's ear, "Adam, this beats my tradition to flinders."

She woke late. She was alone. Her bed was strewn with red roses. Moments later, when Adam appeared with a breakfast tray, he found his wife weeping into her pillow. She raised her beautiful tear-streaked face to his.

"Oh Adam," she sobbed out, "you make me so happy!"

Chapter Twenty-One

Adam and Claire returned to New York when the harvest was in. It was only now that Claire discovered how many hours in each day Adam devoted to his business interests. He worked from a large office at the front of the house. There was a constant stream of gentlemen coming and going. Sometimes, Adam absented himself for long stretches at a time. Occasionally, he made trips to Boston or Philadelphia.

Claire had much to occupy her time. Their rented house on Hanover Square was only sparsely furnished. With Blanche's help, she found a cabinetmaker, a Scotsman by the name of Duncan Pfife, who had opened a showroom on Partition Street. His work was largely of Heppelwhite and Sheraton design. Claire was charmed and ordered several pieces. Adam had given her carte blanche to do as she wished. Claire had married a rich man. Adam wanted her to know it.

The first morning call Claire must make was on Sarah Burke. Claire was highly conscious of the debt of gratitude she owed all the Burkes. She had been treated as a daughter of the house. It was Sarah who had seen to her bride clothes, and Sarah who had arranged her wedding breakfast.

Sarah's conversation was all about her brother-in-law. David Burke had engaged himself to a Miss Duane of Philadelphia, the daughter of one of his colleagues. The wedding was to take place in a matter of weeks.

Claire expressed her pleasure. There was a silence. Though she could not put her finger on it, she sensed an awkwardness in Sarah's manner. Blanche took up most of the slack in the conversation. She inquired after Betsy and the children. Betsy had gone home when Claire and Adam were on their honeymoon. The rest of the ladies' time together passed pleasantly as Sarah recounted some of the adventures of her scapegrace grandchildren. On the walk home, Claire was thoughtful.

Over dinner that evening, Adam wanted to know how Claire had spent her day. She told him about Sarah.

"She seemed . . . distant," she said.

Adam looked a question at Blanche. "She did not seem her usual self," agreed Blanche, "but I would not say that Mrs. Burke was unfriendly."

"What then?" demanded Adam.

"Mmm? Oh . . . she seemed . . . preoccupied."

The following morning, Adam paid a call on Sarah. He found her in her little parlor. There was nothing distant in her manner with him.

It was not long before Adam came to the point. "Sarah," he said. "Claire does not deserve this of you."

Sarah's spine stiffened. "You know?"

"John took me into his confidence some time ago." Ignoring her fierce glare, Adam captured her hands. "Sarah," he said, "Claire has suffered much. No one knows what has become of her parents. I fear the worst. She needs friends. You have been like a mother to her. Must she lose you, too?"

Sarah's eyes filled with tears. "I don't mean to be

341

cruel to the girl," she whispered. "But I can't seem to help myself. When I look at her, I remember, you see."

"Then why did you help Claire with her bride clothes? Why did you open your house for our wedding breakfast?"

Sarah's look was bitter. "Why do you think? John would never countenance a slight to his—to Claire."

Adam's voice took on a hard edge. "Claire is my wife. Any injury to Claire is an injury I take to myself."

The tone of his voice as much as his words shocked Sarah. "Adam," she protested, "I would never injure Claire. I am truly fond of the girl. My quarrel is not with her but with John."

Adam had risen to his feet. "Your quarrel with John is not what is at issue here, Sarah." He regarded her somberly. After an interval, he shook his head and gently chided, "Sarah! Sarah! Don't you know that sooner or later, almost every man has to make a confession to his wife?"

She regarded him mutely. Sighing, he said, "I thank Providence that I have been blessed with a forgiving wife."

"Pooh!" said Sarah. "What does Claire have to forgive? So, you had a roving eye. But that was before you met Claire."

"Sarah, you don't know the half of it," retorted Adam, and left her.

John Burke was descending the stairs as Adam exited through the front doors. John made straight for Sarah's private parlor. He did not wait for an invitation before seating himself in his favorite chair.

"What did Adam want?" he asked.

"He wanted to talk about Claire," said Sarah and fell silent.

John stifled a sigh. In the last number of weeks, he had borne Sarah's long silences with the patience of a Job. He had done everything he could think to re-

342

establish himself in his wife's good graces. Daily, he came to her little parlor and filled in the silences with anecdotes about the cases on which he was working. He chatted about their children and their children's children. He even went so far as to embark on subjects which bored him silly—ladies' fashions and the parties they would attend when the season got underway. Sarah was as cool as snow and equally as noncommittal.

He changed tactics. He brought her gifts. He invited friends to the house for dinners which Sarah must arrange. She did, with her usual aplomb, and arranged it so that she never had to say more than two words to her husband. In that moment, John decided that he had come to the end of his tether.

"Sarah," he began warningly.

"Adam said that sooner or later almost every man has a confession to make to his wife." Sarah was studying her clasped hands.

John was studying Sarah. "Did he?" he murmured.

"He seemed to imply that he was no exception."

"I daresay," said John, not sure where the conversation was leading, only too happy to find that Sarah was finally speaking to him.

"But that's just it, you see," said Sarah. She gazed absently into space, involved in her own thoughts.

"I don't see," contradicted John.

"What? Oh, what I was going to say is this. You haven't told me anything. I know that Claire is your daughter, but that is all I know. When I first confronted you with it, I know I was overwrought. But I'm not overwrought now, and I want you to explain it to me so that I can understand."

John felt as though his heart had stopped beating. "Sarah," he groaned, "why don't you put it out of your mind? Forget that it ever happened? That's the best course."

"I can't forget it," said Sarah. "Don't you think

I've tried?"

"I don't want to hurt you."

"It's too late for that. I'm already hurting."

She looked so calm. She spoke so sincerely. Still, John hesitated.

"I shall always wonder about it," said Sarah.

For a moment John closed his eyes. Then, drawing a deep breath, unsparing of his own part, he related the bare facts of the affair. Sarah heard him out without interruption.

"Is that what you wanted to know?" asked John. Sarah's eyes were downcast. He reached over and grasped her wrist. "Try to understand," he said carefully, "I was infatuated with the girl. You are the only woman who has ever mattered to me."

Sarah jerked out of his grasp. "Do you really suppose that I am thinking of myself?" Her voice was low and trembling with emotion. "That poor girl? You did her as great a wrong, if not greater, than you did to me."

It was the truth. "Yes," he said. "Yes. God forgive me."

Sarah's shock and horror gradually melted in the face of her husband's look of anguish. Even so, she could not reconcile what he had related with the man she loved and respected. It was so much worse than she would ever have believed.

She could not say what it was she had expected to hear, but certainly there ought to have been at least one extenuating circumstance. In her imagination, she had concocted all kinds of excuses to relieve John of some of the guilt. The girl was a Jezebel. John was inebriated. The girl had seduced *him*. There was nothing but a stark story of an older man ruining an innocent girl. John had said nothing to exonerate himself.

That thought calmed her a little. John was not one to shirk responsibility for his actions. In her husband's long political career, she had often chafed because John was too scrupulous for his own good.

Whatever one could say about John Burke, no one had ever accused him of shifting the blame for his own actions. In point of fact, John tended to assume more liability than was his due, and others played upon his benevolence.

She did not know what the future might hold. She could not say if they could ever recapture what they once had. It did not seem possible. They were both changed. The future might lack luster, thought Sarah, but whether she would or no, John was her husband. He was part of that future.

"Sarah!"

She looked up. John's face was white and strained. "We can't help that poor girl," said Sarah. "But we have her daughter. Perhaps God sent her to us. We must think of Claire now."

"Forget Claire!" said John roughly. "She has Adam. What about us? I want my wife back."

"You shall have her . . . in a little while." She swallowed the lump in her throat. "I just need a little time. That's all I ask . . . a little time."

Blanche saw him first. She would have recognized him anywhere.

"Nicholas!" she breathed, then on a more jubilant note, "Nicholas!"

The young man descending from the carriage looked up at the sound of his name. In the next instant, Blanche had hurled herself into his arms. After one startled look, laughing, Millot swung her off her feet in a circle. "Blanche! Is it really you?" He held her at arms' length. "You look stunning. America must agree with you." He kissed her on both cheeks.

Blanche linked an arm through Millot's and began on a spate of questions as she urged him to the front doors of Adam's house.

"Not so fast," said Millot, disengaging his arm. He

turned back to the carriage. "I'm not alone," he said. Smiling, he assisted a young girl to alight.

"Blanche," said Millot, "allow me to present my wife, Janine."

Adam arrived home at the dinner hour. The salutation between the two friends was effusive. Dinner was set back so that Adam could catch up on the news from France. Millot gave Adam a long look which Adam rightly interpreted to mean that he would give a fuller account when the ladies were not present.

There was some good-natured cajolery on the changed circumstances of both gentlemen.

"Married? You? Who would have believed it!"

"Speak for yourself, you incorrigible reprobate!"

Millot's young wife was painfully shy, and never more so than when Adam arrived on the scene. Claire tactfully engaged the timid girl in a quiet tête-à-tête.

Blanche's face was aching from her false smiles. She was putting on the performance of her life and trusted that no one was aware of it. Her veneer of self-control was close to breaking point.

Janine, thought Blanche, was just the sort of girl she would have picked for Nicholas if the choice had been left to her. She was a taking little thing with the promise of beauty yet to flower. Pretty. Innocent. Pliable. And with just a hint of tragedy at the back of those dark eyes.

She was also sickeningly adoring. Those soft brown eyes seemed to seek her husband's for constant reassurance. Nicholas was aware of it. Blanche was left with the indelible impression that Nicholas heartily approved. It made him, she suspected, feel more of a man.

In another year, she told herself, she would look back on Nicholas Millot and think herself lucky to have lost him. He was not the man for her.

Suddenly conscious that tears were standing on her

lashes, she put an end to her reflections and concentrated on the conversation between the two men. Robespierre had been toppled two months before. No one was certain what this might mean for France. Things were still pretty grim. Meanwhile, the war with England continued unabated. Blanche, aware of Adam's penetrating stare, pulled herself together and made some comment.

As the evening wore on, it registered with Blanche that whereas everyone else was blissfully ignorant of her discomfort, Adam was all too aware of it. Several times, she found his eyes resting on her, though in a vague way.

After dinner, the gentlemen did not linger but followed the French custom of accompanying the ladies to the drawing room. Adam pressed a glass of sherry on each of the ladies. Janine's eyes flew to Millot. A silent communication took place. Smiling, Janine accepted the proffered glass. Blanche did, too, but her hand was visibly shaking.

"Are you all right?" Adam asked in an undertone.

"I'm . . . fatigued," she said. "'Tis all."

He must have been watching as she sipped from the glass, thought Blanche, for as soon as it was empty, in the most unobtrusive and natural way possible, he poured her another. When Millot joined her on the sofa she was able to smile without effort.

"Blanche," he said, "you can imagine my surprise when I found you here with Claire. I was sure you would have joined a troupe of actors or some such thing."

His eyes were faintly anxious. "And so I did," she replied. She had recovered her equilibrium and spoke quite calmly. "I was in Philadelphia, and Charleston. I discovered, however, that the traveling life is not to my taste. One of these days, I hope to return to France."

"Or you could come and live with us when we are settled." He threw a quick look at his young bride before continuing in a lowered tone. "Janine was the youngest of five sisters. Her whole family perished during the Revolution. It would relieve my anxieties if she had some female friend in whom she might confide, someone older such as yourself, someone to take a motherly interest in her."

"You do me too much honor," said Blanche, and dropped her lashes to conceal the horror his words had evoked. Fearing that he meant to try and persuade her, she hastily elaborated, "Claire is in much the same case. I could not repay Adam's many kindnesses to me by deserting Claire."

Millot's brows shot up. "Adam? Kind?" he said.

Blanche's eyes flashed fire, then cooled. "Adam Dillon," she said, "is one of the kindest gentlemen I have ever known."

Millot was properly chastened.

In the group by the hearth, Adam listened with half an ear as Claire extolled the merits of New York to Millot's young bride. Occasionally, he offered an idle comment. His attention, however, was largely on the couple on the sofa.

Blanche and Millot? His mind had never made that connection before. That a woman of Blanche's attributes would harbor a *tendresse* for Millot seemed too ludicrous, too preposterous to be credible. On the other hand, if he had discovered that Millot had fallen violently in love with Blanche, Adam would not have batted an eyelash.

Blanche was the stuff of heroines, or martyrs, though no one would know it by looking at her. She dressed and acted the part of a very conventional girl. A cursory knowledge of her history would soon correct that misapprehension.

She had damn near murdered him in his bath, thinking him his half-brother! She had written a letter to the authorities denouncing the commissioner, which, at the very least, had cost Philippe his position, and had almost cost him his head. And

348

when Claire was incarcerated in the Conciergerie, Blanche, discounting every risk to herself, had bribed her way through those impenetrable walls. Adam did not doubt that it was largely through Blanche's efforts that Claire had made the perilous journey to Bordeaux and was subsequently restored to him.

Adam liked Millot, but he did not consider him half the man for Blanche. Millot had found just the right sort of girl. Janine was—Adam's eyes made a leisurely sweep—a quiet, mousy little thing. Millot would have no trouble in ordering her life. Blanche would drive him to distraction. More to the point, before long, Blanche would come to despise Millot. The pity of it was, she could not yet see it.

There could be no question of having them all under his roof for any length of time. That would occasion too much pain for Blanche. Adam was almost certain that it would not be long before Blanche proposed some scheme or other that would take her away from his house. He would not permit it. More than ever, Claire had need of Blanche's support. If anyone were to leave it must be Millot.

He became conscious of Claire's surprised look. Damn, he was doing it again—touching her without even being aware of it! In public, such familiarity was frowned upon.

"There's a loose thread on the back of your gown," he quickly invented.

Claire's smile was demure, but her eyes spoke volumes.

Adam took a turn in the square before turning in for the night. Claire was still at her bath, and the others had retired to their separate chambers. Adam was glad of the respite. He wanted to clear his mind. By and large, as a courtesy to Millot's bride, the conversation that evening had been conducted almost entirely in French. Adam always did his thinking in

English, and after his private tête-à-tête with Millot, he had much to think about.

He began his reflections exactly as Millot had introduced each subject. Without preamble, as soon as they were alone, Millot had blurted out that Philippe Duhet was in New York. The news was shocking, and, at the same time, Adam allowed that he had received the report with near fatalism. He had known that his destiny was entwined with Philippe's. He sensed that the last act was about to begin.

"You are sure it is Philippe?" he had asked.

There was no question of it, though the gentleman who had crossed the Atlantic on the same ship as Millot and his bride had gone by the name of Philippe Vissery. Philippe might be able to conceal his identity from others, averred Millot, but not from him. In Rouen, he had worked with the man too closely. There was also his striking resemblance to Adam.

"What did he have to say for himself?" asked Adam, watching Millot intently.

"He insisted that his name was Vissery and that he wanted to forget the past and start a new life. He is a French refugee, nothing more, nothing less."

"And do you believe that he wants to start a new life?"

Millot hesitated for a fraction of a second before replying, "It seems reasonable. Duhet's estates were confiscated when he fell from favor. It's generally believed in France that he was executed. Everything is in chaos. God, no one knows what to believe anymore, or whose head will roll next. No one knows who is innocent or who is guilty. One day a man is extolled as a hero, and the next he is vilified, yes, and vice versa. It's for that very reason that I came to the New World with Janine. Some people just want to forget the past."

Further questioning elicited little more except that Philippe had kept very much to himself for the duration of the crossing.

From there, Millot moved to the subject of Claire's parents. Adam braced himself to hear the worst. It was exactly as he expected.

"Naturally, I shall leave it to you to break the sad news to Claire," said Millot.

"Naturally," agreed Adam. What he was thinking was that Claire already knew.

She hid her feelings well. But she could not hide them from him. Where Claire was concerned, he had a sixth sense. Before they had sat down to dinner, he was aware of the change in her. And not all her sunny smiles or clear-eyed composure had the power to deceive him.

In some respects, it seemed to Adam that Claire was more the actress than Blanche. The only person present that evening who had not sensed Blanche's wretchedness was Millot, who, himself, was the very source of that wretchedness. Adam could not believe that Millot could be so blind. As the evening wore on, even Janine's eyes kept straying to Blanche.

When Adam entered the foyer of his house, he was met by one of his slaves, a little black girl, whom at first he did not recognize. Then it came to him that she was Sarah Burke's personal maid.

"Dulcie," he said, "what brings you to my house?"

Dulcie gave him a shy smile. "Dis here is my house now. Mistress Burke, she say dat I belong to yor missus."

The frown on Adam's brow lifted. "Mrs. Burke sent you here?"

"Yes suh."

"When was this?"

"Dis mornin'."

By this time, Adam was smiling. "And you are to look after Mrs. Dillon?"

Dulcie's little chest puffed out. "Mistress Dillon, she likes Dulcie. She say ah's to be her maid."

"I see," said Adam. In a day of unceasing tribulation, this one piece of news did much to restore his spirits. Sarah was extending the olive branch. She had taken his words to heart. She would continue to be Claire's friend.

"Mistress Dillon, she sent me to tell yo' dat she's finished with her bath and dat she be waitin' fo' yo', suh."

The message was unnecessary. Adam knew that Claire would be waiting up for him. She had wanted a little time to compose herself—hence the delaying tactic of the bath. "Thank you, Dulcie. Now get off to your bed."

As he idly watched Dulcie tread the stairs to her room in the attics, Adam's reflections took a new turn. He was thinking that his wife had been none too happy when she had discovered that he was a slaveowner. In some respects, Claire was a true daughter of the Revolution. In France, slavery was finally abolished. She could not credit that Americans were so tardy to amend such a glaring injustice.

That day was not far off, Adam had told her. There were men in Congress at that very moment who were actively working to abolish the slave trade. As it was, many slaveowners, himself among them, were following John Burke's example. They were ensuring that their slaves had a trade to fall back on if and when they became emancipated. He was well aware that this route was too slow for Claire.

He entered the chamber so silently that at first she was not conscious of his presence. She was curled up in a chair, gazing into space. As always, there was something about her, something that went beyond her beauty, which arrested him. Slowly, his eyes devoured her, from her halo of flame gold hair to her slippered feet. And it came to him that, even in a darkened ballroom, in the midst of a hundred other women, he would find her unerringly.

She looked up as he closed the distance between

them. Her first words were not of herself.

"Poor Blanche," she said. "And to think I never suspected, not even for a moment. I have not been a good friend to Blanche."

Adam said nothing. Plucking her effortlessly from the chair, he seated himself, cradling her close to his body. "My poor darling," he said.

"I could not bring myself to ask Nicholas about my parents." She nestled her head into the crook of his shoulder. "I would rather hear it from you."

Adam's fingers lifted the weight of hair at her nape, threading themselves through each strand. His lips brushed over her temples. She angled her head back, and he kissed her softly. He did not know how to begin.

"It's all right," she said, sensing the turmoil inside him. She touched one hand to his face. Adam caught it and brought it passionately to his lips. "It's all right," she said. "There was no hope. I knew that before I left France. But I must know what happened."

There was no gentle way to break it to her. His voice was low but steady. "Your mother died of a fever before she could be brought to trial."

"When was this?"

"June, by our calendar. By all accounts, Nicholas says that she did not suffer. It was a blessing, Claire."

She pressed closer to the shelter of his arms. His heartbeat against her breast was strong and regular. She found it infinitely comforting.

He gave her some moments to digest his words before going on. "Your father was very brave at the end. Nicholas witnessed his . . . that is, when Nicholas saw the name of Leon Devereux on the condemned lists, he made sure that he was there."

"My father was executed." It was more of a statement than a question.

"The day after your mother died."

353

Her voice seemed to come from a long way off. "Then my parents must have been transferred to the Conciergerie?"

"Yes."

"And Maman must have been in the infirmary when she died?"

Adam's answering affirmative was barely audible.

Some moments were to pass before Claire said, "I made a very good friend in the Conciergerie. I don't think I ever mentioned her to you. Her name was Madame Lamont. She might have been my own grandmother. I think of her often and what she said to me before she died."

She lapsed into silent reflection, and Adam gently prompted, "What did she say to you, Claire?"

She raised her head slightly. "She said that the best gift I could give my parents was to be safe and to live well."

"Yes," said Adam, not knowing what else to say. He could not believe how calm Claire was.

As though she could read his mind, she said, "You need not be concerned about me. You see, I did all my grieving months ago. Blanche will tell you. There were weeks when I hardly said a word. I could not eat. I could not sleep. I knew there was no hope."

"I understand," he said, and kissed her again.

Without warning, her teeth began to chatter. A violent shudder swept over her, then another. She began to moan, softly at first, and then with dry wrenching sobs. Adam stroked her hair, pressing her head to his chest, murmuring soothingly with words that she neither heard nor understood. Finally she lay weak and shivering in his arms.

By the time Adam had carried her to the bed and settled her between the sheets, she was drifting off to sleep. She wakened when he slipped in beside her, wrapping her in the heat of his body.

A tiny sigh fluttered on her breath. "My shield, my heart," she whispered, and burrowed closer as though she wanted to be absorbed into him.

Her words pierced Adam with something so sweet, so tender, so sublime, that he felt everything inside him melt and then expand. And he knew that, to his dying day, he would remember this moment and Claire's almost unconscious avowal.

"*You* are my heart," he said fiercely.

"Mmm?"

"Go to sleep." He tucked her head beneath his chin. "Go to sleep."

Another sigh. "We shall live well, won't we, Adam? You and I, and Zoë and Leon?"

"Yes, my heart, we shall live well. Do you suppose that I would ever permit anything to touch you?"

Long after Claire was asleep, Adam lay thinking. He was reflecting on the strength of Claire's attachment to her family, and how odd it was that his own family should be so very different. There had never been any love lost between any of the members of his family. He had not grieved for his father, and on being told of his mother's death, he had experienced no more than a pang of regret. Somehow, in retrospect, this seemed wrong to him.

Unconsciously, he tightened his arms around Claire. Where there was grief, there must be a strong bond. He tried to remember a time when he had felt for anyone what he felt for Claire.

The memories were slow in coming, but they were there, and they all centered around his mother. By some lights Mara Dillon might have been judged unfit to have the care of a cat, let alone a child. But Adam, now that he thought of it, had not felt unduly deprived in those early years. In point of fact, he had been reasonably happy.

All that had changed when he had become a member of the Duhet household. For the first time in years, he summoned the memory of that catastrophic day when his mother had made a bargain with his father—hard cash for one bastard son. The picture in his mind lost focus, to be replaced by the vision of another woman on the night when he had begun his masquerade as the commissioner of Rouen. Claire, also, had made a bargain—the use of her body for safe-conduct passes for her brother and sister.

Adam's next thought took him completely by surprise. Might not his mother also have made the bargain with his father, not for herself, but primarily for her son's welfare? Had he damned her all these years without just cause? He let the thought revolve in his mind then lost patience with himself, thinking that such idle speculation served no useful purpose. He had felt betrayed and it had colored all his future relationships with women. Until Claire. And then it was he who had become the betrayer.

My shield, my heart. Claire's words had almost shattered him. By rights, he had forfeited all claim to her trust. In France, he had deserted her, leaving her to fend for herself. In a frenzy of hurt pride, he had deliberately tried to sever the bond which held them together. He had discovered that, for him, the bond was indissoluble. Later, it was only through sheer tenacity that he had forced Claire to give him a second chance. From this moment on, he silently promised her, he *would* be her shield and her heart.

He shifted restlessly, bringing Claire more fully across his body. His wife aroused every protective male instinct in him, as well as a few others he didn't want her to know about. There was a side to him, something dark and primitive, that he supposed must be common to all creatures of his gender. The male of the species was predisposed to violence from the moment of birth. In his own case, there was something more with which he must contend. His veins pulsed with Duhet blood.

In the dark, his lips twisted in a parody of a smile. Philippe. His half-brother was here in New York. For the first time ever, Adam was glad that he had Duhet blood in his veins. In any contest with

Philippe, it must shorten the odds. Duhet against Duhet. No quarter would be asked or given. Honor would not come into it. There was only one way to fight Philippe and win. Adam had learned his lessons in the schoolroom. He must emulate Philippe's example. He must be as ruthless as Philippe.

A moment later, he amended that opinion. No. He must be more ruthless than Philippe, for now he had Claire to think about.

Chapter Twenty-Two

The French community in New York received the report of Robespierre's fall from power with cautious optimism. The tyrant was dead. That did not necessarily mean the Reign of Terror in France was at an end—far from it. A new tyrant might be waiting in the wings to step into Robespierre's shoes. It had happened before. It could happen again. For those with a mind to return to France, to act prematurely might well prove fatal. New York, in the grip of winter, might not be the most pleasant place in the world, but here, at least, a man was not forever looking over his shoulder in fear of his life.

In an upstairs parlor in the Black Boar Tavern, Philippe Duhet twitched aside the curtain at the window and contemplated the spectacle of New York in her winter shroud. He could not accustom himself to the relative quiet of the place after the shock of the city's steady uproar. The snow had brought about this incredible change. Carriages and carts had given way to sleighs and sleds, and the snow naturally muffled the sound of vehicles, a circumstance which was ofttimes hazardous to unsuspecting pedestrians.

He let the curtain drop from his fingers and turned aside to the sideboard against one wall. "You'll have a brandy?" he said to his companion, a gentleman whose youthful, unlined face was at odds with his portly dimensions.

The gentleman absently fingered his lace cravat. "Is it French?"

"Is there any other kind?"

"Philippe! I might have known you would travel in style! Don't you know that good French cognac is as rare in New York as virgins in the precincts of the Palais Royal?"

Philippe smiled. "Gervais, you must know that I've never had the least difficulty in procuring either. Besides, you have been in exile for—what is it now?—more than a year?" His companion nodded. "You would not recognize the Palais Royal." A sneer crept into Philippe's voice. "Robespierre was a moralist, don't you know? The Palais Royal is as respectable as a church."

Gervais Launey, the former Maquis de Jalès, chortled. He raised his glass. "What shall we drink to? The pleasures of yesteryear?"

"Why not? We had many of those in our salad days."

"And virgins," riposted Launey, and Philippe obligingly laughed.

It had been a stroke of luck to find Launey in New York. Philippe and the maquis went back a long ways—to the glittering days of court life at Versailles. As young aristocrats, they had led a wild life, whoring, gaming, dueling, drinking, and those were the least of their vices.

On falling heir to the title, Launey, or Jalès as he had become known, had dropped out of Philippe's circles. His father had left him with a pile of debts. The estate was falling into ruin. He must marry where there was a fortune. The Revolution had taken everything from him. Launey, unlike Philippe, had not learned how to bend with the wind. He must stand on a principle. He and his young wife and their brood of children were lucky to escape with their lives.

The maquis had been living in New York for more than a year. He was well established. No door of any significance was closed to him. Philippe Vissery was a nobody until Launey had taken him up. In point of fact, it was Philippe who had made the overtures, but so subtle was his approach, that Launey wasn't aware that he had been set up.

"But why should you wish to conceal your identity?" Launey had wanted to know. And Philippe had hinted darkly about the Convention's agents being on his trail. The truth was, of course, that it was retribution from former victims that he feared. The name of Duhet was hated in France. Happily, in New York, few seemed to know of him, and those few who did were preserving their silence.

Launey eyed Philippe speculatively over the rim of his glass. "You were commissioner of Rouen, as I understand?" he said conversationally.

Philippe's lids drooped. "What of it?" he murmured.

"Only this. There is a rumor going around that the commissioner of Rouen was either part of a network to help escaping refugees, or he turned a blind eye to what was going on."

Now this was unexpected and might prove profitable. Philippe imbibed slowly before saying, "I did turn a blind eye to what was going on. My sympathies were with the refugees. How could it be otherwise? Many of them were of my own class." He sighed, and slanted his companion a sidelong look. "I lost favor with Robespierre, of course. You know the end result. It is a matter of record that Philippe Duhet was relieved of his command for leniency toward enemies of the Revolution."

"So I had heard."

"Nevertheless . . ."

"Yes?"

"I am not Duhet. I am Philippe Vissery and you, my friend, will oblige me by supporting my story."

Launey inclined his head gravely. "As you wish."

After an interval, Philippe said thoughtfully, "Still, I suppose there is no harm in taking a few, select gentlemen into our confidence. What I mean to say is this. When I am satisfied that the Convention has no longer any interest in me, I may wish to become myself again. In that event, it would be beneficial if there were a few influential men who were party to my secret, gentlemen who would vouch for me."

"In that event, you will be fêted like a hero," exclaimed Launey.

"Shall I?" murmured Philippe.

"The Savior of Rouen, some call you."

"Now that is going too far. I did no more no less than any gentleman of scruples would do in my position."

"You are too modest for your own good, Philippe."

Philippe shook his head and smiled in a self-deprecating way. He sipped his brandy. Behind his somnolent pose, his mind was hard at work. He was beginning to wonder if he had made a tactical error by trying to conceal his identity. From what Launey had told him, it seemed that Philippe Duhet had substantial credit in New York. If so, it was all due to his half-brother. The irony amused him.

Launey's voice broke into his reflections. "When I think of it, it doesn't surprise me that your half-brother has kept your identity a secret."

"Oh?" encouraged Philippe.

"Do you know what I think?"

"What do you think, Gervais?"

"I think he's jealous, that's what. There never was any love lost between you, as I remember. No. It would not suit Adam Dillon's purpose to see you displace him as the unchallenged prince of New York. In point of fact, it suits him very well that you are plain Philippe Vissery."

"There may be something in what you say,"

allowed Philippe. What he was thinking, however, was that it was not nor ever had been Adam's way to tell tales out of school. Adam was far more devious than that. "It's just like when we were boys," said Philippe, and was surprised to find that he had voiced his stray thought.

"What is?" asked Launey.

Philippe laughed. "Adam and I. He was always envious of me. I wanted to be his friend, but he would have none of it. He was the bastard son and could never forget it, you see."

"You are too generous," said Launey, shaking his head. "I am not forgetting that when your father was murdered, suspicion fell on your half-brother."

"Yes, but nothing was ever proved," chided Philippe.

Launey made a small sound of derision. "Just watch your step, Philippe. That's my advice."

"Tell me about Adam's marriage," said Philippe.

"What do you wish to know?"

"Was it a love match?"

Launey gave the notion due consideration. "I should say," he said, "that once caught, the heat of Adam's ardor soon cooled to a more tepid temperature. Your half-brother likes variety."

Philippe laughed. "That sounds like Adam."

Launey nodded. "Yes. No woman holds him for long. But that house of his? That's a different matter."

"House?" murmured Philippe.

"He has a showplace on the Hudson. He's simply poured money into it." Launey laughed, not pleasantly but scornfully. "If you want my opinion, Adam Dillon is aping the modes of his betters. You'd think the damn place was a French château and he a blue-blooded aristocrat."

"That sounds like Adam, too," said Philippe, smiling. After a pause, he went on, "How is it that you were unaware that Adam was my half-brother until I mentioned it?"

Launey shrugged eloquently. "I never met him in France, and if I had known his name, it had completely slipped my mind. You must remember, it's years since I ever gave him a thought."

"But our resemblance? Surely that jogged your memory?"

"No. How should it? Adam Dillon is an American. Your half-brother was French. And if I did remark on his resemblance to you, I put it down to mere chance."

Philippe understood. In much the same way, when he had made his entry into New York society, his resemblance to one of the city's favorite sons was observed, remarked upon, and promptly forgotten. And since he and Adam did not claim a connection, no one pursued the matter.

It was Launey who remarked on the lateness of the hour. Having drained their glasses, Philippe called for his manservant. A young giant, a black slave, entered with their greatcoats. He assisted the gentlemen into them. It was Friday evening and they were engaged to a party at the City Tavern. A sleigh was waiting for them in the inn's courtyard.

The vehicle swayed into motion, setting off the warning bells, and for the short drive, Philippe gave himself over to his own thoughts.

He hated the frigid temperatures of New York, nor had he expected to be wintering here when he had finally decided that he had no future in France. He had been resolved to make his way to warmer climes. New Orleans was his eventual destination. But that was before he had met up with his former clerk aboard ship.

Nicholas Millot, all unsuspecting, had told Philippe what he had feared he would never be able to discover—his half-brother's whereabouts. Adam was a man of influence, Millot had warned him. He would run Philippe out of New York if he tried anything.

And Philippe, at his most humble, at his most charming, had allayed Millot's fears with practiced skill.

The fiction that he was Philippe Vissery could not deceive Millot. He'd changed tactics. Part of what he had told Millot was the unvarnished truth. He had not the least suspicion that Adam was in New York. When he had boarded that ship, revenge was the furthest thing from his mind. He was all alone. What possible threat could he pose to a man in Adam's position?

Philippe smiled into the darkness. Not since he was a boy, since before coming into the title, had he been called upon to employ his gifts as an actor. It was like old times. A smile, a look, a flick of his eyelashes and he had them all eating out of his hand. He would have done well to employ that talent in his later years. Had he done so, he might have averted the fate which had overtaken him.

Charm, be it ever so counterfeit, was a powerful weapon. He had reaped dividends that even he could not believe. Those who should have known better were giving him the benefit of the doubt. He was thinking of Claire.

He had made a beginning with her in the Conciergerie. Since coming to New York, he'd consolidated his position, playing on her sympathies, stirring her softer emotions for his unhappy plight. With Claire, he did not have to act. He really was drawn to her. The girl had a tender heart and could not help pitying him. It had nothing to do with his present circumstances and everything to do with his boyhood. Claire had taken it into her head that he was a victim of parental neglect and he had done nothing to disabuse her of that notion.

He almost laughed out loud. His early years were enviable. He had been petted and indulged to a degree. The advent of Adam Dillon into his young life had marked the turning point. Adam had made an impression on their father. Thereafter the comte had begun to lose patience with Philippe's airs and graces and had ended by exhorting him to emulate his brother's example.

He and Adam had come face-to-face on a number of occasions in the last weeks. Philippe did not think their resemblance was so striking. In any event, he had made it his object to emphasize their differences. Adam's hair brushed his collar. Philippe's was long and tied back with a black ribbon. Adam's garments were sober. Philippe adopted a more flamboyant style. Adam's accent and command of English was faultless. So was Philippe's, but he chose to pretend otherwise. In one thing they were equally matched. In front of witnesses, they were both men of considerable charm. When unobserved, they permitted their masks to slip.

Their first encounter had taken place as strangers. Claire was with Adam. Her eyes had betrayed her. She recognized him. As was to be expected, Millot had forewarned her.

Gervais Launey made the introductions then wandered off. There was a slight awkwardness which Adam's first sally did nothing to smooth over.

"I fear, Mr. Vissery," he said, "that you will find our winters here unhealthy."

Philippe acknowledged the hit with a small smile. "As you may know, Mr. Dillon," he returned, "I have long since learned to tolerate minor annoyances." And then, because Claire was present, he added in an undertone, "I'm sorry if my presence here embarrasses you. Rest assured, when I conclude my business, I shall remove to a . . . healthier climate."

Claire's eyes flew to her husband. "Ah, no," she began. "You are mistaken. We . . ."

Adam cut her off without compunction. "That sounds like a capital idea. New Spain, as I understand, has a perfect climate. You may count on me to do everything in my power to facilitate your removal.

Your servant, sir," and over Claire's shocked gasp, Adam dragged her away.

Philippe had toyed with the idea of simply erasing Adam Dillon from the face of the earth. Though the notion had merit, it was a chancy proposition. Adam must surely be expecting something of the sort. He would be prepared.

That scheme was rejected, not because of the inherent risks, but because Philippe regarded it as too obvious as well as too lenient for the severity of Adam's crimes. Adam had always been a thorn in his side. But his intervention at Rouen had put him completely outside the pale. Philippe had lost not only his position as commissioner, but also his estates and vast wealth. He had been reduced to little better than a pauper—he, Philippe Duhet, who should have been the one to step into Robespierre's shoes. By rights, at this moment, he should be master of France, not a penniless fugitive living off his wits. Adam had deprived him of something of inestimable value. As he had suffered, so must Adam.

He was in no hurry to bring his half-brother to justice. He did not fear Adam. From experience, he knew how Adam's mind worked. Adam did not have it in him to pursue his chosen course with single-minded devotion. He could never bring himself to go the whole length. He was weak. As boys, Philippe had learned how to play upon that weakness. He still knew how to play upon it. And as in the past, he was enjoying every move in their game of cat and mouse.

In Hanover Square, Adam was reading the riot act to his wife. Claire was at her dressing table, putting the finishing touches to her toilette.

"On no account must you allow Philippe to be private with you."

"I understand," said Claire. Peering into the

366

looking glass, she applied a little blacking to her lashes.

"Nor am I gratified by the spectacle of my wife in conversation with that knave whenever my back is turned."

Claire's delicate eyebrows winged upward. "In a roomful of people?" she mildly remonstrated.

Adam's temper wore thin. "God, Claire! I thought that you had more sense than to be taken in by Philippe's flummery. The man is a master of deceit. How many times must I tell you?"

"All I said," said Claire with some asperity, "is that I feel sorry for the man."

"Sorry? For Philippe?" Adam made a derisory sound. "In Rouen, you hated him. Have you forgotten what he tried to do to you?"

"But he didn't do it, did he? Another gentleman, who shall be nameless, got there before him." At Adam's stricken look, Claire's annoyance evaporated. "Darling," she said, and rising, placed her hands on his shoulders, "what possible difference does it make if I feel sorry for Philippe or not? I'm not thinking of eloping with the man. And he would not lust after a pregnant lady, I shouldn't wonder. What do you think?"

Her attempt at humor fell flat. On the contrary, it aroused Adam's ire. "I don't want Philippe or anyone else for that matter to know that you are carrying my child."

"And how long do you suppose I shall be able to keep it a secret?" She gave him a wifely grin. "Adam, I can hardly do up my buttons as it is. I'm more than three months gone. Besides, what need for secrecy? I'm proud to be carrying your child."

"Please, Claire, trust me in this. And it won't be for long."

"What does that mean?" Claire could not keep the alarm from her voice, nor did she try. "Adam, what scheme are you hatching in that maze in your head that you call a brain?''

Adam changed tactics. His arms tightened around her and he laughed. "What a suspicious little mind you have! All I meant was that, according to rumor, Philippe will soon be moving on. And when he does, all my anxieties will be relieved.''

"Moving on?'' Claire's eyes searched Adam's face. She didn't like the way he returned her scrutiny, through the sweep of his lashes, veiling his thoughts.

"To a warmer climate,'' said Adam. "Philippe doesn't much care for our winters, so I've been given to understand.''

"Oh.'' His words should have reassured her. They didn't. Claire was almost at the end of her patience. She could not believe how immutable Adam's loathing was for his half-brother. Somehow, this seemed wrong to her, especially as Philippe had gone out of his way to cultivate Adam's favor.

"Adam,'' she said, "once, a long time ago, I misjudged you. Isn't it possible that you may have misjudged Philippe?''

Adam's answer was a muffled oath.

Claire regarded him somberly. She shook her head. "Adam,'' she said, "you are a hard man.''

"But never with you,'' he said roughly. "Least-ways, not latterly.''

Claire smiled. "No, never with me.'' Her hands moved to his shoulders and tightened. There was an age-old question in her voice. "Adam?''

"No!'' he said passionately. "No!'' But he crushed her to him, one hand moving unerringly beneath her heart, to the swell of her belly where she nourished his child. He was on fire for her. "We can't. We mustn't,'' he said, groaning, and with a supreme effort of will, he set her at a safe distance.

"But I want to,'' said Claire, trying to move closer. Tears stood on her lashes.

Adam held her at bay. "No,'' he said. "Blanche will

be waiting downstairs for us. Besides, it's not safe. You know it's not safe."

It was an argument Claire knew she could not win. She had suffered agonies over the loss of one child. Knowing it, Adam refused to put her at risk again. Since he had learned that Claire was with child he had taken to sleeping in his own bedchamber. Claire was beside herself. She needed Adam more than ever. And she was plagued with the thought that her husband was a virile, lusty man. She did not see how he could be celibate till after their child was born.

"Adam," she said miserably, "if we were to take Dr. Massey into our confidence, if we were to tell him that I had lost our first baby, and if he should say that there was no risk involved, would that set your mind at rest?"

"He will naturally assume that you were my mistress before you became my wife."

"I don't care who knows it," said Claire recklessly.

"You don't mean that," he said. When it appeared that she would argue with him, he quickly interposed, "I believe you mentioned that you had received a letter from Sarah?"

"Sarah?" Claire was lost for a moment by this abrupt turn in the conversation.

"Sarah and John Burke," replied Adam. "They are in Philadelphia to attend David's wedding."

"I know where they are," said Claire crossly. "And?"

Claire bit back an angry retort. There was no persuading Adam when he was in this mood. She might as well argue with a brick wall. "According to Sarah," she said, "Miss Duane is just perfect for David," and she continued in this vein until they had entered the waiting sleigh.

At the City Tavern, Adam was propped against one of the pillars, calmly taking stock of the crush of people. Blanche, he was glad to note, was sticking to Claire like a leech. They were in conversation with an elderly couple who were strangers to Adam. Blanche, feeling Adam's scrutiny, lifted her head. Their eyes met and held for a fraction of a second before each looked away.

Blanche was one of the few who was not taken in by Philippe Duhet. Adam had hoped that Blanche could talk some sense into Claire. But Claire had this bee in her bonnet. Philippe had become an object of pity. He was trying to make a new life for himself. He deserved his chance. They must not be too quick to judge him.

It was all so familiar, thought Adam. Philippe, when he put his mind to it, could charm the birds from the trees. When they were boys, hadn't he taken a leaf out of Philippe's book in the interests of self-preservation? He had learned in the schoolroom that Philippe could worm his way out of anything. It was useless to look to those in authority for justice. Of necessity, he had learned how to shift for himself.

Claire was well guarded, though she would never have known it. Millot was close by. Not that Adam put much stock in that young man's ability to protect Claire. In the first place, he was known to Philippe, and in the second place, Millot, also, had been seduced by Philippe's charm—an engaging mix of frankness and a boyish eagerness to please. Philippe was a consummate actor. Adam studied to match his performance.

By and large, he had succeeded fairly well. When acquaintances were effusive in their praise of Philippe Vissery, Adam managed to dredge up a smile and make some inoffensive comment. With Claire, it was different. She was one of the few who was aware of Vissery's real identity. She must enter into all Adam's feelings. On the subject of his half-brother, however, they were poles apart. And because they did not see eye-to-eye on Philippe, Adam knew

370

he could not take Claire fully into his confidence. If he were to do so, she would think him as deranged as he knew Philippe to be.

Only one person understood. Blanche. If anything, Blanche's thoughts were more extreme than Adam's. She was all for dispatching Philippe on the spot. He deserved it. Adam could not agree more. On the other hand, to murder anyone, even Philippe, was to put themselves on his level. They would be no better than the man they despised.

Blanche could not see it. Adam tried a different tack. If they were found out, he had said, they would pay an exorbitant penalty. Philippe was not worth it. "Yes. But that's not it," said Blanche. "It's more than that. It's because you are brothers, isn't it?"

Adam had denied it, but on further reflection he was beginning to wonder if Blanche had not hit upon something. In Rouen, the rebels had wished to do away with Philippe. Adam had stayed their hand by threatening in that event to abandon the mission. If Blanche was right, if it truly was impossible for him to force himself to that extremity, the advantage to Philippe was incalculable.

It would never come to that, Adam promised himself. His plan was already in motion. In very short order, Philippe would be out of the picture. Then he would explain everything to Claire. Then things between them would be back to normal.

There was a stir at one of the entrances. Lily Randolph entered on Philippe Duhet's arm. Her eyes swept over the throng of people, coming to rest on Adam's tall figure. Adam came away from the pillar. Slowly, deliberately, he slanted her one of his melting grins. She let out a trill of laughter and, after a quiet aside to Philippe, wended her way toward Adam.

Their two heads were bent together, suggesting intimacy. A moment later, Adam led her onto the dance floor. Philippe's eyes trailed their progress,

371

then sought out Claire.

Claire's eyes also trailed Adam and his beautiful partner. A little frown came and went on her brow before she turned her head to listen to the lady with whom she was conversing. Madame Bailly was newly come from England. That fact must necessarily whet Claire's interest. Zoë and Leon were in England.

The Baillys thought to establish themselves in the New World. Though grateful to the English for giving them sanctuary when they needed it, Monsieur Bailly could not be happy where there was an entrenched aristocracy. The young republic of America had drawn him like a magnet.

"I don't suppose," struck in Claire at one point, "that you happened to cross paths with my sister when you were in England?" She'd put the same question to scores of people. No one ever had.

"It's most unlikely," said Madame Bailly, regarding Claire with interest. "We were living in a quiet backwater, Rivard in Kent. I don't suppose you've ever heard of it?"

Claire sighed. "No," she said.

Taking pity on the young woman, Madame Bailly said gently, "What is your sister's name?"

"Zoë," said Claire. "Zoë Devereaux." Madam's face was stricken. "What have I said?" asked Claire, a little alarmed.

"Zoë Devereux!" exclaimed Madame. She signaled to her husband who was in conversation with Blanche. "Emile," she said, "what was the name of that young woman who married the lord of the manor, you know, the Marquess of Rivard?"

"She was a member of one of the great banking families. The last survivor, as I remember."

Claire was holding her breath. "And her name?" she prompted.

"Something unusual."

"Could it be Zoë Devereux?"

"Yes, that's it. Zoë Devereux. Poor little thing. She

lost her whole family to the Revolution.''

"No," said Claire. "She had a younger brother. Leon. He was with her. He must have been." She was visibly trembling.

"Now that's where you are wrong," said Monsieur Bailly, unaware of his wife's warning look. "I know for a fact that she was the only member of her family to get out of France."

"How do you know?" demanded Claire. By this time her agitation was very evident. Blanche laid a solicitous hand on her shoulder. Claire shook her off. "How do you know?" she repeated emphatically.

Monsieur Bailly looked imploringly at his wife. It was she who answered. "I had the pleasure of being introduced to your sister, once, after church services. Naturally, our conversation turned to home. Child, I had it from her own lips. She was the only member of her family to get out of France."

"Liar! Knave! Deceiver!"

"You are repeating yourself, madam wife." Adam's tones were strident. "Now drink that brandy before I pour it down your throat!" He pressed her onto the bed and loomed over her.

Claire wanted to throw it in his face. With trembling fingers, she raised it to her lips and sipped cautiously. The liquid burned a path down her throat. Only when the glass was half empty did Adam allow Claire to set it aside.

"Oh Adam, how could you?" she said brokenly.

More than anything, Adam wanted to gather her into his arms. He dared not. The end of it was all too predictable. He would make love to her.

He cursed savagely under his breath, thinking that the news about her brother could not have come at a worse time. "Look," he said, "I have tried to explain it to you. Won't you at least try to see my side of things? If your brother had not run away, he would

373

have been conveyed to England with your sister. Was it wrong for me to wish only to spare you pain? God, Claire, I have done nothing to deserve your hatred."

"That's not it," said Claire. She pressed a hand to her aching temples.

"Then what is it?" Adam reclined against one of the bedposts. He folded his arms across his chest and regarded Claire steadily.

Claire had to tip back her head to look up at him. "You could have found my sister if you had really put your mind to it. You didn't want to find her, did you, Adam? Then I would have discovered that you had deceived me about Leon."

There was something in what she said, but there was more to it than that. "I am not a magician," he said. "England is a long way off. Where would you have suggested that I begin to look for your sister?"

"I don't know." She shrugged helplessly. A thought came to her. "We could go to England," she said. "It's possible that Zoë knows what has happened to Leon. Her husband? The Marquess of Rivard? He must have connections. Surely, he would help us."

"We are not going to England. For God's sake, Claire, there is a war going on. French and English warships are none too particular about whom they blow out of the waters. American colors are no protection."

"Others have made the crossing," she persisted.

"No."

"But . . ."

"For the last time, no. You are pregnant with our child. I want my son or daughter to be born on American soil. Afterwards, well, we shall see."

Claire ground her teeth together. "As if I cared a fig for that! I am not an American. I am French." Her voice began to wobble, "and . . . and . . . I want my brother and sister."

"You are going nowhere," said Adam, "and that is

ny final word on the subject."

Claire's eyes flashed defiance. "Why am I surprised? You know nothing of the finer feelings. Haven't you always said so? Adam Dillon knows nothing of love. Your parents meant nothing to you. Your half-brother means less than nothing to you. As much as you are able, I suppose you care for me and your unborn child. Well, let me tell you, Adam Dillon, that doesn't hold a candle to what I feel for my brother and sister. I love them. Can you understand that? I *love* them."

Adam's face was ashen. His eyes stared. Without a word, he swung on his heel and slammed out of the room.

Claire's voice broke, "Adam, I didn't mean it. Oh God, I didn't mean it." She covered her face with both hands and wept.

Chapter Twenty-Three

Claire managed to keep the smile pinned to her lips until the front door had closed on Dr. Massey. In something of a daze, she wandered into the music room. There were only the servants to witness the dejected slump of her shoulders. Adam, as ever, was out attending to business; Blanche had slipped out for a few minutes to buy Claire's Christmas present; and Millot had left for Philadelphia with his young bride a week since to take up an appointment as secretary to David Burke.

Absently, Claire sat down at the harpsichord and fingered the sheet music on the stand. Her mind was grappling with the interview that had just taken place with her physician. She was in perfect health, he had told her. The next part was embarrassing, but Claire had managed to steel herself to go through with it. She and Adam had lost their first child, she had told Dr. Massey. In France, she'd had a miscarriage. For this reason, Adam had decided not to exercise his conjugal rights. Was he perhaps being overcautious?

If Dr. Massey was shocked by her indelicacy in raising such a subject, and she knew he must have been, he covered it well. Of the two, she was more shocked than he, for his response had floored her. It seemed that he had already had a similar conversation with her husband a month before. As he had told Adam, so he would tell her. There was no reason in the world why they should deny themselves the comfort of the conjugal bed.

The thoughts that chased themselves through Claire's head were laughable, she tried to tell herself. Only she wasn't laughing. Adam was tiring of her. He had never been faithful to one woman for long. He had a roving eye. He was not a safe man to love.

She moaned under her breath. She would not accept that. These were merely the lunatic ravings of a pregnant woman. Adam had changed. If he were ever to discover what was going on inside her head, he would be hurt to the quick. There was a reasonable explanation for his refusal to make love to her. He was more cautious than was necessary. That must be it.

The thought did not cheer her to any appreciable degree, not when she considered that her relations with Adam were at their lowest ebb since Rouen. Adam was keeping his distance from her. She had said some unforgivable things to him when she discovered he had concealed the truth about her brother. Nevertheless, she had begged his forgiveness. He'd said all the right words, but what use were words when his actions told her a different story? He was no longer the doting husband. At every gathering, he had barely settled her when he was off like a shot, flirting with anything in skirts that moved. Claire thought of Lily Randolph and she ground her teeth together.

When she heard someone at the front door, she thought it must be Blanche. She went into the foyer to find Philippe Duhet, or Vissery, as he would have it, brushing snow from his hat.

"It's a beautiful day out there," he said. "I have a sleigh waiting. I would be honored to have your company for a turn around the Collect Pond."

Her first impulse was to refuse. Adam had warned

377

her in no uncertain terms to keep her distance from his half-brother. This was easier said than done, for Philippe was invariably present at every social event that she and Adam attended. It was impossible to ignore him or give him the cut directly without occasioning suspicion. And it seemed that the last thing that either Adam or Philippe wanted was for events in Rouen to become public knowledge.

"Well, fair lady, what is your answer?" drawled Philippe quizzically.

Claire's reflections had not put her in a frame of mind to heed her husband's explicit commands. Besides, she reasoned, a turn around the Collect with a maid in attendance would not raise a single eyebrow, except for Adam's. Adam deserved a set-down.

Another thought came to her. Leon. Philippe might know something about Leon. "I'll get my things," she said.

"And don't forget your maid." To her blank look, he elaborated, "A chaperone, Claire, a chaperone." Laughing, he went on, "May I suggest Dulcie? My man has taken a bit of a fancy to your young maid. Surely there's no harm in promoting that little romance?"

As she ascended the stairs to her chamber, Claire's thoughts drifted to Rouen, when fate had thrown her in the way of both Philippe and Adam. Adam insisted that no one must ever know about his masquerade as commissioner. He had explained it very carefully to Claire. It had to do with American foreign policy. She could not see it. Adam had done a very fine thing. To her way of thinking, he should be acclaimed for it, and so she had told him.

But that was before Philippe's advent on the scene. It seemed to Claire that both gentlemen were more than a little anxious to put the past behind them. After due consideration, she amended her opinion. She sensed that the past was there like a simmering volcano, waiting to erupt when one least expected it.

It was so sad. They were brothers. Brothers should not hate each other. She understood Adam's aversion to Philippe, an aversion that was shared by Blanche. She knew that Philippe did not deserve her compassion. Yet, she could not help pitying him.

When she had confessed her sentiments to Adam, he had lost patience with her. Her sympathies were wasted on that scoundrel, he had flung at her. Philippe did not dare use his own name. He must pass himself off as Vissery for a very good reason. The name of Duhet was poison to all right-thinking men.

Claire was silenced, but she could not help wondering how things might have turned out if Adam had been the elder son and Philippe the younger.

His master was in one of his more mellow moods, decided Ebony, gazing with rapt appreciation at the small coin which glinted in his dark palm. It was a reward for a job well done, his master had intimated. The coin was English, a half sovereign, and as acceptable to shopkeepers in New York as any American currency. Ebony was from St. Croix in the West Indies. He could not get used to the system in America where both English and American money circulated.

Feeling quite in charity with his master, unbidden, Ebony began to clear away the remains of a late lunch. Philippe made some idle comment, and stretched out his long legs to warm them at the blaze in the grate. He composed himself to carefully sift through everything that Ebony had ferreted out about the Dillon household in the last several weeks.

It seemed that Adam Dillon was a great disappointment to Claire's maid. Dulcie had a romantic turn of mind. Adam Dillon was an indifferent husband. He and Claire had separate chambers. Marital relations were nonexistent. If anything, Mr.

Dillon, by Dulcie's account, showed more partiality to Mrs. Dillon's little friend who lived with them.

Philippe's thoughts moved from there to the sleigh ride just past. Everything seemed to bear out the maid's confidences. Claire did not seem like a woman in love. Of the contrary, when they had halted to take in the spectacle of the skaters on the frozen Collect, her conversation had been all of Rouen and her young brother and sister. She seemed to be waiting for him to say something of grave import. If she was setting a trap for him, he was not about to fall into it. In Rouen, she had feared him. He had subtly moved the conversation on to Paris when they had both been incarcerated in the Conciergerie. Though he was careful to couch his language in inoffensive terms, the implication was clear. Adam had betrayed them both. After that, Claire had fallen into a reflective silence.

He had just given the order to Ebony to make for Hanover Square, when, by the merest good fortune, whom should they happen to come upon but Adam with Claire's little friend in tow. Claire gave a start. She raised her hand to catch the attention of the couple who were walking along the boardwalk. Adam and Blanche did not notice. Suddenly, Blanche was in Adam's arms and they were embracing. Claire's hand fell to her lap. As the sleigh passed, Adam's head lifted. His eyes locked on Philippe then darted to take in Claire's shocked expression. Adam's eyes flared, and Philippe had his answer.

His half-brother was clever, Philippe allowed, chuckling, but not nearly clever enough for him. Adam had laid a false trail, and he, Philippe, was the only one to have seen through it. In spite of Launey's avowal that Adam's interest in Claire was tepid, in spite of Adam's interest in a former mistress, in spite of poor Adam's cold bed in Hanover Square, in spite of Dulcie's innocent confidences, Philippe had his answer. Adam Dillon was deeply in love with his wife.

Poor Claire. It was very evident that Adam had not taken her into her confidence. In this, Adam was wise. Claire was too transparent. He would soon have tricked the truth out of Claire. With Adam it was otherwise. Adam knew him as no one else did. Adam's mind was impenetrable. It was the spectacle of Claire with the last person he had expected to see her with that had shocked him into betraying himself.

It put Philippe in mind of another occasion, years before, when Adam had fallen in love with some inn-keeper's daughter. He could not remember her name. The girl wasn't important. He had taken her away from Adam. That was what was important.

Evidently, Adam had learned his lesson from that experience. He did not want Philippe to know how much Claire meant to him. He'd gone one step further. He had dangled another carrot in front of Philippe's nose. Adam Dillon's house on the Hudson was reputed to be his pride and joy. He had spent a fortune on it.

Philippe smiled. He was perfectly sure that the house was significant to Adam. But next to Claire, it meant nothing. Ebony had learned something today which had added one more piece to the puzzle. According to her maid, Claire had required the services of a physician twice in the last month to treat an ankle that she had turned while out skating with her husband.

Ankle be damned! thought Philippe. Claire was carrying Adam's child. He would stake his life on it.

Claire was in her bedchamber, in the act of removing her fur-lined wraps, when she heard Adam come storming up the stairs. When he burst through the door, she did not deign to spare him a glance. It was the little maid who retreated a step and swallowed convulsively.

Adam's voice was low and abrasive. "You may go, Dulcie."

Dulcie did not wait for a second telling. In her day, she had seen Mr. Adam in a taking a time or two. She wasn't about to wait around for the explosion. Mumbling incoherently, with head down and arms clutching her mistress's precious ermine-trimmed garments, she went scooting out the door.

In the ensuing silence, Claire was almost sure she could hear the sound of her husband's teeth grinding together. Knowing that she was in the wrong in this instance did nothing to check her own temper. All the resentment which Adam's inexcusable conduct had provoked seemed to ignite like a flash fire. Blanche was merely the spark that had set fire to the dry tinder. If Adam was angry, she was beside herself.

Her spine stiffened. Her chin lifted. Her features might have been set in ice. Only the blue fire leaping from her eyes betrayed the violence of her temper.

"You, sir," she suddenly erupted, "have gone your length! And with my very best friend of all people! Oh, not that I blame Blanche. Adam Dillon must always be chasing after anything in skirts. Haven't I always known it?"

Adam was momentarily deflected from his purpose. His first thought had been to make sure that Claire was safe. His second was to give her the tongue-lashing she so richly deserved for disobeying his orders.

Not without some difficulty, he forced his anger down. He knew that there was more to Claire's outburst than the mere sight of Blanche in his arms. By her lights, she had just cause for complaint. He was neglecting her abominably, not only in public, but also in the privacy of their own home. But he had good reason for what he was doing.

With all his heart, he wished that it was possible to take his wife fully into his confidence. More than once he had made a start, only to be brought up short by Claire's refusal to face facts. He could never make her believe that there was not a particle of saving grace in Philippe Duhet. He could never make her believe that the extraordinary lengths to which he was being driven were very necessary if he was going to beat Philippe at his own game.

Adam had long since decided that ignorance was Claire's best protection. Nevertheless, it galled him to think that she would immediately jump to the conclusion that he was a fickle husband. He knew he was being unreasonable, but he could not seem to help himself. He wanted Claire's faith in him to be so unshakable that it would fly in the face of the evidence—a vain hope, Adam told himself savagely. That Claire did not demonstrate complete confidence in him was a bitter pill to swallow. But that grievance was paltry compared to what he suffered when it had become evident that his half-brother had wormed his way into his wife's good graces. There was no greater betrayal in Adam's eyes.

"If you are wise, you won't provoke me," he said tautly. "I warn you, I am just about at the end of my tether. Good God, Claire, you must know that you are making a mountain out of a molehill. I admit I met Blanche by design, but it was only to help her choose a suitable gift for *you*. And if I did embrace her . . . well . . . you know as well as I do that Blanche needs the support of all her friends at present."

"You were comforting her?" derided Claire, though with a little less heat than formerly. She knew that Blanche would never betray their friendship. But now that she had let loose her wrath, she did not wish to contain it. Haughty with dignity, she went on, "Oh, I don't doubt that Blanche is innocent. She has ever been a true friend. Whereas you . . ." She let her words trail away suggestively.

Adam's smile was bitter with mockery. "So," he said, "I've played the gallant a little too eagerly for my wife's comfort. I've flirted a little, and paid court to the odd beauty." His eyebrows rose eloquently. "Madam, I do not remember promising that I would never *look* at another woman. I suppose I should be flattered by this unwarranted display of jealousy."

"Unwarranted!" she scoffed. "And what of Mrs. Randolph? Do you tell me that you have done no more that *look* in that quarter?" She was tempted to tell him about her interview with Dr. Massey. But that wound was too fresh, smarted too keenly for her to mention it without bursting into tears. She had been humbled, but it was a private humiliation. Already, she had revealed too much.

"Think what you will," he said unpleasantly. He combed his fingers through his hair. "God, what's the use?" he gritted. "There is no persuading you! You are like all the rest! I might as well save my breath. Philippe . . ." He shook his head. "Yet, you once told me that he made your skin crawl!"

Claire was ever afterwards to regret the reckless and misleading words which sprang to her lips. "That is no longer the case," she said. "I fear that I misjudged Philippe."

Adam's face was vivid with color. He swung away from her and went to stand by the window, staring out on the square.

When he had himself in hand, he said under his breath, "It's of no consequence, now. I betrayed myself. He knows." Expelling a long breath, he went on in a more normal tone, "You are overwrought, Claire. I've thought so for some time. You have been attending too many functions. For the sake of our child, as well as for your own health, I've decided to send you away."

"What are you saying?" asked Claire uncertainly.

Adam turned to face her. "My estate," he said.

"Tomorrow, you and Blanche must go to my estate."

"Blanche and I?"

His hand was on the doorknob. "All going well, I hope to join you for Christmas."

"But . . . aren't you coming with us?"

"Unfortunately, there is business in town that requires my attention."

Her head jerked up. "And if I refuse to go?"

He laughed, a soft, infinitely insulting sound. "I wouldn't advise it," he said. And then, because he knew what was going through her head, knew that she expected him to play the part of the dissolute libertine in her absence, he added with soft sarcasm, "Have no fear, my love. I shall do my best to live up to your expectations."

Moments later, when Dulcie entered the room to assist her mistress to pack for the journey, she found Claire sitting on the edge of the bed. Her look was thoughtful.

Sarah Burke calmly surveyed the glittering throng of guests in her magnificent ballroom. This was to be the last party of any note before New York's finest retired to their country places for the Christmas season. The Burkes' boxes were packed in readiness for the journey to New Jersey where a grand family reunion was to take place. Sarah's eyes fell on the tall figure of her brother-in-law. David Burke and his young wife, Mary, newly arrived from Philadelphia, were to make up two of the party. As David's black head bent to his wife, and the girl laughed and blushed at the same instant, Sarah's lips curved in a smile. Everything had worked out for the best, she was thinking.

That thought prompted her to search the throng for Adam Dillon. When her eyes found him, her smile faded. As ever of late, Adam was paying assiduous court to Lily Randolph. And now he could do so with impunity, thought Sarah crossly, having packed Claire off with her inseparable friend, Blanche, to his place in the Hudson Valley. To the world it seemed obvious that the Dillons' marriage was running a predictable course. Adam had reverted to form. Yet, Sarah was not quite satisfied with that explanation.

Adam and Claire had been invited to spend Christmas with the Burkes. Adam had declined. This was his first Christmas as a married man. He knew he was being selfish, he had laughingly told Sarah, but he wanted to spend it alone with his wife. He would be joining her in a matter of days.

Sighing, frowning, Sarah slipped away to the grand formal dining room to confer with her French chef, her thoughts still occupied with the sad spectacle of Adam and Lily Randolph. At that moment, her thoughts about men in general were not very charitable.

Satisfied that everything was in readiness, Sarah paused at the dining-room doors. In the foyer, she came upon her husband. John was in conversation with two other gentlemen. He was unaware of Sarah's presence until one of those gentlemen said something in his ear. John looked over his shoulder. At the sight of Sarah, pleasure leapt into his eyes. He came to her at once.

Sarah's eyes flashed to John's companions, one of whom was instantly recognizable. It was Alexander Hamilton, a member of Washington's cabinet. Without acknowledging her presence, the gentlemen entered her husband's bookroom.

"John, what is going on?" Sarah demanded, though in an undertone. "We never invite Hamilton and Burr to the same party. They cannot be civil to each other for more than a few minutes at a time. Yet you must know that Aaron Burr is at this very moment in our ballroom at our express invitation."

"No need for alarm, my dear. Hamilton will not be

joining your party. He is here on a...eh... diplomatic mission. No, I am not at liberty to say more. Will you do something for me, Sarah? Will you ask Philippe Vissery to come to my bookroom? He's expecting the invitation."

The foyer was deserted. John made capital of his opportunities. He kissed Sarah full on the lips before he, too, entered the bookroom. Lost in thought, Sarah remained where he had left her.

She was remembering another party, more than a year before, when her husband had come to her in acute agitation, fearing that Hamilton and Burr had been inadvertently invited on the same night. Sarah sighed, thinking that she was not the same woman she had been a year ago. For a moment, tears stood on her lashes. She dashed them away with impatient fingers. When she entered the ballroom, she was her usual, serene self.

Chapter Twenty-Four

Philippe received his host's invitation to join him in his bookroom with an expression of acute pleasure.

"I have you to thank for this, Gervais," he said to his companion as they wended their way to John Burke's bookroom.

Launey smiled. "That would be going too far," he demurred. "I am not the only one who wishes to see Philippe Duhet receive his due."

Philippe gave a self-deprecatory shake of his head and smiled faintly. Inwardly, he was exultant. He had never foreseen this turn of events—that the American government would wish to honor him, albeit mistakenly, for the part Philippe Duhet had played in Rouen. When Launey had first broached the subject, Philippe had been wary. It did not seem likely that Adam would maintain his silence if Philippe were to receive honors for something his half-brother had effected.

By degrees, Philippe came to see that Adam's silence played into his hands. For whatever reason, Adam had been at some pains to conceal his part in the affair. Philippe thought he understood. The story was so farfetched that no one would give it credence. He had to give Adam his due. The plot had been well executed. Adam's masquerade as commissioner had gone undetected, and was, to this day, undetected. That fortuitous circumstance was not only Adam's doing. He, himself, had maintained his silence, even after he had been released from the rebel camp when most men in his place would have created a hue and outcry. The thought that he would most assuredly become a laughingstock was what had induced him to hold his peace. And how he thanked his lucky stars that he had chosen that course! For if Adam suddenly decided to challenge him on this, even if he could produce witnesses, who would believe him?

But Adam would never challenge him now, thought Philippe. For should he do so, Claire's role as his mistress must be revealed. He would make sure of it. And Adam would do nothing that would bring shame on Claire. For that very reason, Philippe knew he need not be troubled by witnesses. For Claire's sake, Adam would ensure their silence.

Honors were within his grasp, and he owed it all to Adam. He almost laughed out loud. The government of the United States wished to honor him. It did not matter that the honor might be nothing more than a handshake from the President. It was what followed that was of significance. He would have the goodwill of men of influence. He would be fêted and taken-up. His future would be assured. He would have the financial backing of well-wishers should he embark on some enterprise. Hadn't Launey intimated that his own fortunes had followed a similar course? Americans were the most openhanded race on God's earth. Their generosity was almost legendary, so Launey averred. Philippe had no reason to doubt him. In fact, his own experiences confirmed his friend's observations. Even as plain Philippe Vissery, a nobody with nothing to recommend him but graceful manners and an easy charm, he had found a ready welcome wherever he went. As Philippe Duhet . . .

He felt a faint stirring of caution and shrugged it off. The role of Vissery had served its purpose. He had not known what to expect when he had first set foot on American soil. For all he knew, his notoriety might have preceded him. Instead of which, thought Philippe dryly, Adam's intervention at Rouen had turned the tide of diplomatic opinion in his favor.

His mind raced ahead to what would be the fruition of all his hopes. He had yet to even the score with his half-brother. That day was not far off, even supposing Adam had sent Claire away. At the thought of Claire, amusement gleamed in Philippe's eyes. The girl was an innocent. She had made an eloquent though vain appeal to everything that was fine in his nature. She had no conception of a hatred so obsessive that a man would risk everything, even life itself, to pay off old scores. But Adam understood. He must not underestimate Adam.

It was Launey who held open the door to their host's bookroom, motioning Philippe to precede him. At their entrance, several gentlemen rose to their feet. John Burke came forward and made the introductions.

Philippe's eyes were immediately drawn to Alexander Hamilton. This dapper little gentleman with ruddy cheeks and piercing blue eyes held no less a position in Washington's Cabinet than Secretary of the Treasury. Like Philippe, he, too, had once been an immigrant. It was public knowledge that Hamilton had scarcely arrived as a youth from the island of Nevis when he had caught General Washington's eye. With Washington as his patron, Hamilton's rise had been meteoric. The thought brought a gleam of interest to Philippe's eyes. If he had had the least suspicion that his host, in his day, had served as Adam's patron, Philippe might have had second thoughts about remaining in this select company. But he did not know it. The subject had never come up, and those who might have enlightened him chose not to do so.

Next in line to be introduced was John Burke's brother, the young congressman. As Hamilton was to Washington, so David Burke was to Hamilton. There were two other gentlemen who needed no introduction to Philippe. Like Launey, they were fugitives from the Terror in France and had made themselves very useful to Philippe since his arrival in New York.

The gentlemen seated themselves. The brandy decanter was handed round. Conversation was desultory and tended to be dominated by Hamilton and John Burke. Philippe had known that Burke and Hamilton went back a long ways, to the time when they both had law practices on Wall Street. What he had not known and what became very evident from their idle chitchat was that Hamilton held the elder man in the highest esteem. They had worked together in smoothing out wrinkles in the Constitution before it was ratified. Philippe gathered that Hamilton was trying to lure Burke back into the stream of federal politics, without success. Law was Burke's first love. New York was his home.

Presently, there was a lull in the conversation. All eyes looked expectantly to Alexander Hamilton. Smiling pleasantly, he said without preamble, "Let me say at once that, before we can proceed, we must have done with subterfuge." Though the words held a faint threat, the smile was reassuring. His eyes held Philippe's. With almost shocking directness, he went on, "Think very carefully before you answer this question. Am I addressing myself to Philippe Vissery or Philippe Duhet?"

Thoughts and impressions flashed warningly in Philippe's mind. His eyes drifted from person to person. Slowly, he took a long swallow from the glass in his hand.

"And if I say that I am Philippe Duhet?" he temporized.

Hamilton's bark of laughter was spontaneous. "Spoken with all the subtlety of a true diplomat!" he exclaimed, and flashed an amused grin at John Burke.

The comment seemed to ease the tension. Others joined in the laughter. John Burke made haste to replenish his guests' glasses.

Hamilton's piercing gaze returned to Philippe. With surprising gravity, he said, "I presume you can prove your identity?"

At this point, Launey struck in, "I can vouch for the gentleman. He is Philippe Duhet, the Comte de Blaise. Good God, I've known Philippe since we were in shortcoats."

Launey was not the only one to voice his endorsement. The other gentlemen from France both spoke out, crediting their escape from the guillotine to the good offices of the commissioner of Rouen.

Hamilton merely shook his head. "It won't do," he said, and silenced the querulous outburst with a warning frown. Philippe appeared to be amused. "It won't do," Hamilton repeated, "and for a very good reason. Our friend here has established himself as Vissery. Yes, yes, I'm aware of the circumstances that forced him to that course. He assumed, wrongly as it turns out, that agents of the Convention were on his trail. That is, if he is Philippe Duhet."

Philippe's long fingers, which were toying with a button on his waistcoat, stilled. Hamilton observed the gesture.

"I assure you," he said, addressing Philippe directly, "Philippe Duhet's name is no longer on the proscribed lists from France. If it were, you may be sure, the government of the United States would offer the gentleman sanctuary, but to honor him publicly or unofficially would be out of the question. My government will do nothing to jeopardize its cordial relations with France, especially since Robespierre has been toppled."

"As I understand," said John Burke, "the Terror has come to an end."

"Quite," assured Hamilton, his eyes still locked on Philippe. "But I am waiting for my answer—an unequivocal answer, that is."

Philippe smiled, thinking that he had nothing to lose and perhaps a great deal to gain. "A man who is not cautious in these desperate times is a fool," he said, and slipping his hand inside his coat pocket, he produced a ring. It was no ordinary ring as every man there could see.

"It bears the crest of the Comtes de Blaise," offered Launey, addressing Hamilton.

"Then you are Philippe Duhet?"

"Naturally."

Hamilton sat back in his chair. "Thank you," he said. "That is what I wished to know."

At a nod from Hamilton, David Burke slowly rose to his feet. Philippe sensed the fine hairs on the back of his neck begin to rise.

The young congressman's tone was sombre and formal. "Philippe Duhet," he said, "it is my duty to inform you that, under the provisions of the Aliens Bill, you have been declared a political undesirable. In short, sir, you are not welcome on American soil. Passage has been arranged for your immediate return to France aboard the packet *Mariner*.

"These words are not mine, sir, but come to you directly from the President of the United States of America. President Washington's decision is final. No appeals will be permitted."

The silence was long and unbroken. Philippe looked from one to the other of his companions, as though expecting an outcry. None was forthcoming. A mask of indifference seemed to have settled on each unrevealing face. Not even a flicker of surprise registered.

His voice betrayed nothing of the rage which almost choked him. "You, too, Brutus?" he said, addressing Gervais Launey.

Launey answered in a less restrained tone. "As I said, Philippe, I have known you since we were in shortcoats. You sickened me then. You still sicken me. Did you really suppose that your past would never catch up with you? Some of us have long memories."

"And Rouen?" intoned Philippe politely.

Launey's smile was grim. "We know about Rouen," he said. "In point of fact, I was one of those who prevailed upon your half-brother to take your place."

"Ah."

Without haste, Philippe rose to his feet. His look was amused. "In all this, I sense the hand of Adam Dillon," he said. "I should have expected something of the sort. Adam has always hated me."

Hamilton refused to rise to the bait. He merely said, "You will go along with these gentlemen, if you please, Monsieur Duhet. They are charged with your safety."

"Am I under arrest?"

"Certainly not! You have committed no crimes on American soil that I am aware of. As I said, these gentlemen are charged with your safety until the *Mariner* sails. I might add that it is not the wish of my government to embarrass you in any way. Whether you return to France as Vissery or Duhet is up to you. I meant what I said. The name of Philippe Duhet is not on any proscribed list that I have ever seen."

"In that case," said Philippe, as though he had not a care in the world, "I should prefer to go by the name of Vissery."

"As you wish."

When the door had closed on Philippe and his escort, only three gentlemen remained, John Burke, his brother David, and Alexander Hamilton. Of those three, only David Burke appeared to be disturbed by the little drama which had just taken place.

"If it ever gets back to the President or Congress," said David Burke gloomily, "that we took it upon ourselves to send Duhet back to France, our political careers will be over, and that's the least that will happen to us. We are conspirators, that's what we are."

Hamilton laughed. "Who is there to betray us? Duhet, you may be sure, will keep his own counsel. A man of his consequence would not wish to lose face."

"You seem very pleased with yourself," observed David Burke sourly.

Hamilton shook his head. "No," he said. "What amuses me is your part in all this, John. In all the years I have known you, unlike me, you have never lent your support to anything that could not be examined under a magnifying glass. You are not usually so devious."

"Devious!" scoffed David Burke. "That is a *tepid* word for our part in all of this! I would not say that *treasonable* is an exaggeration! Yes, and I am not only referring to what took place here tonight. I still find it hard to believe that a man of your principles, John, would have encouraged Adam in this Rouen affair."

"I'm of the same opinion," said Hamilton, enjoying himself immensely.

"Surely all men of principle must deplore recent events in France?" murmured John Burke.

Ignoring this observation, David Burke went on in the same censorious tone, "We were fortunate tonight that Duhet took us at face value."

"He had no reason not to," pointed out the elder Burke mildly. "You are both known to have considerable influence with the President."

At this remark, David Burke visibly winced. "The President would never have sanctioned Duhet's removal," he said. "His powers are not so far-ranging."

"And so I told Adam. This was the best I could

come up with at short notice."

John's reasonable tones, far from appeasing his reluctant accomplice, seemed to have the opposite effect. "And where on earth did you get the idea of an Aliens Bill?" he demanded shortly. "It's the first I've heard of such a thing."

"I borrowed it from the British," answered John. "Gentlemen, you have my thanks. I don't think I can express adequately how much your support has meant to me."

"John! We trust your judgment implicitly!" exclaimed Hamilton.

There was an odd silence as the eyes of the two brothers met and held. After a moment, the younger Burke's face split into a wide grin. "I second Mr. Hamilton's sentiments," he declared. "And even if I did not, you know that I would never fail you."

"Do I?"

"Good God, John, don't you suppose that I know how much I owe you?" If anything, his grin intensified. "And not least," he said softly, "for my present domestic happiness."

John's lips curved in an answering smile. In a more expansive mood, he handed round the brandy decanter. "I must say, gentlemen," he said, "that you played your parts to admiration. And may I say, Alex, that the way you handled Duhet was positively masterly? For a time, there, I was beginning to fear that he would never admit to who he was."

Hamilton, who had been observing the interesting byplay between the two brothers, smiled at this and said, "Yes. We could hardly have had any reason to deport so harmless a creature as Philippe Vissery." After an interval, he went on musingly. "I suppose Duhet is as black as he has been painted? What I mean to say is . . . I found myself in sympathy with the fellow as the interview progressed. And at the end . . . well . . . he conducted himself with admirable restraint. In his shoes, I think I would have been foaming at the mouth."

John Burke sat very still. "Yes," he said, "to all appearances, Duhet is a charming fellow. No one disputes it. It's what makes him so . . ."

". . . dangerous?" supplied Hamilton.

". . . diabolical," came the swift retort.

Philippe managed to maintain his air of nonchalance until he was safely behind the closed doors of his bedchamber in the Black Boar Tavern. The three gentlemen who formed his "escort" had made themselves comfortable in his private parlor. He could hear the chink of glasses as they made free with his stock of brandy. It seemed that they were settling in for the duration. A card game was soon in progress.

Moving to the window, Philippe twitched the curtain aside. It was as he expected. Sentries had been posted. If he tried to go out the window, the alarm would be raised.

He could scarcely credit his own gullibility. Rouen! There was never any question of the American government rewarding him for his services as commissioner. It was all part of Adam's plot to entice him into admitting his true identity. If he had only clung to his story from the very beginning, if he had only insisted that he was Vissery, no one could have proved him a liar.

He had been overconfident. He thought he knew how Adam's mind worked. Never, in all their battles as boys and as young men, had his half-brother ever taken the initiative. Adam played a defensive game. He, Philippe, would make the moves and Adam would try to check them. It was a pattern that was well established. He had been counting on it.

Again, he thought of Rouen, and he gnashed his teeth together. In Rouen, that childhood pattern had been broken. Adam had taken the initiative there.

Why had he not foreseen that the same thing could happen here?

His face twisted in fury. He had not foreseen it because Adam had set the stage to allay his suspicions. Launey and all the rest, the men in high places whom he had believed he was so subtly cultivating, they had all been deceiving *him!* They were all in Adam's pocket!

If Adam only knew it, he was sending him back to France to face charges on a spate of crimes from one end of the country to the other. The amnesty which Robespierre's successors had inaugurated was not for the likes of him. His crimes were not only of a political nature. And if his name was not on any proscribed list, that was because it was generally presumed in France that he had perished on the scaffold. He could never return to France under his own name.

Perhaps Adam knew it. No, thought Philippe a moment later. Adam did not have it in him to pursue his goal so ruthlessly. Adam had proved that he was a formidable foe. But he had an Achilles heel. He must always allow the ties of blood to stand in his way. He would stop short of sending a brother to his death. He, Philippe Duhet, accepted no such constraints, as Adam would soon discover to his cost.

Whistling under his breath, he moved to the gentleman's commode. He dispensed with the ribbon which tied back his hair and surveyed himself critically in the mirror.

"Ebony," he roared.

It was Launey who came to the door.

"Might I presume on your good nature?" said Philippe politely. "Would you be so kind as to inform my man that I wish him to draw my bath? He usually hangs out in the kitchens, making himself useful."

*   *   *

398

Adam returned to Hanover Square in the wee hours of the morning. Without Claire's presence, the house felt as cold and unwelcoming as a morgue. There was no question of him seeking his bed. He was too wound up, too restless. He made for his study. The fire had been allowed to die down. Snatching a glass and a decanter from a side table, he made for the stairs, assured that the fire in his bed-chamber would be banked up.

Ensconced in a wing armchair flanking the grate, he poured himself a generous shot of whiskey. There was a slight tremor in his hand. He noted it with dispassionate interest before taking several long swallows in quick succession. The whiskey had a steadying effect.

It was almost over. In a day or two, as soon as there was a break in the weather, the *Mariner* would set sail for France with Philippe on board. Though everything in him revolted at the thought, Adam was resolved to see his half-brother one last time before, hopefully, they parted forever. He closed his eyes, trying to envision that scene.

He had, quite deliberately, kept himself out of the picture as the jaws of his trap had closed around Philippe. Adam did not wish his half-brother to think that he was gloating, or that he wanted to humiliate him. He had stolen a march on Philippe, that was all. And though they had come too far for the possibility of a reconciliation, he hoped that his moderation had paved the way for a truce of sorts. It was time to bury the past and get on with the business of living, if only Philippe could be persuaded to see it that way.

He would tell Philippe that he was sending him back to reclaim his estates and fortune. There was an amnesty in France. That must count for something. But something more was required, a threat to stay Philippe's hand. He had friends in France, Adam would tell Philippe. If some untimely accident were to befall himself or anyone close to him, it would be the signal to unleash his hounds upon him. Any sane man must heed such a warning in the interests of self-preservation.

Was Philippe entirely sane?—that was the question. Adam sincerely doubted it. In the first flush of rage, Philippe was capable of anything. It was for this reason that Adam could not settle. Until, with his own eyes, he saw the *Mariner* sailing out of New York Harbor, he would find no peace.

His fears, he tried to assure himself, were groundless. He had a dozen men patrolling the environs of the Black Boar. Launey and his associates were safely ensconced inside. Hadn't he just come from there, having satisfied himself that the place was as tight as a drum? There could be no escape for Philippe. And Claire was miles away.

Claire. When Philippe was safely away, he would go to her. He would tell her everything—how he had tried to throw Philippe off the scent by feigning indifference to the one person who was everything in the world to him. He would tell her about Dulcie's role, how she had been Philippe's innocent dupe, and how necessary it had become to maintain the fiction that he was an indifferent husband even in the privacy of his own home. He would tell her how he had betrayed himself with that one revealing look when he had looked up to find her alone in the sleigh with Philippe, and how imperative it had suddenly become to send her away for her own good.

She would think that he had exaggerated the danger, of course. The kind of evil that Philippe represented was so entirely beyond Claire's ken. Her next thought would be for Philippe. And Adam would be happy to reassure her on that point. For her sake, he was being more generous than Philippe deserved. Surely she must see that?

And when they had done with talking, he would send the servants away and lead Claire to their bedchamber. Though he was starved for her, he would take her with gentleness, with reverence, binding her more closely to him with the inevitable rapture they found in each other's arms. And Claire would give herself freely, withholding nothing from him, because she knew how desperately he needed her. And afterwards, in the afterglow, they would talk in whispers of the future, anticipating with awe the birth of their child. Before long, he would want to take her again, but he would deny himself. Claire came before anything, Claire who had brought joy and radiance into his life, Claire who had taught him the meaning of . . . love.

Adam came awake instantly. The door knocker was pounding. He glanced at the timepiece on the mantel. Dawn was still hours away.

Two strides took him to the door of his chamber. He could hear the bolt of the front door as it was pulled back. There were four gentlemen milling around in the foyer. It was Launey who ascended the stairs to meet Adam halfway.

"He got away from us," he said tersely. "He and that man of his tricked us."

"Tell me what happened as I get dressed," said Adam, leading the way upstairs.

"He wanted to bathe," said Launey. "I could see no harm in it."

"No," said Adam. "Go on."

"His man fetched the water. We were playing cards in the other room. Everything seemed normal. We could hear him, you see."

Adam found what he was looking for—a warm riding cloak to keep out the winter chill. He threw it over his shoulders and motioned his companion out the door.

Launey continued his narrative as they descended the stairs. "When I finally went in to see why Duhet was taking so long at his bath, only his manservant was there."

"How did Duhet escape?"

"Over the roof. No, he did not go out the window. The most damnable thing! We found a trapdoor in the closet in his chamber. It gave onto the attics."

"The men I posted to watch the inn—surely they must have seen something?"

"That's just it, Adam! They swear that the only person they encountered was—you!"

Adam broke his stride and turned to give his companion his undivided attention. "What do you mean—they encountered *me*?"

"They thought it was you. It must have been Duhet masquerading as you. He'd cut his hair, of course, and changed his garments. In that half-light, it's impossible to tell the difference between you."

"How much of a head start does he have?"

"An hour. No more than two. We searched everywhere for him. He seems to have vanished into thin air."

A muscle clenched in Adam's cheek. "I know where to find him," he said.

Chapter Twenty-Five

At Adam's place on the Hudson, Claire and Blanche had hardly unpacked their boxes when Mark Clay and his mother appeared on their doorstep. Claire, remembering how she had once tried to make Adam jealous by playing up to this local Romeo, was a little reserved in her manner. She need not have troubled herself. Mark took one look at Blanche and appeared to be entirely smitten.

Before a week was out, Claire had divined Mark's purpose. It was all a sham to allow Mark and his friends unlimited access to the house and estate. A man bent on courting did not arrive with a sleigh of young bucks in tow, all of them strapping lads and sporting ferocious looking firing-arms.

"This is Adam's doing," said Claire. She made no attempt to hide her agitation. "He has set Mark and his friends to guard us. Something is afoot, Blanche, something to do with Philippe. I wish I knew what it was. Well, I'm not staying here if Adam is in some kind of danger. I don't care what he says, I'm going back to New York."

"You're imagining things," said Blanche soothingly. "And it's hardly flattering to me when you imply that Mark's interest is spurious. Look, if you return to the city, I shall have to go with you. Then I'll lose my chance to attach Mark. Besides, Adam

403

will soon be here. You're alarming yourself unnecessarily."

"Then why must Mark always bring his friends?"

"They are just being neighborly. We should be grateful for their presence. We are, after all, only two defenseless females in an isolated house."

Claire might have argued that they were scarcely defenseless. The house had a full complement of servants, two of whom were strangers to Claire, brothers, big burly Irishmen whom Adam had hired to do the rough work. They seemed to spend most of their time chopping wood or working in the stables.

As for the firing-arms, this was soon explained away. This was the hunting season, and these young bucks were avid sportsmen. In the woods around the house was a plentiful supply of game. Grouse, quail, and partridge, as well as venison were a welcome addition to the winter table. Claire almost believed it, until Mark Clay warned her in no uncertain terms that she and Blanche must stay close to the house unless he or one of his friends accompanied them. There was always danger at this time of year, he said. Careless hunters were sometimes known to shoot first and ask questions later. Every other year, some innocent trespasser lost his life in a hunting accident.

Claire fretted, but soon came to see that there was no point in arguing. Adam's friends and hirelings knew their duty. If she rebelled, she had no doubt that she would become a virtual prisoner in her own house. She gave in gracefully, but that did not stop her worrying about Adam.

If it had not been for Mrs. Clay and her daughters, she would have become as broody as a mother hen. But Christmas was fast approaching, and there was much for a conscientious chatelaine to oversee. And since Claire was unfamiliar with Adam's traditions, and she wished to please him above anything, Mrs. Clay and her daughters were invited to instruct her. There were pies to bake and puddings to steam, and he game that Mark and his friends bagged must be plucked or skinned and hung from the rafters in the larder. Americans, it seemed, followed the English custom of sitting down to an elaborate dinner on Christmas Day. There would be no Midnight Mass on Christmas Eve, Claire was thinking, and no *réveillon* to follow, with pâté, *tartes* and *gâteau*. She shrugged philosophically. She was an American now. She was even beginning to think in English. Her sons and daughters would be Americans also. It was fitting.

Some traditions were entirely new to her. Taffy-pulling was one of them. Claire and Blanche spent an enjoyable evening as guests of the Clays learning how to prepare this delectable treat from maple sugar. Taffy-pulling parties were great social occasions where young people, so Claire was given to understand, could do their courting with impunity. Blanche and Mark certainly seemed to avail themselves of this liberty, for they spent almost the entire evening in each other's company. Claire was tempted to believe that they were sincere. But when it came time to go home, and their sleigh was escorted by no less than six armed gentlemen on horseback, she reverted to her former opinion. Mark's courtship of Blanche, and at which Blanche connived, was merely a pretext for his unwavering vigilance.

Claire was pondering these things the following morning when Mark and one of his sisters drew up at the front doors in his sleigh. He was accompanied by his customary escort of outriders. Claire and Blanche, snatching at their cloaks, went out to meet them.

Mark was in fine fettle. "No hunting today," he called out. "My mother has sent me to forage in the woods for evergreen boughs and cranberries. In these parts, we make them into wreaths and garlands to decorate our homes. There's room for two more in the sleigh."

Blanche was eager. Claire hung back. It was a

405

glorious day, but she was fatigued. That she was suffering all the discomforts of her pregnancy was something Claire kept to herself. She might have been persuaded, however, if Mark had not produced the strangest-looking objects which he called snow-shoes. The girls listened with interest as he explained their usefulness in deep snow.

"The exercise will do you both good," he said finally. "And it won't be too strenuous. We'll take the sleigh. If you become bored, or you can't get the hang of snow-shoeing, I'll let you take a turn with my team, if you like."

Nothing was going to persuade Claire to don those absurd objects. And it wasn't only her dignity she was thinking about. In her delicate condition, she wasn't about to take any chances. Besides, she could not see why any sane person would wish to trek through snowdrifts when it could be avoided very easily by adhering to well-trodden paths.

Blanche, on the other hand, was intrigued. The end of it was that Blanche went off in the sleigh with Mark and his sister, while the gentlemen dismounted and trooped into Claire's kitchen. Claire was not quite sure of the propriety of this turn in events. She debated with herself for a moment then followed them inside. It seemed pointless to argue. They were there to protect her. They knew it. She knew it. The least she could do was offer them the hospitality of her home.

"You'll be ready for your breakfast, gentlemen?" she said.

When she awakened, she was disoriented. She had been dreaming of Adam. The dream was so real, she could almost sense his presence in the room. She felt safe and cherished.

"Adam," she said, and gave a little sob. She missed

406

…im dreadfully. Tears squeezed from beneath her …ashes.

Before she gave in completely to self-pity she …wung her legs over the edge of the bed and took a …moment to get her bearings. In the kitchen, when …ook had set the bacon in the pan to fry, she had suddenly turned nauseous. Her protectors must be …wondering why she had left them so precipitously.

The nap had restored her depleted strength. She …elt that she could tackle anything. Stretching, …awning, she rose to her feet. Sounds from outside …drew her attention. She moved to the window and …ooked out through one of the small frosted panes. Horses and riders were milling about. She scratched …he surface of the glass, clearing a spot to get a better …ook. There could be no doubt about it. The young …men who had sat down at her table so shortly before …were all mounted up. Someone was directing them. …Someone was shouting out orders as though he had …hat right. As she watched, the riders wheeled their …horses and rode off. Only one rider remained.

"Adam!" breathed Claire.

She rushed to the door and flung it wide. "Blanche!" she cried out. "Blanche! Come quickly! Adam's home."

There was no answer. It registered vaguely that …Blanche was off gathering evergreens with Mark …Clay and his sister. Claire could hardly contain her …impatience as she flew down the stairs. She made for …the kitchens. Adam must stable his horse before he …entered the house. He would use the back door.

Cook and her helpers were clearing away the …breakfast debris. "Adam's home!" Claire cried out …with more gaiety, more animation than she had …evinced in an age.

It was second nature for her to reach for her soft, …fur-lined moccasins and the warm cloak which hung …on a hook by the door. In these frigid temperatures no one left the house without dressing appropriately. She pushed into the arctic cold summer kitchen, taking a moment to pull on her leather mittens. Once outside, she lifted the snood of her cloak to cover her hair. Within minutes, she had crossed the distance between house and stable. "Adam?"

There was no one there, not even one of the burly Irishmen whose watchful eyes unfailingly trailed her, yes, even when she had occasion to use the outside privy.

"Claire!"

She spun on her heel to face him. As she watched, he carefully dismounted. Hoar frost clung to his garments. His mount was steaming, quivering, on the point of collapse.

"Don't come any closer," she said as he advanced a step toward her.

Philippe halted and studied her quizzically. "Do you know," he said easily, "you are the first to challenge me? No really! This was easier than I would ever have believed. Everybody I have met has taken me for my half-brother. I'm not surprised that Adam had an easy time of it in Rouen if even his friends can't tell the difference between us."

"You are mistaken," said Claire, surprised at how steady her voice was when her pulse was racing like a runaway carriage. "Those gentlemen you sent away are not well acquainted with Adam. No one who knows either of you intimately could ever mistake your identities."

"You did once," he answered softly. "In Rouen."

"What have you done to Adam?" she asked sharply.

He laughed, almost gaily. "You should ask rather what Adam has done to me!" His face suffused with sudden anger. "He has been plotting against me from the first, Claire. I'm to be returned to France to face certain execution. That's what Adam has done to me."

"I don't believe it," she said flatly. "And if you believe that about Adam, you don't know him at all. You're his brother, for heaven's sake. Adam could never do what you are suggesting."

His crop came down on his knee so violently that Claire jumped. "We are not brothers," he said savagely, "we are half-brothers, and there has never been any love lost between us." He shook his head and said in a more normal tone, "I haven't the time to explain things to you. Go into the stable, Claire. I must saddle a fresh mount and then I shall be on my way."

Her voice dwindled to a thin whisper. "What have you done to Adam?"

"I've delayed him," he said, then gave a blood-curdling laugh. "I've sent his own men to ambush him. They believe that they are converging on me, you see. By the time he fights his way clear of that one, I shall be well on my way to Canada."

Her mind fastened on the one thing that really mattered to her. Adam was safe. Her lashes swept down, concealing the wild surge of elation that swept through her. Adam was safe.

Caution returned in full force when he took another step toward her. "Go into the stable, Claire," he said.

Nothing was going to make her enter that stable. "Let me go," she said. "I have never done anything to hurt you. You have no quarrel with me."

His smile was almost tender. It terrified her. "That is not important," he said. "What is important is that Adam loves you. And you are pregnant with his child, aren't you, Claire?"

He laughed, and Claire's skin began to crawl. Her mind had finally begun to make connections. Every able-bodied man on the place had been sent off on a wild goose chase. Blanche had not yet returned from her outing with Mark Clay. The only people in the house were three female domestics.

Adam's words came back to her. Her pity was misplaced. There was no saving grace in Philippe. He would stop at nothing to hurt Adam. Whatever Adam loved, Philippe had always taken away from him.

But all was not lost. Even at this moment, Adam was in hot pursuit. Claire fastened on the hope that if she kept her head, she would yet be rescued from the deranged man who was studying her with an odd little smile.

She moistened her lips and made an involuntary movement.

"Don't try to escape me," he said gently. "You would not stand a chance."

"Save yourself," she burst out. "For God's sake, Philippe, save yourself before Adam finds you."

"What an odd choice of words," he said. "Are you referring to heaven and hell?"

"No. Yes. I don't know what you mean."

He smiled sadly. "In any event, it's too late. I chose my path a long time ago."

His words confused her. She tried another tack. "There are armed men set to guard me. If I scream, they'll come running and find you."

"Ah Claire, you are so transparent. Don't you think I made sure that there was no one here to help you?"

She forgot about keeping her head. "Adam was right about you," she said. "You don't care who gets hurt in your lust for revenge. Give it up, Philippe, before it is too late."

"I thought I told you? It is too late. Do you know, you almost had me convinced that you understood my point of view? You lied to me, didn't you, Claire? You don't see things my way at all. It was all a charade. Do you know what I think, Claire? I think Adam can do no wrong in your eyes. You are just like my father. You can't see past Adam."

She wasn't really listening. A plan of action was

410

forming in her brain. Philippe stood between her and the house. The only other cover close by was the stand of trees behind the stables, bordering a creek. If she could get to the trees, and if she followed the bed of the frozen creek, she would come eventually to a true forest where she could hide herself indefinitely.

She had not a hope in heaven. She knew that even as she took the first step. And just as surely she knew that to stay with Philippe was unthinkable. The man's mind had snapped. He was unpredictable. He would kill her as soon as look at her.

She took off like a startled deer. At her back, Philippe cursed vehemently. Some sound alerted her to the fact that he had remounted. It was this that saved her. As he dug in his spurs, he cocked his pistol. The exhausted animal took one step, then another, and staggered to its knees. At the same time, Philippe pulled the trigger. The shot went wild.

Again, Philippe cursed and kicked the downed beast as he fought to free his trapped foot from the stirrup. He did not waste time in reloading his pistol. Discarding it, he reached in his waistband for its mate.

Claire did not take the time to look back. The report of the pistol shot acted on her like a keg of gunpowder in a raging inferno. She went shooting into the trees. There were no sounds of pursuit. She had to steel herself for what came next. Though everything inside her screamed that she should hide herself, she left the cover of the trees for the frozen bed of the creek. Ice left no footprints. Philippe would be able to track her in the snow.

With heart-wrenching terror, frequently looking over her shoulder, she picked her way over the ice, carefully avoiding the odd drift of snow. She had progressed for thirty yards or so when a slight sound alerted her. She gave a stifled gasp and flung herself into the underbrush.

Panting, shoulders heaving, she crouched down,

411

flattening herself against the hard trunk of a maple. When Philippe appeared on the ice, twenty paces away, spurs jingling, she pressed her fist to her mouth, terrified that the harsh rasp of her breath would betray her presence.

Without haste, he removed his spurs. "Claire, this is foolhardy beyond permission." He spoke softly, soothingly. "I won't hurt you. I promise."

Claire said nothing. Her gaze was fixed on the pistol which Philippe held in one hand. He turned to the right, thinking no doubt that she was trying to make her way back to the house.

"Claire," he said again. "Come out of your lair. You can't get away from me. You know you can't. I shall make this as painless as possible."

She held her breath. As soon as he was out of sight, she was on her feet, hoisting her skirts to her knees. Then she was off like a shot. How she managed to move at breakneck speed without attracting Philippe's attention was something she would ponder later. A time or two, she took a tumble. The snow seemed to absorb every sound.

Occasionally, she paused to listen and to catch her breath. Nothing was moving. The silence around was like no silence she had ever heard before. It was deep and complete, as though the very forest were holding its breath for something momentous to happen. She shivered and pushed on.

By degrees, the impetus that had carried her along began to dwindle. By this time, she felt more secure. She was hedged in on every side by a dense wall of pines and thick undergrowth. The stitch in her side was so painful that she did not think she could take another step. She must rest or she would collapse.

She was to discover that terror is a miraculous restorative. "Claire!" The ghostly voice was behind her. She whimpered. The snow had swallowed the sounds of both hunter and hunted. Concealment was impossible. Her tracks gave her away. She must keep moving. She forced herself to take one step and then another, and she did not know where her strength and determination were coming from.

"Claire, it's Adam. Can you hear me? Don't panic, darling! Just stay where you are. I'll find you."

Joy leaped to her throat. In the nick of time, Adam had come to save her! A wild sob of thankfulness almost burst from her. She choked it back, biting down on her lip. It was a trick. Philippe was trying to lure her into a trap! The man was a devil!

"Claire! Come to me!"

Wildly, she twisted her head to the left, then to the right. She didn't know where the voice was coming from. She only knew that it was behind her, and that Philippe was closing in.

Blind panic engulfed her. Like a doe with the hounds at her heels, she sprang forward. There was no strategy now, no forethought. Running, stumbling, dragging herself from tree to tree, she pushed forward. Tears froze on her lashes. There was the taste of blood in her mouth. Her garments were soaked through, not with melting snow, but with the perspiration from her exertions. Claire was oblivious. In a queer detached way, an odd thought had taken possession of her mind. If by some miracle she were to survive, she would never again permit anyone to hunt defenseless creatures on her lands.

Suddenly, she checked. She had come to the edge of the forest. Before her was a vast expanse of pristine white snow which sloped down to the river road. Gasping, sobbing for breath, she sagged against the trunk of a tree.

"Claire!"

"Claire!"

Philippe's mesmerizing voice seemed to echo from every side. She didn't know which way to turn. There was the sudden report of a gunshot, not from close behind, but from far ahead of her. And then she saw them, on the river road, men, spread out, waving,

413

moving slowly uphill, like ants on a white sheet. She would never reach them in time. She knew that for a certainty even as she burst like an arrow from her cover.

Plunging, sliding, rolling, she came to an abrupt halt only twenty paces from where she had begun her mad descent. In her terror, she had miscalculated. In the open, the wind blew the snow into odd drifts, treacherously masking natural depressions in the ground for unwary trespassers. She sank to her knees, sobbing with hysteria. All she could think of was "snowshoes." At length, she turned at bay to face her hunter.

She did not have long to wait. Philippe's pursuit was as crazed as her flight. He came bolting out of the trees not thirty feet away. She crouched there, shaken and terrified, waiting for him to end it all.

"Claire," he shouted. "Claire! Come to me!" Like a man demented, he moved toward her. The pistol glinted wickedly in his hand.

She thought she was prepared for death. She thought that she didn't care anymore. She was mistaken. With a despairing cry, on hands and knees, she crawled away from him. Suddenly, miraculously, she found herself on firmer ground. Hope quickened inside her.

There was a road of sorts across the pasture. She vaguely remembered it from the time she had been there before. She had no idea where it led, nor did she care. Half crouched over, she pulled herself to her feet and took a few stumbling steps toward it, steeling herself for the bullet that would enter her back.

She was hallucinating. She must be. Philippe was there before her, facing her. Stupefied, almost fainting with exhaustion, she looked straight into the barrel of his pistol.

"Claire!"

The warning cry came from behind her. She looked over her shoulder. And then she understood everything. Adam was there. It was Adam who had been pursuing her. And while she had been fleeing from Adam, Philippe had circled ahead of them both.

As though she had all the time in the world, she looked down the slope of the valley. Help was at hand. Adam's men were closing in. The pity of it was, they would be too late.

She felt a great sense of peace settle over her. It was almost as though she were detached and exalted at the same time.

"Claire," said Adam, softly, carefully, "move out of the way, my dear. You are standing between Philippe and me. Don't say anything, just move out of the way."

Philippe laughed, and even that demented sound had not the power to sway Claire. She moved closer.

"Philippe," she said, fighting for breath, begging with him, raising both hands in unconscious supplication, "this is your last chance, your very last chance. Do you understand? Think carefully before you choose. Save yourself, Philippe. For the love of God, save yourself." As she spoke, she inched forward, closing the distance between them.

Adam heard her words, observed her gestures, saw the determination in the set of her shoulders, and it was as though he stood at the edge of a great precipice. "No!" he said. "Oh God, no!"

He threw back his head and sucked air into his lungs. "Cl . . . ai . . . re!" His cry was the scream of a creature in torment.

He knew that he was moving at the speed of lightning. He felt as though his limbs were weighted with lead. As he bore down upon her, every second seemed like a minute, every minute seemed like an hour. He sprang at her at the same instant that Philippe's pistol spewed out fire. They went rolling into a snowdrift. *Rose petals*, thought Adam as the crimson from her wound seeped into the driven snow. His face was as ashen as hers. "I love you," he said brokenly, damning himself to hell for having left it for too late. "I love you, Claire."

Her eyelashes fluttered. A fleeting smile touched her lips. "It's all right," she whispered.

Adam drew his first conscious breath in a long while. Crouched over his wife's prostrate form, shielding her, he leveled his pistol. Tears blinded his vision. He blinked them away.

Philippe stood his ground. "I've won!" he cried exultantly. "I've won!"

Adam's eyes flared. Behind Philippe, like a great charging predator, a sleigh erupted from between two stands of trees. For all its speed, it moved soundlessly. Blanche was at the reins. She had lost control of her team. Her mouth opened, but no sound came. Mark Clay's look was one of horror. Philippe did not stand a chance. It happened so quickly, he did not even have time to call out. His body went flying with the impact and came to rest with a sickening thud.

When Adam bent over him, Philippe was still breathing. There was no wound that Adam could see. But Philippe's eyes held the glaze of death.

"Papa!" he said. "Papa . . ." Blood spurted from his mouth, choking off the sentence. It was finally over.

Chapter Twenty-Six

Claire was not the best of patients. She was chomping at the bit. And it was no wonder, she told Adam, glowering at his tolerant grin. She had been forced to forgo her very first Christmas in America. There was not the least necessity for it. The wound was superficial. The bullet had not even entered her arm. It was so unfair. While others had sat down at her board, eating their heads off, she had been confined to her chamber on short rations.

"Chicken soup," she disparaged, "and custard! For Christmas dinner!"

"I'll make it up to you," said Adam, and silenced her protests with a long lingering kiss. "If you are a good girl, and promise not to overtax your strength, I might be persuaded to allow you to come downstairs for a little while tomorrow."

She grinned impishly. "Autocrat!" she said.

He seated himself at the edge of the bed. Before he could say another word in the same light-hearted vein, she captured one of his hands and pressed it to her breasts. "We must talk," she said. "No really, Adam. I have regained my strength. I am not an invalid. I think I shall go mad if you say one more time that you'll explain everything to me when I am more myself. I've never felt better in my life."

Adam studied his wife's face intently. As it had

turned out, the wound to her arm had been the least of his worries. She had come through a harrowing experience. When he brought her home, she had been in shock. He did not want to say or do anything to cause Claire a moment's unease.

"Please, Adam?"

"Very well. What is it you wish to know?"

"Everything," said Claire, laughing. "But you may begin by telling me how you came to find me and save me at the very last moment."

The smile left Adam's eyes, and a muscle clenched in his cheek. "I think," he said, "that I have relived every moment of that chase a million times over in the last week."

"Darling, don't," she said. "Forget about the chase. Tell me how you found me. I could scarcely believe my eyes when I saw you standing there."

"Yet, you did not recognize me," he said gently. "You thought I was Philippe."

She faltered a little under his stare. "Only for a moment or two, and only because it was Philippe I expected to see. Please, tell me what happened. I know that Philippe sent your own men to ambush you. I watched from this very room as he sent them away."

"Yes," said Adam. "They thought they were following my orders. They pinned us down at Coulter's farm. If I'd had all the time in the world, I think I could have persuaded them that I was not Philippe. Or if Mark had been with them, he would have vouched for me. The long and the short of it is, while Launey created a diversion, I slipped away on a fresh horse. The rest you may imagine. When I got here, I found Philippe's mount and a spent pistol. Thank God for the snow! I was able to follow your tracks."

A shudder passed over her. "If you had not known to come looking for him here, I can't think how it would have ended. Forgive me, Adam. You were right and I was wrong."

"Don't reproach yourself. Philippe was always a master of deception. Even when we were boys, he had a whole repertoire of smiles and looks which he employed to incredible effect."

"I was not taken in by Philippe's charm," she said with surprising passion.

"No? What then?"

"I never liked him. I never really trusted him. It was only . . . ," she hesitated as she put her thoughts in order. "I misjudged you once, Adam. I learned my lesson. I had made up my mind, you see, that I should not be as quick to judge others. It is a flaw in my character. I was trying to correct it."

She looked so contrite, so woeful, that Adam could not resist the temptation. He kissed her softly. "Next time, steer a middle course," he said. "How is the arm?"

"A little stiff, nothing more. If you had not pushed me out of the way . . ." Aware that she had made a blunder, that she had brought to mind something she wished him to forget, she quickly changed direction. "Did Philippe . . . did he say anything at the end?"

For a moment, she thought that Adam was about to take her to task. Then he said simply, " 'Papa.' He said, 'Papa.' "

"I thought it might be something like that."

"Why? What can you mean?"

"Oh . . . nothing definite. He said something to me about your father. He seemed to think that you were the favorite son."

Surprised, Adam said, "I hardly ever saw my father. I was the bastard son. Philippe was the heir. All his hopes resided in Philippe. What else did my half-brother say to you?"

"He said that you had been plotting against him from the beginning, that you were sending him back to France to face certain execution. I told him that if he believed *that* he didn't know you very well."

"I *was* plotting against him from the beginning. I *was* sending him back to France. But not to his death. He *must* have known he had nothing to fear in France. No, Philippe was simply trying to destroy your confidence in me."

"Nothing could do that," said Claire so quickly that Adam's eyes gleamed in appreciation.

For a time, they became lost in reflection. It was Claire who broke the silence. "I expect we shall never understand what drove a man like Philippe." She shivered. "I don't think I want to know. What . . . what story have you given out about his death?"

"That Philippe Vissery met with a tragic accident while he was my guest."

"Vissery?"

"To reveal Philippe's identity now would serve no useful purpose. It's better this way."

"Poor Blanche! I can't be sorry, of course, that we were saved, but at the same time, I can imagine how she must be feeling."

Adam knew perfectly well that Claire could not imagine what Blanche was feeling. Blanche's first horrified thought, so she had told him, when the sleigh had run down Philippe, was that she had run down Adam. Later, when everything became clear to her, she was inclined to credit Providence with taking a hand in things. If she had not gone out with Mark that day, if she had not taken a turn at the reins, if the horses had not bolted . . .

"Do you know what I think?" said Claire. "I think Providence took a hand in things. And so I shall tell Blanche."

Adam was startled into a smile. A moment later, a new train of thought led him to ask solicitously, "You are sure you are feeling better?"

"Oh quite. I feel as right as a . . . I forget the expression."

"Trivet," supplied Adam helpfully.

"Yes, whatever that means." She smiled happily.

"Then tell me this," he said, and there was no levity in him. "Why did you put me through that hell? And spare me the innocent look! You know what I'm talking about! I told you to move out of the way, instead of which, you positioned yourself closer to Philippe. You knew I would not have a clear shot at him."

"I knew," said Claire.

In a different tone, he said, "Then why did you do it? What fool thought took possession of your mind?"

She closed her eyes, blinking back moisture. "I knew you could not shoot your own brother," she said. "And just as surely, I knew that Philippe had no such scruples. It seemed I had nothing to lose."

"Not shoot my own brother?" Adam looked to be stupefied. "Claire, that may have been true once upon a time. But the moment he acted against you, he put himself beyond the pale. I was ready to tear Philippe limb from limb even before he shot at you. If the sleigh had not finished him off, you may take my word for it, I would most definitely have shot to kill."

"It's easy to say that now," she said. "But you did not shoot him, did you?"

"No, but . . ." Comprehension suddenly dawned. He grasped her shoulders with enough force to make her wince. "And believing that I was too scrupulous to take Philippe's life, you were prepared to sacrifice yourself to save mine?"

"Not consciously," she cried out, stunned by the wild look in his eyes. "It was instinct. It must have been. I don't think I knew what I was doing."

Gradually, his grip slackened. "Claire," he said, "you foolish girl! Don't you know that I love you better than I love my own life? If anything had happened to you, what would I have had to live for?"

"But don't you see, Adam? It's the same for me. Without you, my life would be empty."

421

"But . . . our child. I know how much our child means to you. My God! Do you think I shall ever forgive myself for what happened the last time?" His strong hands moved protectively to the swell of her abdomen. "Claire," his voice was unsteady with emotion, "you should have been thinking of our child."

Tears were flowing unchecked down her cheeks. "In that moment, all I could think of was you. Besides," she went on, throwing logic to the winds, "I was doing it for our child, too. You are going to make a perfectly wonderful father, Adam Dillon. My child would never have forgiven me if . . . if . . ."

By this time, she was sniffing and gulping. Adam had a lump in his throat. He produced a large snowy handkerchief and tenderly mopped his wife's cheeks. She blew her nose and stuffed the handkerchief under her pillow.

"Thank you," she said, and chanced a quick look up at him. His expression was still very grave. She fidgeted and looked away, then looked at him again. This time, he was smiling.

"Hungry?" he asked.

She thought of chicken soup and custard. "Not particularly," she demurred.

"I think I know how to tempt your appetite. Cook has prepared something delectable for supper. I shall ask her to serve it in here, shall I?"

A small oval table was soon set with two places. Claire donned a warm robe. Adam served her personally. The first course had her gasping with delight—cream of asparagus soup—her favorite.

"Asparagus!" she exclaimed. "In December? Where did it come from?"

"It's better not to know," said Adam, and poured her a glass of white wine.

The subsequent courses surpassed the first. There was pâté, and meat *tortiers* and fruit *tartes* and a *gâteau* that was so light it practically melted in

422

Claire's mouth. Her eyes were dancing. She was beginning to catch on. These were all her favorite dishes. This elaborate supper was the prelude to an apology.

They sipped their coffee in companionable silence. Claire waited expectantly.

"I have an apology to make," said Adam.

"I thought you might," murmured Claire.

"Well, actually, it's more in the nature of a confession."

"Confession?" The word might once have alarmed Claire, but no longer. She smiled serenely.

Her smile was not lost on Adam. He twirled his wine glass before imbibing. "You must understand, Claire," he said, "I had to make Philippe believe that I was indifferent to you. Need I say more? I've gathered that you've worked everything out to your own satisfaction, else you would not be giving me the time of day."

"Are we talking about Lily Randolph, and the way you dangled after her?" she asked archly.

He frowned at her choice of words. "That and a few other things."

"Such as Dr. Massey?"

"Dr. Massey?"

She could not prevent the faint flush. "I . . . I approached him and he told me that there was not the least necessity . . . that is . . . I am in perfect health and there is no reason . . . oh, you know what I am trying to say!"

His eyes were bright with laughter. "And did you also know that your own maid, in all innocence, was carrying tales to Philippe's man? For your sake, I had to play my part convincingly, yes, even in the privacy of my own home."

"Yes, I thought it must be something of the sort, though I wish you had taken me into your confidence."

He made no reply to this, and after a moment or

two, he removed the cup from her fingers. "It's bed for you, my girl. You are falling asleep where you sit."

He swept her up in his arms and carried her to the bed.

"It's just as well," she said, stretching like a cat, helping as he wrestled her from her garments. "I'm all talked out."

"I'm not," he said. He stretched out beside her, turning her face up to receive his kisses. His lips were warm and soft and surprisingly chaste. "I love you. Do you hear me? I love you, Mrs. Dillon."

"And I love you."

He pulled back slightly to get a better look at her. "And that's all you have to say on the subject? For more than a week, I have been confessing, over and over, that I love you, and you simply give me my own words back?"

"What more should I say?"

"Well, you could say, 'I told you so'! You could say that I'd behaved like a damned idiot, keeping the words from you. You could say . . ."

She stopped him with a kiss. "Words are all right in their way," she said. "But actions speak louder than words. Adam, I've known for an age that you love me." She yawned hugely.

He nudged her awake. "You can't stop there," he protested.

"Mmm? Oh, I know you love me because . . ." another huge yawn, "when I am with you, you make me feel ten feet tall, and though you sent me away . . ." Her voice faltered then rallied. "How could I not know it? I could not have been better guarded if I were money in the Bank of . . . Adam, is there a Bank of America?"

"Bank of the United States," he corrected, nuzzling her throat. "We have Alexander Hamilton to thank for that . . . among other things."

In two minutes, she was asleep.

*　　*　　*

Adam was dreaming. She was scattering soft, open-mouthed kisses over his throat and bare shoulders. The scent of roses filled his nostrils. He could never inhale that scent and not think of Claire. He knew he was smiling absurdly. Claire had that effect on him. He was the most fortunate man in Christendom. A star had drifted into his orbit. And though he was not worthy of her, she was his destiny. He would never let her go.

Her caresses became bolder. In his dreams, Claire was never shy, or modest, or shocked by what he wanted to do to her. She was never afraid of the violence of his possession. In the sober light of reality, as much as he was able, he ruthlessly suppressed this primitive side of his nature. He could never forget that once, in their first coming together, he had forced himself on Claire. He was going to make her forget that other Adam Dillon. For Claire's sake, he must cultivate some of the softer virtues. Tenderness, Restraint, Moderation.

His dream-Claire was climbing all over him. Adam laughed exultantly. He wound one hand in her hair, arching her head back. One arm closed around her waist. He bent to her breasts, sucking hard on first one engorged nipple then on the other, making her moan and writhe in a frenzy of desire.

Claire's fingers tangled in his hair. She dragged his head back. Her lips came down on his. Hard. Insistent. Primitive. She loosed the full fury of her passion against him. Her tongue plunged into his mouth.

Adam came fully awake. His senses were leaping. His body was ravenous for her. The primitive side of his nature was clamoring to get out.

"No," he said, making a supreme effort to check himself. "Not like this."

She didn't give him time to think. "Yes," she said,

"like this," and she stroked him voluptuously till he was crazy with wanting her.

There was never any doubt who would carry off the victory in this contest. Claire was too skilled, too experienced not to push her advantage.

She positioned herself above him. "Yes," she said, pleading with him. "It's all right. Don't be afraid for me. The doctor says it's all right. I want it. You want it. Give in to me."

"Claire!" he groaned. He made his entry as smooth and as gentle as he could make it. He wasn't taking any chances, not with Claire.

She began to move. Bucking, rolling, arching, she rode him to a furious and rapturous finish. When it was over, when they were both panting as though their lungs would burst, she collapsed against him. Adam's arms tightened even more.

"You made me," he said fiercely. "You know you made me." He could feel the smile on her lips as he smothered her face with kisses. "Why did you do it?"

She stretched languidly and tucked her head into the hollow of his shoulder. "It was wonderful," she said. "Wasn't it, Adam? It was just like the first time, in Rouen, when you made me give in to you." A long replete sigh fluttered on her breath. "You've met your match, Adam Dillon," she said. "Why won't you admit it?"

She raised her head to look at him. "Well?" she demanded.

Adam seemed to be in a daze. It was a moment before he came to himself. He angled her a sleepy grin. "Tigress!" he said, and kissed her again.

Epilogue

Claire's eyes kept straying across the expanse of lawns to the treelined path which led down to the river. At any moment, she expected to see Adam's tall figure come striding toward her. At his side would be a slighter figure, her brother, Leon—Leon whom she had always known in her heart of hearts would somehow manage to survive the carnage in France.

Sighing, striving for patience, she threw herself down on the grass at Sarah Burke's feet. Sarah was dangling her namesake on her knee. Claire's infant daughter, as dark as her mother was fair, looked about her with interest. She gurgled when her mother tickled the soles of her tiny bare feet with a blade of grass.

"It's a perfect day for a barbecue," said Sarah Burke to her adopted grandchild. "Papa's favorite, roast turtle. Aren't we the lucky ones?"

Claire made a face, and Sarah laughed.

"How long has Adam been gone?" asked Claire for the hundredth time in the last hour. "That's a stupid question," she said, answering herself. "You told me not a minute ago."

"It won't be long now," said Sarah. *Valclair* is, after all, practically on New York's doorstep."

Valclair. Claire could never hear that name

without having to swallow a constriction in her throat. Adam had named his house after *her*. If she lived to be a hundred, there could never be another gift to match it. It put her in mind to do something extraordinary, something on the same scale, for Adam, something to demonstrate the height and depth of her love for *him*. She'd wracked her brains but no thought came to her. Some gifts, she had decided, were simply beyond compare.

"When did you last see your brother, Claire?"

Claire squinted up at Sarah. "A little over eighteen months ago. In Rouen. Yes, darling, Papa will soon be home with the best present in the world for his precious little lamb. Uncle Leon is going to love you on sight. I just know it."

"Eighteen months," mused Sarah.

Claire knew what the older woman was thinking. Adam had said as much when Leon's letter had arrived from Boston by way of New York.

The letter said little enough. The boy had run away from school in Rouen to fight with the rebels. A year was to pass before Zoë's husband, the Marquess of Rivard, had found him in Paris. Leon had come to Boston to search for Claire because it was her letter from Boston which had finally caught up with them at Rivard Abbey.

It was what was not in the boy's letter that troubled Claire. What sort of life must Leon have led as a young rebel soldier? How had he passed his time in Paris when the Terror was at its height?

They must not expect answers to these questions, Adam had warned her. In point of fact, it was better not to ask, but to let the boy tell them as little or as much as he wished. And Claire, seeing the sense in what he said, had acquiesced.

Adam's last words to her before setting out to fetch her brother from his lodgings in New York revolved in her mind. "He won't be the same boy, Claire. You must expect to see changes. Eighteen months is a long time."

There was something in Claire's expression which prompted Sarah to strike out on a different tack. A propos of nothing, she interposed, "How is your friend, Mrs. Clay, going on?"

The question had to be repeated before Claire came to herself. "Blanche? Last I heard, she and Mark were in Charleston. I see his mother and sisters quite frequently. We are neighbors, you know. They are a charming family, and so relieved to see that Mark has finally settled down."

"Yes," said Sarah, "sons can be a terrible burden, so I've been given to understand. The right girl can be the making of them. Look at Adam."

"No," said Claire, grinning hugely. "That's where you are wrong, Sarah. Adam was the making of *me*."

"I won't quarrel with you," said Sarah, her expression one of supreme complacency.

Baby Sarah decided she wasn't getting enough attention. She caught her mother's hair in her little fists and pulled gleefully. Laughing, disengaging herself, Claire held her child at arm's length. "Did you ever see such a shock of dark hair?" she said. "You are your father's daughter, Sarah, and no mistaking!"

"Hmmph!" snorted Sarah Burke. "She may have her father's hair, but she has the unmistakable Burke eyes." Suddenly conscious of her gaffe, horrified, she looked at Claire.

Claire was studying her daughter intently. "I believe you are right," she said. "John's eyes, my eyes, true blue with not a shadow of green or gray." And she turned a smiling face upon Sarah.

"You knew!" accused Sarah. "All the time, you knew!"

"No, not all the time. Not at first."

"Then when? Who told you?"

"Nobody told me, exactly. But when so many remarked on my extraordinary Burke eyes, I began to put two and two together."

"And you never said a word!"

"How could I? The last thing I wanted was to hurt *you*. And I could not be sure that *you* knew."

Claire stretched out a hand. Sarah grasped it and bent to kiss the younger woman on the cheek. "Oh, my dear," she said. "I could not love you more if you were my own daughter."

"I know," said Claire, laughing and crying at the same time. "Don't you think I know? And Adam, too? Why do you think he wanted his daughter named for you? Sarah Mara Juliette Elise was to be named for her grandmothers. And since you are as near a mother to Adam, to us both, as makes no difference, our child must have your name, too."

"And John?" said Sarah with an odd catch in her voice. "You won't judge him too harshly, will you, Claire?"

Shaking her head, Claire could only manage a choked, "No!" When she could find her voice, smiling through her tears, she went on, "Adam would not permit it. There is no one whom Adam esteems more. And I have learned to trust my husband's judgment."

Again, the two women embraced.

This was the scene that met Adam's eyes as he and his companion took the last turn in the path. He halted.

Time seemed to be suspended. The sun made a halo over the canopy of oaks and maples which edged the lawns. Adam was conscious of grace and beauty and peace, as though Valclair, so aptly named, was his own private sanctuary.

"Welcome to Valclair," he said to the young man at his side and gave him a nudge in Claire's direction.

The boy moved swiftly, Adam following at a

430

slower pace. Again he halted. His eyes took in the figure of John Burke as he sauntered down from the house. Sarah, feeling her husband's hand on her shoulder, covered it with one of her own and turned a dazzling smile upon him. Circumspectly, Claire set her baby on the grass and became involved in counting fingers and toes.

"Claire!" cried the boy. "Claire!"

In that moment, Claire's face was transformed. She leaped to her feet. With a little cry, she came racing across the lawns. There was a slight hesitation as her eyes devoured the beloved face. He was the same boy she had always known, and yet he was a stranger. This darkly handsome youth with the patrician features carved in proud lines had matured out of all recognition. He had the look of a pagan warrior.

"Leon?" she whispered, then with a cry of joy, "Leon!" and she threw herself into his arms.

Laughing and talking together, arm-in-arm, they moved toward the little group under the trees, Adam following in their wake. He had not taken many paces when again he halted. An odd sensation, a glimmer of something he did not quite understand, came upon him. He felt as though he were standing on holy ground.

He absorbed everything in the scene before him. The buzz of conversation pulsed with warmth and laughter and intimacy. Claire's eyes were brilliant. She picked up her daughter and raised the child for Leon's kiss. John Burke's arm was around his wife's waist. Adam was content just to watch from the wings.

As though she sensed that all was not quite perfect in her world, Claire's brow wrinkled. She looked over her shoulder and caught sight of Adam. Shaking her head, holding her baby to her breast, she came toward him.

Adam gathered his infant daughter in his arms.

431

Claire slipped one hand into the crook of her husband's elbow.

"I love you," said Adam, mouthing the words.

Claire's dimples flashed. Everything that Adam could have hoped to see was shining in her eyes. Wordlessly, she urged him into the charmed circle.